Hannah Brennan lives in South East London, where she was born and raised.

She studied English Literature at Durham University alongside British Sign Language, which she uses in her role as a trustee for the Royal Association for Deaf people. After returning from the North East, Hannah has turned her love of pubs into a career, working in marketing and technology for many fantastic British hospitality brands.

Hannah is a fanatic book-collector, with a passion for crime fiction and television. She is also one of the organisers of Greenwich Writers, a South-East London writing group.

Hannah developed OCD as a teenager, and hopes that her debut novel, *No Safe Place*, may give readers a fresh insight into a frequently misunderstood and misrepresented condition.

# NO SAFE PLACE

## HANNAH BRENNAN

avon.

Published by AVON
A division of HarperCollins*Publishers* Ltd
1 London Bridge Street
London SE1 9GF

www.harpercollins.co.uk

HarperCollins*Publishers*
Macken House,
39/40 Mayor Street Upper,
Dublin 1, D01 C9W8
Ireland

A Paperback Original 2025
1

First published in Great Britain by HarperCollins*Publishers* 2025
Copyright © Hannah Brennan 2025

Hannah Brennan asserts the moral right to
be identified as the author of this work.

A catalogue record for this book is available from the British Library.

ISBN: 978-0-00-877806-4

Typeset in Sabon LT Std by Palimpsest Book Production Limited,
Falkirk, Stirlingshire
Printed and bound in the UK using 100% Renewable Electricity
at CPI Group (UK) Ltd

*For Mum*

# Prologue

The knife slipped easily into his stomach, just below the ribs.

David stumbled, already reeling backwards into the shadow of the birch tree next to them.

The knife swung again, meeting sinew, bone.

He clutched at his neck as he fell to the ground.

'Why?' he managed to gasp, tipping his head back, blood bubbling from between his fingers. 'Why are you—'

He whimpered, eyes alive with fear.

Seventeen years ago, he had made promises, assurances. Pretended to care about the people everyone else was leaving behind. He'd scooped up the most vulnerable to become their protector.

Such a good actor, this man.

The perfect doctor act had everyone fooled.

David Moore thought he'd got away with it. Thought his secret had died with her.

He didn't deserve to die quietly.

None of them did.

# Chapter 1

## Wednesday | Early hours

## Field

In seconds, the night went from dull routine to life and death.

They'd just got back in the car after a call to assist during kicking-out time at a pub, when the radio crackled into life.

'Circulation of an I-Grade. Ambulance Service requesting assistance for a male found with multiple stab wounds on Ancona Road, Plumstead. Is anyone available to respond?'

The easy atmosphere, their chat about swapping back to day shifts after a run of nights – it was forgotten.

Field put her coffee into the cupholder and pulled the radio from the dash. 'Control – Hotel Charlie Six-Four, we're round the corner. Show us en route.'

She punched the street name into the car's satnav, but Riley was already pulling away – his superior sense of direction the reason he was often behind the wheel.

Blue lights. Siren.

The radio crackled again. 'Hotel Charlie Six-Four received.

Update from LAS: subject is unresponsive. Sending further LAS and locals.'

Adrenaline was already pumping, making the tips of her fingers tingle and her heart beat harder in her chest.

Riley took a corner at speed and Field threw out a hand to stop herself smacking into the passenger window. The radio went off constantly with patrol cars responding.

'Show Two-One.'

'Eight-Zero-One.'

Riley glanced at the satnav. 'I'll have us there in two minutes, boss.'

'Six-Four, any update, Control? Are suspects on scene?' Field said into the radio.

An Audi in front of them chose to speed up instead of pulling over. The pedestrian crossing to their right meant they couldn't overtake – and Field smacked her hand against the dashboard.

'Say that again, Hotel Charlie Six-Four?' Control said, finally.

'Are suspects on scene?' Field shouted.

She shot a look at the speedometer. Riley was doing fifty down Plumstead Common road, the dark street oddly lit as they flew down it.

'Unknown at this stage. We've passed to Metro Alpha for review.'

Metro Alpha – serious enough to need firearms on standby, then.

Riley put his foot down. 'One minute.'

She wiped her hands on her black trousers, smoothed her hair. Pulled an extra set of handcuffs from the glove box and secured them to her belt.

Heading up a Major Investigation Team didn't involve as many sirens and active scenes as Field's civilian friends assumed. She couldn't deny the thrill of a boring on-call night shift interrupted.

4

'We're here, boss,' Riley said, indicating and swinging onto Ancona Road, and braking hard.

An Ambulance Response car was parked across the other end of the street, doors still open.

Control spoke over the radio. 'Two cars on their way to you, Hotel Charlie Six-Four. Five minutes out.'

Field threw her door open, and the heat hit her, like the first step off a plane abroad. She popped the boot, grabbed her stab vest and pulled it on.

She didn't wait for Riley before running towards the scene, clipping the radio to the left panel of the vest.

A huddle of people in pyjamas and dressing robes blocked the victim from view.

'Police—' Field pushed through the gathered crowd. She could hear the victim wheezing before she could see him. 'Police – stand back.'

They parted, stumbling.

Two paramedics were already working on the victim. One was by his head, a young girl with dark hair back in a bun, listening to his chest through a stethoscope.

The older paramedic was cutting through the man's shirt like it was made of tissue paper. 'He's unresponsive. Collapsed airway – at least five stab wounds.' He looked up at Field, pink scissors frozen by the man's collar. 'This is nasty.'

Field grabbed her baton and flicked her wrist to extend it. A woman next to her jumped and clung to her husband.

There wasn't as much blood as she'd been expecting. A pool of blood meant arterial, death in minutes.

'Any sign of the attacker?' Field barked at the paramedics. Neither spoke, but both gave one shake of the head.

Riley appeared on the victim's other side, baton out, and nodded at Field.

*Protect the medics.* Always the first duty of the police on an active scene.

Field held her radio to her mouth. 'TOA Hotel Charlie Six-Four. We've got an IC1 male, approx. fifty years old. Not conscious, trouble breathing. Male appears to have multiple entry wounds, including one to the neck.'

Field turned so she was facing outwards, scanning up the street towards the ambulance, while Riley faced their unmarked car. It was impossible to see much beyond the pool of light cast by the headlights. 'Chase firearms, Control. We might need a chopper so get HEMs on standby, and identify a suitable landing location.'

'Is he going to be okay?' asked one of the neighbours, the husband of the scared woman.

Field glanced down. The female paramedic was talking soothingly to the patient, while unwrapping a large needle, which Field suspected would be going straight into his chest.

Her stomach flipped.

She turned and the small crowd were still standing there, gawping. Unable to look away.

'I need everyone to get back inside,' Field shouted. 'We don't know it's safe out here.'

No one moved.

'I've got a major internal bleed here, Lea,' the male paramedic said. 'Coag bandage.'

People were craning round her, trying to see, and Field snapped. 'Get back in your houses, *now*.'

They jumped – scurried away.

'You—' Field pointed at two men with bloodstained arms and T-shirts, who must have tried to help before the paramedics arrived. 'Go inside, but don't touch anything. Don't take those T-shirts off.'

She scanned the street again, gripping the baton tighter.

The front gardens were small, tiny patches of grass and some window boxes – not big enough for someone to hide.

She hoped.

More front doors were opening.

Field turned the volume up on the radio and spoke into it, eyes still ahead. 'Control, I need that backup, *now*.'

She didn't hear the response.

'Detective, I'm going to need you to give us a hand here,' the male paramedic said. He kicked a box of gloves towards her.

Field gritted her teeth, passed the radio to Riley.

As she kneeled, Riley moved closer to them, baton up.

She looked at the victim properly, for the first time, as she pulled the gloves on. His skin was grey, and his breathing was erratic, rattling. He was hooked up to a portable monitor and his BP was low – the red numbers glowing.

The fingers of his left hand were twitching. He was wearing a wedding ring.

He had collapsed below a silver birch tree, bark glowing in the gloom. Its leaves were casting dappled shadows across his bare chest.

The paramedic snapped her back to the present. 'Right, I need to deal with the neck wound while Lea intubates, so I need you—' he handed Field a thick wad of gauze '—to apply pressure here.'

The top of the man's jeans had been cut away too, and Field saw a deep gash in his thigh, blood oozing down into the space between his legs.

How many times had this guy been stabbed?

She pushed down firmly on the wound and watched the man's face, hoping to see him flinch or groan.

No response.

'I'm Lea,' the female paramedic at the man's head said. 'This is Mike.'

7

'Field,' she said with a nod, glad to have names for them. 'That's Riley.'

The exposed skin of the victim's chest was patchy with bright blood, smeared by the medics. It was hard to see the wounds, but Field could count at least five.

The blood on the pavement looked darker, congealed. Field's knee was an inch from the slowly growing pool.

'Right—' Lea spoke loudly but with a soothing tone. 'This is going to hurt but we need to get this needle in, okay? It's going to help with your breathing.'

She might as well have been talking to the tree.

Field focused her gaze on her own hands as the needle pierced the man's chest plate.

'Cars are arriving, boss,' Riley said, somewhere above her. 'At least one ambulance too.'

And then they were surrounded by uniforms – officers with batons out, forming a proper ring around them.

Two more paramedics joined, unfazed by the gasping, dying man, unzipping bags and pulling out dressings.

'Keep that pressure on, Detective,' Mike ordered. 'Don't ease up until someone's ready.'

Field's arms were starting to shake with the effort, sweat running down her face.

She pressed harder and looked up at Riley. 'Firearms?'

He looked pale in the moonlight. 'On the way from Lewisham. Three minutes out.'

Then blue-gloved hands were taking over from hers, and Field sat back on her ankles, panting. She had an iron taste at the back of her throat, like she'd breathed the blood in.

There were five medics around the victim, now, and a sixth unpacking a defibrillator.

Her gloves were sticky with blood, hands sweaty inside

them. A young PC materialised – evidence bag already outstretched.

When the gloves were off and bagged, Field felt her sense of control return. She could concentrate on being a police officer, leave the lifesaving to the professionals.

*Where is the knife?*

*Which direction was he attacked from?*

*Which route is the attacker most likely to have taken?*

Mike's voice: 'He's going into shock.'

Field turned back to watch them. Lea was still speaking in a low, soothing voice, right by the man's ear.

*This is going to end up a murder investigation.*

The thought had popped into Field's head before she could stop it.

Upstairs windows were opening all along the street, shocked figures leaning out, holding up phones.

Riley strode towards her, thumbs tucked into his vest. 'We've got six PCs and a skipper. Told four to stay with our victim, got one at each end of the road. Cordon going up now.'

'Good. The blokes who found him – bag their clothes.' Field pointed at one of the houses – door still wide open, like there wasn't a madman with a knife on the loose. 'Take a quick statement – timings, whether they know the victim – anything that's going to be helpful *now*.'

Forensics was going to be tricky with the paramedic intervention. She pulled a torch from her belt and shone it at the ground.

There was more blood than she'd realised, stretching down the street, towards their car. Their attacker must be covered in it.

A different pitch of siren in the distance, the wide headlights of a black van and then firearms officers were pouring onto the road.

It was progress: they had the bodies – and gunpower – to keep the scene safe.

'Detective?'

Field jogged back to the paramedics.

Mike stood, breathing hard. He had dark stains on his uniform. 'We've got five minutes to get him stable enough to get into the van or—' He gave a grim shrug and returned to crouching.

As a rule, if a stabbing victim wasn't in the back of the ambulance or a chopper within twenty minutes, chances of survival were slim to none.

The scene was a mess. Boot marks in the blood, bandage wrappers littering the street.

The victim had tubes in his throat, the needle in his chest rising and falling rhythmically, now – the paramedics breathing for him. One medic had his hand inside the slice to the thigh.

Field retrieved evidence bags and gloves from the car. She needed to ID the victim.

Time was elastic, and in seconds she was back by the paramedics.

Trying not to get in the way, Field dived into the man's pockets – the job made easier by the fact his jeans were in ribbons. Her hand closed around a wallet, and she teased it out between the green jump-suited bodies.

Field sat back and flicked it open, squinting to read the name on the driving licence.

David Moore.

There were three £20 notes inside.

*Not a mugging.*

Heart racing, Field bagged the wallet.

'His name is David,' she called, and Lea looked up, flashed her a grateful smile.

'David?' Lea said, over the low urgent chatter of her

colleagues – passing each other equipment and negotiating for space. 'David – my name is Lea, okay? I'm right here with you.'

The medic next to Field stood up. He had been kneeling on a sheet of paper. It seemed so out of place, a piece of bloodstained A4 tangled in the detritus and ruins of his clothes. It wasn't Field's, and it wasn't something the paramedics had used.

She caught the page by one of the corners.

*The Disordered Approach to Diagnosis:* a pilot study of—

Field was distracted from the sheet by the raised voices of the paramedics.

'He's coding. I've got no pulse – I need epi and fluids now; get ready to charge—'

Field twisted, seeking out Riley. Ancona Road was now swarming with people. Police tape was going up, more paramedics were on standby to support. There was a slight whine as the defibrillator charged.

'Clear.'

Riley was a few metres away, looking sombre. She was glad. She wanted him here to witness this, to understand the magnitude of what they were dealing with.

'You're okay, sweetheart,' Lea intoned, stroking David Moore's hair while her colleagues alternated chest compressions. 'You're okay.'

Field looked away from the bloody mess of David Moore's chest, and went to bag the items she was holding.

# Chapter 2

## Wednesday | Early hours

## Field

Field glanced at her watch: 4 a.m.

Most of the response cars had been called away. DS Riley had started the case log and PCSOs were speaking to witnesses. DS Wilson had just arrived. Field had called in a decent DC to act as crime scene manager.

The hours had passed quickly, and they now had a good picture of the scene, an idea of who their victim was. Traffic police were tracing all cars and motorbikes seen in the area at the time of the attack.

Privacy screens had been erected around the more gruesome areas, although as the sky started to lighten, Field had still seen a few people aiming their phones out of upstairs windows.

Field walked the crime scene in reverse, starting from where they'd found David collapsed, and working outwards. He was found at the side of the road, outside number 19.

There was blood spatter on the pavement and on the

wooden garden gate. An officer had already informed the homeowner that they'd be taking the whole gate away with them for testing. Field couldn't imagine they'd want it back.

In total, their victim had only travelled a few steps between the first wound and where he collapsed. The attack had been vicious, efficient.

*Dr David Moore.*

A therapist and lecturer. Already there was speculation among some of the younger uniforms that it might have been one of his patients – chatter Field put a swift stop to.

They found a receipt for the twenty-four-hour petrol garage on Plumstead High Street in his wallet, timed for 12.14 a.m. A packet of cigarettes and a lighter – found in the gutter outside number 17.

It was between a nine- and sixteen-minute walk from the garage to where he was found, depending on which route he took. The shorter cut through an alleyway. Back at the station, five officers had been pulled off other cases to trawl CCTV on both routes.

David's jacket was on the ground next to that first blood spatter. Possibly dropped as he backed away from his attacker.

Field squatted next to it.

'I've got that,' the crime scene photographer called over, holding up his camera. 'If you want a look.'

'Ta.' Field lifted the jacket with a gloved finger. There was a book underneath it, and Field called the photographer back.

It was a crime novel, a pulpy police procedural.

A few clicks of the camera, and then the book and the jacket were both ready to be bagged.

Field was shattered, but running on adrenaline. She sat down on a garden wall. She'd worn new shoes, expecting a quiet night to break them in – and her feet were killing her.

A few metres away, SOCO were briefing the last of the

paramedics on which bits of kit and uniform would need to be kept as evidence. Mike and Lea, the two who had been first on scene, were among the small group.

'All right, boss?' Riley took a seat next to her, adjusting the knees of his suit trousers.

'You shouldn't have taken your vest off yet,' she said, mildly.

He scoffed. 'I was about to pass out. And I don't think our nutjob is getting through this circus.' He gesticulated with his coffee mug. 'Not any time soon.'

Field's radio crackled and she tensed – expecting every broadcast to be "*suspect apprehended*".

It was a domestic call in Thamesmead. Riley's shoulders relaxed.

Opposite them, the group of paramedics broke up. Some of them went back to their vehicles, night carrying on as normal. At least some of them must be off shift by now.

'My son is a paramedic, you know,' she said, offhand.

Riley looked at her in surprise. Before he could ask any questions, the older paramedic, Mike, had walked over to them. They must be similar in age – early fifties.

He was in a too-large grey tracksuit, and Field couldn't help smiling.

'Don't,' he said, putting a hand up. 'Your SOCO has my uniform. A mate had to bring me his gym kit, and let's just say he's a strapping young lad.' He waved his phone in the air. 'I thought I should let you know as soon as we heard – he's out of surgery and they've stabilised him.'

Field felt the knot of tension in her stomach loosen, just slightly. 'That's great news.'

'He's still in ICU.' Mike tucked the phone away. 'But yeah – he's stable.'

From down the road, a crime scene photographer was waving for them. Field nodded at Riley to go.

'Right, well, pass on our thanks, won't you?' Riley stuck out a hand and Mike shook it. 'All the best.'

Riley went to speak to the photographer and Field felt a flash of irritation. He could get a bit public school with paramedics and community support workers, liked to puff himself up with his detective status.

Mike looked unperturbed. He yawned. 'I'll sleep well when I get in, I tell you. Sun will be up soon.'

Field cleared her throat. 'Thank you, for tonight.'

'All in a day's work.' Mike took Riley's spot on the low wall, with a slight groan.

Nights like this, Field really did marvel at the differences in their jobs. Both on hand for the most horrific things – LAS there to save lives, the Met there to pick over them.

'The girl who was with you, when we arrived,' Field said, and Mike turned to her. 'Lea, was it?'

Mike nodded, smiled.

'She was—' Field hesitated. 'She did a really good job.'

'Would you believe she's a trainee?' Mike asked, sitting a little taller. 'She's going to be bloody brilliant. I'm getting ready to hand my job over to her.'

Like Field, Mike was the old hand tasked with training up the newbies.

It was still dark, but the sky was starting to take on that grey tinge that meant dawn was round the corner.

'All debriefed and cleared to go?' Field asked.

Mike nodded. 'Nothing else for me?'

'There was one thing, actually,' Field said. 'A sheet of paper.'

'Yeah,' he said. 'I saw that. He was clutching it to his chest, when we arrived. Didn't get a chance to look at it – obviously.'

She made a note.

'Do you mind if I put that in your statement?' Field asked, and he waved a hand. 'Great, well – pass my thanks on to Lea.'

Mike stood to leave but she put a hand on his arm.

'Can I ask—' She looked down at her notebook, like this was something else she would need to note down. 'The way Lea was talking to him, all the way through – do you think he could hear her?'

He spoke softly. 'Your hearing is the last thing to go. And maybe he couldn't hear a word she said. Maybe he was already out of it before we arrived.'

Field's grip loosened on her pen, and she almost dropped it. She looked up at Mike.

'But if he could hear us, he would have been scared. And wouldn't you want a kind word in your ear, Detective Field?'

# Chapter 3

For as long as there have been human beings, there has been a need to keep records.

We have a pathological need to leave a mark behind. Something that says *I was there* – something that will survive us.

This is my record. I hope it survives me.

**P:** Do you wish we could take it back?
**D:** Look, P—
**P:** Because I don't. Is that okay? That I don't regret it?

*Pause*

**D:** It was wrong. It was my fault.

*Pause*

**D:** I don't know. I don't know how it happened.

*Pause*

**P:** You should have stopped me.
**D:** I know.

*Pause*

**P:** But you didn't, and I didn't want you to.

*Pause*

**P:** It's all right, D—. It is.
**D:** It's not all right. How is it all right?
**P:** It's not that big a deal. It doesn't have to be a big deal, okay?

*Pause*

**P:** I promise I won't tell anyone.

# Chapter 4

## Wednesday | Morning

## Callum

The sun was coming up, and the walls were closing in.

They always did, first thing in the morning.

His sleep patterns were fucked. He'd barely slept all week, finally passing out properly yesterday afternoon. He must have slept for thirteen hours, and now it was five, maybe six in the morning.

There was no way to be sure. There were no clocks in this house.

The sun threw weak beams of light through the cracks in the curtains and Callum counted dancing dust particles until his heart rate slowed.

Most days it took him hours to leave his bedroom – battle one of many.

But today, Callum had slept, and he felt better. The good days were getting fewer and further apart, so it was important to make the most of them. He'd do some tidying, take his dirty plates downstairs and wash them up.

His fingers itched to pick up the pen on the bedside table, but he wouldn't let himself write until he'd achieved something.

Six deep breaths, Callum decided, and then up.

He paused outside Lily's door, listening for voices, but they weren't awake yet. Of course they weren't.

Callum crept down the stairs, skipping the second from bottom because it creaked.

He hated it when Scott stayed over. Dr Scott with his slicked-back hair and hand-ground Fairtrade Nicaraguan coffee.

Callum crossed his arms and frowned down at the neatly polished shoes in the middle of the cramped, cluttered hallway.

Callum didn't need to keep shoes in the hallway, because he never went anywhere.

Scott's brogues were next to a haphazard pile of Lily's eclectic footwear – blue pumps, pink Converse, battered Doc Martens – threaded with lime-green laces stolen from Callum, a long time ago.

They didn't *go* together, those shoes, Callum thought sadly, staring at the brogues.

'Twat,' he said out loud to himself, picking up Scott's wallet and dropping it down the back of the radiator cover.

# Chapter 5

## Wednesday | Morning

### Field

One of the benefits of being the Senior Investigating Officer was the power to follow whatever thread you deemed most important, without having to answer to ten people first.

Next on her list, and a persistent gripe at the back of her mind: the sheet of paper she'd recovered from David's torn clothes. Field strode over to the car that the evidence was being placed into, nodded at the squeaky-voiced youngster in charge of the exhibits.

She rifled through the paper bags, finding the one she wanted at the back.

The sheet of typed A4, badly bloodstained, but legible through the plastic. She scanned the first page.

*The Disordered Approach to Diagnosis:* a pilot study of the impact of misdiagnoses on young people with

complex presentations of obsessive-compulsive disorder,
and subsequent group-therapy treatment

It was the title page of a paper or an article. It didn't have an author's name, but she assumed it was something David was working on, possibly brought home from work with him in a pocket.

Not necessarily the smoking gun she'd hoped for. The attacker's bank statement or something, dropped as he legged it.

Field leaned closer to the sheet, flattening out the plastic window of the evidence bag. Most of the bottom half of the page was smeared with blood.

There was always a chance that the attacker dropped it deliberately. Pointedly.

Field's phone buzzed in her back pocket.

She answered the call reluctantly, and only because she had no excuse not to.

The superintendent didn't wait for her greeting. 'Quite a morning you're having over there, DCI Field?'

'Yes, sir,' she said, then stopped speaking.

Field put the sheet of paper back in the boot, and walked to a patch of road where there were fewer people to eavesdrop.

'I can have this case reassigned. Say the word.' The superintendent was using his best kindly-and-calming voice, and Field could picture his smug smile on the other end of the line.

*Prick.*

She kicked at a crumbling garden wall and didn't answer.

'You've got a lot on, and that case coming up at the Bailey, *and* you've got the most junior team. We can get someone else—'

Meaning someone male.

'—to take over from you, if you'd prefer. DCI Raynott, maybe?'

Field did not prefer. DCI Raynott was an arse. They were basically the same age, but unlike her, Raynott had never had children – and unlike him, Field had never had Botox.

Field had been the DCI for Major Investigation Team 4 for six years, and a DI for another seven before that – but somehow MIT4 still ended up with the shit cases. Reassigned from anything meaty and given the months-old dregs. It didn't help that they were a DI and a DS short compared to the other South London teams, and there was no budget to fill out the ranks.

Field had also ended up in the awkward in-between career position of giving keen newly transferred DSs their first run-around. Just as the young fuckers knew what they were doing, they'd get promoted to a growing task force or a different MIT with a juicier caseload.

'Like I said,' the super simpered down the phone, 'it's a big case, could be national news.'

Because how could a perimenopausal DCI with twenty-five years' experience be expected to handle a case of this magnitude?

'It's fine, guv,' she said, finally. He hated being called guv. 'I was first on scene, and anyway, I'm about to go and inform the wife. It should be me.'

Field shouldn't use informing a woman her husband was in a coma to points-score against her boss, but needs must.

The super let out a deep sigh. 'Field—'

'Sorry, I need to go. Briefing.'

She ended the call before he could object.

It wasn't exactly a lie. The team were gathering for an improvised briefing in one of the front gardens. An elderly lady tottered through the front door with a tray of more coffees and teas, and Wilson rushed forward to help her.

Field took a particularly garish mug with frolicking kittens on. The black coffee was cool enough that she could gulp it, imagining the caffeine fizzing through her veins.

Most of the sixteen officers she'd been assigned were on house-to-house. Two DCs and a community support officer had been held back.

DS Riley was leaning against the house with his hands in his pockets, and DS Wilson was standing upright next to him.

The five of them stared evenly back at her.

Wilson and Riley had clashed ever since Riley joined the team, six months ago. They were fiercely competitive, determined to be promoted before each other.

After three years of Criminology at Manchester and a master's at UCL, Riley had worked a boring private sector job for a few years, before joining the Met on a direct-to-DC scheme. Wilson, on the other hand, had started her career as a PC at eighteen and spent years on Response, before her DC posting. Despite being in their thirties now, Wilson resented Riley for taking what she saw as a shortcut, and she wound Riley up about his lack of experience in the "real world" of policing.

It was evident that even with his degrees, Riley found Wilson intimidating. She had achieved ridiculously high scores in every exam. She made a name for herself among the higher-ups, while she was still a PC in Hackney, by voluntarily leading the local widening participation programme. On her days off, Wilson visited schools and chatted to pupils about her experiences as a young, black officer.

They were two of the most impressive officers Field had welcomed onto her team for years, and she doubted either of them would be with her long.

Despite that evening's dramatic turn of events, Riley still managed to look immaculate, his sharply pressed shirt tucked into grey suit trousers, sleeves rolled up to the elbows.

Wilson's wardrobe was a lot less try-hard – thrown-on monochrome clothes, paired with Doc Martens.

Some DCIs would demand that they sort out their differences, but Field approved. Their need to outdo each other made them work harder.

'Right,' Field began. 'It hardly needs stating, but let's all remember that this is an attempted murder inquiry. Evidence logs, witness statements – everything about how we conduct this case needs to be impeccable. Wilson, can you give DC Ayres a call? She can act as family liaison officer.'

'She's already on her way in,' Wilson said. Behind her, Riley rolled his eyes.

'We identified Moore from his driving licence,' Field went on. 'The victim was wearing a wedding ring and has a photo of a woman in his wallet – presume that's the wife. We'll need to inform her as a priority.'

Riley straightened up, tired eyes calling for her to pick him, but this was a big case. Field couldn't let him cut his teeth on this particular distressed spouse.

'Wilson – you and I will go to the address as soon as we're done here.'

Wilson's face remained impassive.

'What else do we know about Dr Moore?' Field asked.

Riley reached into his suit jacket for his daybook, but Wilson was already on the page.

'Dr David Moore, forty-nine. Married. He came up on the King's College University website. He's a lecturer in clinical psychology – a specialist in obsessive-compulsive anxiety disorders, but he also works for the NHS trust.' Wilson read on. 'There's a news article on the site too – last year he received a medal at Buckingham Palace for his charitable work, as well as his part in numerous academic studies, research projects.'

A good man, then. Field took a beat.

'Nikki, Cat—' Field turned to the DCs. 'I'd like you to co-ordinate door-to-door. We've got no CCTV on the street itself, but they're not cheap, the houses around here. There'll be private cameras, Ring doorbells.'

The uniforms nodded.

'Anything noteworthy, email me. Riley – make a start on the decision log and open a case file on the system. Crack on with making a list of his patients, okay?' She made a snap decision. 'And there's an exhibit in evidence – a page of an article or something, that he was working on. Check it out, please.'

'Yes, boss,' he drawled, snapping his notebook shut without writing anything down.

A cloud shifted and Field had to raise a hand over her eyes. 'Wilson, we'll leave in five.'

# Chapter 6

## Wednesday | Morning

## Field

The address on David Moore's driving licence was a narrow townhouse on the edge of Greenwich Park. Every house on the street was well maintained, freshly painted – and Moore's was no exception.

David couldn't have been walking back to this home last night – they were more than a twenty-five-minute drive from the scene.

Wilson performed a neat parallel park and Field let her lead the way up the path to the house. Field's face felt flushed and sweaty, from the heat or hormones – she couldn't tell. She glanced across at Wilson, whose dark skin was wrinkle- and sweat-free.

They turned the volume on their radios down before knocking.

A woman opened the door, holding a wooden spoon and wearing an apron covered in flour.

'Penelope Moore?' Wilson asked, and the woman nodded, the spoon dropping to her side. They both held up their warrant cards. 'My name is DS Wilson, and this is DCI Field. Could we come in?'

Penelope took a moment to look closely at their cards, cleared her throat. 'Can I ask what this is regarding?'

She was a tiny slip of a woman, younger than Field had been expecting, with vivid red hair, in a short bob. The calm demeanour, the baking – this wasn't a wife who'd been up all night, wondering where her husband was.

'I think it's best we come in, Penelope, and take a seat,' Field said.

She looked between them, gave a curt nod, and stepped backwards into the house. 'It's Penny, by the way.'

In the hallway Penny untied her apron, and placed it on a side table with the messy spoon on top. She led them into a high-ceilinged living room, and they took their seats.

Wilson spoke softly. 'Penny, your husband is David Moore – is that correct?'

A split-second hesitation, then: 'Yes.'

Instinct made Field glance at Penny's left hand, clutching her bare knee below the hem of her summer dress. She wasn't wearing a wedding ring.

'David was involved in an incident in the early hours of this morning. A stabbing.' Wilson lifted a hand as Penny's face crumpled. 'It's okay, he's at the hospital now. We've been told he's stable. But we are treating this as an attempted murder.'

Penny stayed very still, apart from the rise and fall of her chest. Her pale collarbone looked vulnerable.

Wilson did well – delivering the facts in a kind, but firm voice, as the incongruous, sweet smell of baking cake drifted into the room.

Penny was stoic, still. Taking in the information being offered without reacting.

'Is there anything you want to ask us?' Field asked, indicating to Penny that Wilson was now finished.

Her eyes were wide. 'Which hospital?'

'King's,' Field said. 'In Denmark Hill. We'll take you straight to the hospital, but first—'

Penny's head snapped to look at her.

'—it'd be really helpful if we could ask you a few questions. It'll only take a few minutes.'

Penny nodded, then sagged back into the overstuffed sofa. Her legs curled up and she wrapped her arms around her knees, like she was trying to take up less space.

'DS Wilson, make us all a cup of tea, would you?'

Wilson took the dismissal without hesitating and stood up.

'The kitchen's at the back,' Penny said, her voice a whisper. Her eyes, unfocused, moved to the window.

To give Penny a moment of privacy, Field stood, as if stretching her legs for a moment.

Penny wasn't crying, but that wasn't unusual. This sort of news did strange things to people.

The living room was expensively furnished, tasteful but still homely, with bookcases of battered paperbacks on either side of the chimney. There were photos of Penny and David on the mantelpiece – one in a park or garden, a couple on holiday. In all of them David was grinning goofily, arm thrown round a tight-smiling Penny.

Field wondered about the age gap again. There had to be ten years between them, at least.

Field heard Wilson's steps in the hall, and then she was back in the room.

'I turned the oven off,' Wilson said, quietly.

Field took a mug from the tray, and then sat again, this time taking the spot on the sofa closest to Penny. 'I know this has been a terrible shock.'

Penny turned wide, blank eyes to her.

'You'll be assigned a family liaison officer today – you might hear us refer to them as a FLO,' Field said. 'They'll be your main point of contact as our investigation progresses. She's called Zara and she's a star.'

Penny gripped her tea but didn't drink any.

'I'm going to ask you those questions, now. Is that okay?' Field asked.

Penny nodded.

'Take your time,' Field said quietly. 'When did you last speak to David?'

Penny looked up at the ceiling. 'Not for a while. We're—'

Field waited.

'We're separated. He's been staying in a flat in Plumstead somewhere. I don't have – have the address.'

The words tumbled out of her. It explained why David had been so far from the house.

'We're getting divorced,' Penny said, finally.

'I'm sorry to hear that,' Field said.

'It's amicable,' Penny said. She looked to Wilson, and the notes she was taking. 'We were taking some space. I last spoke to him maybe – maybe three months ago?'

Penny put the mug down on the coffee table, placed her hands on her knees.

The living room, with its pictures of the couple, didn't feel like Penny had gone in for the clean break. Field made a mental note to check the download of David's phone for communication with his wife.

Field moved on. 'Do you know if David has any after-work routines? He was walking home quite late.'

Penny shook her head. 'No.'

Wilson pressed the point. 'Did he have a local?'

'I don't know. He drank in The Mitre while he lived here, but I don't know about now.'

'That's okay, Penny, thank you.' Field kept her next question nonchalant. 'Were you with anyone last night, Penny? Did you go out?'

'No,' Penny said. 'I was here, on my own.'

'Okay, thank you.' Field shut her notebook. 'Do you have any questions for us, Penny?'

Penny tipped her head back and looked at the ceiling. 'Was it a mugging? Why would someone—'

Field waited a few seconds, to see if Penny would keep talking, then answered. 'I'm sorry, Penny, but it really is too early to draw any conclusions. I'm afraid at this stage, I can't be more specific with the details.'

There would be time for details. Field wanted to ask about the study mentioned on the scrap of paper. Make a start on victimology, dig into what made David tick—

But that could come later.

There was a knock on the front door.

'That'll be the FLO. DS Wilson, could you get that please?'

Wilson bobbed her head and left the room again. She came back in with another female officer, DC Zara Ayres.

Introductions were made that Penny seemed to barely register. She sat in silence, picking at dried flour on the hem of her dress.

Ayres had been in MIT4 for a couple of years, but was relatively new to the FLO role. Field had no complaints so far. She was as petite as Penny, smartly dressed in a grey blouse and cream trousers, dark hair in a neat bun.

'I have one last question, if that's okay,' Field said, turning back to Penny with what she hoped was a reassuring smile.

31

'Was David worried about anything? Was there anything unusual going on – or any reason you can think of that someone might want to hurt him?'

Penny shook her head. 'No one could – could want—'

For the first time, her voice cracked.

'Thank you, Penny. You've been so helpful. That's all I need for now.' Field put her hand over Penny's. 'I'm going to talk you through what happens next, okay?'

A crease appeared between Penny's eyebrows, and she pulled her hand away. 'Next?'

Field kept her tone light. 'David is in ICU – intensive care. I'm going to the hospital now, to meet with Dr Young – a forensic medical examiner. That's just so we can get a picture of David's injuries, to help with our investigation.'

Penny's grey eyes were intense, unblinking and unnerving.

'We should be finished with the examination by—' Field looked at her battered Casio. 'I'd say by around 1 p.m. Zara will drive you to the hospital, and she'll wait with you until—'

'No.'

'Penny—'

'I'm not going to the hospital.' She pushed herself to standing, swaying a little. A beam of sunlight fell across her face, making her expression hard to read. 'And I don't need a family liaison officer.'

Penny moved quickly, taking four strides across to the door, almost knocking into Wilson and her second tray of tea.

'Thank you, for coming to let me know.' Penny's voice was strained, and high-pitched. 'But it really is nothing – nothing to do with me.'

Wilson turned to Field, confusion written plainly on her face.

32

'Let's just sit down and take a moment, shall we?' Field put her hands up. 'You don't have to come to the hospital, Penny.'

Penny closed her eyes and took a deep breath. Her cheeks and neck were pink, and she tucked her hair behind her ears before opening her eyes again. 'I'd like you all to leave.'

Wilson and Zara looked to Field.

She kept her movements slow, like she was in no hurry to go – offering Penny plenty of time to change her mind.

Field flicked to a blank page at the back of her notebook, set it down on the coffee table. Reached into her bag to get a pen, then tore out a page. Wrote down her mobile number and email address.

She didn't give it to Penny straight away. Field led Wilson and Zara Ayres back into the hall. Field was hit by a wall of heat as they stepped back out into the morning sun.

She paused on the top step. 'Here's my number, Penny. Call me any time.'

The woman hesitated, then took it.

'Could you give me a contact for someone I can call?' Field asked quietly. 'A friend of David's or a family member, perhaps? We don't want him to be on his own in the hospital.'

A moment of uncertainty, but then Penny disappeared into the house, leaving the door open.

She was back in under a minute, with a business card in hand. 'David's mentor.'

Penny thrust it into Field's hand, nodded at Wilson – and then shut the door.

The whole thing had taken thirty minutes. It always threw her, how quick it was – turning someone's life upside down.

Field and Wilson walked back to the car in silence, and

Zara followed, getting into the back for a quick debrief. No one spoke until all three car doors had slammed.

'That was—' Wilson hesitated. 'Weird. Right?'

'Shock?' Zara said. 'No part of her was expecting that news today.'

'Well, they were getting divorced,' Wilson said, craning her neck to look up at the house. 'Maybe she secretly thinks he deserved it.'

Penny's response had been muted, certainly. Not all victims' families sank to the floor in spasms of anxiety.

Field turned in her seat. 'Thanks for making it so quickly, Ayres.'

Zara smiled. 'Of course, boss.'

It had felt unnatural earlier, calling Ayres by her first name – but it was important in front of the family.

Field's use of surnames for her team was horribly old-fashioned, but a quirk she'd become known for, and secretly enjoyed. A hangover from having a military father, and hating her own first name.

Field chose her words carefully. 'I'm surprised Penny doesn't want to come to the hospital. It might be a tricky one, Zara – but I think you'll need to persevere with her. Try and get her to open up.'

They had a quick chat about timings and logistics. Zara took the business card, and responsibility for contacting Dr Simon Dawes. Then she headed back to her own car, and Wilson started the engine.

Something about Penny made Field uneasy. The fact David had a ring on, but she didn't. The long period of no contact – it was all a little odd.

She glanced back at the house as they pulled away. Closure had its role in all of Field's cases. Families needed the closure of a perpetrator caught and imprisoned.

Field also knew about the closure of a divorce. The relief of it, when it was final.

As long as David pulled through, that was something Penny might still get to have.

# Chapter 7

## Wednesday | Afternoon

## Lily

Lily had been awake for hours, curled in a ball next to the gently snoring form of her boyfriend.

Scott woke up slowly, arching his back and blinking himself into consciousness.

'Morning,' Scott said, his voice husky. He still had his eyes closed.

She shuffled closer to him. 'Afternoon.'

He let out a low groan but smiled. 'What time is it?'

'Almost two o'clock,' Lily answered, pushing his hair away from his sweaty forehead. 'You got home so late last night, I thought you needed the rest.'

Scott stretched, reaching for the ceiling, and then draped a heavy arm over her.

'What're you going to do today?' he asked, eyes still closed.

'I should probably write some lesson plans.'

He grunted. Opened one eye and tried to look down her

shirt. 'I'm not at work until eight tonight. We could get a late lunch?'

'Tempting.' Lily reached up to play with a lock of his hair, twisting it round her index finger. 'But I don't think I can face food.'

He frowned. 'You still feeling beneath the weather?'

'First of all,' Lily sighed. 'It's under the weather, not beneath the weather. Don't they teach you that at medical school?'

Scott rolled his eyes.

'But yes.' She put a hand to her stomach, which was churning. She'd felt a bit hot and sick-y in the mornings for a few days.

Scott lay back down, his hands behind his head, and inspected her cracked ceiling.

'What?' Lily sat up. 'Why do you look all pensive?'

'You don't think—'

There was a loud creak from the hallway, footsteps, and then another door closed with a quiet click. Cal was up.

Neither of them spoke, not wanting Callum to overhear. Lily waited for the familiar gurgle of the taps running, then prompted Scott to continue.

'It's just, you know. You.' He didn't look at her. 'Feeling sick in the mornings.'

Lily's stomach lurched at the idea of it.

She'd already panicked and done two, mercifully negative, pregnancy tests. Thirty-one wasn't particularly young to have kids, but she was far from ready.

She took Scott's hands and pulled him into a sitting position. 'Between the pill and our good friend, latex, I think we're pretty safe.'

Scott still looked worried, and Lily threw her arms around him.

'Besides, who'd want to have your baby?' She laughed into his neck. 'You fucking stink.'

He growled into her shoulder and pushed her flat onto the bed, a hand already inside her pyjama top. He nudged her legs apart with one knee, but her stomach clenched, and she gave him a pat on the shoulder.

He stopped at once and sat back.

'Sorry.' Lily smiled.

Scott's hand moved from her chest to her stomach, letting it rest there for a split second, and then he kissed her lightly on the cheek.

'Got it,' he said, softly. 'None of that until you're feeling the full ticket.'

She felt a twinge of guilt, and relief, and blew her hair out of her face.

Scott climbed off the bed, picked a T-shirt up from a pile on the floor and dragged it on. 'Have you thought about a date? For the move?'

Heat rose in her cheeks. She had been putting off anything to do with moving in together. 'There's still three weeks of the holidays left. Loads of time.'

'I have no idea where all your stuff is going to go.' Scott turned, taking in the room. 'You're not going to be able to bring all this with you.'

She had boxes of old clothes under the bed, wicker baskets full of winter scarves on top of her wardrobe – shelves and windowsills crammed with photo frames and knick-knacks. Small, precious items from places she'd been, the people she'd loved.

Scott's flat was a minimalist one-bed. The only books he bought were coffee-table books and big hardbacks, chosen because the spines looked aesthetic, lined up on the sideboard.

Her eyes went to the sprawling devil's ivy, hanging in a macramé sling. A gift from Callum, years ago, that had slowly taken over one sunny corner of the room.

Scott moved the bric-a-brac on her shelves aside and pulled out a big book of brutalist architecture, picked up on the Southbank years ago.

'I could always just take the essentials to yours.' Lily flopped back onto the bed. 'Cal won't mind me storing some stuff here.'

'Or maybe you should be ruthless, babe. Although we both know how hard you find it—' He flipped through the pages, and then paused, peering closely at a photograph of the Barbican centre. 'Letting go of things.'

# Chapter 8

## Wednesday | Afternoon

### Lily

Lily went to the kitchen to make Scott's toast, and bumped into Cal.

He was constructing an elaborate sandwich, his back to her. Lily stared at the back of his head. He'd buzzed his hair short last week. Lily quite liked it. The buzzcut owned his slight baldness, where the brushed-forwards flyaway mop apologised for it.

He'd been receding since he was twenty-four, his hairline deteriorating at roughly the same rate as their relationship.

'All right?' Cal asked, without turning round.

He'd lost more weight.

Scott was right. It was going to be hard letting Cal go.

'Not bad. Still feel sick-y.' She leaned against the counter, still talking to Callum's back. 'Are you going to get some writing done today?'

He ignored her. 'Loverboy here, is he?'

'Yes,' she answered, demurely, opening the cupboard above the toaster. Her Hovis was half-undone and upside down, confirming the suspicion that Callum was using her bread. The only thing that irritated her more was when he borrowed her leftie scissors, and took them to his room.

She took two slices from the packet and dropped them into the toaster.

'I don't know why he has to stay here so often.' Callum turned to face her, dark circles under his eyes. He was wearing the same clothes as yesterday, and they hung loose on him.

Before she could answer, a sharp stabbing pain in her abdomen made her gasp, a hand going to her side. Callum frowned but didn't say anything. After a few seconds, the pain ebbed away, and Lily straightened up.

'He was on a night shift.' She shut the cupboard door with more force than she meant to, and Cal smirked. 'And ours is closer to the hospital.'

Cal lifted the uncut sandwich in one hand and took a bite.

'If it bothers you, I can always move out.' She let the challenge hang in the air.

'Scott's welcome here any time,' he said, sweetly, through a mouthful of ham.

They both jumped at the knock on the front door.

'Shit.' A large drop of mayonnaise had escaped the sandwich and was dripping down his chest, a white parody of a Halloween stab wound, right above his heart.

The loud knocks on the door continued, but this time it was the pop of the toaster that made Lily jump. Her stomach gave another painful clench.

'Oh, for God's sake,' she muttered, mentally shaking herself and heading for the hall. '*Yes*, I'm coming.'

She rattled the handle, but it was locked.

They had an old-fashioned door you needed the keys to

open. Lily riffled through the junk on the dresser, hunting for them. Broken scissors, chocolate wrappers. A thick wad of pizza and burger leaflets made a break for it, cascading to the floor.

Her keys fell with them, and she snatched them up. If there was ever a fire they'd burn to death.

She was so dazed that it took a second to register that the woman at the door was in police uniform. Her patent leather shoes were shining in the August sunlight.

'Hi there. Last night there was an attack in the area, and we're just knocking to see if you may have seen or heard anything. Could I come in?'

Lily shot a glance at the closed dining room door. 'Not really. Sorry.'

A raised eyebrow. Lily checked over her shoulder. 'It's my,' she hesitated. 'Housemate. He's not well.'

Lily tried to nudge some of the leaflets under the cabinet with her foot.

The policewoman – police officer Lily should call her – checked her notebook. The heat outside was stifling, and Lily thought she must be sweating in her bulky uniform.

Lily wiped her forehead with the back of her hand.

'What's going on?' Cal emerged from the dining room, a cigarette between his lips. He stood behind Lily, a fraction too close.

Even a year after the break-up, they hadn't quite lost that overfamiliarity. Sometimes they'd catch themselves and Cal's hand would be on her waist, or she'd have touched the nape of his neck, like she used to.

'We're knocking to ask if you saw or heard anything suspicious last night. There was an attack in the area, on Ancona Road.'

Lily blinked. 'No – nothing.'

'Me neither.' Callum stared blankly ahead, not quite meeting the woman's eye.

They stood in silence for a second, and Lily was about to suggest that the officer come back later, when she smiled and took a step backwards.

'And you haven't seen anyone suspicious in the area? Nothing that's made you feel uncomfortable or seemed out of place?'

Lily felt Callum shuffle behind her. Not the time to tell this woman that he hadn't left the house in two years.

'No,' Lily said. 'Not that I can think of. Was the person – were they okay?'

The officer smiled a benign smile, tucking her notebook into her vest. 'It's good of you to ask – not everyone does. I can't give out any details, though.'

Lily's stomach churned, and made embarrassing noises. If the officer heard, she didn't react. Lily put a hand on the doorframe to steady herself.

The officer leaned back and scanned the walls. 'Does that camera work?'

'It's a dummy,' Callum answered.

The woman nodded, hooked her thumbs into her vest and took a step back. 'Okay, well, thanks anyway. If you think of anything that might be relevant, you can dial 101, or pop into the station.'

'Okay,' Lily said, already shutting the door. 'Thank you.'

The hinges creaked, and the hallway fell into its usual gloom.

'I'm going to make a brew,' Callum said in monotone, not meeting Lily's eye. His hands shook as he lit his cigarette. 'Want one?'

'No, thanks,' she said.

Lily felt the weight of all the things she *should* say.

She should go to Callum, comfort him. Congratulate him. A stranger at the door – and he'd come and spoken to her.

Lily was so proud of him, she wanted to pull him into a hug. She could imagine the pressure on her chest as he pressed against her, his heart thudding away behind his ribs.

But Callum walked to the kitchen, and Lily stayed frozen, leaning against the front door and holding her aching stomach.

# Chapter 9

**D:** P—, breathe . . .
**P:** I can't breathe. I haven't been able to breathe for years.

*Pause*

**P:** I'm tired, and I'm sad and I'm *angry*. I am so – fucking – angry.

*Pause*

**D:** It's okay. You're safe, here.
**P:** Don't. Don't do that, D—.
**D:** Listen, just take a seat.
**P:** No.

*Pause*

**P:** I need to get out of here. I shouldn't be here, not with you. I need to go home – *move*. Seriously.

*Pause*

**P:** I'm not joking. Get out of my way.

*Pause*

**P:** If you don't move, I'll fucking tell.
I'll tell anyone who will listen.
**D:** P—, please . . .
**P:** Don't touch me.

# Chapter 10

## Wednesday | Afternoon

### Field

As Wilson swung into the King's College car park, Field checked the time on the dash. With lunchtime traffic and blue lights, they'd made it from Plumstead to Denmark Hill in thirty-five minutes. Wilson stopped the car just short of a cross-hatch yellow box, so Field could jump out.

'So you're okay to get back and go over all the CCTV?' Field checked her appearance in the sun visor, and rubbed at a smudge of mascara with a dry finger.

'Yep, no worries. Will you be back to the station today?'

'I don't know. Maybe.' Field flicked the visor up. 'Either way, keep in touch.'

Field didn't stop to watch Wilson pull away. She jogged into the building and went straight to ICU, taking the stairs instead of waiting for a lift.

The clean, medical smell got stronger on the intensive care

ward, and Field stopped at the desk. There were no nurses, and it was eerily quiet.

'Detective Field?'

She turned to see a tall, dark-haired man in scrubs walking towards her.

'Dr Wheatley,' he said by way of introduction, holding his hand out.

Field shook it, briefly wondering how many lives it'd saved.

'David Moore?' she asked, but Wheatley was already nodding his head. She was glad he wasn't one of those doctors who liked to leave a long pause for dramatic effect.

'He's stable, but critical,' he said bluntly, crossing his arms. 'The blood loss was severe. We've put him in an induced coma and he's on a ventilator. The medical examiner is in with him now.'

Still alive.

After a detour to the vending machine on the corridor outside, Field opened the door to David's hospital room with her back. She had to be careful to avoid spilling scalding instant coffee from the lidless polystyrene cups.

'It'll have to be black coffee, I'm afraid,' she said. 'The machine doesn't do bloody oat milk.'

Dr Debra Young looked up. 'You know you sound like a proper boomer when you say stuff like that?'

In spite of everything, and where they were, Field cracked a smile.

Field and Young had worked a case together over twenty years ago, and been friends ever since.

Their boys were the same age, and Young's divorce had come a year or two after Field's. Now they were both single empty-nesters in their early fifties. It was always good to have someone to split a bottle of Pinot with on a Friday night, even if Young's vegan phase was dragging on.

Young nodded at her gloved hands and then at the bedside table, and Field put the coffee down on it.

'Right,' Young said. 'Let me talk you through what I'm thinking.'

Young lifted the covers away from David Moore, folding them over the end of the bed. 'We have nine wounds in total.'

Field looked solemnly down at his injuries.

She was sure that David was a healthy, active ordinary bloke, but in the bed, against the sterile blue sheets, his legs looked thin and pale and vulnerable. The machines he was hooked up to were breathing for him, and the rise and fall of his chest was exaggerated.

'I think I have a reasonably good idea of the order they were inflicted. The tearing of the skin on these makes me think we're looking for a kitchen knife. Incredibly sharp, with a serrated blade.'

'So, someone with access to a kitchen,' Field said softly. 'Great.'

She didn't mean to sound ungrateful. At least Young got straight to the point. Most forensic examiners described how they reached conclusions in excruciating detail, while loading their findings up with arse-covering caveats. Field was impatient at the best of times and, as a trainee detective, would physically bite her tongue to stop herself from snapping at them.

'I think this is the first wound.' Young pointed to his abdomen, just below the ribs, the slash now neatly stitched together. 'It's on the right, which suggests a left-handed attacker. It's hard to tell, because of the treatment he's received but, from the bruising, I think the knife was angled slightly upwards. A shorter attacker, perhaps.'

Young mimed the action. Fist raised, a sharp jab upwards.

'Then the wound pattern becomes – unusual.'

'Unusual how?' Field prompted.

Young frowned. 'Well, with this number of injuries I'd expect to sense that it was frenzied, uncontrolled. I think the second injury was the neck.' She mimed a slashing motion. 'The perpetrator wanted to do maximum damage, but the victim took a step backwards, perhaps, and the wound wasn't as deep as they expected.'

Field looked at the man's face. Under all the tubes he looked older than forty-nine, his features sunken and withered compared to the photos on Penny's mantelpiece.

Young straightened up. 'Then he collapses to the ground. There are slashes to his left arm, which he raises to defend himself.' Young pointed to David's bandaged hands with a gloved finger. 'And here to the hand. I think he grabbed the blade with his left hand. The skin between his thumb and index finger is cut down to the bone.'

Field felt a little sick.

'So our victim is on the ground, hands over his head. Probably twisted over onto his right side, trying to protect the wound he'd already sustained.

'That's when the attacker uses a sweeping downward motion—' Young mimed '—to stab him four more times on the left side, where his leg was raised.'

'So, he stabs him below the ribs, then goes for the neck as David stumbles backwards,' Field said slowly. 'David falls, raises a hand up to protect himself – gets those injuries. Then four more, in quick succession.'

'That's right. The bruising on those four is particularly bad. They must have been standing over him. That would allow a lot of room to swing their arm back and bring it down hard.'

Field frowned. 'And how many times did you say he was stabbed? As in – how many wounds total?'

'Nine,' Young said. 'If he was found even a few minutes later, I'd say it's unlikely he'd still be here.

'What I find interesting—' Young continued, as she replaced the sheet; Field noted the care and respect in the gentle actions as she repositioned the many tubes and wires covering David's chest '—is that the first wound, that one to the ribs – it's an injury typical of males. Face to face, close contact. But the downward stabbing motions when he's on the ground – that's much more typical in acts committed by a female.'

Field hadn't considered that.

She tuned back in to Young's commentary.

'I've drawn blood, although he's had transfusions, so the blood alcohol level won't be accurate. Scrapings from his fingernails will probably take a week, and your team are sending over his clothes, right?'

'They're on their way to your office,' Field said. 'Order whatever tests we need.'

'Great. I'll have an interim report with you by tomorrow, with a list of outstanding bits, and a timeline.'

Dr Wheatley appeared at the door, and he and Young exchanged a few words, before she snapped her gloves off, grabbed her coffee and followed Field out of the room.

There was no respite from the smell of hospital and sickness in the corridor.

Field checked her phone and found a text from Wilson.

*Simon Dawes will be at King's by half two.*

She'd just locked her phone when the screen lit up with a call from the super. Field pushed it back into her pocket. 'Got twenty minutes until David Moore's mentor arrives.'

'Do you want me to stay? To talk to him?' Young took a gulp of the cooled coffee.

Field shook her head. 'It'll be fine. Shoot off if you need to.'

Young shrugged. 'I always have ten minutes for you.'

They ducked into the family room, which was both mercifully empty and air-conditioned. Unlike the rest of the hospital, there were no posters in here. Nothing declaring the importance of handwashing or the dangers of smoking.

Field took a battered brown leather armchair and Young sank into a coral-pink sofa.

Young had trained as a pathologist, but her expertise was the still-living. Across South East London and beyond, it was Young people called when their victim survived their injuries. She had a formidable reputation in court, her scientific rigour and the clarity of her reports leaving little room for defence lawyers to discredit her.

Field asked her once, when they were halfway through their third bottle of Merlot at Young's kitchen table, why she'd taken that route. She thought maybe her friend would say it was about making an impact to living victims, or the scientific complexity of wounds that have been treated, or partially healed.

'It was just because no one was giving me interesting murder cases.' She'd shrugged. Field knew the feeling.

Now Young put her coffee down and started rummaging in her handbag. She pulled out her purse, a novel and two water bottles – leaving them on the coffee table. 'So, you were first on scene?'

'Yep. Just happened to be round the corner. My lucky night, I guess.'

'I mean, you were in Plumstead. If it's going to happen anywhere—' Young said, still excavating items from her bag. 'I'm from there, so I can say that.'

Field was unfazed by the chaos. 'Do you know Ancona Road?'

Young rolled her eyes, scooping items back into her bag.

'Yeah, of course. I lived on Mineral Street until I was about ten. Aha—' She pulled out an oversized pair of sunglasses, and jammed them on her head. 'Can't see a bloody thing when I'm driving in the sun.'

'I forgot about your encyclopaedic memory for road names,' Field said, swallowing a yawn.

Young narrowed her eyes. 'You look done in.'

'Charming.'

'Have you slept?'

Field just looked at her.

'You're getting too old for this, you know,' Young chided. 'But if you *insist* on working these stupid hours, then I've got just the thing for you, somewhere in here.' She thrust a hand deep into her bag, and Field rolled her eyes.

'You work as late as I do—'

'Yes, but I work in a lab, and labs are civilised.'

Field snorted. She'd heard too many of Young's stories about ruined experiments and petty vendettas to buy into that.

Young pulled out an Yves Saint Laurent under-eye concealer with a flourish.

'I hate you,' Field said. 'But I actually am going to borrow that.'

Young grinned. 'Gotta dash.' She downed her coffee, put the empty cup in Field's other hand, and aimed an air kiss near her cheek. 'Will get all the David Moore stuff to you ASAP.'

'All right. I'll call you tomorrow.'

Young aimed a stern look over her shoulder as she hoisted her handbag up. 'Don't forget to sleep.'

# Chapter 11

## Wednesday | Afternoon

### Field

Field was so engrossed in responding to emails on her phone, she almost didn't register the door to the family room opening. When she looked up, in came a man who, to Field, looked like the walking stereotype of a shrink.

Grey cords, even in this weather. Shirt neatly tucked in, a tie that was old in the Noughties. A brown leather weekend bag, monogrammed with his initials. If it was winter, she'd put money on him wearing a tweed jacket with elbow patches.

'Dr Dawes?' she asked.

'Yes, that's me. Call me Simon. You must be Detective Field.'

Field got to her feet, and they shook hands. 'Where have you come from?'

'Cambridge.' He let out a shaky breath, and eyed the mismatched furniture. 'Sorry if I'm a bit—'

Field sat back down, and he followed her lead.

'Can I get you anything to drink? Coffee, or a water?'

'No, thank you.' He put his hands on his knees. 'I expect I should find out what room David is in.'

He spoke with clipped vowels and pinpoint precision, and Field's own South London twang felt conspicuous in comparison. If she didn't watch herself, she'd end up using her customer-service voice.

'Simon,' she said. 'I appreciate you're keen to see David, but it'd be helpful to have a quick word.'

Simon pushed his glasses higher up his nose and frowned. 'With me?'

Field offered a reassuring smile. 'It's nothing formal. It's just helpful to build up a picture of David. The more we know about him the better.'

Simon sank back into his chair with a sigh.

'Penny said you were David's mentor?' Field offered.

'That's right. We met when he was on his very first placement. For the last five years, I've been his therapist.' He smiled at her confused expression. 'Oh yes, DCI Field. A lot of therapists are in therapy. It's practically mandatory.' He folded his arms. 'So. How can I help?'

Field turned to a new page in her notebook. 'I didn't know anything about OCD, before this morning,' she said. 'That might be a useful place to start, before we speak about David.'

'Ah. Yes. Well, for a condition half the population claims to have, OCD is very little understood,' Simon said, his tone reassuring. 'It's partly why it's such a difficult illness to treat. Why don't you tell me what you *do* know?'

It was like being put on the spot at school.

'Well, I know some people wash their hands to excess. Or check the house before they go out, flick on light switches.' Field knew enough not to say anything about keeping things tidy or lining pencils up in a row. 'Like I said – I don't know anything, really.'

'What you've described there are the *compulsions*, Detective. It goes a lot deeper than that, I'm afraid.'

It wasn't a rebuke. She felt uncomfortable, the room warmer than a moment ago – but she did need to understand this stuff. For the case. 'How would you explain it? To a lay person, I mean.'

He puffed out his cheeks. 'Okay. Take your handwashing example. A person may be convinced that their hands are dirty, even though they have just washed them and can see quite plainly that their hands are clean.'

Simon looked down at his own palms. His tone was patient, not patronising.

'They know that thinking their hands are dirty is irrational, but the anxiety is building. If they move about the house with these dirty hands, how many surfaces might they touch? What might they contaminate? What if that previous handwash wasn't thorough enough?'

He looked up at her, over the top of his glasses. 'So? They wash their hands again. And performing that compulsion brings relief – albeit temporary relief – from the anxiety. It's like taking paracetamol for a headache. But—' he held up an arthritic finger '—and this is the crucial part, the relief that the compulsion brings *reinforces* the idea that there was actually something wrong in the first place.'

Field nodded, her impatience biting at her. She needed to move on to practical and tangible questions. *Who were David's friends? How had he seemed in the past few weeks?*

But Simon Dawes wasn't done.

She suspected that this speech was something Dawes had delivered before, for an audience of students, maybe. He was expressive, hands constantly moving, illustrating his points.

'Now this pattern of thinking, the decision to perform the compulsion – it can take place in seconds. Imagine spending almost every waking moment of the day, bargaining with yourself. If I act out this compulsion – wash my hands, check the gas again, perform that ritual, avoid touching that, say that phrase out loud, ask my partner for reassurance – then I can dampen down the anxiety enough to go about my day.

'And they're not always big things. They can be tiny, seem insignificant on their own. But the whole cycle can be playing on a loop, multiple times a minute, hundreds of times an hour – with little to no respite.'

'That sounds exhausting.' Field spoke quietly.

Where could you escape to, she wondered, if you were under attack from your own thoughts?

'Quite,' he agreed.

They sat in silence for a moment.

'I don't think I could do it.' Field sat back in her chair. 'Your job, I mean.'

'Not my job anymore.' Simon sighed. 'I got out years ago, took the academic route. David could have done the same. Any university would have bitten his arm off. Cushty teaching job, contributing to papers, wood-panelled office.'

She was glad he'd brought them back to David. It felt like terra firma, compared to the last five minutes.

Field cleared her throat. 'Why didn't he go the academic route?'

Simon hesitated. 'Well, he always did solid research, and he taught modules at KCL. But he always kept an active practice, had patients. It was like he *needed* to be doing the doing, you know?'

'I know a few coppers like that, to be fair,' Field said. 'Would rather die of a heart attack during a drugs raid than ride a desk.'

Was that her? Would she be one of those old hands who had to be managed out?

Simon carried on. 'Some psychologists avoid treating OCD, you know? Don't like it.'

'Really?'

He leaned towards her. 'You give a lot of yourself to OCD patients. You're always searching for the real fear. The obsessions might manifest in any of those things we discussed – but there's always something deeper at play. You deal with all the anxiety and the compulsions *and* at the same time, you have to work back to where it all comes from in the first place.

'And what is the difference between healthy fear, and what's OCD? There's no clear line.' He raised his hands to the ceiling. 'We can't promise them they won't get sick, or their family member won't get hit by a car.'

Her head was reeling. She was too tired for this level of philosophical conversation.

'But David . . .' She hesitated. 'He was good with OCD patients?'

'Oh yes.' Simon nodded emphatically, like a proud father. 'One of the best.'

Field opened her mouth, then closed it again. An image of Toby as a teenager came to her unbidden.

*No.*

She turned over a new page in her notebook, even though the previous one was still blank, and gripped the pen more firmly. 'Were you aware of David and Penny's separation?'

For the first time, Simon looked uncomfortable. 'Well, yes. I'd spoken to both of them, as it happens.' He uncrossed and recrossed his legs.

'She didn't want to come to the hospital,' Field said, gently. 'That's unusual, in my experience.'

'She hasn't always had an easy time of it,' Simon said. The warmth was gone from his voice.

Field examined his posture, the new hunch of his shoulders. She waited for him to continue.

'Penny wouldn't wish David any ill, whatever was going on between them. She gave you my details, didn't she?' He waited for Field's nod. 'Well, then.'

Field wasn't sure the erudite doctor had quite made his point, but she let it drop.

From then on, the rest of the conversation was perfunctory, and straightforward. A list of colleagues it might be useful to speak to. David's mood, his favourite pubs. He wasn't dating. He hadn't had any issues at work.

They spoke for another ten minutes, and as far as Simon Dawes was concerned, there was no reason for anyone to wish David harm.

'That's been really useful, thank you, Simon.' Field drew the conversation to an end, feeling less perturbed than she had at the beginning.

'Of course, if there's anything else I can do . . .' He got out of the low seat with a slight groan.

'Well, actually, I do think we need to speak to Penny again today. Briefly.'

His expression darkened. Was that protectiveness?

'But it may help her to have you there, for support.' Field held the door open for him. 'I'll let you spend some time with David. I'm going to head back to the station for a few hours.'

'But you want me back at the house later, when you speak to her again?' he asked.

'I think it might help.' Field gave an apologetic shrug.

Simon picked up his bag, and Field registered that if he'd come from Cambridge with a bag that size, he might be planning to stay in the area.

'Are you heading back home today?' she asked.

'I was thinking of staying with Penny, for support. That is, if she would like me to,' he said stiffly. 'So I suppose I shall see you later.'

# Chapter 12

## Wednesday | Afternoon

### Field

Riley and Wilson had run a full team briefing while she was at the hospital. By the time Field got back to the station, her DCs were talking in hushed voices, moving busily between desks – getting on with the job at hand, while Raynott's bored officers looked on enviously.

Field went straight into her office, which had the same sterile, over-bright strip lighting as the hospital, and chucked her handbag under her desk.

She felt like she had jet lag, but there wasn't time to go home and sleep. The first few days would be crucial, and she had plenty of ironed shirts ready on the back of her office door.

A quick knock, and Riley's head appeared round the door. 'Cup of tea, boss?'

'Coffee,' Field said, and then added as an afterthought, 'Please.'

Riley left without needing to ask how she took it.

Field pulled her phone from her handbag, answered a few emails that couldn't wait for her computer to warm up. Toby's number flashed up on the screen, and she answered on the second ring.

'Christ,' Toby said, startled. 'I wasn't expecting you to pick up.'

'Had the phone in my hand,' Field said. 'Everything okay?'

Her pulse quickened in the few seconds it took him to answer.

'Yeah, everything's fine, Mum. I just got off shift and saw your text. You were at that Plumstead stabbing?'

'I'm the bloody SIO, and Young's on it too. Do you know any of the paramedics who were there?' she said, leaning over to power on her laptop. Nothing happened. The screen stayed black.

'Nope, not our station. Word got round about it, though. Miracle they kept him alive, by the sounds of it.'

Her charging cable was curled innocently under the desk. She swore under her breath and plugged the laptop in.

Toby laughed. 'You're really not listening to me, are you?'

'Sorry, sorry.' Field leaned back into her desk chair. 'There's a lot on. How was your shift?'

'Oh fine. Mostly dealing with old ladies. You know the type – early fifties, can't operate an iPhone—'

Field grinned, and her laptop blinked into life. 'You're not too old for a smack, you know?'

'Oh, I know. So, can I assume our dinner date is cancelled tonight?'

Her stomach sank. Toby's boyfriend, Billy, was away for the weekend. She'd booked their favourite Italian for a catch-up, and to give Toby a break from revising.

He was only a few weeks away from sitting the final exams

for his paramedicine degree, meaning he would go from being an ambulance technician to a fully fledged paramedic.

'I'm sorry – I totally forgot. I was supposed to be off today—'

'Don't apologise, Mum,' he said, gently.

Field stabbed in her password, her cheeks hot. 'I shouldn't have forgotten.'

Riley returned with two steaming black coffees, and took the seat opposite. She nodded her thanks and looked down at the mug, a beacon of syrupy hope amid the unfiled paperwork.

'I've got to go,' she said. 'I'll call you later, okay?'

Riley tapped his fingers against his mug.

'Sure,' Toby said – and he sounded fine. 'Love you, Mum.'

'You too,' she said, and hung up.

'Everything okay, boss?' Riley asked.

'Fine,' she said. 'Where's Wilson?'

'I think—' He spun in his chair and craned his neck to look out over the office. 'She's printing some shit off.'

'Right, okay.' Field took a large gulp of the coffee, and her laptop finally turned on.

'Have you spoken to the super yet?' Riley asked, his voice tight.

Field contemplated her answer. For Riley and Wilson, this case could be career-defining, but there was still every chance the super would allocate it to a DCI with a more senior team, and they'd end up working the fringes of it.

'He hasn't called in the last hour, so that's a good sign,' she answered, finally.

Wilson burst through the office door already speaking. 'Boss – you're going to want to see this. It's about the document you found – oh.'

Wilson caught sight of Riley and stopped short in the middle of the room. He smiled up at her from his chair, and Wilson's eyes flicked upwards. She'd clearly hoped to share her find without him.

Wilson laid a thick printout on Field's desk. The title page matched the sheet found tangled in David's clothes. *The Disordered Approach to Diagnosis.*

'I thought I asked you to look into this?' Field said to Riley, eyebrows raised.

'I delegated.' Riley shrugged, and behind him Wilson's jaw clenched.

'Well, *I* got someone to look this up, like you asked, and it wasn't something Moore was working on recently.' Wilson leaned over and tapped the date at the bottom of the sheet. 'The paper is fifteen years old.'

'So why would he be carrying it round with him on a Tuesday night?' Riley said, through a yawn.

'I've given it a quick glance,' Wilson said, breathless. 'The paper was published in 2010, after a pilot study with five teenagers, all sectioned.' Wilson turned to a patient list and tapped it. 'Five kids, all let down by the system, all hospitalised at the Maudsley between 2008 and 2009.'

Unbidden, an image of Toby flashed into Field's mind. Fifteen and unable to get out of bed. Barely saying ten words per day, refusing to eat.

'Oh God, we're going to be looking for some schizo, aren't we?' Riley muttered.

The look Field gave Riley would have withered even her most senior colleagues, and he looked cowed.

'Is it relevant though?' Riley asked. 'What does this have to do with the stabbing?'

'Well, it was in his pocket, or under the body or whatever,' Wilson snapped. 'That makes it pretty relevant.'

Field thought back to that morning, the moment she found

the sheet in the torn-away clothing. She woke her computer screen up, flicked through the crime scene photographs.

David had been clutching it to his chest, the paramedic had said. There was nothing to hint at whether the sheet of paper had been deliberately placed on the body by the attacker.

Riley and Wilson were still bickering.

'Maybe Moore has some sort of saviour complex. Carries it round to show off to people.'

'He's done much more impressive work since then.' Wilson's voice rose. 'Why would he be showing people page one of a paper from fifteen years ago?'

Field was scanning the witness statements of the residents who found Moore.

'Fifteen years. That's the point, Wilson. It's good background but it's hardly motive for murder, is it?'

'How do you know?' Wilson scoffed. 'You haven't read it.'

'Enough,' Field said, and they both snapped their mouths shut. Wilson had her arms folded. Riley feigned nonchalance.

'I want us to assume that this wasn't something David dropped. It may be a long shot, but if the attacker left it for us to find, then it's our first real lead.'

Wilson's mouth twitched at the corners.

'So—' Field sighed. 'This study will have been totally anonymous, and it's old. Is there anything in here we can identify the five kids with?'

'Well,' Wilson said slowly, picking up the stack of paper again. 'They all had different presentations of OCD. Like, there was one who was scared of noise, one who had the germs kind. There are details in that sense.'

'Write up a summary, and Riley – speak to the Maudsley and see if there's any record of who these kids were.' He went to speak, and she cut him off. 'I know, I know they won't tell us anything – but just try, okay?'

65

He nodded.

'How are we getting on with tracking down Moore's current patients?' Field asked.

'Precisely nowhere.' Riley huffed, flicking his notebook open. 'Someone told me that all therapists have something called a "clinical will" – which means Moore had a plan for all his current patients, in case he got ill or – well, died. I've asked to see it – but without a court order no one will send me anything. Reckon it'll be next week, earliest. Patient confidentiality—'

'Right, okay,' Field interrupted. 'Stay on it, anyway.'

The two of them sat forward in their seats, anticipating her next instruction.

Field geared herself up for one of her mentoring monologues.

'We need to be sensitive,' she said firmly. 'There will be press coverage in a case like this – and I don't want to be accused of jumping to conclusions. OCD is not an illness that usually presents with delusions or violence.'

Field delivered this fact with more confidence than her conversation with Dr Dawes actually afforded her.

'If anyone we identify as a person of interest does suffer from a mental illness, I still want us to look for a motive.'

Wilson glanced down at the academic paper.

Field leaned forward, directing her next comments to Riley. 'The whole team – not just us three, everyone – I want us to be mindful that we might not be conducting run-of-the-mill witness interviews. We are dealing with potentially vulnerable people, who may be deeply affected by what's happened to their therapist.'

Nods all round. It felt like enough arse covering, and enough of a warning.

# Chapter 13

*The Disordered Approach to Diagnosis:* a pilot study of the impact of misdiagnoses on young people with complex presentations of obsessive-compulsive disorder, and subsequent group-therapy treatment

## Background

Cognitive-behaviour therapy (CBT) is the recommended psychological treatment for obsessive-compulsive disorder (OCD) in young people. However, research shows young patients with complex OCD presentations (e.g. misophonia, body-focused repetitive behaviours) spend 18–36 months longer seeking a diagnosis and treatment via the NHS. (McLaren, 2008)

Access to a correct early diagnosis may be limited by several factors, including lack of trained therapists, and geographic or financial factors preventing access to a specialised service. This pilot study describes outcomes for a group-based cognitive-behavioural treatment for OCD in young people who have experienced lengthy misdiagnosis, and explores the impact this delay has had on their subsequent illness.

## Method

Five participants, aged 13 to 16 years, received up to 25 hours of CBT per month. This was supported with weekly talking therapy sessions in a group setting. All five participants were hospitalised at the time of the pilot.

## Participants

**Patient A** – ritualistic eating, compulsions around food. Misdiagnosed as body dysmorphic disorder (BDD).

**Patient B** – severe dermatillomania. Misdiagnosed as generalised anxiety disorder (GAD).

**Patient C** – harm OCD coupled with severe misophonia. Misdiagnosed as autism-spectrum disorder (ASD) and post-traumatic stress disorder (PTSD).

**Patient D** – counting and magical thinking. Misdiagnosed as borderline personality disorder (BPD).

**Patient E** – contamination OCD and magical thinking. Misdiagnosed as GAD.

## Results

Improvements were found for OCD symptoms across all informants. All five participants were discharged from hospital care at the end of the pilot, with continued support taking place in the community. Follow-ups will be carried out at 3-month intervals for 24 months.

## Conclusions

The findings suggest that group therapy is a clinically effective, feasible and acceptable means of service delivery that offers the potential to make CBT a more accessible treatment for young people. This therapy requires further evaluation in randomised, controlled trials to compare effectiveness with one-to-one CBT at the point of the eventual diagnosis, which currently represents the usual care model. Furthermore, the study highlights the need for greater education of general practitioners and therapy services, to ensure complex cases of OCD are diagnosed effectively and as early as possible.

# Chapter 14

**P:** I'm sorry.

*Pause*

**P:** I can't live like this anymore.
**D:** You can, P—. It'll get easier, I promise.

*Pause*

**P:** I'm so tired.
**D:** I know.

*Pause*

**D:** But I'm here. I won't let anything happen to you. You know that, don't you?

*Pause*

**P:** Take this away. Please?

*Pause*

**D:** I can't—
**P:** I don't want it anymore. I can't do it. Please, D—, *please* - give it to someone else.

*Pause*

**D:** It's okay. It's all going to be okay.

*Pause*

**D:** You're a brave girl, aren't you? You're going to be brave.

# Chapter 15

## Wednesday | Evening

## Lily

'Callum,' she yelled over her shoulder. 'Callum.'

'What?' he shouted back, and the direction of his voice surprised her. He wasn't in the dining room – he was on the toilet.

There was a flush and she waited impatiently. He sauntered in, drying his hands on a tea towel.

She raised her eyebrows and nodded her head in the direction of the washing-up. 'Well?'

He looked from her to the sink, and back again.

'I'm sorry,' he said with a shrug, and clearly no idea what he was apologising for.

'You're not fucking sorry.' She pulled the towel out of his hands. 'I've asked you so many times, *not* to leave washing-up soaking in cold, dirty water.'

'In my defence,' Cal said, stifling a yawn. 'When I put the dishes in there, the water was hot and clean.'

It was the sort of conversation they had a hundred times a year, but the mood in the room was wrong.

Callum hadn't spoken since the policewoman left. His eyes looked shiny, and his skin was red. He might have been crying, but if he had he'd never admit it to her. His anxiety hung in the air between them.

'Fine,' Lily snapped. She gritted her teeth and put her hand into the sink, to pull the plug out. 'Fucking fine.'

Callum sifted through the biscuit tin on the side, coolly unconcerned.

She lifted a plate out of the water and slammed it down on the counter. 'It's not enough that I do everything for you, and all I ask is your help with this one thing. Who fucking cares if I don't want dirty plates sitting in the sink? What do I fucking know?'

He still didn't react, just extracted a bourbon from the tin.

She pushed past him and stalked out of the kitchen. The house smelt of stale cigarette smoke and sweat.

She took a seat at the dining table, still littered with Callum's empty cans from last night. There were rings on the polished wood. Dark circles with fainter satellites. Ghosts of yesterday's poor decisions.

The room was depressing. There was shit everywhere, crap filling up every space. Junk mail, old magazines. The band posters they'd picked out in Greenwich market were wonky in their cheap frames.

She looked up at the yellow ceiling as a creak came from above – Scott moving around her room, getting ready for his shift.

'Look, Lil.' Callum followed her into the room. 'I am sorry, okay? About the washing-up.'

'It's okay,' Lily said, after a pause.

Cal took a seat at the table, put his feet up. The bottoms of his socks were black. 'Do you want a Mars bar?'

73

He lifted a multipack out of the fruit bowl.

'You know they're mine, right?' Lily said. 'You're literally offering me my own shit.'

He took one from the packet, made direct eye contact, and peeled the wrapper off.

'Don't you fucking dare,' Lily warned, trying not to smile.

He didn't speak. He took an enormous bite and then let out a bark-like laugh.

'You're an arsehole,' she said with a laugh, flinging a handful of crumpled napkins in his direction. Cal ducked and stood up, chewing with his mouth open, rolling the gummed-up nougat in his mouth.

Lily jumped from her chair, her laughter making her stomach ache worse. She made a snatch for the Mars bar.

Then she tripped, and Cal shot an arm out, catching her round the waist, just before she hit the floor.

Scott entered the room, dressed for work in dark scrubs. He looked at them both. Took in the mess, the ashtray they'd knocked over.

Lily shot away from Callum. She caught Cal's eyeroll as he stalked off to the kitchen.

'Have you seen my wallet?' Scott called, fumbling around for his shoes.

She scanned the dark hallway. 'No.'

The bulb had blown months ago, and Cal hadn't bothered to replace it. Lily hadn't changed it as an experiment, to see how long it would be before he sorted it out. He'd been promising to fix the broken back door for months, too.

'I must have left it at work. What are you doing tonight?' Scott asked.

Lily shrugged and passed Scott one of his brogues.

He leaned against a wall as he pulled it on. 'Bye then.'

'Have a good shift,' Lily said, over-bright, standing on tiptoes and planting a kiss on his cheek.

He caught her round the waist and held her to him. She felt his solid warmth through his shirt, his hair tickling her cheek.

'Take this,' he said, pressing his door key into her hand. 'I've got a spare in my locker. Go to my place tonight, have some time to yourself, and then I'll see you when I get in.'

'I can't,' she said, into his shoulder. 'Not today. After the police knocked earlier, he's stressed – I need to keep an eye on him.'

Scott let go of her and turned to the door. 'Right. Whatever.'

'Scott.' She leaned forward to grab his arm. 'Don't be like that.'

'Like what? Like it bothers me that we've been dating for almost a year, and you still live with your ex-boyfriend?'

Scott looked down at her, his jaw set and his eyes cold. He still had one hand on the door.

'I never pretended the situation wasn't a mess,' she answered, keeping her voice even.

Scott dropped his voice to a loud whisper. 'Have you even told him you're moving out?'

Lily glanced at the door to the living room. 'Can we not do this right before you leave?'

Scott turned without speaking and slammed the front door behind him. She was still clutching his key in her fist.

Lily put off seeing Callum for as long as possible.

She attempted to work on some lesson plans. Gave up and cleaned the sides in the kitchen instead, and the bath – anything to avoid the living room.

Finally, gearing herself up to go and talk to him, she had a fag on the front doorstep.

After she closed the front door, Lily leaned against it, standing on the junk mail, hemmed in by dusty coats on hooks. She reached out and held on to the corner of Callum's red parka, as if it could bring her comfort.

She'd always known Callum to wear a parka. He'd wear it too late into spring, when everyone else was in light jackets and overshirts. You always could see him coming down the street, head down, fur facing forward.

For the last two years it'd hung on the same hook in the hallway. Sometimes with one of her coats over it, sometimes slipping onto the floor, but never worn.

She let the parka go and rapped on the living room door.

After a full day with all the curtains in the house closed tight, Cal had thrown the living room windows wide open.

He'd pushed the sofa right back against the wall and twisted the armchair, so it was facing the window and the street. He had his feet up on the sill, ankles crossed in his thick sports socks.

There were a few candles lit, guttering in the breeze, and the lamp was on in the corner. A Beatles vinyl was playing, the one she'd bought for his birthday a few years ago, crackly from constant use.

'All right?'

He twisted his head to look at her. 'Hey.'

'I like the living room like this.' She sat on the sofa, stretching her own legs, and following his gaze out of the window, to the orangey sunset beyond. Cal didn't speak.

'Are you okay, Cal?'

He drew in a deep breath. 'Yeah,' he said, on the exhalation.

Cal's notebook was on the floor, between them. Lily hadn't read any of his writing since their break-up. The gold nib of the fountain pen winked at her.

She leaned back into the worn cushions, letting some of the tension in her shoulders melt into them.

A moment of silence in between songs.

The record crackled into life again and they sat, side by side, listening to "Revolution" and the traffic from the main road.

Cal had a flair for the dramatic. A knack for being impulsive in the midst of self-destruction. When they were younger, finding Callum contemplating an open bay window like it held the meaning of life would have left Lily feeling inspired, by his depth and capacity to feel. She had been slightly in awe of him once, of his ability to blow up his life and make it look like a lifestyle choice.

Now, it all left her slightly sad.

'David phoned yesterday,' he said. 'They're taking my disability living allowance away again.'

She didn't say anything.

'You knew?' he asked, still looking dead ahead.

'I spoke to him on Monday.' Lily sighed. 'We can appeal it. I've got all the paperwork. There's that bloke at the helpline that we used last year.'

'David will write me a statement, won't he?' Callum asked.

'He's already sent it over.'

Cal nodded. 'They think I'm fit to go and look for work, apparently. Proper work, they mean.'

Lily reached across the gap between their chairs and took his hand. The skin of his palms was rough, and her hand felt tiny in his. The tips of her fingers barely reached his knuckles when they were palm to palm.

'We'll appeal it, Cal,' she said again. 'It'll be fine.'

'Lil?' He squeezed her hand and then let it drop. 'Shall we get really fucking drunk?'

# Chapter 16

## Wednesday | Evening

## Field

Field pulled up at the Moores' house a little after six, after a detour through a McDonald's drive-thru for a large fries. She was running on fumes.

She'd phoned Simon Dawes on the way, but he was still at the hospital. Field wondered if he was avoiding her.

Penny answered the door, still looking dry-eyed and composed. Her hair was pulled back into a small ponytail, and she'd taken off her make-up. Her feet were bare, her toenails painted pink.

Field noted that she wore her watch on her right wrist.

'I'm sorry to turn up again so soon,' Field said. 'I have a few more questions.'

Penny led Field through to the garden. She'd have preferred to have Ayres with her. It helped a family to bond to the FLO, when they were there throughout the process, and usually families clung to their liaison for far longer than the officer was supposed to stay.

Field let out a soft "oh" at the patio doors. The walled garden was small but bursting with colour. Around the edge of the cobbled patio were raised beds, planted with poppies, wildflowers and luscious green shrubbery. Ivy and jasmine climbed the walls – the latter giving the garden its heavy perfume.

'This was David's pride and joy,' Penny said, flatly.

Penny took a seat at the wrought-iron table in the centre of the garden. She was still wearing the same floaty summer dress, and it clashed with her shock.

Field took a seat opposite Penny, steeling herself for the questions she needed to ask. 'Firstly. Are you sure there's no one who can confirm you were home last night, Penny?'

Penny shook her head. She was spaced out, like she'd taken something. A beta blocker, or maybe diazepam. Field would ask Zara to have a discreet look in the bathroom cabinets next time she was at the house.

'And are you sure you're okay to be on your own? Simon Dawes said he could come and stay with you.'

Penny reached out and pulled a dead flowerhead from its stem, with her left hand.

'Well, it would be good, if he could come over,' Field said, keen to press the idea. Penny's ambivalence was hard to read. 'Now – I know this is the last thing you want to talk about, but I'd like to ask you about your relationship with David. When did you separate?'

Penny's voice was flat. 'Six months ago. He stayed in the spare room for a few weeks, before he found his flat and left.'

A long pause.

'We haven't spoken for a while,' Penny said. 'He thought – we thought it would be easier. Clean break, for now.'

David's phone download was back from Digital Forensics already. Field had checked it herself before she left the station – it had been three months since their last contact.

Field filed the word *estranged* away for later.

Penny was coming across as cold, possibly uncaring. But was that just shock? Was she just the buttoned-up repressed type who found it hard to process things?

Field gave a supportive smile. 'Do you mind telling me why you split up?'

Penny gave a jerky shake of the head. 'No. I don't want to talk about it.'

'I know,' Field urged. 'I'm divorced myself, and I know it's awful. But it might help us.'

Penny nodded and covered her eyes with her palm. 'I was jealous.'

Field waited.

Penny shook her head behind her hand, then pushed her hair away from her face.

'I was jealous of his work, his obsession with his work. Jealous of his *patients*, even.' Her voice was clipped, and she turned her head slightly, not meeting Field's eye. 'He kept up his NHS clinics, still lectured long after all his colleagues stopped. Private patients in the evenings, even weekends sometimes.'

'That must have been hard for you,' Field said, shifting forward in her chair, to avoid a ray of sun that kept blinding her. 'Had you tried to resolve it?'

'I gave up work a few years ago – with *stress*.' Penny said the last word like it was a source of great shame. 'He didn't mind but that made it worse, just sitting around all day.'

Penny straightened in her chair, sitting straight-backed and rigid.

Field could sense her distress beneath the stoicism. 'What did you do, Penny?'

'Community work. A nurse, for the British Heart Foundation.'

'Okay, thank you. Sorry, you were saying—'

Penny sniffed. 'I told David to take a sabbatical. He was nearly fifty – he needed a break. We could finally spend time together, do some work on the house—'

Field took a second to process what Penny was saying. She had been awake for almost twenty-four hours and the warm, scented air wasn't helping her focus. 'And David said no?'

She nodded, hands clenched in her lap. 'That's when I told him I wanted a divorce. He wanted to be their doctor more than he wanted to be married to me.'

Penny had given David an ultimatum and she'd ended up with the unfavourable outcome – but he was still wearing his wedding ring when he was attacked. He hadn't let go of the marriage yet.

'You said you had to give up work with stress, Penny. Did that contribute to the situation, do you think?'

Penny gave her a puzzled look, as though trying to gauge the relevance of this question. Finally, she responded, in a low voice. 'I supported David through everything. I met him when I was young and spent the best part of two decades supporting him. But when I needed support?' Penny lifted a hand to her forehead and rubbed at it, like she was getting a headache.

The thought seemed to trail off. A lawnmower started up in the distance.

Field moved on, raising her voice to be heard. 'Penny, this next question may seem confusing, but it's our job to investigate all possibilities. Our attention has been drawn to a paper David published in 2010—'

It was a clumsy, abrupt shift in topic – but there was no natural way to bring up David's study.

Penny blinked, slowly. 'That was fifteen years ago.'

'I know—' Field hesitated. 'And I know it seems strange,

me asking about it. Do you remember that paper, by any chance?'

'I – yes, of course. It kick-started his career.'

'Okay, great,' Field said. 'And, could you tell me your impression of the study? What it meant for David at the time? Anything you think is relevant – I'd love to hear it.'

Penny folded her arms. 'It takes years to become a psychologist. After his master's, while he was an associate psych, he worked on a mixed inpatient ward – adults and teenagers. CAMHS wasn't really a thing everywhere yet—'

'CAMHS?' Field asked.

'Child and Adolescent Mental Health Services,' Penny replied, automatically. 'He was only on that mixed ward for a year, but after that he wanted to work with teenagers.'

A nectar-drunk bee passed by Penny's shoulder, but she didn't notice it.

'And of the five patients David worked with for that pilot study – they were all teenagers with OCD, is that right?' Field prompted, nudging them back on topic.

'Yes, although most of them didn't know it. Misdiagnosed – until David.' Penny leaned forward. 'He just seemed to *get* them. And David, he threw everything at those kids, and that study. Got buy-in from the Maudsley, met with their GPs, drew up new treatment plans – he worked himself half to death. Two years, that trial went on.'

Field waited and shifted uncomfortably on her iron chair.

Five teenage patients who had been the foundation of Moore's career. He got them better and they got him attention. Together they must have changed countless lives.

Talk about intense relationships.

She'd been on a course, recently, about transference. Some prick of a DI at another station got too friendly with a victim and she declared her love for him, so they packed the whole borough off on an away day.

It was a train of thought for another time.

'I know this seems odd, but we really do need to contact those five patients, from the study,' Field ventured again.

Penny was twitching one foot under the table, her stare fixed on a point above Field's head. Back to the spaced-out expression she'd had at the start of their conversation.

Finally, she shrugged. 'I don't know their names.'

Penny knew a lot about the trial, and Field found it hard to believe they'd never once discussed the individuals involved.

'Did he ever speak about them? Even anonymously—'

'I don't know their names,' Penny said again, and her voice rose in pitch. 'All of this, David – it's nothing to do with me.'

She looked flushed, her cheeks red.

Field couldn't be sure she was telling the truth.

But for now, she had what she needed, and what Penny needed was rest. 'Okay. I'll leave you to it.'

Field closed her notebook. When she looked up and stood to leave, Penny was studying her intently.

Penny followed closely behind her, all the way to the front door, as if scared Field was about to duck into one of the rooms and start poking around.

Field hesitated on the doorstep.

Penny had downplayed having to give up work, but whatever had led to it must have been pretty severe. Field wanted her to open up, let the cold exterior drop and admit she was scared for her husband.

But Penny was chewing the inside of her cheek, distracted – and Field was tired. She could come back tomorrow and try again then.

# Chapter 17

## Wednesday | Evening

## Lily

Lily could hear Cal singing as he climbed the stairs to the upstairs toilet. She frowned to herself. It was hard to imagine him living in the house without her.

She picked up her glass, swilled the last few mouthfuls of whisky around in it.

One wall of the living room was covered by bookcases. Floor to ceiling.

They spent the night Lily officially moved in pulling all his books down from the shelves and unpacking hers from boxes. They'd eaten Chinese from the containers and arranged the books by theme.

The bottom shelves were the books they were both a little embarrassed to admit they owned. Dan Browns and *Game of Thrones* for him, the *Twilights* and *Fifty Shades* for her.

The vast Mills & Boon collection, which Callum's nan had built over fifty years, had pride of place across the top shelves.

There was a whole section dedicated to children's books – mostly hers. A sombre run of grey and dark green titles on First World War poetry of Callum's, with a separate shelf for Edward Thomas.

He had a shelf of books about OCD that David had recommended over the years. Invariably he got a few chapters in, and then lost interest. Lily had read them all.

There were thin volumes of plays above those. Cookbooks on the right. Books about art on the left.

Lily bought Cal a stand for one particularly beautiful coffee-table book about the Sixties, and he had propped it open on a double-page spread about Woodstock.

Then their life together. Years and years of pulling books from shelves and shoving them back at random. More books bought and crammed wherever they would fit. Loaned to friends, while they could still visit.

Lily looked over her shoulder, then stepped up to one of Cal's shelves. Took down his battered copy of *Hamlet*. The faded cream cover was well worn along the spine, and an illustrated theatre mask grimaced up at her. She opened it carefully, his most precious book.

On the inside, in looping handwriting, was the message Lily had seen so many times before:

> Dear Callum,
>
> I thought you should have a copy
> of this, as it's my favourite.
> Remember: 'There is nothing
> either good or bad but thinking
> makes it so.'
> All my love – P

Lily put the book back, tipped more whisky into her glass and took a step backwards from the shelves.

Tried to imagine them full of gaps.

'It's not funny,' Lily protested, still laughing. 'I have to teach that kid for the next two years.'

Cal threw his head back and laughed, almost knocking his whisky flying.

They'd moved to the dining room. It was in the middle of the house, between the living room at the front and the kitchen in the extension at the back. A large, square space with a round table in the centre and booming speakers, where the world was put to rights.

Callum hadn't redecorated since his nan died. She'd left him the little two-up two-down six years ago, mortgage paid off. It had been a lifeline to both of them, especially as his OCD had got worse again over the past two years, and he'd stopped going out.

'Incredible.' Cal downed the rest of the whisky and winced, taking a swig of beer after.

'I thought you liked whisky.' Lily took a demure sip of wine, eyebrows raised.

'I do.' Cal pointed the bottle at her. 'But I'm very proud of my Scottish heritage, and *you*, Lily Stewart. You bought Jameson's.'

'It all tastes like nail varnish remover to me, Scottish or Irish.'

'Take that back,' he exclaimed, mock outraged.

'What if I don't?' She smiled.

He stared at her for a second, the breeze from the window ruffling the tablecloth.

'What?' she prompted.

'Nothing,' he said, eyes closed. 'Just thinking about how much better we are at flirting, now we're not a couple.'

Her stomach muscles clenched.

'But either way, this is pretty spot on.' He splashed more whisky into the tumbler. 'Me, you, booze. It's like the good old days.'

She got up and busied herself with the wilting spider plant in the corner, tipping stale water from a forgotten glass into the pot.

He surveyed her over his drink. 'I've been writing again. Properly.'

She didn't admit that she'd noticed.

'Proper writing.' His eyes lit up.

'Picking up that second novel again?' she asked, a little coolly. She scratched at a stain on the tablecloth with her thumbnail.

'Nah, can't be arsed with that pile of shit, although if I get sectioned again, I'd have a shot at the Booker.' He cracked open a cider. 'It's a short story. It's about you.'

Lily blinked. 'Callum—'

'It's nothing like that, Lil. Do you remember—' He shifted his weight on the dining chair, so he was crouching on it, looming over her a little. 'When we went to that farm? In Wales?'

'When we went camping?'

He nodded, eager.

It'd rained, incessantly. They were pretty much the only people at the farm's open day. The owner gave them a personal tour. She and Cal held hands the whole way round, except to pet the animals. There was a lot of standing in the rain, gazing into each other's eyes.

On the last night of the trip the weather had cleared up and they'd packed the tent away, back in the car. Slept under the stars. Cal counted them for her: 12, 24, 48—

'It's about the farm,' he went on happily. He licked the

Rizla of a cigarette that she hadn't noticed him rolling, then handed it to her.

She took it, wincing inwardly. Scott had made her swear to start cutting down.

'What's there to say about the farm?' she asked, voice a little unsteady.

He spread the tobacco along his own cigarette and didn't look up at her as he spoke. 'The story is about something you said, just before we left. Do you remember?'

She shook her head.

'Well, I do. Right before we got back in the car, you said to me that we'd go back one day. To the farm. You promised we'd see it again. Remember?'

'No,' Lily lied.

He arched an eyebrow. 'Yes, you do.'

She shrugged.

'Anyway, that's what the story is about.' He lit the cigarette. 'It's about not going back.'


Lily felt woozy. She shouldn't drink spirits.

'I'm going to get better,' Cal said, his eyes unfocused. 'I am. I'm *getting* better. I feel better every day.'

Lily didn't say anything. She picked at the label on the edge of a wine bottle, trying to scrape off the sticky adhesive.

Callum licked his lips. 'I've been doing more exposure therapy. I've been carrying this phone around. Look.'

He pulled it out of his back pocket and threw it down on the table between them. Drank deeply from his can.

His OCD had always manifested in numbers. Even when it cropped up in other forms – contamination during the pandemic, harm OCD after his nan died – the numbers and the counting were always there.

Number six? Good.

Number nine? Bad bad bad.

Lily blinked, trying to pay attention.

'I will work on leaving the house, but if I can concentrate enough to *write* – if I can get back on a computer.'

Lily made a noise of agreement.

Some of the sticky on the side of the bottle came off under her nail.

'Look at Andy, look at Sam.' He licked his lips again. 'If they can do it, I can.'

Lily didn't rise to the bait of that sentiment.

Callum nodded, firmly. 'I'm getting there, I really am. Aren't I?'

Lily looked past him, to the patch of darker wallpaper where the clock used to be, and didn't answer. 'I need to go to bed.'

She pushed herself to standing, swayed a little.

Detour to the kitchen. She glugged a pint of water, refilled the glass.

She could hear Callum yelling at Alexa, cursing her for misunderstanding his song choice.

They'd given up on playing records, because they were too pissed to get up and change them. Cal had finally shut the windows, so they could blare music through Alexa.

Alexa was a godsend as Callum's fear of numbers got worse. It was how he searched Google, got the news, played music, the radio – all without ever seeing a keypad.

She was on her way to say goodnight, when the song finally played.

Lily froze in the dining room doorway, her stomach plummeting into her socks.

'Remember this?' he asked, smiling.

It was an old song.

A song they'd sing on summer road trips with the windows down. *Their* song.

'Cal—'

He didn't hear her. He had his eyes closed, swaying and mouthing the words.

Those familiar chords tore something open in her chest.

'Alexa – next,' she snapped. The song changed, to something she didn't recognise.

Cal looked down at his hands, pulling a face that suggested he found the exchange comically awkward.

Anger, always close to the surface when she was pissed.

'Don't play that,' Lily said, wanting him to react. Wanting listening to it to hurt him, like it hurt her.

Cal stretched, eyeing the empty Jameson's bottle. 'We're going to have to start on the Advocaat.'

The happy bubble of the evening had burst. She was tired, woozy and she wanted to fade into sleep.

'I'm going to bed.' She gathered her stuff, spewed from the pockets of her jacket as she hunted for spare Rizla. 'I need to get up early tomorrow, I'm meeting Scott for lunch.'

The corner of Cal's mouth twitched.

'What?'

He shrugged, stifling a laugh.

Drunk Cal could be your best friend. He'd listen intently to you while you talked about your dreams, make you believe they were just within your grasp. He'd listen to songs from your childhood with you. Lie on the floor of the living room and hold your hand, staring up at the ceiling like it was the Northern Lights.

But Lily knew all too well that, more often than not, he ended up mean. Maybe it was the writer in him, but drunk Cal knew how to phrase his joke so that it stung. How to inflict wounds in an argument.

'Goodnight, Callum.'

She had one foot on the bottom step when he called out to her.

'Has he made you come yet?'

She was glad she wasn't in the room, so he couldn't see how deeply red her cheeks went.

Going upstairs was an option. Ignoring him, not rising to it, was an option. Not giving him the satisfaction.

He was in self-destruct mode, and he wanted to blow up a really nice evening.

*'He's just deeply unhappy, babe,'* Scott would say to her. *'He's sad and he wants to make you sad too.'*

But Cal knew her, and he knew that she couldn't leave it.

'I told you that in confidence.'

He hadn't moved from the table, but he was smoking again. After her brief respite in the hallway, she realised the room stank of smoke.

'I'll take that as a no then.' Cal's grin widened.

Lily drummed her fingers against her thigh. Trying to think of something to say and failing.

'It's not an issue you ever had with me,' he said, putting his hands behind his head.

'Don't fucking tell him,' she snapped.

Cal pulled a sympathetic expression. 'Still faking it then? I thought so. I heard you the other night when I got up for a piss. Can he really not tell you're putting that on?'

She wanted to pick something up and throw it, but she was working hard, really hard, not to do shit like that anymore.

It was good. They'd had a lovely evening, but she needed this reminder. It was good to keep this side of him fresh in her mind.

'That's enough, Cal.'

'Again, not something you used to say to me very often,' he said, smirking.

Her hands were fists at her sides, and there were angry

tears in her eyes. The dining room suddenly felt hot, like the heating had been turned up to full whack.

'I always knew Scotty wouldn't be up to much.' Callum sighed. 'It's not his fault. He's only, you know, got a—'

He held up the limp, half-smoked cigarette.

'No, Callum.' Lily's cheeks were still red, but her voice was steady. 'You can't fucking talk about him like that.'

He still smiled, but his eyes were fixed on hers, his jaw set. 'Why not, Lil?'

'Because *you* left *me*.' She was breathing heavily. 'And Scott is nice and he's there for me, and he's—'

'He's what, Lil?' Cal tapped the volume button on the Alexa, six times, so the music was barely audible.

He got to his feet, slowly, deliberately. Stubbed his cigarette out in an old yoghurt pot that no one had binned.

On his way out of the room, Cal stopped next to her. He smelled of smoke and washing powder and familiarity.

He leaned in, the stubble on his jaw millimetres from her cheek. She could feel his breath as he spoke.

'Fuck you.'

# Chapter 18

## Wednesday | Evening

## Field

When Field finally got home, she was still mentally running through tomorrow's to-do list.

Interview more of David's friends, colleagues. Ask them about the divorce – explore what Penny had said about being jealous of his patients.

Then there was CCTV and forensics and a meeting with the super first thing.

And trying to trace the five patients from the paper David had written – teenagers at the time, but Toby's age now.

She opened the front door and was surprised that the living room was lit by the flickering light of the TV. Toby twisted on the sofa, smiling at her, sleepily.

'What are you doing here?' Field kicked her shoes off.

'Hello, son,' he said, grinning. 'Lovely to see you, son.'

She flopped onto the sofa and Toby leaned the top of his

head towards her so she could kiss his hair, like she always did when he was little.

At thirty-two he was too old for this action, but they'd done it so instinctively, for so long, that there'd never been a natural stopping point.

'I was home alone anyway, and I had no plans after *someone* bailed on dinner,' Toby said, through a yawn. 'So, I thought I'd make sure you were okay.'

Toby looked knackered. There were dark circles under his eyes, and he'd lost more weight. He put it down to long shifts, no time to stop for lunch between calls. His ambulance station was particularly short-staffed, he claimed, but it would calm down soon.

'You thought you'd raid my fridge, you mean?' She sat next to him.

Toby made no denials, sitting up so she could claim a corner of the blanket.

'How's the case then?' Toby said, pressing mute on the remote and turning to her. 'Caught the guy yet?'

Field shook her head. 'Give me another day or two, at least.'

Toby smiled. 'You can have four.'

'Thanks, boss.' She touched his hand. 'How's work been?'

'Pretty rough. Hit-and-run,' he said, grimly. 'Twenty-year-old kid.'

'Christ. I'm sorry, Tobes.'

'It's okay.' A shadow crossed his face.

Field wanted to take away some of the darkness. Toby always asked her, when he was little, whether he could join the police when he grew up. She'd wanted to shield him from this kind of work.

He forced a smile. 'Did I tell you we delivered a baby in the van last week?'

'Yep,' she said, adjusting the blanket. 'Amazing.'

She braced herself for the next question. 'And how is the revision going?'

'Yeah, good,' he said vaguely, suddenly engrossed in the drama on *Married at First Sight*.

All the horrific things she'd seen at work – abuse victims and mutilated bodies and people wasting away from drugs or disease or sheer poverty – and nothing had terrified her more than Toby's illness. There was no darker period in her life.

It was the speed of it all that scared her – one day he was a happy fourteen-year-old and almost overnight he was catatonic, unresponsive. Locked in his own brain. The pressure of exams, and coursework – the long essays he found it difficult to concentrate on.

She'd made it clear that she couldn't give a shit whether he passed or failed the lot; he didn't need to make himself ill over his marks. But it made no difference.

Toby had forgiven her, for the things she'd said to him when she was at her most desperate. The day she'd cracked and screamed at him.

*You're selfish. Attention-seeking.*

*It's not that hard. Just get the fuck up.*

And worse.

Toby forgave her, but his father never had. During their divorce he'd made bitter swipes at her, accused her of being an unfit mother.

It was all ancient history now – more than half of Toby's life ago. But Field was always watching, always looking for evidence that they were on the precipice of another downturn.

Toby laughed at something on the screen, and she shot a sideways look at him.

Three years ago, he'd given up his comfortable job, working

in phlebotomy at the hospital, to do a Paramedic Science degree at Greenwich Uni.

She'd seen less of him, in the last year, as the workload intensified, and he went out on more placements. Harder to keep a gauge how he was doing when he was on a run of nights, and she was in court for a week straight.

As if he could sense her thoughts on him, Toby turned to her. 'You okay, Mum?'

'Yeah,' she said. 'Tired. Thinking about work.'

Was he still going to therapy? Still taking meds? She didn't know how to ask him.

What would she do, if it happened again? If Toby got ill? He wasn't a child anymore. She couldn't force him to get help.

Maybe if Toby had met David Moore when he was ill, if she'd taken him to a good psychologist, it would never have got as bad as it did.

*No.*

She couldn't entertain those thoughts, and she couldn't let this case get personal.

'You look done in, Mum,' he said, touching a hand to her cheek. 'Bed?'

Field wanted to be in at the crack of dawn, and she could barely keep her eyes open.

She liked it when Toby stayed over. On the phone he never called it "her house", it was always "our place", even though he hadn't lived here for years.

She liked knowing he was safe and warm in his childhood bedroom – painted magnolia now.

She kissed the top of Toby's head again, unable to resist. 'Bed.'

# Chapter 19

## Wednesday | Evening

## Lily

*Fuck him.*

She jammed a pair of trainers on her feet. She'd had enough.
*He's bad news, Lil. He'll drag you down. He's not your problem.*

Lily heard it from all angles. Scott. Her friends, the ones who still spoke to her. Even her workmates.

*I think you like it*, Scott said once. Their first fight. *You like that everyone hates him, and you like being treated like shit. You love being a fucking martyr.*

She hunted around in her tote bag for Scott's key. Thank God he'd given it to her – it had to be there somewhere. She knocked an old lamp off the side, heard it crack, and left it there.

Lily sometimes tried to imagine being Callum. Knowing what people thought of him.

Through the fog of the alcohol she knew, for a fact, that

Callum would never change. It wasn't because he was worrying about his benefits; it wasn't his OCD. Alcohol dredged up the darkness and the spite and the *bile* he carried around. His contempt for her.

She found the key. The night was probably still warm; she wouldn't need a jacket.

'Lil?' he called.

She shouldn't turn around. She should walk straight out the door and slam it.

Hating herself, and hating him, she went back to the dining room.

Callum hadn't moved. He had his feet up on the table, an unlit cigarette between his lips.

'What?' Lily snapped, the key hot in her fist.

Callum's jaw was set, his eyes unfocused. 'I think it's time you moved out.'

# Chapter 20

**P:** I'm not afraid of being alone.

*Pause*

**P:** I'm afraid of being left alone.

# Chapter 21

## Thursday | Midnight

## Callum

"How Soon is Now?" blared through the speakers and Callum sang at the top of his lungs.

Fuck the neighbours.

Fuck it all.

He'd lost track of the time, but it was late. Could be four in the morning – he didn't know.

He'd lost track of how much he'd drunk, but around his tenth can of cider he'd decided he didn't care.

He spun in a dizzy circle – arms spread – imagining he had Morrissey's branch in his back pocket.

Lily should live with her perfect smug-faced-cunt boy-friend.

And it would be all right. Because eventually Lily would have to tell the prick that she was mental too.

And if she didn't, Scott would work it out.

There was a sound, under the music. Callum turned his

head, to the hallway, squinting into the darkness. He flicked the light switch, forgetting nothing would happen.

The song was fading out, but before "Handsome Devil" could start up, someone knocked again.

He stumbled in his haste to get to the door before whoever it was got to nine knocks. It'd be next door, the timid wife sent by her uptight husband to tell Callum to keep it down, remind him that *they* had work tomorrow.

Well so did he, Cal thought, as he fumbled with the locks. He had work to do – he had to write a book that would prove to Lily – to everyone – that he was *fine*. Fine on his own. Better.

But once he'd managed the key, the door wouldn't open. Lily must have locked the bottom bolt.

He frowned at it, stumbling again.

Fuck, he was drunk.

He groped on the side for his keys, knocking things over. Really, he should keep a torch in the hallway, or learn to cope with the one on his bloody phone.

He found the keys, finally, and after a few wobbles, got the bottom lock undone.

And opened the door.


He must be dreaming.

Callum pressed his hand harder into her throat, but it slipped from under him. She let out a low moan. His palm was already slick with thick, hot blood.

He gagged.

'Help—'

His voice sounded pathetic, thin in the night air. Not loud enough to raise the neighbours.

Less than five minutes ago he was in his living room, safe, angry-drunk. Then the knock on the door and the body in the street, the blood . . .

Callum shouted again, louder.

Then again, and again.

Apart from her gasping, the night fell back into silence. He looked up and down the street, waiting to see a light go on in a window.

He hadn't seen Sam in over a decade. And now she was here, on his street – bleeding to death.

Sam's eyes were frantic, her hands scrabbling weakly at Callum's wrist, like he was strangling her.

'I'm sorry, Sam,' Cal choked on a sob. 'I've got to.'

Callum twisted to look at the wounds to Sam's stomach, her thigh.

*Don't count them.*

In spite of himself, he counted.

*One* – the wound to her neck. *Two, three, four* – down her side. There was a deep slash in her jumper, and the blood was staining the blue fabric black.

*Five. Six.* Cuts to her forearms. *Seven* – the thigh, visible below her denim skirt.

Stop.

Cal forced his attention back to Sam's face. She was trying to cough, and Callum considered twisting her onto her side.

He should phone an ambulance. His phone was in his back pocket.

The cough exploded out of Sam and Callum felt blood spatter his face.

Callum gagged again, pressing the back of his wrist to his mouth. In the dim streetlights the blood looked more black than red. Fake, Hollywood gore. It was everywhere – his T-shirt soaked, his jeans.

Her feet scrabbled feebly, kicking out at the air. She'd lost a shoe, one foot bare.

The effort of pressing down on Sam's neck was making him sweat, beads of it dripping down his forehead.

*Phone an ambulance. Do it.*

Sam's head moved and Callum's hand slipped again. In the split second he broke contact, a new rivulet of blood sprang from the wound.

'You've got to stay still, Sam,' Callum urged.

*Call an ambulance.*

*Call 9-9-9.*

'I can't,' Callum gasped. 'I can't, I can't.'

Callum screamed for help again, threw his head back and let rip. Not even words, just a desperate noise. It could have been an animal.

The blood had reached paving slabs over a metre away. A tear leaked out of one of Sam's eyes.

There was a shift in the darkness, a few houses down. A square of light in a window.

'Please,' Callum said. 'Please, fucking please.'

The light stayed on.

'It's all right, Sam. It's all right, someone is coming.'

*They* could phone – they could ring for help.

Sam's eyes were unfocused now. Staring at a point in the sky, over his shoulder.

A door banged open.

'What the fuck—'

'Ambulance,' Callum spat at him. 'Call an ambulance.'

Callum squeezed his eyes shut. Not wanting to see the man dial. Not wanting to see Sam's now vacant expression.

Then there were strong arms on his shoulders, pushing him aside. Clean hands taking over from his bloodstained ones.

A voice shouting into the night, down the telephone.

Callum scrabbled backwards, away from the pool of blood.

The man was bare-chested and barefoot in jogging bottoms.

'She looks about early thirties – maybe younger. I can't tell. There's blood everywhere. Yeah – multiple stab wounds.'

Callum tried to breathe, but the oxygen wasn't reaching his brain.

'No – there's someone else here. A guy.' The man didn't turn to look at him.

Callum wiped his hands on his jeans. The blood didn't come off, just smeared. When he clenched and unclenched his fists the creases of his palm stood out white against the red-black blood.

A siren in the distance.

He lay backwards on the pavement. The mirror of Sam next to him.

From above Callum imagined that, with the bloodstains, he'd look like he'd been stabbed too.

Minutes ago, he'd been sure the night was oppressively hot, but he was cooling quickly. The rough concrete of the ground pressed against his phone.

His eyes flicked back to Sam. The man was kneeling over her. Attempting CPR.

Callum closed his eyes.

The ringing in his ears.

Sirens.

The rhythmic counting of the man, as he performed the chest compressions.

*One*
*Two*
*Three*
*Four*
*Five*
*Six*

# Chapter 22

**P:** Breakdown.

*Pause*

**P:** The rules don't work. There aren't enough rules.

*Pause*

**P:** There are too many rules to cope with.

# Chapter 23

## Thursday | Early hours

## Callum

He sat on the sofa, his sofa.

'We need to take some photos of you,' a gentle voice said, from the doorway, and he turned.

He'd forgotten the detective's name. She must be in her early fifties, her face the only thing visible in her full protective forensic gear. Kind face, but stern. Flecks of grey visible at her temples under the hood of her paper suit. She'd been asking him questions about himself, his writing, who he lived with.

She was with a younger man, also in white overalls, who smiled at Callum and held up a DSLR camera with an apologetic shrug.

Callum looked down at his hands, then held them out in front of him.

The man walked over with a rustle and put the camera to his face, and the detective stayed in the doorway. Callum closed his eyes as the shutter sound started, willing himself not to count how many photos he was taking. Trying to dampen down the panic that was still beating below his breastbone.

'Turn them over for me. That's it.'

More shutter clicks.

Callum wanted to ask someone if Sam was okay – if she was still alive, but if he opened his mouth, he'd immediately throw up.

He'd retreated into the house as soon as he heard the sirens, but left the door open as an invitation. The first police there had asked him questions and he'd stuttered out answers.

*I didn't see anything.*

*I don't know who stabbed her.*

*I tried to help.*

'Can you stand up for me?' The man reached out to put a hand under his elbow, but Callum flinched away.

He took photographs of Callum's torso, then picked up the bags. Not clear plastic bags, like you saw in detective programmes on TV. Paper bags, like you'd get at a farm shop.

Callum followed his instructions. Pulled his T-shirt over his head, dropped it into the first bag. His trainers went into the second. The man smiled at him encouragingly, like he was a toddler undressing himself before bed.

Before Callum took his jeans off, he pulled out his phone from one back pocket, and his small red Moleskine from the other. The man had to go and find more bags for those, smaller ones. Then his jeans went into the third large bag, and he sat down on the sofa in his boxers.

The skin of his chest was stained lightly red in some places, where the worst of the blood had been, but otherwise it was clean. Under the bare seventy-watt light bulb the bloodstains up to his elbows looked comical, like part of a gory Halloween costume.

'Can I have a shower?' he asked. His voice was a croak.

The forensics man turned to the woman.

'We'll get you cleaned up at the station, Callum,' she said gently.

The man took a step back, collecting up the bags of his belongings.

'I can't leave.' Callum's voice cracked. 'I can't leave the house.'

'I'm afraid you can't stay here, Callum,' the detective said. Field – that was her name. She moved into the room, to allow the photographer to get past, and then it was just them. 'This is a crime scene now, and we need to do everything we can to catch whoever hurt Sam.'

*He had to leave the house.*

A breeze lifted the curtains up into the air.

*He had to leave the house.*

'Is she dead?' he asked, in a whisper.

Field shook her head. 'No, Callum. She's with the paramedics now.'

Sam was alive.

'You recognised Sam, didn't you, Callum?' Field asked. 'How do you know her?'

He couldn't concentrate.

*He was going to be taken away.*

'Met when we were teenagers.'

Field's eyes were wide. 'Were you in hospital together, Callum? The Maudsley?'

Callum felt numb, couldn't feel his fingers. Managed to nod.

'Did you take part in David Moore's trial together, Callum? In 2010 – did he write a paper about you?' she asked, and her voice was more urgent.

The weight of his exhaustion and anxiety was threatening

to bury him, and his shock at the question was dimmed, overwhelmed by everything else.

'Yes,' he choked out.

*They were taking him back there.*

'Last question, Callum. What alerted you to what had happened outside?'

Callum sat on his hands, to try and stop them from shaking so badly. 'There was a knock on the door.'

Field's eyebrows shot up. 'Really?'

'I didn't see anyone, when I answered it. It took me ages to get the door open, I had the bottom lock on, or something. Then Sam was just—'

He squeezed his eyes shut. He couldn't go on, couldn't say anything else.

'It's going to be okay, Callum,' Field said firmly. 'We'll get you cleaned up. We'll find out what happened to Sam. This will all be okay.'

There was a silence, and Callum supposed he should say something, but all he could think about was leaving. Leaving the house, the street, the road.

The panic was still fighting to break through the numbness and the shock.

'I'm going back outside now, Callum.' Field's voice was far away, distant. 'I'm going to find someone to sit with you, and then I promise, we'll sort this all out.'

# Chapter 24

## Thursday | Early hours

### Field

The similarities between the scenes made the night surreal. Like déjà vu come to life.

Tonight's attack was on Conway Road, less than a five-minute walk from where David was stabbed on Ancona. The houses were similar, the same birch trees at regular intervals, the kind of streets that all look the same unless you know the area.

Field watched from the cordon as the paramedics continued to work on the victim. From this distance she couldn't see how young their victim was.

Twenty minutes: the golden rule, at a stabbing. Twenty minutes to get the victim stable and in the ambulance, if they were going to stand any chance of surviving.

The paramedics had been on scene for over an hour.

On Field's drive over, she'd made the split-second decision to call Riley over Wilson. He lived closer and drove like a lunatic, and Wilson had been to plenty of stabbings during her days on Response.

Wilson wasn't happy about it, but she was on her way to the station, prepping the decision log, compiling what little they knew about the *Disordered Approach to Diagnosis* paper and co-ordinating the wider team.

Field heard her name and turned. Riley was ducking under the crime scene tape.

He was in his usual pressed grey suit, but his blond hair wasn't slicked back, a shade lighter without gel.

'Well?' he said, striding over to her. 'Is it linked?'

No preamble.

'It's linked,' she answered, grimly. 'Our victim was found in the street by a Callum Mulligan. He told the skipper who was first on scene that he can't leave the house – OCD.'

'Fuck,' Riley breathed.

'I've only managed to get a few words out of him. He's in shock, but he's confirmed he was in the Maudsley with Sam. They were both part of the trial.'

'So that's two of our five missing kids—'

Field nodded.

'Fuck,' Riley said again.

He followed her gaze fifty metres up the road, to where the huddle of paramedics blocked the figure in the road from view.

Field lowered her voice. 'Victim is a woman this time. Samantha Hughes. Still alive, but barely. It's not looking good.'

'So that's two attacks in twenty-four hours.'

Field took a steadying breath. Everything was turned on its head, now they were looking for a serial offender. Prioritising the right lines of inquiry was crucial, when you had an attacker who could be poised to strike again.

Multiple attempted murders, potentially escalating. The only

111

link between them a completely anonymous medical study from fifteen years ago.

Field turned back to Riley, and caught the gleam of excitement in his expression. 'Where do you want me?'

She shot a glance back at the house. 'Sit with Mulligan. Keep him calm, and don't question him until I'm there, okay?'

'Boss,' he said.

Riley adopted a more solemn expression and hurried towards the house.

A tall, red-haired paramedic was in charge of keeping Field up to date. She kept her focus on him, and not the victim.

Field clenched her jaw as he put his hands on his knees and pushed himself up to standing.

A few paces, and he was next to her.

'Anything?' she asked in a low voice.

He shook his head. 'No. No response.'

After twenty-five minutes of sustained CPR, defib, epi, fluids – the victim still had no vital signs.

'Time?' Field asked, simply.

He nodded. 'I'm going to ring the medical director. He needs to call it.'

The CPR continued, the paramedics sweating – pushing themselves like it had only been thirty seconds, like there was every chance she'd pull through at any moment.

Field exhaled. She took out her notebook, flicked it open, made a note.

*Time of death:*

Her pen hovered over the page.

# Chapter 25

## Thursday | Early hours

## Field

The scream could have belonged to another stabbing victim.

Field was halfway through checking the evidence log, bending over in the boot of the car as she checked the reference numbers. It made her jump, and she smacked her head.

'What the—'

She extracted herself from the boot as a second scream tore through the night. The PC cataloguing the evidence was staring, open-mouthed, towards Callum Mulligan's house.

'Get off me,' Callum shrieked, twisting and turning against the arms that held him. 'Get the *fuck* off me.'

Riley was shouting and the scene was chaos. Field sprinted over, accidentally barging a PC out of her way.

Riley and a muscled Territorial Support Group officer were dragging Callum away from the house and from the crime scene tent, which was shielding the body from view. They were heading towards an unmarked car that had all four doors thrown open.

'What are you doing?' She could barely make herself heard over Callum's desperate yelling.

Riley and the TSG were shouting over Callum, telling him to stop moving. Even with two of them, they were struggling to keep hold of Callum's arms and shoulders, until they managed to push him down against the bonnet.

'Stop fighting,' Riley barked at Callum, as Field shouted, 'Get off him.'

Doors were opening along the street, people in dressing gowns appearing, phones out.

'Get off me, get off me, get off me.' Callum drew his head back and smacked it into the bonnet with a sickening thud.

It was like trying to contain a wild animal, and their grip was only making Callum struggle harder, fight more. He let out another wild scream.

'Stop pushing him into the car, for fuck's sake,' Field ordered. 'Lower him to the ground.'

The TSG glanced at Riley, but didn't hesitate to follow orders.

Callum kept writhing as they wrestled him to the ground. Field knelt and grabbed Callum's head, gripping it hard, to prevent him hurting himself.

'I can't,' Callum panted, still struggling. 'I can't – don't make me, please.'

'It's okay—' Field started.

'I don't want to have to cuff you, Callum.' Riley was sweating with the effort of trying to restrain him, now pressing his weight onto Callum's legs. 'Can we get a medic over here?'

Riley had barely got the words out before a green jumpsuit appeared.

'Callum,' the paramedic said over the noise. 'Callum, I need you to try and calm down for me, okay?'

'He told me he's agoraphobic,' Field said, stroking Callum's hair, even as he continued to thrash. Tears were streaming down his face. 'He hasn't left the house for years.'

Riley swore and jumped to his feet. His trousers were wet – Callum had wet himself with fear.

They were all wearing bodycams. Field's was blinking steadily in her eyeline. Field could feel the prying eyes of the neighbours on them. They could be – probably were – filming the whole episode.

Riley brushed his trousers and kneeled back down, next to the paramedic, still trying to assume some kind of control.

Suddenly Callum went totally still, his eyes rolling between Field and the medic.

'Callum,' the paramedic said again, and Callum's eyes followed the voice. 'Tell me what's going on with you.'

'It hurts,' Callum said in a whisper.

Field shot a look at the TSG officer, and he eased off Callum's legs a little.

'I can't leave the house.' Tears streamed down his face. 'Please. I can't.'

'It's going to be okay, Callum,' the paramedic said, taking his left hand and holding it. 'It's going to be okay.'

Callum's head swivelled to look at Riley. 'He's taking me away.'

Callum moved without warning, limbs waving, and Riley's head snapped back as a fist caught him in the lip. Callum was screaming again, and the TSG was struggling to keep him pinned down.

'Ten milligrams diazepam,' the paramedic shouted over his shoulder, but his counterpart already had the syringe ready.

Riley pressed his sleeve to his lip, trying not to let blood drip onto the pavement as the needle pierced Callum's neck.

'We need to protect his head,' the paramedic barked, taking over from Field.

Gradually, Callum calmed down, going glassy-eyed and rolling up into a ball.

Riley stood awkwardly by Field, nursing his face and not looking down at his piss-stained trousers. She forced her rage down, kept her face neutral.

A docile Callum was stretchered onto the ambulance, while the uniforms urged people to go back into their houses.

'Think he's faking it?' Riley asked a passing paramedic.

The medic threw him a filthy look and didn't answer.

# Chapter 26

P: We are monsters, in our own right.
   The people we get close to, the people we
allow ourselves to love.
   We hurt them.
   We destroy them.
D: You're not a monster, P—.

*Pause*

P: We destroy them, before they can destroy
us.

# Chapter 27

## Thursday | Morning

### Lily

Lily wanted to stay in bed, hiding from the hangover and her nausea under Scott's Egyptian cotton sheets. The argument played on a loop inside her head, Cal telling her to move out. She had nowhere else to go – it was Scott's or nowhere – but the thought of actually moving into this flat, being with him every day, made her feel profoundly lonely.

Scott had made her promise they'd do something nice with his day off, so she dragged herself into the shower.

Lily pressed her aching forehead against the tiled wall and let the water run down her back. The sickness was worse than yesterday – no surprise given how much she'd drunk last night.

It was a while before she realised the faint banging noise wasn't in her own head.

She turned the water off.

'Babe?' Scott called, voice strained. 'The police are here to see you.'

Lily stepped out of the shower, pulling a towel round her. The drop in temperature made her head swim, and she had to sit on the toilet.

*Something has happened to Callum.*

She struggled to untangle the twisted legs of her tracksuit bottoms and grabbed Scott's jumper from the laundry hamper, so she could get away without a bra.

Scott's hallway was bright white, immaculate. A dish for his keys on the radiator cover, a special cupboard for his trainers. The detective was slipping her shoes off.

'DS Wilson,' she said, smartly, holding up a police ID in a wallet. She was probably around Lily's age, with big, dark eyes and her hair back in a ponytail.

Lily pretended to peer at it, then Scott waved them into the living room.

'How can we help?' he said, taking the seat next to Lily on the sofa.

'What's happened?' Lily asked, her voice a croak. She crossed her arms over her chest.

Wilson hesitated.

*Callum.*

Had her worst fear finally come to life? The intrusive images of finding Callum dead, or having hurt himself, were so frequent they were routine. And yet, a police detective knocks on the door the night after she and Cal have a big argument—

Her heart was in her throat as the detective began to speak.

'Last night there was an incident on Conway Road – outside the house you share with Callum Mulligan.'

*Outside?* A bubble of hope – that this couldn't be about Cal.

'Lily, do you know Samantha Hughes? She's a—' The detective hesitated. 'She's a friend of Callum's.'

It took a moment to register what DS Wilson had said,

119

because it was so unexpected. Her hangover throbbed behind her temples.

'Yeah, I know Sam,' Lily said slowly. 'Why?'

Scott's head was on a swivel, looking between them.

'I'm afraid that last night Samantha was attacked outside your house.'

'What?' Lily jerked upwards in surprise and her headache worsened.

For something to do, she gulped from a cold cup of tea Scott had made her earlier, and winced at the taste. He never remembered she didn't take sugar.

'Samantha was stabbed,' Wilson said. She was examining Lily now, scrutinising her. 'Unfortunately, she passed away at the scene.'

'Shit.' The mug slipped in her hand, cold tea slopping over the side. Scott let out a gasp, but Lily managed to catch it, and only spilt it on herself.

'Sorry. Sorry,' Lily said, weakly. She put the mug down and turned back to Wilson. 'She was outside our house?'

'Unfortunately yes. It was Callum who found her.'

'Oh God.' The fear was back and Lily rose from the sofa. 'Is he okay? Is Cal all right?'

Wilson hesitated and every muscle in Lily's body braced for bad news, the worst news.

'Callum wasn't injured,' Wilson said finally. 'But after the ordeal it was necessary to take him to a secure unit for his own—'

'You sectioned him?' Lily cut across her.

It had been over ten years since Callum was last in hospital. Only a short stay, a relapse – after the news about Paige. The accident.

'I need to see him,' Lily said, getting to her feet. Her stomach twisted painfully but her head had stopped pounding.

She looked about for her phone, her keys. It probably wasn't safe for her to drive. She felt like shit. Scott would take her.

'Please, Lily. Sit down,' Wilson said.

Scott put a hand on her arm and pulled her back down.

'I understand that you want to see Callum, but you should also know—' The detective took a breath and Lily braced herself. 'In the early hours of Wednesday morning, there was another attack in the area. Dr David Moore—'

'Is David dead?' Lily breathed.

'No, Lily. He's in hospital. I understand he's Callum's therapist, and I do have some questions about that, but first—'

'I need to see Callum,' she said again.

Why wasn't this woman listening to her?

Scott was on his feet, moving purposefully towards the door.

*Sam. David. Callum.*

Her head was swimming.

'Lily, before you go, I need to ask.' Wilson's voice was urgent. 'Where were you, early this morning? Who were you with?'

# Chapter 28

## Thursday | Morning

### Field

Callum Mulligan's house was small and unremarkable.

The search was well underway. DI Bellamy was co-ordinating the joint effort between Forensics and PolSA – the Police Search Advisors – who were already taking each room apart, an item at a time.

Field moved between them, trying not to get in the way. While they searched for a weapon, for evidence, she wasn't looking for anything specific. Field wanted to understand what made Callum tick.

She'd noted Callum's movements last night. Right-handed. Next check would need to be the girlfriend.

Even with all Dr Simon Dawes' insight into OCD from yesterday, and despite knowing that it wasn't just about being tidy, Field was shocked at how messy the house was. It reminded her of student accommodation – drawers overspilling with junk, scuffed skirting boards, walls covered with posters and postcards.

And there were books everywhere. Floor-to-ceiling bookcases covered a wall in the little living room, at the front of the house. There were food-splattered cookbooks in the narrow kitchen, and boxes of books from the cupboard under the stairs were being picked through, pages rifled one by one.

Field was looking for one book in particular.

It always helped to get people talking about the easy topics when they were in shock. Stunned and blood-spattered up to the elbows on his sofa, Field had asked Callum what he did for work. He told her he was a writer, a novelist. She assumed that was code for 'unemployed' – but a quick google of his name had thousands of results.

A *Guardian* article described his novel as *The Bell Jar* meets *The Breakfast Club*.

Field couldn't find Callum's book on any of the shelves downstairs. There were none on display anywhere.

PolSA hadn't made it upstairs yet. There were two doors on either side of the hallway, leading to the bedrooms. The first Field tried smelled of perfume, and the floor was covered in women's clothes. She found Callum's book on the windowsill, sandwiched between *Perks of Being a Wallflower* and *Looking For Alaska* – both novels she recognised from Toby's teenage reading.

Field picked up the slim purple paperback.

*Darlings, Obsessed* by C. Mulligan.

She turned it over. Instead of a blurb on the back cover there was a long list of praise from newspapers, and people Field had never heard of. She opened it to the dedication page.

For P

# Chapter 29

## Thursday | Morning

### Field

The sun was already burning hot in the sky.

Field waited outside the crime scene tent, arms folded, scanning the houses on either side of the street. Despite the hot August morning, the curtains in every upstairs room were drawn, windows closed.

The blood on the road had dried a deep rust colour, the ground littered with sterile packaging and medical gauze.

David Moore attacked in the early hours of Wednesday morning.

Less than twenty-four hours later, another stabbing. A murder.

'All right, ready.' Young's voice carried from inside the tent.

Field took a breath and stepped inside.

It was stiflingly hot, the air thick with the scent of blood.

Young hadn't worked a murder on-scene for years – there was too much demand for her elsewhere. But she'd seen

David's injuries up close, so her examination of Sam was a shortcut to a comparison.

Sam's clothes had been cut away, still pinned under her body. The paramedics had left the breathing apparatus in; the packing material was still in the wound to her throat. Young was kneeling by her midriff, knees resting on a stepping plate.

There was hardly room to move, and Field trod carefully as she took up the same position on Sam's other side.

Young sat back on her heels. No preamble. 'Wounds to both legs, as well as her arms and torso. Seven total, so a comparable number to the attack on David Moore.'

Field leaned closer to look at the wounds to her side. They were much closer together than David's had been.

Young followed her gaze. 'Bruising has formed here.' She picked up a torch and shone it onto the skin, revealing a reddish tone. 'That will be from the handle of the knife hitting the flesh. We should be able to get an idea of the blade's length from that wound, specifically.'

Field looked at the woman's face. Even with all the tubes and the blood, Field could tell Sam had been pretty – and she looked younger than thirty-two. She had light silvery-lilac hair, and a few small tattoos on her arms. Her skin was grey and waxy, with a sheen to it that could be mistaken for sweat.

Field tried to look at the slim frame on the ground as evidence, rather than a human being. Only for now, while she needed objectivity.

'It can't be a coincidence,' Field said. 'I mean – look at the state he's left her in.'

Young gently moved a lock of Sam's hair, looking closer at her neck. 'This wound to her throat will be the cause of death. From what I can see it looks like a similar, if not identical, weapon to the attack on David Moore. Similar wound pattern, too.

'First wound below the ribs, on the right-hand side. Then a wound to the right of the neck. But Sam wasn't as lucky as David – this wasn't a glancing blow.'

Field's forensic suit rustled as she dabbed at the sweat on her forehead. 'If he'd called the ambulance earlier, do you think she might have made it?'

'I don't think so,' Young said. 'That kind of injury, it's not something they could have got to outside of an operating theatre.'

A grim thought occurred to Field. Could David and Sam have been dating? There was a big age gap – but then his wife was younger.

'One point you may find interesting,' Young said, straightening up. 'Her face.'

Field frowned. There were a few tiny drops of blood on her cheeks, but no wounds to the face.

'Have a look at this.' Young pointed to Sam's hairline with a gloved finger.

On closer inspection, the skin at the edges of Sam's face was heavily scarred. Small but deep pockmarks, and raised bumps in some places. Field frowned. 'Chicken pox?'

'I don't think so. I know you haven't had her notes through yet, but I think Sam might have historically had a condition called dermatillomania. Skin picking disorder,' Young added, for Field's benefit.

Field already had Moore's paper bookmarked in her emails, and she had it up on her phone in a few swipes. She scrolled to the participants list and read aloud. 'Patient B. Hospitalised at fifteen years old with severe—' she stumbled trying to pronounce the word '—derm-a-till-o-mania. Brackets – excoriation disorder.'

Field held the phone up to Young, so she could read it without needing to change gloves. 'It makes sense. Body-focused repetitive behaviours are often classed under OCD, although not all clinicians agree.'

'When I spoke to Callum Mulligan last night, he confirmed he'd been in the Maudsley with Sam,' Field said.

Until that moment, she hadn't thought about piecing together which of the five they each were. They were so focused on finding the names, but they also had to match them to the symptoms described in the paper.

Young turned back to Sam. 'It was a severe case of dermatillomania, judging by the scarring. There are much larger patches on her shoulders. There's also these—'

Field leaned in. Sam had a line of small round scars on her left wrist.

Young went on. 'Over a decade old, I'd say. About the right size to be cigarette burns.'

'Could she have been abused, then?' Field asked. She had met plenty of damaged adults, with physical and mental scars from childhood torture.

'It's a possibility,' Young said, quietly. 'But they're only on her left arm. If she's right-handed, then it's more likely they were the result of self-harm.'

Young got to her feet. 'There's one more thing.'

'Love it when you say that.' Field stood up too.

She took a deep breath, and a last look down at the battered body of their victim, before they stepped out into the slightly fresher air. 'Tell me you've saved the best until last.'

Young had stopped just outside the tent, moving the fabric slightly for a better look at the dried bloodstains on the road.

Field stared down at them with her hands on her hips.

'It's this.' Young pointed at two parallel smears of blood, maybe the length of Field's palm. Young's brow was creased with concentration, and Field could sense her brain firing connections and calculating possibilities.

'Right.' Field waited for the mark on the tarmac to reveal its secrets to her, but it just looked like a smudge.

'That's a shoe mark, believe it or not,' Young said. 'Specifically, it's a shoe dragging through the blood as someone gets to their feet.'

The penny dropped. They weren't two parallel, separate stains. The toe of a shoe, or the tip of a sole, had streaked through the blood.

'We know the first two wounds were designed to get the victim to the ground—' Young stood in front of Field, then grabbed onto the front of her forensics suit. 'What if she pulled her attacker down on top of her?'

Field pictured it in her mind, trying not to dwell on the image of Sam's terrified face.

Young was working her way up to her point.

'If Sam pulled her attacker to the ground with her, and they didn't stand up until there was a significant pool of blood, it explains why the wounds to her side are so close together, compared to David's. If you're kneeling over someone, there's a lot less room to swing.'

'Could the shoe mark have been a paramedic?' Field reasoned. 'One of our officers maybe—'

Young was already shaking her head. 'I've checked their shoes, even the knees of their uniforms. The paramedics' boots are all bagged.'

Field didn't have the same fizz of excitement yet. 'Okay, so we've got an absence in the blood caused by a shoe, which we can match to our victim when we find our killer.'

'If he fell on top of her—' Young turned to Field, eyes bright. 'Then we could have contact DNA on the body, sweat maybe. But there's also this—'

Field should have known there was more.

More turned out to be tiny droplets of blood. 'These droplets of blood fell from a height, onto the ground,' Young announced, triumphant. 'I think they belong to your killer, and they cut themselves when they fell.'

'Will we get DNA from the blood?' Field asked.

'There's a good chance, but you'll have to send them to Teddington.' Young blew out a breath. 'We'll do everything we can.'

The Met's new lab in Lambeth could run basic tests quickly, but the complex stuff had to be outsourced to labs in Teddington. It could take a few days, even fast-tracked.

'Thank you,' Field said, meaning it sincerely.

She needed a moment to process the mass of information, and she sought the shade on the far side of the road, for relief from the heat.

The droplets of blood indicated the attacker was injured, to some degree. If they couldn't retrieve DNA from those, falling over meant there was at least a hope of finding their DNA on Sam's body.

Forensically, it was a win compared to David's attack. If – *when* – the case went to court, there were now more opportunities for irrefutable physical evidence.

But the results would take at least a few days, and their perpetrator was escalating.

For all the uncertainties and unanswered questions, Young's evidence proved one thing beyond doubt.

Samantha Hughes had fought for her life.

# Chapter 30

## Thursday | Afternoon

### Field

The station was packed. Phones rang constantly, and Field nodded at various people as she weaved through the crammed-in desks and chairs with her mug, towards the privacy of her office, where DS Riley was waiting for her.

Field had left the crime scene tent, and the crime scene itself, feeling her usual level of slightly queasy. Seeing bodies had never become routine for her, not that she'd admit it.

'Briefing in the conference room,' she announced to the room at large. 'Ten minutes.'

She turned a corner and saw Riley leaning against her door, laughing with a young DC who'd recently transferred from somewhere up north.

He touched a finger to his fat lip and winced, and the girl laughed again.

Riley clocked Field and stood up straight. 'All right, boss?'

Field said nothing. Held the door open for him.

Riley took a seat opposite the desk and Field let the door close.

She stood with her back to him, looking out over the car park through the grimy window. 'We need to talk about the witness. Callum Mulligan.'

'Witness?' Riley scoffed. 'Prime suspect. He's a nutter from what I can make out.'

Field turned and slammed a fist into the desk. Riley jumped.

She took a moment to gather herself. 'DS Riley. Do not use words like "nutter", in front of me.'

She sat down, heavily, and caught sight of Toby's school photo, propped against her monitor.

Riley blinked and didn't speak.

'You decided Mulligan needed to be removed for questioning, without asking me. Mr Mulligan became extremely distressed. He'd just dealt with the wounds of a woman who'd been brutally stabbed—'

'He went berserk,' Riley interrupted.

'At which point,' Field said through clenched teeth, 'Mr Mulligan makes it known to you, *again*, that he suffers from anxiety and hasn't left his house for God knows how long, and is in therapy and on benefits and is basically—' she thumped the desk again '—extremely vulnerable.

'Now,' she went on. 'Mulligan was surrounded by officers, he wasn't a flight risk, and the interior of his home was not, at that time, considered to be involved in the crime scene. Without consulting me, your fucking SIO, what did you decide to do?'

'I took him outside to put him in the car, boss, but—'

'You forced him out onto the street, in full view of the whole damn circus.' Her voice was rising. 'When he had to be sedated and taken to a psychiatric ward, did you follow him in? Make a phone call to the Maudsley to see how he was?' She went on without waiting for his answer. 'No, you came back to the station and hung around up here, flirting.'

Colour rose in Riley's cheeks. 'I don't see the issue. We needed to bring him in. The stabbing was on his doorstep, and he didn't call an ambulance, plus he was one of the trial kids. He's a suspect—'

'He is a person of interest. But he's also an extremely vulnerable young man, who was in your care. And, for fuck's sake, Riley, no one at that scene was impressed with how you handled it.'

Riley lifted his chin. 'I'll feel sorry for him when we establish that he's not the one stabbing people in the neck.'

'And how are we supposed to do that, with him on a psych ward?' Field's voice rose to a shout. People outside would be able to hear, but she didn't care.

Field picked up the newly purchased copy of *Darlings, Obsessed* from her desk and Riley flinched, like she was going to throw it at him.

'Top priority for every officer on this case is tracking down the people involved in that study. Callum Mulligan was the only person who could tell us who we should be fucking looking for.'

That wasn't the only reason she was angry – she could admit that much to herself. Field was angry that someone on *her* team could get it so wrong – could treat Callum Mulligan that badly.

Riley had gone red, but to his credit, maintained eye contact. She threw the book down on the desk between them.

'If he is guilty—' She was speaking at a normal volume again, and through the glass walls she watched people turn back to their computers. '*If* he is guilty, nothing he says while he's on that ward will be admissible.'

She drained her lukewarm coffee in one and stood up. 'I'm placing you on restricted duties.'

132

Riley's eyes bulged. 'Seriously? Boss—'

'I'll make a decision about serving you with a Reg 13 after I've reviewed the bodycams.'

She didn't want to look at the footage. Already couldn't get Callum's screams, his tortured expression out of her head.

He'd reminded her of Toby, on those darkest days.

Field took a steadying breath. 'I'm placing you on restricted duties,' she repeated. 'You'll be office-bound until further notice. Count yourself lucky I haven't removed you from this case, DS Riley.'

His cheeks flamed, but he didn't argue.

'Now get out of my sight.'

# Chapter 31

## Thursday | Afternoon

### Field

The meeting was bigger than yesterday's. For the first time since she made DCI, members of Raynott's team were being loaned to their MIT. Only DCs, but even so.

Riley was leaning against a desk, chatting to a couple of the newer uniformed recruits, but his smile didn't reach his eyes. He was putting on a brave face after his semi-public bollocking, but he wasn't wincing over the split lip anymore.

Wilson was firing off emails on her laptop.

'Afternoon, all,' Field barked.

She held up a hand and indicated everyone should sit down.

'First things first, David Moore is still in critical condition at King's, but he's stable. The initial report from the forensic medical examiner should be with us by tonight. Due to catastrophic blood loss, he was technically deceased for several minutes, which could mean permanent brain damage. We can't rely on him waking up and telling us who did this.' She glanced at Sam's file on the desk. 'Today I want to focus on our second victim.'

The room was silent.

Field pulled the file towards her and took out Sam's photograph, pinning it to the centre of the whiteboard, next to David's work headshot.

'Samantha Hughes, or Sam to her friends. Thirty-two years old, healthy, no criminal record. She worked at a local pub and was studying for an English PhD at Goldsmiths.' Field steeled herself. 'Her parents live in Rickmansworth. Hertfordshire police delivered the death notice this morning. They'll be here this evening.'

Field uncapped a marker and wrote "PATIENT B" above Sam's photograph. 'According to Callum Mulligan, she was a patient in Moore's study, and Dr Young found scarring consistent with Patient B's described dermatillomania.'

Field held up a photograph of Callum, cropped close onto his face.

'She was found by this man. Callum Mulligan, also thirty-two. The ambulance was called by a neighbour.'

A few frowns around the room.

Field glanced at Wilson, who cleared her throat and said: 'From some interviews and articles he's written, I think Callum is Patient D. Something called magical thinking – about numbers.'

'Thanks,' Field said, adding the label "PATIENT D" above Callum's photograph.

'Any leads on the other three kids?' A voice – Field didn't catch who it belonged to.

'No. As soon as Callum Mulligan is fit to be interviewed, he may be able to shed light on that. Either way,' Field said. 'Any of the other three patients could be our perpetrator, or our next victim.'

Wilson nodded, and opened her mouth to ask a question, before sticking her hand in the air.

'Yes?'

'We should go through the hospital admissions in the local area, in case this person has committed other stabbings, but not on our patch.'

'Yes, good point, Wilson.' Field paused. 'Early blood-spatter analysis suggests that the perpetrator cut themselves during the attack. It's unlikely they'd seek medical attention, but it's also worth pursuing.'

Wilson nodded and made a note.

'I also want us to look for any link between David Moore and Samantha Hughes. If they have been targeted in connection to each other, let's not take for granted it's solely related to the 2010 trial. We didn't find anything on Samantha's phone download, but I'd like to get a download of her home router, too. We need to search Samantha's home for a second phone, and I'd like cell-site mapping done on her and David in the past three weeks, to see if they were together at any point.'

She directed most of this to a red-haired digital forensics specialist at the back of the room.

Field turned back to the board. 'We need to expand door-to-door to include more streets, in all directions, from both scenes. Even if no one saw or heard anything, there'll be something on one of those bastard doorbells. I want everyone and anyone who was out walking or driving on the streets of Plumstead at that time of night traced, interviewed and ruled out. We have a violent, unstable perpetrator out there.'

'Unless they're not "out there" anymore,' Riley said, in a low voice.

'Right.' Field snapped. 'Yes – Callum is, of course, a person of interest.'

Field had seen him, shaking in the middle of his living

room. The state he was in, the state of the house. That animal fear – it wasn't something you could fake. Field's gut said that he was caught up in something much bigger, which none of them understood yet.

Field tapped the board marker against her palm. 'Mulligan is currently undergoing an assessment in a psychiatric unit. If he did it, he's not going anywhere, but right now we have no motive and nothing concrete placing him at David's murder.'

'And why is he in the unit?' Wilson muttered.

Riley flushed. 'Does he need a motive? He's had a breakdown, lost it and stabbed his therapist. Then, what if Sam guessed Callum attacked the doctor, and went to confront him about it?'

He shot a look at Field, knowing he was pushing it. Wilson opened her mouth to retort, but Field put a hand up.

'I know none of you listen to anyone round here, but if you pay attention to any instruction I ever give you, then let's make it this one. Do not make assumptions. Let's not assume that because Mr Mulligan has a mental illness that he's somehow taken leave of his senses and decided to attack people—'

Wilson nodded, emphatic.

'And at the same time, let's not assume that Mr Mulligan is a blabbering, incompetent wreck. It could be a very clever, considered ploy for diminished responsibility, if he is guilty.'

Field's gaze moved between Wilson and Riley.

'Let's make sure this case is dictated by the evidence, shall we? DS Wilson, you're with me. Dismissed.'

Wilson followed Field out of the room. With all their officers back in the briefing room, only DCI Raynott's team were sat at their desks. A few of the DIs eyed Field as she walked past.

Wilson shut Field's office door behind her. 'What's the plan, boss?'

Field checked the time. 'We're going to inform Penny Moore about this second attack. It'll have to be brief, though. I want us to be back here when Mr and Mrs Hughes arrive.'

Wilson scratched the back of her neck. 'Am I going to be handling that—'

Field shook her head. 'It should be me.'

She scanned her desk for anything she would need. Notebook, a lip balm and Young's concealer were all plucked from the mess and thrown into her bag.

'I guess it means more, hearing from another parent.'

Field's stomach dropped at the mere suggestion of Toby having a bearing on the case.

'It's not that.' She sighed, and allowed herself a brief sit-down in her chair. 'I need to ask them to refrain from talking to the press. We need to keep a lid on Sam's identity.'

There had been some coverage about David, but it hadn't caught the attention of the nationals.

A pretty thirty-two-year-old stabbed to death? That would be a front-page story.

The thought of speaking to the parents tonight was like a physical weight on her chest. She was already scanning for phrases, condolences.

'Right. Let's get out of here.'

# Chapter 32

## Thursday | Afternoon

### Lily

'A girl murdered,' Scott said. 'Right outside your place.'

He drove over a bump at speed and the jolt to her stomach made Lily double over, the seatbelt cutting into her neck.

He shot a glance at her. 'You okay, babe?'

She nodded, breathing through the sickness. Scott carried on.

'Even you have to admit,' Scott scoffed, 'it's all a bit weird, isn't it? You two have a massive argument and suddenly—'

'How did you know we had an argument?' Lily twisted in her seat. 'I never told you that.'

Scott gave her a pitying look. 'Why else would you have been at mine when I got home?'

'Oh,' Lily said, softly. It made sense.

'Plus,' he went on, turning the radio down as he spoke. 'You stank of booze and fags.'

Her cheeks flushed.

The road sign in front at the traffic lights had two red H symbols. One pointed towards King's College Hospital, where David had been admitted. It might be where they'd taken Sam – her body. Heat crept up Lily's neck.

The other pointed to the Maudsley psychiatric, and Callum.

Another disapproving sideways glance. 'I'm going to have to change the sheets. I can't stand the smell of stale smoke.'

Lily wondered whether her hair still smelled. It sometimes did, after they smoked indoors, even after a shower. It didn't help that Scott refused to buy proper shampoo, and used environmentally friendly blocks of antiseptic-smelling hair products that never managed a proper lather.

'While you're visiting Callum,' Scott went on, taking the left at the lights. 'I'll go to work, do a few hours on the ward. They're short-staffed; they'll appreciate an extra pair of hands.' He put a hand on her knee, squeezing the joints. 'I want to be there, to bring you home.'

Lily stiffened in her seat, and he took his hand back to change gear.

*Focus.*

She shouldn't be thinking about Scott, and his suffocating, stressful brand of affection.

Callum needed her.

# Chapter 33

## Thursday | Afternoon

### Lily

Lily waited on a hard plastic chair, for a nurse to take her to Callum.

It wasn't the first time she'd been on a psychiatric ward, but she was struck again by how unlike the TV stereotype it was. There were no patients shuffling along like zombies with wide eyes and caved-in faces. No bars on the windows.

The only thing that felt true to her once-imagined version of the ward was the smell. Sterile, dentist-like.

Two children were playing on a rug in front of their dad, who looked completely at ease, the plastic bracelet on his left wrist the only thing that marked him as a patient.

How was Cal going to cope with the news about Sam? He fell apart when Paige died.

They had all agreed to go to the funeral – Lily, Cal, Sam and Andy.

Lily was living in West London, near her uni, and the tubes

were fucked so she was late, stumbling towards the crematorium in her black pencil skirt and low heels. But she never made it to the service, because she found Callum curled in a ball on a bench outside, sobbing his heart out.

It took years after that for them to finally admit they had feelings for each other. They told themselves Paige would be thrilled, that she wanted them to find each other at the funeral, to become friends again, to fall in love.

Paige and Callum had always been close. At the Maudsley, Lily had sometimes been jealous of their bond. She'd never told Cal that.

No one could have predicted Paige's accident, but David and Sam had been targeted. Maybe even hunted. And the police didn't seem to know why.

Lily didn't know how much time had passed when a voice behind her was saying: 'Do you want to follow me?'

Lily got to her feet.

The nurse was Lily's age, dark shadows under her eyes.

'Callum hasn't eaten, but he has had some water,' the nurse said, smiling kindly. 'Hoping to get him to have a lie-down and a sleep. I'll have to stay with you, I'm afraid. I'm Erin.'

Erin buzzed them through a security door with the badge on her lanyard.

'He was beyond lucky we had a bed, with all the shortages. He'd have been looked after in police custody, usually.'

Lily watched Erin's ponytail swing as she walked.

'But we heard there was a bit of a cock-up at the scene. Better that he's with us. Okay, we're just here.' Erin paused with a hand on the door, her voice dropping to a whisper. 'We don't usually let visitors into the rooms, but Dr Maxwell has made an exception. I'll just be in the corner – okay?'

Erin held the door open.

142

Lily breathed in from her diaphragm, fixed a smile on her face.

Cal was sitting on the edge of the bed, deep in thought, wearing a grey T-shirt and jogging bottoms that didn't belong to him.

Lily sat next to him and reached for his hand. 'All right, dickhead?'

He turned to her, his smile on delay. 'Hey, Lil. Hey.'

His speech was slurred, but Lily was prepared for that. They'd given him strong meds.

A pair of shoes were lined up next to the bed, the kind with no laces.

'The nurse says you won't eat anything,' Lily said, shooting a look at Erin, motionless in the corner on a plastic chair. 'That's my trick.'

A long pause.

'You should eat, Cal. Even if it's just a biscuit or something.'

Cal didn't move.

He gazed back at her, seeming to process what she'd said, then pulled his hand from hers and shuffled sideways, away from her.

How was she going to tell him about Sam?

And David – he had to pull through. She couldn't look after Callum without him.

'I'm really sorry.' Lily looked down at her hands. 'I'm sorry I wasn't there last night.'

He sucked in a deep breath, and Lily held hers, waiting for him to say something.

He nodded towards the corner. 'Spider.'

Lily twisted to follow his gaze. She couldn't see anything. 'You need to get some sleep, Cal. You'll feel so much better, if you can have a sleep.'

Cal was picking compulsively at a thread on the cheap

T-shirt, and Lily watched his fingers working at it. They'd been clipped short – either by the staff, so he couldn't scratch himself – or maybe by the police. She'd seen that on a documentary once.

The nausea that'd sat low in her stomach for days was churning again when Cal finally spoke.

'I did it, Lil.'

It was like all the air had been sucked out of the room.

He turned to her, alert now, scratching his buzzed head with those short nails.

'It was me.'

Lily glanced at Erin, in the corner.

'Will you tell them?' Cal demanded. 'Will you tell them for me?'

'Cal I—' She let out a hiss of pain as he grabbed her wrist.

'You have to, Lil. They won't believe me; they won't get it.'

He was squeezing her wrist hard, and pain shot up her arm as she tried to pull it away.

'But you can make them understand. You can tell them for me.'

'When you say you think you did it, Cal . . . ?' Lily chose her words carefully. 'You don't think that it was you, who stabbed Sam?'

He let out a bark of laughter. 'Of course I didn't stab Sam. I didn't *stab* anyone. But it was my fault.' He spoke so quickly that spit flew from the corners of his mouth.

She had pins and needles in her fingers.

Erin was up, out of the chair, on Callum's other side.

'You don't get it,' Callum said. 'The counting, I've been trying to stop the counting for months, years—'

'Let go of Lily for me, Callum, come on,' Erin said.

'—and I felt like something bad was going to happen if I

did stop and I knew as soon as I saw her. She was outside our house Lil, she was stabbed on our doorstep.'

Callum carried on speaking, words tumbling out of him as Lily finally managed to pull her hand away.

'I did that to her; I did it. I tried to stop the counting and I was trying to fight it and that's why this all happened, isn't it? Will you tell them, Lil?'

Lily hid the red marks from Erin's view, tears in her eyes. She stood up and held Cal against her. Wrapped him up, head against her chest, and held on tightly. 'You just need more sleep, Cal. You're confused. A glass of water, maybe some food. Then sleep.'

Erin still looked concerned, hovering near the door.

Callum nodded in her arms. 'Will you make them understand that I didn't want to hurt her, but I must have?"

'I'll explain it to them, Cal. I'll explain it to them.'

# Chapter 34

## Thursday | Afternoon

## Callum

'Come on,' she said, pulling the covers back. 'A little lie-down.'

He noticed some of his things on the bedside table and couldn't remember putting them there.

'That's it, Cal. Get into the bed for me, come on.'

He put his hand out to the wall to steady himself.

He wanted to close his eyes. Shut them and be in darkness, be alone and be asleep.

'Here we go.'

Lily gave a gentle tug on his hand.

He sat on the bed again. On the edge.

He wasn't going to lie down.

There was a figure in the doorway, someone watching them, but he was too tired to look at who it was.

His breathing felt funny, and he counted.

*One – in. Out.*

*Two – in. Out.*

*Three – in. Out.*

'Hey, hey.' Lily kneeled in front of him, tried to pull his hands away from his face.

*Four – in. Out.*

*Five – in. Out.*

She let out a deep sigh and it took him out of the counting, just long enough. He lifted his head and met her gaze.

'I'm sorry,' he managed, one fat tear rolling down his cheek.

'Oi,' Lily said, with a smile. 'We've got through worse than this, haven't we?'

*Had they?*

'You don't worry about anything, Cal, okay? You've been so brave. You're doing so well. Let me do the worrying. You'll feel better after some sleep.'

'I want to—' His voice hitched in his throat. 'I want to sleep.'

She lifted the covers up and he slid underneath them.

The light switched off, and Callum rolled over, looking at the smooth white wall. It might have been the sudden darkness, or lying down, or being exhausted, but he was crying again. His face was hot, and he counted the drops rolling sideways down his face, collecting on the pillow by his cheek.

Then the blanket lifted, and she was climbing into bed behind him. Her thin arm wrapped round his chest as the sobs came.

'It's okay,' Lily whispered. 'It's okay.'

She stroked slow little circles below his ear, the one not against the pillow, until he calmed down.

Empty, dry-eyed, he finally felt like he could sleep.

'I love you,' he whispered to the wall. The slow circles in his hair didn't stop. His eyes were closing.

'I love you.'

147

# Chapter 35

**D:** I only ever wanted to help people. I knew that's what I needed to do, what I was good at.

*Pause*

**D:** I just want to make broken people better.

*Pause*

**D:** I don't know what I'd do, without this job.
**P:** I don't know what we'd do without you.

*Pause*

**D:** I needed to hear that today.
**P:** Well, you know – this is a safe space.

# Chapter 36

## Thursday | Evening

## Field

Field drove, needing an excuse not to look at her overflowing inbox for twenty minutes. Wilson was quiet next to her, and a Radio 4 show Field wasn't listening to filled the car. Zara met them outside the Greenwich townhouse, elegantly dressed and unflappable, as always.

Penny opened the door to the three of them. She looked like she'd just stepped out of the shower. Her red hair was still wet, slicked back, and she was dressed in a pair of matching floral pyjamas. She was also wearing perfume.

'Hi, Penny,' Zara said. 'Is Simon still here? We need to talk to you both.'

'He's – he popped out.' Penny glanced between them. 'Sorry, but can we do this later? I don't feel up to talking.'

Penny started to close the door, and Field put out a hand to stop her. 'It's important, Penny. We need to come in.'

Penny's resolve crumbled, her shoulders falling forward as

she opened the door wide. Zara went first, heading for the kitchen. Penny trailed after her like a scolded child, and Field shut the door behind them.

Time to deliver more bad news over another hot drink.

'Penny.' Zara pulled a chair out, the one next to Field, and took a seat. 'Were you home all night?'

Penny wiped her hands on the legs of her pyjamas. 'I was here,' she managed, after a long pause.

Zara leaned forward across the table. 'Talk me through what you did, please, Penny.'

Field glanced to her left to make sure Wilson was taking notes.

'I—' Penny stopped, looked at Zara. 'You called me, at around ten o'clock last night. Then I turned my phone off, after we hung up. Didn't want to keep reading the condolences texts. What's happened?' Penny demanded. 'Tell me.'

Zara leaned forward. 'There's been another incident. A stabbing.'

Penny pushed her chair back from the table but didn't stand up. She kept her gaze locked on Zara.

'It was a young woman involved this time. We have reason to believe it's linked to what happened to David. It's possible she was one of the patients who took part in David's 2010 trial.'

'One of David's patients?' Penny said – and her voice sounded mechanical, emotionless.

'Her name is Samantha Hughes. Had David ever spoken about her?' Field said.

Penny shook her head.

'Unfortunately, she passed away at the scene,' Zara said, voice grave.

Penny sucked in a breath, and it seemed to catch there. She put a hand to her chest and gripped the front of her pyjama shirt, twisting the silk. Zara moved around the kitchen table, put a hand on Penny's back.

'Breathe, Penny. It's okay.'

Field kept her face blank, but her mind was whirring. Penny was having a bigger reaction to Sam's attack, a person she'd apparently never heard of or met, than the one she'd had to the news of her own husband. Even if they were getting divorced, that seemed unusual. 'Will Simon be back soon? Was he here last night?' she asked.

Zara took a step away, and Penny gripped the marble counter. 'He went home. I told him to go home.'

Penny looked like she was struggling to hold it together.

'We'll get in touch with him,' Field said. 'And with your permission, we'd like to take your phone for a day or two. It can help confirm where you were.'

Penny turned, scanning the kitchen as if looking for her mobile. 'I didn't turn it back on. I don't even know which room it's in.'

Wilson wrote several exclamation marks on her pad, which Field acknowledged with a nod.

It could be grief, or delayed shock. For all they knew Penny had spent the time she was alone in paroxysms of sorrow, but she was trying to keep that in, at least in front of them. But she had no alibi for either attack, and her reactions were odd, to say the least. At the minimum it called for a voluntary interview.

'Penny, do you think you'd be able to come into the station, tomorrow?' Field asked. 'I'd like you to answer some questions, to help us get a better picture of David. Help us understand why someone might—'

'I need to go.' Penny was staring out of the patio doors, into the colourful garden, stems waving in the dappled evening light.

They waited.

'You need to go somewhere tomorrow?' Zara asked.

But Field already knew what Penny was about to say.

'No.' Penny looked down at her pyjamas, put a hand to her cheek. 'I need to go to the hospital. Now – I need to see David, now.'

# Chapter 37

## Thursday | Evening

### Lily

Scott wasn't in the car, and Lily moved to the shade of a gnarled tree. The roots were pushing up through the concrete, and she balanced on one uneven patch of ground, teetering back and forwards.

Her phone buzzed.

*Sorry, babe. Two cardiac arrests today. Just getting changed - 10 mins.*

Scott's ward had been relieved when he turned up for an impromptu shift, while she was visiting Cal.

Lily pulled Callum's tobacco from her pocket. She rolled a cigarette, a precise if slightly thin cylinder.

Lily inhaled deeply. Scott hated smoking. She hadn't eaten and by the time she exhaled her head was already spinning.

She hadn't seen Callum in that catatonic state for a long

time. The memories slammed into her, pinning her to the side of the car.

Callum facing the wall in bed, refusing to move. Catching a glimpse of Callum in David's office, sobbing so hard his shoulders shook. Callum, dead-eyed, telling her about the night he stood on a bridge, aged twelve, and debated whether to jump.

The memories – of her being ill, of Callum being ill – it was all a world away from their lives in his little house. He wasn't *well* now, but he was okay. They had their day-to-day routines – washing up and playing records and never hoovering.

The cigarette crackled as she reached the filter and she flicked it towards the kerb, debating rolling another. It was only a matter of time, before it would all come out.

Maybe it would be in the press, or maybe the police would speak to the school. If people at school found out, then it would get out to the parents. Would they want her teaching their kids? Would she lose her job?

She put a hand up to her chest.

Lily was so wrapped up in Callum she had barely thought about Sam. Her poor parents.

Two stabbings in two nights. The police couldn't think it was a coincidence, not with all the reminders to lock her doors and call them if she saw anything suspicious.

Lily shivered, despite the warm night. The hairs on the back of her neck tingled, like she was being watched.

'Lily.'

She jumped, yelping and scrambling away from the voice.

Scott held his hands up, wide-eyed. He was clutching a bedraggled bunch of flowers.

'Shit.' Lily put a hand over her pounding heart. 'You scared me.'

Scott didn't speak. He pulled her into a hug.

'I hope those are for me,' Lily mumbled into his chest. He was warm and smelled like antibac.

'Of course they are.' He laughed, handing them over. Spray carnations. Not the splashiest flower, certainly not the most expensive. But her favourites. 'How are you, babe?'

She clutched the flowers as she thought. After a pause she shrugged and said, 'I actually don't know how I am.'

But Scott wasn't listening. He took Lily's arm and pulled it towards him. The bruises looked worse in the daylight.

A muscle in Scott's jaw twitched. 'Did he do that?'

She shrugged. 'He didn't mean to. It was an accident. And it doesn't even hurt.'

Scott didn't say anything. He let her go and they got into the car. Lily was drained.

Lily leaned back in her seat and felt the first stirrings of panic. She was going to have to tell him everything – her past, the paper. Her throat closed and she felt the pressure behind her eyes that meant she was going to cry.

'Scott,' she said. 'When we get home, we need to talk.'

# Chapter 38

## Thursday | Evening

### Lily

Scott drove them back to his flat in silence. His hands gripped the wheel, his shoulders rigid.

Tears dripped steadily down her face during the drive. She knew Scott thought she was about to break up with him, but she didn't trust herself to speak. Too anxious to offer him reassurance.

They climbed the stairs to the flat. Scott always took the stairs, never the lift. She trailed behind him, still crying.

He let her in and went straight to the sofa. Sat down heavily. Lily wished they were back at hers, in the safety of her own room.

Scott's face was earnest, full of concern, and Lily felt guilty.

Scott didn't speak as she sat next to him. He reached over and picked up her hand. The gesture made her cry again.

'I'm sorry.' She sniffed. 'Do you mind if I tell you all of it really quickly and get this over with?'

Scott nodded.

'It's not just Callum,' she said, eyes squeezed shut. 'I have OCD too.'

Silence.

'And I didn't meet him in my twenties,' she went on. 'I met him when I was fourteen. I met him at the Maudsley.'

She had spent the last decade trying not to think about the Maudsley.

Lily might be Cal's carer now, but he had looked after her first, on the ward. He was a year older, fifteen going on twenty-eight. Cal wore band T-shirts and smoked with the night porters. She'd finally got an OCD diagnosis after years of utter misery and confusion, and she was terrified.

Callum got Lily through it. Callum understood her.

Lily only met Callum again because of Paige's death – and it unravelled him. It was slow, but Cal recovered, and they were happy. Their little life, in their safe little house. They were good for each other.

Until they weren't.

Callum got ill again, but this time there was no life-shattering event to point to, no root cause. And this time, Lily couldn't make him better.

Scott was sitting very still, waiting for her to keep talking. She felt sick.

'I developed OCD as a child. About food. How it was prepared and what was safe to eat and what was bad. Mashed potato? Good. Boiled potatoes? Something terrible would happen.' She sucked in a breath, aware it sounded flippant, aware it sounded ridiculous. 'My parents thought I was fussy, at first, then thought I was anorexic when I got to secondary school. And I was slowly going mad, because I had all these crippling rules to follow around food.'

Scott had a deep furrow between his concerned eyebrows.

He went to reach for Lily's hand, but pulled it back when she flinched.

'I was in and out of hospital from eleven to fourteen, in eating disorder clinics.'

'All this – is this why you don't speak to your parents?' Scott asked in a whisper.

'Yeah. They were scared I'd pass my behaviours on to my little sisters. I haven't spoken to my mum since I was sixteen and she said I was using OCD as an excuse. She accused me of making it all up. For attention.'

'Fuck.'

'Yeah.' She shrugged. 'But, by then our doctor – he was called David Moore – David told me I had OCD. I joined the support group, and did this intensive course of CBT. It was a fucking lot.'

'That's why you can't let go of Callum.' Scott said it as a statement, in a kind of hard voice.

Lily gave Scott a hard stare. She would not stand for him being jealous of a sectioned teenager.

'Cal started writing his novel while we were still in the Maudsley. The first half is during treatment. The second half is after. David wasn't the only one to get published off the back of it.'

Scott looked confused, and she realised he didn't know about David's paper. She was too tired to explain that as well.

Lily thought back to the books on her bedroom windowsill. Her copy of *Darlings, Obsessed* was mixed in with other books on madness. *One Flew Over the Cuckoo's Nest*, *The Bell Jar*. *Perks of Being a Wallflower*. Woolf, Vonnegut, Kane. Paige *loved* Sarah Kane. Always aspired to act in a production of *4.48 Psychosis*.

Lily kept cuttings about David's career tucked inside the madness books, like pressed flowers. *Psychiatry Monthly*'s first write-up of their study, articles in the local paper, David getting his medal from the king – safe between the pages. She wondered if the police would search her room, move the books around.

Scott cleared his throat.

'It's all fiction,' she said looking down at her hands. 'Callum's book, I mean. The story and the characters were made up, but the charm of it was that the actual OCD and stuff – that was really us.

'We did lots of creative stuff. David encouraged us to write fictional versions of ourselves.' She sniffed. 'Write out the best-case scenarios. The worst-case.'

She twisted to look at Scott. He hadn't moved. Through the wide window behind him, the sky was beginning to darken, turning blusher-pink at the edges.

'I can't believe she's dead,' she whispered. 'Sam – she was there when I arrived. We were together on that ward, every day, for almost two years—'

The sobs came and Scott wrapped her in his arms, squeezing her tight until they subsided, patting her firmly on her shoulder like she was a burping baby.

The nausea was building again, and she twisted her body to try and ease the feeling, pulling away from his hug.

Scott swallowed. 'Can I say something?'

Lily nodded.

'I think on some level, I already knew.' His voice was deeper than usual. 'I knew there was something about you that you were holding back. Holding back from me, I mean.'

She wiped her nose on her sleeve.

'You know I would never have judged you, Lily.'

'Of course.' She frowned. 'Why would you judge me?'

'That's my point,' he said, a note of frustration in his voice. 'I never would.'

# Chapter 39

## Thursday | Evening

## Lily

She asked Scott to go to the shops for almond milk and peppermint tea – two things she could be sure he didn't have in – and he reluctantly obliged. Lily eased herself out of the bed, to look in his fridge.

The shelves were gleaming, not a speck of food or dribble of sauce on the glass. His cleaner's work.

Scott took pride in eating healthily.

Where the vegetable drawers in her and Cal's fridge were empty, apart from slabs of chocolate and a few sugary yoghurts, both of Scott's were full.

The first was fruit. Red apples, one lemon.

Lily opened a paper bag. It was full of fat, seasonal strawberries. Bought at the market, not Tesco, to save using a plastic carton.

She dropped them back in the drawer.

She didn't want to open the vegetable one. Spinach and

kale and cucumber – never cooked but blended to a thick, ripe pulp and downed at breakfast.

He was so *good*, this man. Fucking perfect.

Lily's stomach twisted again, and she put a hand to it. She knew something wasn't right, and the sick feeling was only getting worse.

Ginger was good for nausea. Cal always kept a bottle of ginger ale on standby for her, even though she hadn't been on meds, and suffering the side effects, for a long time.

She slammed the fridge door, put a hand to her mouth and turned to the kitchen sink. There was nothing left for her to throw up, but she retched, dry-heaving over the coffee cups in the washing-up bowl.

Her phone was buzzing on the side – unknown number. Lily wiped her mouth. 'Hello?'

'Hello, is this Lily Stewart?'

'Speaking.' Weak again, she slid down the cabinets and sat on the floor.

'Great. This is DS Wilson.'

Another stab of cramp, her stomach clenching hard.

'I wanted to check, Lily, are you staying with your boyfriend again tonight?'

Lily stared at the phone, wondering whether something was wrong with the speaker. The voice sounded faint and far away.

'Yes,' she said, finally.

'Okay, good. Now with everything going on, I'd advise you to lock the windows and put the bolt on the door. I'm sure you're perfectly safe, but—'

The "but" hung in the digital air between them.

'We're hoping to interview Callum tomorrow, Lily. Could you come down to the Maudsley, in the morning? He'd like you to act as his appropriate adult.'

'Oh. Yeah, I'll be there.'

'Great. We can pick you up.' Wilson sounded relieved. 'I'll aim to get to you for around 10 a.m.?'

Lily made a noise of agreement and Wilson ended the call.

She checked the time. Scott had been gone a while, and she didn't want him to wander through the door while she was on the phone to the hospital. But she wanted to see how Cal was, whether he was in bed.

She moved to the bathroom; ran a bath she didn't want to get into. Dialled the number to the sound of the water.

Dr Maxwell couldn't come to the phone, but Lily had a short conversation with a nurse. All she would say over the phone was that Callum was safe, and they'd take good care of him.

'Okay,' Lily said, weakly. 'Thank you.'

She sat on the closed lid of the toilet, phone in her hand, and stared at the bath slowly filling.

Part of her could sense the fridge, looming in the kitchenette. Almost hear its low buzzing, its shelves full of health and vitality mocking her from inside it.

# Chapter 40

**P:** I am not reliable.

*Pause*

**P:** I am not stable. I am not rational. I am not always kind.

*Pause*

**P:** I say the wrong things. I ask the wrong questions. I waste my doctors' time. I don't try hard enough. I think too much. I struggle with simple tasks. I don't take care of my belongings. I don't take care of my personal hygiene. I don't take an interest in others.

*Pause*

**P:** I am difficult, and I am difficult to love.

# Chapter 41

## Thursday | Evening

## Field

Field let herself out onto the fire escape at the back of the building, and took in a lungful of air. The sounds of Lewisham were loud below her. Sirens, faint shouting. The usual chorus. Field had a hard lump in her throat, that a cup of tea and a glass of water hadn't shifted. Her voice was fine, but she could feel it every time she swallowed. The threat of tears.

Mr and Mrs Hughes were crushed, and the forty minutes she'd spent with them had wrung Field out. Field always came out here for a break after the really difficult interviews, even after she gave up smoking.

She'd never cried in front of a victim's family, although she'd come close a few times. She used the selfie mode on her phone, for a quick glance at her reflection. The lump in her throat was still there, but she looked normal.

A safe pair of middle-aged hands, with decades of experience.

Exactly who you wanted working on your daughter's murder investigation.

At the last minute, Field had told Zara that she wasn't needed for the meeting, and she'd called in DI Bellamy instead. Zara and Sam were too close in age.

Mrs Hughes hadn't been able to speak. She spent the whole forty minutes with a handkerchief pressed against her mouth, staring bug-eyed at the table as tears dripped onto it.

Sam's father had asked a series of practical questions, gripping his hands together tightly. Then he told Field stories about Sam.

He spoke about her kindness. Sam was a volunteer at a children's hospice on Sundays, cleaning the rooms at the end of weekend stays for new families to come in on Monday.

She played in a women's football team at uni. Her PhD was on Emily Dickinson. She'd never had a long-term partner, but there had been a couple of people who came close.

Her dad asked Field if she had kids, and she told him yes – just one.

Sam had a sister. She was in Australia, travelling. They'd spent thousands on a last-minute flight home.

Field looked up at the darkening sky, wondering if she was up there now.

Mr Hughes had remained stoic as Field asked question after question about the trial, Sam's time in the Maudsley, whether he knew of any recent contact with David.

He was resolute on all points. Sam had fully recovered from OCD and dermatillomania. She had been healthy and happy, and they all had nothing but respect and gratitude for Dr David Moore.

When the interview was over, and the family were on their way back to Hertfordshire, Bellamy had slapped Field on the back. 'That was brutal, boss. Well done.'

It meant a lot more to her than she'd ever admit to him.

The lock screen on Field's phone was the generic one that all iPhones had, but once she'd unlocked it, there appeared a picture of Toby on his first day of work, at Queen Elizabeth. Eighteen and thin as a rake inside his hospital scrubs, beaming from ear to ear. Thrilled to spend eight hours a day extracting blood from patients, nattering to them and holding hands with the squeamish ones.

She wished he'd stayed there.

Field had seen the slightly haunted, vacant expression on the faces of coppers and paramedics for nearly thirty years. The dazed look of someone who knocked for a routine welfare check and found something horrific.

She'd never wanted to see that on her son's face.

Field felt guilty for even dwelling on Toby, after the conversation she'd just had with Sam's parents.

*Even if he does get ill – he'll be alive.*

But she couldn't help the nagging feeling that he wasn't strong enough for this job. He couldn't study for the exams and work all the shifts, maintain his steady home life with Billy, take care of himself.

*He'll get through it*, she told herself.

She would get him through it. Patiently, this time.

Something Sam's father told Field came back to her:

'I thought seeing Sam like that, a teenager in that hospital – I thought that would be the worst thing we'd ever had to live through as a family.'

The only thing Field could do for Sam now, was to minimise her family's suffering by giving them answers and bringing the culprit to justice.

Field would let herself take five more minutes, out in the night air.

And then she would get back to catching the bastard who did it.

# Chapter 42

## Thursday | Evening

## Field

At nine, Field packed up her stuff and dropped her car home, then walked to the Volunteer pub.

Tonight, it was full of football fans, packed at the front of the bar in front of the screen. They exploded with screams of fury as she ordered a gin.

A lot of police officers used the Volly. It was loud enough that you could have a discreet conversation, and Field had a favourite booth that was usually free. She found it helped to get out of the station, and talking things over in a different setting.

Her booth was in the corner near the toilets, at the edge of the bar. She liked having no one sat behind her. From her premium vantage point, Field saw Riley and Wilson enter through a side door.

It was always weird, seeing them in their civvies. Wilson was bare-legged in a short dark dress, and Riley wore blue jeans and a tight white T-shirt.

'All right, boss?' Riley said, nodding at her half-empty glass. 'Another G&T?'

'Better not,' she said. 'Might have to drive later—'

Field was cut off as a huge cheer erupted. A bald man at the back of the crowd twisted round to look at them, fists aloft, waiting for them to join in with the celebration.

Wilson glanced at her watch. 'A single G&T is one unit; you'll be fine to drive by 11 p.m. if you have another.'

Riley gave her a bemused smile. 'DS Wilson, are you actually *fun* when you're not in work?'

She ignored him. 'I'll have a white wine spritzer. You can go to the bar, since you've been sat at a desk all day.'

Wilson threw her phone, keys and warrant card onto the table and dropped into the booth, while Riley went to get the drinks.

'Do you think I've been too harsh on him?' Field asked.

'No.' Wilson shrugged. 'He knows he fucked up. I caught him watching the bodycam footage earlier.'

'Really?' Field said, in surprise.

Wilson nodded. 'He seemed pretty stressed out by it.'

'This case—' Field sighed. 'We're going round in circles.'

'Yeah,' Wilson said, sympathetically. 'It's a headfuck.'

Field watched Riley navigating football fans with their drinks. Another gin, Wilson's wine, and a vodka soda for him.

'How did it go with her parents?' he asked, as soon as he was sat down.

'It was horrible,' Field said, with feeling.

Wilson turned to her, surprised. She didn't usually let on if she was affected by something.

'Her mum was in bits,' Field went on. 'Sam didn't even have OCD anymore, apparently. She'd put all that behind her, after the trial.'

'I didn't think that was a thing,' Wilson said. 'So she was like, cured?'

'Yeah. They think David is a hero,' Field added.

Riley drew patterns in the condensation on his glass.

Field was so relieved to have got the meeting with Mr and Mrs Hughes out of the way, she was practically melting into the cushions.

They tried, for a while, to talk about something other than the case. Once Riley realised Field wasn't here to bollock him again, he relaxed.

One of the recently retired DCIs had been working on a crime novel, starring himself. He'd asked everyone to read it, and to Field's surprise, Riley had said yes.

'I thought it'd be shit and I could post bits of it on the fridge in the tearoom.' He grinned. 'But it's actually pretty good.'

They laughed easily, swapping stories and upcoming holiday plans.

Wilson and Riley were more at ease with each other in the informal setting, shoulders almost touching in the booth. Field was full of warmth for her two imperfect detective sergeants, already ruing the day they'd fly the nest, when all three phones on the table pinged in unison.

Wilson got to it first.

'The super wants an update.'

Field rubbed her temples. 'I'll call him on the walk home.'

A loud groan from the football crowd. Field glanced up at the clock in the corner of the screen. The ninety minutes were almost up. The clock made her think of Callum, on the ward – trying to sleep away from home for the first time in years.

'So – do we think there'll be another attack later?' Wilson asked, setting her glass down. 'If he's escalating, our man, there'll be a third victim come one o'clock this morning.'

'Depends,' Riley said, turning back from the football. 'Whether they're planning to do one a night, or they just got lucky, jumping out on them on their way home.'

'Although we don't know how they got Sam to walk down Callum's road,' Field countered. 'That would take planning. They wanted Callum to find her, because they knocked on his door.'

'So Callum says,' Riley said, darkly.

Wilson rolled her eyes.

'I'm telling you,' Riley said, leaning back into his booth. 'There'll be no attack tonight – nothing until he's out of the loony bin.'

'Riley—' she snapped.

'Sorry, boss.' He held his hands up. 'Shouldn't have said that. But the point stands.'

'It wasn't him,' Field said, matter-of-fact. 'You're missing the obvious.'

Riley turned his head, and Field noticed his neck was pink above the collar of his T-shirt.

Wilson was frowning in thought.

'The attacker was bleeding. Callum wasn't injured, was he? Not a scratch on him.'

They sat in ominous silence for a few minutes. The football ended, and people hurried to the bar, jostling to be served first.

'I still think there's something off about the wife,' Wilson said, eventually. 'You haven't seen her yet, Riley. She went weird after we told her about Sam. Couldn't get a straight answer out of her.'

It gave Field a thought, and she checked her phone. No response from Dawes, when she asked him to stay with Penny tonight. If there was another attack, she wanted Penny alibied.

She put the phone back down. 'We'll speak to Penny tomorrow, even if we have to go to her.'

'I'd caution her for obstruction, if she refuses to come in.' Wilson folded her arms. 'It's weird. She didn't want to go to the hospital yesterday, but as soon as we have questions about Sam, she's desperate to be by his bedside?'

'Maybe the second attack brought home how close she came to losing David,' Field reasoned.

'Can we just go back to Mulligan?' Riley broke in. 'That blood, couldn't it have been a nosebleed, or something? It could have been Sam's blood. It's not one hundred per cent certain.'

'If you want to argue with Young tomorrow, Riley, be my guest.' Field finished her drink. 'And whether he's a witness or a suspect, Mulligan isn't going anywhere tonight.'

Riley looked mollified.

'So, what're the odds that we get another phone call at two o'clock in the morning?' Wilson said darkly.

No one answered her.

'I know we're focusing on the five patients,' Wilson reasoned. 'And that does make sense. But they went for David first, didn't they? We need the names of the staff too. The cleaners, the social workers – God knows. They could all be targets.'

'They specifically left that sheet, at the scene,' Field countered. 'It's about that paper, isn't it? The people involved?'

'Or it could just be about Sam and David—' Riley's eyes were on the melting ice cubes in his glass. 'An affair maybe?'

Field exhaled.

They were all exhausted, and they needed to be with it tomorrow. Talking around the possibilities would get them nowhere.

Either there would be an attack tonight, or there wouldn't.

# Chapter 43

## Thursday | Evening

### Lily

The front door closed with a click, and Lily sat up on Scott's sofa, switching off *EastEnders*. The movement made her stomach clench, her throat still sore from the bile she'd spat up while he was gone.

'Lil?' Scott's voice was light, and relief spread through her.

He'd been gone ages, but he must have gone for a walk, to clear his head.

'Hello,' he said, poking his head round the door and smiling at her.

There was rustling in the hallway and then he came into the room. He took her hands in his and pulled her to her feet.

'Hey,' he said, softly. He moved her arms and put them round his neck.

She let out a low growl and put her head on his chest. He smelled like soap and fresh laundry.

'I've got a surprise for you.'

She didn't look up. 'Is it my own door key? Because I'm going to need one.'

He chuckled and planted a kiss on the top of her head. 'Wait there.'

She waited in the middle of the room, her grubby socks out of place against the polished wooden floors. Scott re-entered, laden with tote bags, holding them aloft like a fisherman with the catch of the day.

She felt sick again. Anxiety-sick or sickness-sick she couldn't tell.

'I bought your favourite.' Scott bounced on the balls of his feet. 'I couldn't get sprouts for the bubble and squeak in Sainsbury's, so I went to M&S and got pre-made stuff. It'll be better than what I could make anyway, so I thought fuck it.'

Lily pushed past him, back to the hallway.

'Lil?'

*Lil. Lil. Lil.* She'd spent the past two days lurching from one crisis to another, and Scott was always there, right behind her, calling her in that confused little-boy voice.

'I need some air,' she said, stumbling and putting a hand out to catch herself.

'You shouldn't go out, the police said. Did I do something wrong?' Scott grabbed her arm as she reached for her shoes. 'I wanted to show I wasn't bothered about the food thing. That we can fight it together.'

'It's not a "food thing"—' Lily wrenched her arm from his grip. 'And I don't need you to fight it. This – this stuff – it's too much. You've only just found out, and your first reaction is to do a big shop? What the actual fuck?'

He looked hurt and confused, and it made Lily angrier.

'Do I not have enough going on? The man who got me better is in hospital, and I'm processing the fact that my—'

Scott's concerned expression hardened into something ugly.

'That *Callum* has been sectioned,' Lily corrected. But the fight was over.

'I was doing a nice thing,' Scott said, his voice hard. 'I thought we could cook together. It hasn't escaped my notice that you've barely eaten today.'

He took a step towards her, and Lily shrank back, another painful wrench in her abdomen making her double over.

It wasn't just anxiety. Scott's bathroom was by the front door, and she lurched into it, making it to the toilet as the first heave hit her.

Scott was behind her, trying to hold her hair back. Lily pushed him away. She'd rather get sick in her hair.

'You're not well, Lil. You need to rest, drink some water. I've got rehydration sachets.'

She turned, wiping her mouth on her sleeve. She never did get into her bath. The bubbles were slowly dying in the cooling water, leaving a ring of scum around the edge.

She flushed the toilet. 'I want to go to bed. I want to be on my own.'

# Chapter 44

## Thursday | Evening

### Field

Her house was in darkness, when she got back.

When she was married to Chris, they'd had a four-bed semi-detached on a sleepy street in Kidbrooke. It was boring, but the schools were good, and the commute wasn't bad.

After the divorce she wanted a complete change, along with her downsize. Toby was nearly eighteen by the time the house sale went through.

Her little house on Market Street was perfect. A row of tiny Grade 2 listed Victorian houses, probably built for munitions workers in the Arsenal. It looked like a shoebox from the outside, but inside it was plenty big enough for the two of them. Cosy, that's what they called it, that first day they unpacked.

Field stood on the step, key in hand.

Each of the five houses had its doors and wooden window frames painted a different colour. Hers were aquamarine blue, the paint now beginning to fade.

Inside it was hot. The windows and doors had been shut tight all day. She turned the fan on with the remote, and then went to open the back door for a minute.

Her galley kitchen wasn't dissimilar to Callum's in shape. Cabinets on either side, barely room for two people to pass each other. Back door at the far end, next to the fridge. Field's kitchen was always spotless and gleaming, from lack of use rather than effort.

Not today, though. Pans were piled in the sink, a dribble of milk on the counter. In two strides she was by the open microwave, pulling the door back.

A dinner plate was inside. Three sausages, a mound of mash, and some peas. Gravy poured over the top, thick and congealed. A note in Toby's handwriting read, *Don't forget to eat x*.

It was thoughtful, and it shouldn't have pissed her off, but it did.

She scraped the cold food into the bin, and stepped out into the backyard for her first cigarette in months.

That was where Field was when she got the call from the hospital. Halfway through an illicit cigarette, bummed off a drunken football fan at kicking-out time.

She didn't stub it out, but she didn't take a drag either. The cigarette burned in her hand as Dr Wheatley explained that David Moore had suffered multiple system organ failure, and died without regaining consciousness.

# Chapter 45

**D:** You said you felt unsafe, but you are safe here. This place – it's designed to keep you safe. That's our job.

*Pause*

**P:** There isn't a safe place for me, D—.

*Pause*

**P:** I am the danger. My brain, it's hardwired to make me suffer. I'm not safe anywhere.

# Chapter 46

## Friday | Midnight

## Andy

He opened his eyes.

Andy didn't know how long he'd been lying on his bed, headphones on, eyes tight shut. Days?

*You need to go.*

The room was still spinning, and he looked down at his chest. His T-shirt was stiff with blood.

He removed the headphones, wincing in pain.

*You can't stay here.*

The house was silent.

He got up from the bed, breathing heavily, dragged his large rucksack from under it, and placed it on the bed.

*It's going to be okay. It's going to be okay.*

He carefully added black clothes, a few books and his late father's pocket watch. Last in was £1,000 in cash, which his mother had given him for emergencies, before she went into the hospice.

Anything that could be used to trace him was left in the drawer of the desk, in orderly rows. Phone, cards, Oyster. A short note on top of the desk said he was going to his mother's house, if any of his housemates even noticed he was gone.

He hoisted the rucksack over one shoulder.

# Chapter 47

## Friday | Early hours

## Field

Zara opened the door to Field, expression grave. Even at one in the morning, she managed to look well put together.

'How is she?' Field asked quietly.

Zara just shook her head.

The lamp in the living room was casting an incongruous cosy glow. Simon Dawes was sitting just beyond the puddle of light, tears on his cheeks.

'If she won't talk to me, she won't want to talk to you,' he said, voice hoarse.

'She's upstairs,' Zara said. 'In David's office.'

Field took a seat next to Simon, careful not to touch him, but sitting close. 'We're not here to question her, or you.'

Simon exhaled, shakily.

'We're just here to lend support,' Zara added.

Their heads snapped up in unison, as glass shattered somewhere above them.

# Chapter 48

## Friday | Morning

### Callum

Callum stretched out on the bed, feeling the aches in each limb at a time.

He remembered being awake for a few hours last night. He'd spent some time speaking with Dr Maxwell, been given a higher-than-usual dose of his normal meds, then went back to sleep.

Slowly, it felt like he was coming back to himself.

The last time he was sectioned was twelve years ago – when he was twenty. His nan got sick, and then they lost Paige, and everything became too much. He didn't remember being admitted to the adult unit, or his first few weeks there. David immediately took Callum back on as a patient. Lily visited, once he was up to seeing people.

There were just so many compulsions, and they were so contradictory that he was entirely unable to function. It mostly felt like it was happening to someone else.

Callum sat upright. Being sucked into memories wasn't going to help. David's usual words rang in his ears:

*OCD-brain wants you to dwell on those times, to obsess over them – rather than focusing on tackling today.*

At their next session, David would praise Callum for recalling his voice, his advice, despite everything. *CBT is alive and kicking.* One of his favourite phrases whenever Callum showed the faintest sign of resisting a compulsion.

Callum hoped someone had seen David's name on his file, and put a call in. He'd forgotten to ask Maxwell.

Callum closed his eyes. He was tired. Dog-tired.

A hangover from the sedative.

Closing his eyes brought back images of blood and the sound of Sam's gasping breaths.

His eyes flicked open.

It didn't make any sense. He hadn't seen Sam for years, hadn't spoken to her – although she was probably friends with Lil on Facebook. Then she was outside his house.

*What if they think I did it?*

His brain went into overdrive and within seconds he had lived an entire lifetime as a guilty man. What if Sam never woke up, or she didn't remember who attacked her? What if he went to prison? What if he died in prison? What if he had done it, but he couldn't remember doing it? What if—

Two knocks on the door.

Dr Maxwell edged his way into Callum's room like he was intruding on a private moment – which, in a way, he was.

Callum sat up, and Maxwell took the hard plastic chair opposite the bed.

'The police are here.' Maxwell spoke in a very soft, very gentle way. The way you might address someone with advanced Alzheimer's, Callum thought. 'They want to speak to you.'

He rubbed his head, trying to clear the last of the sedation-fog. 'Okay.'

'I've been asked to explain that nothing you say will be admissible in evidence. They can't do a proper interview until you've been signed off by the unit.'

Callum didn't know whether to feel guilty, angry or relieved. *Being fucking batshit does have the odd advantage*, Lily always said.

'But they need to talk with you, to establish what happened.'

He wanted to ask Maxwell about Sam, but he was scared of the answer. If she was fine, surely they'd have told him that? He'd know by now.

Which meant maybe she wasn't fine.

Callum stared at his feet in the unfamiliar, cheap plimsoles. 'Who's here, then? It's not that bloke in the suit, is it?'

His anxiety spiked at the memory of the hands on him, pressing him into the car bonnet, the ground.

'It's two women,' Maxwell said. 'And if you're not comfortable, you can stop at any time. The interview will be here, on the ward.'

'Okay. Will the room have a number on it?'

'No.' The doctor didn't blink. 'Your friend Lily suggested the dining room.'

*Lily.* Always one step ahead, taking care of him so he didn't have to take care of himself. His cheeks flushed, as he remembered her putting him to bed.

'She's here, and she'll be able to sit in on the interview with you.'

'Okay,' Callum breathed. 'Great.' He picked up the cup on the bedside table. His mouth was dry as dust. Swallowing the water was difficult. 'Let's do this.'

Maxwell got up from his plastic chair. 'I do mean it – if

you need to, just stop the interview. And if there's anything I can do while you're here, please ask.'

'Okay.' If Callum could cry any more, he would have welled up at the kindness.

Instead, he walked out of the room, wincing in the doorway, and followed Maxwell down the hall.

Lily was already sitting at one of the dining tables. She looked pale, dark circles under her eyes. He knew it wasn't his place anymore, but he still worried about her.

As they waited for the police, Callum's lawyer repeatedly told him everything was going to be fine. Lily agreed that *everything* was going to be *fine*.

It was a good job he was deliberately *not* counting how many times it was all going to be fine, because he'd be struggling to keep up by now.

The room smelled faintly of minced beef and onions. The view from the windows, of the grounds and the footpaths and King's in the distance – was reassuringly familiar, even from the second floor, instead of the fifth.

Maxwell returned with two women – the police. One was the kind middle-aged detective from that morning. She had the authority of a headmistress or a traffic warden.

She re-introduced herself, sticking her hand out for him to shake. 'Mr Mulligan, I'm DCI Field. We met yesterday.' She gestured behind her. 'This is DS Wilson.'

He nodded at them, and they sat down opposite him.

DS Wilson took out an A4 pad and a pen, then waited, eyes on Field.

'Great,' Field said, briskly. 'So, Mr Mulligan—'

'Callum is fine.'

'So, Callum. I'm going to ask you eight questions.'

Callum nodded, sensing Lily's interference there too.

'There'll be no more than eight, although if I don't feel

we've got to the bottom of something I might ask you to expand on your answer.'

'Okay.'

Field paused, and broke eye contact. 'Before I do that, though, there's something we need to tell you.'

*Sam. She was dead.*

He looked at Lily – she looked nervous, unsure.

'There was another incident in the area in the early hours of Wednesday morning. Unfortunately, the victim of that attack has passed away.'

He'd forgotten – the policewoman at the door, asking questions, wanting to know if their CCTV camera was real. *Why wasn't it real?* If it was real, the police could see who stabbed Sam. They would have seen it wasn't him.

'So, Sam wasn't the first person they attacked?'

Field ignored his question. She looked like she was choosing her words carefully. 'I'm really sorry to tell you this, Callum. It was Dr David Moore who was attacked, on Wednesday. He passed away this morning.'

The room seemed to bend in and out of focus, and he thought he was slipping out of his chair. Callum turned to Lily and saw his own shock mirrored back at him.

*David.*

'David? No.' Callum heard his words but wasn't conscious of speaking them. 'No. David isn't – he can't be.'

Lily had gone very still.

'I'm sorry,' Field said.

The other detective, Wilson, lowered her head.

'But – I have a phone appointment with him on Tuesday.' Callum's voice came out in a whine. 'He's—'

Callum didn't know how to end that sentence.

Field's voice stayed low and calm. 'He was attacked on Ancona Road, while walking home. We found the cover sheet of the *Disordered Approach to Diagnosis* paper he published in 2010, at the scene.'

She pressed on, like this conversation was a plaster she needed to rip off.

'I'm sorry to tell you, Callum, but Sam also died of her injuries.'

It was too much, and Callum didn't know if they were waiting for him to say something.

Did they think it was *him*?

'We'll give you some time, Callum, to gather your thoughts.' Field stood up.

Through the fog of the medication and the shock, it finally hit him. *David and Sam.* If it was a coincidence, it was a big fucking coincidence.

'I'm sorry for your loss.'

# Chapter 49

## Friday | Morning

## Callum

They came back after a ten-minute break, which presumably was supposed to be enough time for Callum to absorb the news.

The label of his T-shirt was scratching his neck, but he didn't want to rub it. He didn't know much about body language, but was pretty sure there was something about touching your neck.

'So, if we go back to Wednesday evening, before you found Sam outside the house.' Field cleared her throat. 'What were you doing that evening, Callum?'

'Drinking.'

Wilson's pen was poised over her notebook, but she didn't bother writing his one-word answer.

He was tempted to leave it there. To be unhelpful and obtuse and say fuck it, fuck all of them. David was dead, and someone had attacked Sam on his doorstep, and what was it all for? Why were they interviewing him instead of catching the psycho who did it?

But Lily had a wide-eyed panicked look, and he wanted the interview to be over, for her as much as for himself.

He heard David's voice in his head saying *breathe, Callum* – and a wound opened behind his ribcage. It occurred to him that every time he heard David's voice, which was several times an hour, recalling his advice and his mantras – the grief would hit him again.

'Lily and I had an argument. I was pissed off – I wanted to get pissed. I was listening to music.' He frowned, trying to remember the order of things. 'Lily left at midnight, maybe?'

Lily nodded, but Field and Wilson weren't looking at her. Really, he wasn't sure why they'd let her in here.

*They don't know.*

He went to take a sip of water, but his hand was shaking so badly that he had to put the cup straight back down.

'Okay,' Field said. 'That's good, Callum, thank you. Now let me know if I've got any of this wrong – you were drinking beers and whisky, and at around midnight, Lily left the house, and you were there alone.'

'Cider,' he said. 'It was cider.'

Wilson made a note.

Field didn't seem overly comfortable. Callum imagined she was usually much more together than this, more with it. But maybe the setting, or the fact he was mental – something was throwing her off her game.

*You and me both*, he thought.

'Okay. So – my next question. When you found Sam on the ground, why didn't you call 999?'

Lily stiffened as Field said it, but the army of Maxwell's drugs swimming through his system must be doing their job, because it wasn't the gut punch he would usually expect.

'I couldn't.'

Field's eyebrows shot up. 'Really? Your phone was in your back pocket.'

Callum didn't speak.

'What happened next?' Field said. 'As in – I'd like you to expand upon your answer.'

Field didn't want to waste one of her questions. She was trying to find an OCD loophole. He was all too familiar with the practice.

'I don't use the phone, not properly. I can't explain it, but I just couldn't do it. That number—'

He couldn't finish the sentence. A muscle in one eye was twitching, his foot tapping under the table, like his whole body was betraying him, tuning in to the high-frequency note of panic that was vibrating through him.

He was surprised when Field moved on. 'Thank you, Callum. I know it must be hard to talk about.'

Callum shot a look at Lily, who was staring wide-eyed at Field, like she was a fascinating TV show.

'Question three – how did you know Sam, and was it via David?'

She'd asked him that at the house. 'I met Sam in hospital, when we were teenagers.' He looked around the room. 'Here, actually – the Maudsley. Different ward, though.'

Wilson and Field exchanged a look and waited for him to carry on. Next to him, Lily cleared her throat.

'I haven't seen Sam since we were teenagers.' He paused. 'The people you go through that shit with, you don't always want to be around them when you get better. Or they don't want to be around you.'

Lily was wringing her hands in her lap, but looked calm otherwise.

All this – it was all something to do with the paper, David's fucking crusade against shit therapists that had got him promoted and talked about and launched his career.

'My fourth question—' then Field smiled. 'Halfway there now.'

It felt like they'd only been talking for a few minutes. Callum was relieved, at the thought of it being over, of going back to bed.

'When was the last time you saw David, before Friday? And how did he seem?'

Callum shut his eyes. Technically two questions, which would make the total nine.

He steadied himself. It was part of the same question; it was all one thing she wanted to know. It was fine.

*And anyway*, he thought, already not believing it, *it doesn't even matter if she does ask nine questions. It's just a number.*

'I don't see him, I speak to him on the phone,' Callum managed, his voice strained. 'I spoke to him on Tuesday morning. He called me—'

'But that wasn't your usual appointment slot, was it?' Field frowned. 'You were only on the phone for five minutes, and you terminated the call.'

They had been looking at David's phone records. It made him feel sick again. The unreality of the situation, its bizarreness, kept being punctured by the realisation that this was an investigation. It was real.

'Next question,' the lawyer prompted.

'Actually, Mr Greyson,' Field said, with a tight smile. 'I was waiting for Callum to expand on that last point.'

'It wasn't an appointment. Sometimes I speak to him when I needed to. It was a benefits thing.' They looked at him blankly. 'He was letting me know that they were stopping my disability living allowance.'

'Okay,' Field said.

190

God. Madman on the loose and she wanted to talk about his fucking dole money. Today of all days, they must believe he was mental enough to deserve it.

Under the table, Lily put a hand on his thigh. Gentle squeeze.

The room was heating up, the smell of food getting stronger. The label in his T-shirt was infuriating him, and he had a layer of sweat on his skin. Lily squeezed his leg again.

*Two.*

He nearly missed Field's next question.

'When you found Sam, on the doorstep. What did you do?'

He blinked. Her tone was harder, like she was getting impatient.

Well, he was getting impatient too. Impatient for this to be over. To be back in the dark where it was cool and he could take the T-shirt with the itchy label off, and be left in peace.

He jerked his leg and Lily took her hand away.

'It wasn't the doorstep. She was on the pavement, beyond the gate.' He shut his eyes.

One moment he was totally fucked, but then he saw the figure on the ground, and he was instantly sober. Like he'd not had a drop.

They were waiting for him to speak. 'I didn't recognise her at first because of the blood. Straight away I could see her neck was the worst, so I pressed down on it and then I realised it was her. Sam.'

Everyone was looking at him, rapt.

'And I shouted for help, and I tried to stop as much of the bleeding as I could. I was scared I was strangling her, but I had to, didn't I? Press down?'

The room was dim enough that he could imagine himself back in the dark again, with Sam. Crying out for someone to help, the unbearable *need* to take his phone out and call an ambulance.

If he had . . .

'It's okay,' Field said, finally. 'There was nothing more you could have done, Callum.'

His heart was beating fast, like it had done that night.

And he was back here. Back at the Maudsley. The police thought it was him – he could tell. He could end up in prison and then what?

His brain kicked in and he was catastrophising, playing out every scenario, from his arrest to his imprisonment, to his dying alone in a cell – all in a split second.

He couldn't hear what Field was saying and his panic levels were rising, and then Lily was speaking, the words muffled. Field's lips stopped moving and Lily's face was in front of his, and he took a proper breath of air.

He was tempted to ask for Maxwell to bring him a beta blocker, a little life raft of calm. But he needed to be able to focus.

'Sorry,' he managed. 'Could you say that again?'

# Chapter 50

## Friday | Morning

## Field

Callum was getting stressed. The lawyer looked like he was considering getting the doctor back in.

'We're nearly there, Callum. I promise.' Field kept her tone calm. Keep everything calm, that was all this would take. 'Question six. Did you see anyone else on the street at all, before your neighbour arrived to help?'

Callum shook his head.

He wrapped his arms tighter around his thin frame. Callum was dressed in cheap, grey clothes, and Field wondered what he wore normally – it was hard to get a read on him in the drab, too-large hospital outfit.

'Okay, that's fine.' Field smiled.

Time for the big question.

'So, Callum, there's a link between you and David, and Sam. I'm sure you understand, we need to know who else was involved in the trial – the other patients David referenced in the paper.'

Callum's eyes flicked to the girlfriend. *Ex*-girlfriend.

Field's gaze followed. Lily Stewart was looking down at her lap, her breathing fast. She had a soft, heart-shaped face – the opposite of Callum's sharp angles.

Field pressed the point. 'They could be involved in what happened, or they could be in danger. Can you tell me who they are?'

Callum didn't respond.

Field kept her voice level, not letting herself speak as rapidly as instinct wanted her to. 'Callum, I need those three names. We need to make sure they're safe, and you're the only person who can tell us.'

Callum's physical reaction, the jolt that ran through him, was the confirmation she needed, before he'd even spoken.

Lily moved closer to him.

'I can't – I can't tell you that.' He shook his head. 'It's private. They might not want you to know.'

'Callum. They could be in danger.'

He closed his eyes and wrapped his arms around himself.

He was pale and his eyes were flicking left to right. His hands had been shaking since he sat down and his whole body was tense. As he considered his answer he started rocking back and forward, only slightly – tiny movements.

Whatever he had, mental-illness-wise, he wasn't faking it.

She was pushing him too hard, but she needed answers. Field pulled the sheet from a folder and pointed at the list of participants. 'Patient A. Patient C. Patient E. They could all be at risk, Callum.'

'I need to go,' he said, abrupt.

'I really think my client—'

Field spoke over the lawyer, pushing Callum. 'Two stabbings

in two days, Callum. Who were the other patients? Help me keep them safe.'

Callum stood up from the table, unsteady on his feet. He swayed, and Lily caught him under the arm.

'Okay, that's enough,' the lawyer said.

'You need to tell us the truth,' Field pressed, leaning across the table. Pushing Callum was the only way to get the answer. 'Unless you tell us, we can't protect—'

'I can tell you,' Lily snapped. 'I was there, okay?'

They all turned to her, and Field sat back in her chair.

'I'm Patient A. I'll answer your questions, or whatever, but let me get him out of here first.'

Lily led Callum out of the room. The doctor was outside, waiting. The three of them left in a bustle of jerky movements and soothing voices.

Wilson let out a low whistle, barely audible. 'I did not see that coming.'

# Chapter 51

## Friday | Morning

### Field

Lily was back five minutes later. Wilson turned to a new page in her daybook.

Field had assumed Lily was worried about Callum, but it was suddenly apparent how much distress she was in. The news of David's death had been a shock for her. He had treated her too.

And Lily should never have been present at Callum's interview.

They ran through the formalities first.

Lily's alibi for the night David was killed was being home with Callum, but they were in separate rooms from seven o'clock. Her boyfriend, Scott, got home from work sometime after 3 a.m.

No alibi for Sam's stabbing, either. After the argument Lily left the house and went to her boyfriend's empty flat.

'Lily,' Field said, finally getting to the question she needed to ask. 'You understand – how Callum was found, the fact he didn't call an ambulance. The circumstances, well—' She let the sentence hang for a moment. 'Do you think there's any way that Callum could have done this?'

Field didn't believe Callum had done it, but she wanted to see how Lily responded.

Lily laughed, caught herself, stopped. 'No.'

'Then why didn't he call an ambulance?' Field prompted. 'I know he found it hard to answer that question, but I'm struggling to understand it.'

'You've read David's paper, right?' Lily took a deep breath. 'One of the ways Cal's OCD manifests is numbers. To him the number six is safe, and nine is bad.'

Field didn't react, but it sounded implausible, at the very least.

As if she'd read her thoughts, Lily continued. 'My birthday is the 19th of the month, and we have to celebrate a day early.

'He can't go into shops because the prices make him so anxious, he can't breathe. He doesn't go on the internet, read books. We put tape over the nine on the clocks at home, before we had to get rid of them all.'

To Field, it seemed like well-trodden material. Something Lily had perfected over the years, explaining Callum's behaviours, learning what people would respond to.

Field looked down at her notes, letting Lily speak at Wilson – the more sympathetic face.

'If he could leave the house, he wouldn't be able to go more than two doors down. We live on the odd side of the road,' she said. 'But he's making progress. David recently got him using a mobile phone again. Just owning one, carrying it round, is a huge step for Cal.'

'And how long has David been Callum's therapist?' Wilson asked.

'Since he was a teenager,' Lily said, wiping away a tear. 'Well, since *we* were teenagers.'

'And what was your relationship like, with David?' Field asked quietly. 'When you were part of the trial.'

'He believed me,' Lily said, her voice barely above a whisper. 'I'd told so many doctors that I thought it might be OCD, but they told me I was wrong. I'd given up on getting better, when I met David.'

'They didn't believe you?' Wilson echoed.

How many times had Field told Toby that he was just going through a phase? That he didn't need medication – he just needed to get out and do some exercise.

'Four.' Lily turned to Wilson, a note of challenge in her voice. 'Four eating disorder clinics, before I ended up on David's ward. You can check my medical records, if you don't believe me.'

'I'm going to ask you the same question I asked Callum, now, Lily. I need the names of the other two patients.'

Lily looked down at her hands. 'Callum is right. This stuff, it's private. My work don't know, about my OCD. I told my first few schools, but after the initial conversation with the head, it never came up. It doesn't affect my work, so I stopped telling them.

'I have colleagues I've worked with for five years who don't know, and I like it that way.'

Wilson sighed. 'Lily, we're not going to go around telling people's employers—'

'It's not about that,' Lily snapped.

Field gave a tiny shake of her head, and Wilson sat back in her chair. She waited.

'I can tell you about Patient E. Her name was – it's Paige Jacobs. She had contamination OCD.'

'Was?' Field prompted, gently.

'She died. She was – she was nineteen.'

'How did she die, Lily?' Field asked, fearful that she knew the answer.

Lily closed her eyes. 'Car accident.'

Not what she was expecting. Field thought Lily hadn't meant to be blunt; she could only bear to say it that fast.

'And Patient C?' Field asked, but Lily was already shaking her head.

'No. Callum was right, and that paper was anonymous for a reason.'

They had four out of five names. Lily was distracted and sweating, and Field came to her decision easily.

'Okay, I think that's enough for now.' Field closed her notebook. 'When Callum is feeling up to it, we will need a formal statement, and we'll need to formally interview you, too.'

'Callum – would he have to come to the station for that?' Lily asked.

Field shook her head. 'We can arrange to hold it wherever works for him.' She turned to the list of questions she'd prepared. 'There's one last thing I need to ask, Lily. I had meant to ask Callum, but – as you were there too – you should be able to help.'

Lily folded her arms.

'David's wife, Penny. Have you ever met her? Has Callum? While you were in the Maudsley, perhaps.'

Lily didn't hesitate. 'No. Why?'

Field smiled, shrugged. 'Not important.'

# Chapter 52

## Friday | Afternoon

### Field

Maxwell's office was barely bigger than a supply cupboard. Field's glass box at the station was palatial, in comparison. They'd had to relocate when the patients started filing in for lunch.

'Callum is settled now,' Dr Maxwell said with a sigh, dropping into his chair. 'What happened to a few gentle questions?'

Wilson squirmed, but Field stayed still in her hard plastic chair.

'This is a double murder investigation,' she answered, finally.

'Yes,' Maxwell replied, with forced politeness. 'And that's an extremely traumatised young man, whose mental health was already in a precarious state, to put it mildly.'

'You signed him off for interview,' Field snapped, wound up by his tone. 'You claimed he wasn't "too anxious" to talk to us.'

'No, I did not *claim* that,' Dr Maxwell said, his fist clenched on the desk. 'Callum is always anxious. Patients with OCD can't choose to switch off. He was facing his anxiety, because he wanted to help you.'

Field didn't speak and the doctor held out a packet of custard creams. She shook her head, and he gave a little sigh, as if offended.

His officious attitude was pissing her off. His assumption that she was totally ignorant, a stone-hearted copper who couldn't fathom doing his job, even though she'd been called out to help hundreds of ordinary people with psychosis or delusions or depression, over the years.

Behind the desk was a wall of thick patient files, organised alphabetically in neatly labelled brown folders. Everything in the room was old or badly repaired. The computer monitor was chunky and the blinds on the small window hung at an odd angle. The cords to straighten them were curled neatly on the windowsill, patiently waiting to be reattached.

'How is he?' Field asked, finally, accepting a biscuit.

'Bottom line is: he's coping. Still counting, but I think with his usual medication and some rest, he'll be okay.'

There were no photos on his desk, although there were personal touches. A few thank-you cards, a stress ball in the shape of a llama.

'And you're convinced he's genuine?' Field asked.

'Yes.' The lines between his eyebrows deepened.

'Because—' Field paused. 'Callum had the same therapist for a long time. My understanding is that he was one of Moore's private patients, so you don't have access to those notes, is that correct?'

A curt nod.

'So, with all due respect, Doctor, you don't have much experience of Callum to draw on, do you?'

Wilson shot her a sharp look.

The doctor exhaled fussily and shook his head. 'I've carried out an assessment. Callum is lucid. He's witnessed something incredibly traumatic. Add the news about Dr Moore to that, and he's now grieving. Overall, his emotional response is completely in keeping with what I'd expect to see.' Maxwell smiled, expression cold. 'I'm not going to sit here and pretend to know anything about running a murder investigation. I'd appreciate it if you'd extend me the same professional courtesy.'

She resisted the temptation to roll her eyes.

'I've also spoken to Callum about his experience at his house, before he was brought here,' Maxwell said. 'You should know that he would find it potentially triggering, dealing with that officer again.'

Field saw no point in lying. 'DS Riley is on desk duty for the rest of this case.'

To his credit, Maxwell just nodded. 'I'll let Callum know. Are we done?'

Maxwell and Wilson got to their feet, but Field stayed in her uncomfortable chair.

'No. I've been told you're considering releasing him.'

'Releasing?' Maxwell scoffed. 'I think you mean discharging. This is a hospital. Your lot seem to have forgotten that.'

'*My lot* haven't forgotten anything,' she said, coldly. 'We haven't forgotten the knife wounds of our two victims.'

He stared down at her. 'Providing nothing changes over the next couple of days, I'm going to suggest Callum is discharged on Sunday. I'm going to recommend beta blockers for the panic attacks he's been having, but otherwise his prescription will remain unchanged.'

She almost didn't catch herself. Nearly snapped at him.

There was a thick folder of crime scene photos in her work

bag that she would love to slap down on the chaos of his desk. Ten, fifteen years ago, they'd already be out, and she'd have been forcing Maxwell to really look at them.

'Is there anything else?' Maxwell rooted around on his untidy desk.

'I want to have him assessed,' Field said. 'Independently.'

'And you can,' Maxwell said, moving to the door. 'You can assess him at his home, because unless you're arresting him, you can't detain him here.'

Field was still pissed off when they got back to the car. She had the post-mortems down the road in a few hours, but DI Bellamy was going to accompany her, so Wilson was driving back to the station.

Field grabbed her bag from the boot and waved her off.

It was a relief to be alone for a while. Plus, it made sense for Wilson to go back. She could relay the news, kick-start the new lines of inquiry.

Lily was Patient A. They'd need to look into her boyfriend, her relationship with Callum – her non-existent alibis.

Paige Jacobs had died a few years after the trial. Riley was already working on tracing her family, and pulling the road traffic collision reports from the incident.

Possibly most significant, there'd been no attack last night. Two stabbings in the space of twenty-four-hours and then just – nothing. Either the attacker couldn't get to their next victim, or they only ever had two intended targets.

Field walked in the opposite direction of both the Maudsley and King's – rubbing her forehead to try to ease some of her tension. When she arrived, Ruskin Park was full of laughing children, picnicking students and NHS workers on their lunchbreaks.

Field found a bench in the shade and checked her emails.

The blood-spatter experts definitively agreed that Samantha Hughes had been stabbed directly outside Mulligan's house. What wasn't definitive from their perspective was whether Callum Mulligan stabbed her.

In trying to save Sam's life, Callum's clothes had become so drenched in blood, and so smeared, that it was impossible to tell whether he had been near her when the wounds were inflicted. There were microscopic airborne particles, apparently, but as Sam had sustained an arterial wound, they could have been deposited in trying to save her life, rather than in taking it.

But either way – it didn't matter. Callum wasn't injured – they'd photographed his chest and hands, and Field had studied the images. Callum had no injuries.

'Perfect alibi,' Field mumbled, flicking onto the next email.

The droplets of blood that they presumed belonged to the attacker had been sent to Teddington for processing, and fast-tracked. They should have the results on Sunday – Monday at the latest.

Even in the shade of the oak tree, the afternoon sun felt laser-targeted on her back, and she could feel her neck burning.

The phone rang.

'Fuck's sake,' she muttered. She debated putting the phone next to her on the bench and not answering, but the super had a view of her calendar – he'd know that she was free. 'Afternoon, guv.'

'Field,' he said. 'I've got five minutes. Give me the headlines.'

She told him they had four of the five names. Good progress being made processing the scene. Several new lines of inquiry. Zara Ayres establishing a good relationship with David Moore's wife. Mr and Mrs Hughes being kept up to date by Herts police.

'But no suspect?' he barked.

She gritted her teeth. 'The trial was anonymous, and well over a decade ago. Forensics is the best chance we have of catching him, Sir. I've fast-tracked—'

'I saw that. I approved it. But what if he's on a mission? Why's he stopped at two?'

She still had a horrible feeling that it was because Callum was in hospital.

'It's early days, sir—'

'Yes, it is. I'll level with you, Field. I've got the chief super breathing down my neck already. If you haven't made progress by Monday morning, at the case review meeting – I'll have to reassign this to MIT2. Your team can support, of course.'

She could hear the super breathing down the phone, as his words sank in. She said she understood, and then they said a polite but tense goodbye.

The burning sensation in her face was nothing to do with the sun.

If she had to hand this case over to Raynott's MIT – or worse, work under them – she might as well just quit there and then.

# Chapter 53

## Friday | Afternoon

### Andy

He hadn't slept.

His plan had been to get a train to Brighton from Victoria, but there was a problem on the line. He spent the morning on the busy station concourse, back to a pillar, scanning the crowd – but there was still nothing running.

He'd hoped the 11 a.m. coach would be half empty, but it was packed. He had to put his AirPods in, underneath his noise-cancelling headphones.

It didn't occur to Andy that the B&B wouldn't still be there, up a steep side street a few minutes from the beach, until he was getting off the bus.

His parents were from Brighton, and the family spent two weeks by the beach every summer holiday. Until Andy was too unwell to go anymore.

But there it was – still there, same crumbling façade and faded 'rooms available' card in the downstairs window.

He remembered the old woman, but she didn't remember him.

Andy paid for his room in cash. Asked for one at the top of the house, locked the door behind him and sat down on the creaking bed. He barely noticed the peeling flocked wallpaper and the threadbare rug on the old floorboards.

He did spot an ancient TV on one wall, which would be something to do, at least.

At the Sainsbury's in Victoria station, Andy had bought enough noodles and other no-cooking-required food to last him several days. Paid in cash.

After taking a moment, processing where he was and what he was doing, Andy shrugged his rucksack off and removed his jacket.

Blood had seeped through his makeshift bandages. He took the dressings out of the shopping bag, where they were nestled between the noodles, and braced himself.

The cut was the length of his forearm. The skin was tight and hot to the touch.

Stupid. He was so stupid.

He had Savlon in the bag, and Andy went to the sink in the corner, to clean the wound out.

He couldn't go to a doctor. As far as he was able, Andy wasn't planning on leaving this room.

# Chapter 54

**P:** Everyone lies. Are you lying to me?

*Pause*

**D:** What would I be lying to you about?
**P:** About what's wrong with me. About what's going to happen.

*Pause*

**P:** About whether you love me.

# Chapter 55

## Friday | Afternoon

## Field

Wilson had been disappointed not to come to David's post-mortem, but if Field was going to spend hours trying to concentrate while feeling sweaty and nauseated, she wanted an old faithful – not someone she needed to put a brave face on for.

She'd got into a good rhythm with DI Bellamy over the last five years. He hated being at the station, and the staffers at Lewisham called him the phantom, because he was barely ever there. He ran scenes, co-ordinated SOCOs and pathologists and forensics, and Field left him to it.

A mortuary assistant held the door open for them, and Field and Bellamy stepped inside the pathologist's basement office.

Inoffensive modern art hung on two walls, with a bookshelf of physiological textbooks and medical journals covering a third. The lighting was low – the near-silent air-con kept the room comfortable. It could have been 5 p.m. on a winter's evening, for all they would know down here.

Young smiled and gestured to the man behind the desk. 'This is Professor Robinson, senior forensic pathologist. He was one of my lecturers.'

'Many, many years ago,' the professor said with a grimace. 'Call me Prof – everyone does.'

Professor Robinson stood to shake Field's hand. He had neatly parted white hair, and was probably in his seventies. Young and Field took seats on the other side of the desk, and Bellamy stood, arms folded.

'I'll start the post-mortems shortly,' Prof said, sitting back down. 'But I did an external examination of both bodies yesterday and I can provisionally say there are similarities.'

'Provisionally?' Field prompted.

He extricated a sheet with the outline of an adult male. There was one line drawn across the neck, a few on the left arm, one on the right-hand side of the abdomen, and four on the left.

'Well, there are a comparable number of stab wounds, and the pattern is similar,' Prof said. 'Especially if you factor in Young's theory about the attacker falling on top of Samantha.'

Prof extracted two photographs of David's chest. The first was taken in the street and the second was under the full glare of mortuary lights. The violence and depth of the wounds was obvious.

Field rubbed the heel of her hand into her forehead. 'So, almost exactly twenty-four hours after David is attacked, Samantha Hughes is stabbed a few streets away, but they fall over. What does that mean?'

'Samantha Hughes' attack feels less controlled,' Prof said. 'Maybe David's murder was thrilling but left him scared of being caught. Made him nervous.'

'The wounds to the neck and stomach,' Field said, pointing to the charts. 'Both on the right-hand side?'

'Correct,' Prof said. 'Suggesting a left-handed assailant.'

They sat in silence for a moment, staring at the sheets on the desk.

'I'd like to know if there are any signs of sexual activity, or sexual assault, when you examine her,' Field said.

'Of course,' he said. 'Let Young and I get scrubbed in, and we'll get started. I'll be conducting both post-mortems, but with Young's assistance we should be able to get them done in good time. How are you with PMs, DCI Field? Do I need to have a bucket on standby?'

Field got to her feet. 'I should be all right.'

'They all say that,' Prof said with a sigh.

'Let's just hope these are the only ones I have to watch,' she said, thinking of Callum Mulligan, and his discharge on Sunday.

# Chapter 56

## Friday | Evening

## Field

In the end, the post-mortems took six hours.

Young told Field to wait for her to shower, and they could get a drink – but she was too desperate to get out of the hospital.

Outside it was still hot and airless.

David's PM was first. No real surprises there. No evidence that he'd been sexually active on the day he died. Estimated blade length confirmed as ten inches. The smell hadn't been too bad, because the lab was state-of-the-art, with an extractor fan system that worked minor miracles.

But then Sam.

Field took an unsteady step out the way of the main hospital doors, towards the taxi queue.

Sam looked so young, and vulnerable, under the bright lights. There were no signs of sexual assault, but she'd had sex in the past forty-eight hours. Young had fast-tracked the samples, with David's DNA for comparison.

It had occurred to Field that the attacker intended to terrify Sam. Ensure she died in a state of panic.

*For God's sake.*

She couldn't breathe properly.

Undoing the top buttons of her shirt didn't help.

Sam and Toby were the same age. They'd been ill as teenagers, and had both come through it. Both happy, both doing well.

The thought of a police officer watching on as her son was picked over by doctors was unbearable. She couldn't look Young in the eye after Sam's PM, let alone meet her for a drink.

A thin man in a hospital gown was eyeing her thoughtfully, taking slow drags on a cigarette, and then considerately blowing the smoke away from her. Field took her phone from her pocket and went into her call log, scrolling down to Toby's name. If he was on shift it would go straight to voicemail – his phone would be in his locker.

It started ringing. Field leaned against a wall.

He answered on the fourth ring. 'Mum? Everything okay?'

His voice. As familiar as anything, but still strange – deep and grown-up when she expected to hear a little boy.

'Yes,' she said. 'Everything's okay. I just – I missed you.'

He gave a tinkly laugh. 'Who are you and what have you done with my stone-hearted mother?'

*He's okay. Toby is okay.*

She smiled at a passing paramedic, someone she vaguely recognised.

Toby wasn't going to get ill again. Being a paramedic was stressful, and the final exams would be hard – but wasn't her job stressful? He had support – a great boyfriend, a nice flat. And even if he did get ill – he had never been ill like Callum and Sam, never been in hospital.

'Mum?'

She needed to get a grip. Pull herself together.

'I love you, Tobes.' Field pushed her hair away from her face, the phone hot against her cheek.

'Christ, this case is really getting to you, isn't it?' he said – then, after a tiny pause. 'Are you sure you're okay?'

She pressed a hand to her chest. 'I have to go.'

# Chapter 57

**P:** Who picked the word "disorder"?

**D:** You know what? I don't know.

**P:** It makes it sound like – like a minor skin irritation. Something you can pop to the chemist for. Pick up a cream.

*Pause*

**P:** That'd be nice, wouldn't it?

**D:** Well, I'd be out of a job.

**P:** Disorder. *(Scoffs)* It had to be a man. I think he was taking the piss.

# Chapter 58

## Friday | Evening

## Lily

She sipped tea on the sofa and nibbled on digestives, while googling her symptoms. Scott was next to her, reading a dry non-fiction book about economics.

He kept making comments about her "getting her colour back", enthusiastically commenting on the fact she seemed to have turned a corner.

Lily nodded along, but she still felt like shit.

Nothing seemed to fit. It wasn't food poisoning. Could be a bug – but she didn't have a temperature.

A few times an hour she would still get cramp. They felt like hunger pangs. The old, familiar feeling, which still brought an undeniable scrap of comfort.

She'd never had bulimia. Her problem with food didn't stem from a desire not to eat, or to be thin. She just needed to control how it happened. What she ate and when and with what cutlery. On which table, or in front of which person.

How she cleaned her teeth afterwards, how quickly the dirty plate could be removed from sight.

But she'd never wanted to be sick, or to get rid of what food she had managed to eat.

The rules built up slowly, at first. Imperceptible little decisions, like not to eat peas from the plates with the green pattern on them, and not to make tea in the mugs with the coloured insides. The sorts of quirks she thought everyone had.

And always – the fear that no one believed her.

It became harder and harder to follow and obey all the rules, to keep them straight in her mind, to keep them placated even when they were self-contradictory and illogical. And as that became harder, her one defence, the ace up her sleeve, was not eating at all.

Her tea had gone cold.

Scott also liked control. He didn't have OCD – Lily was certain of that. David always called OCD the doubting disease. It made you doubt everything. Intrusive thoughts defied logic; they made you question the evidence of your own eyes, hands – even science. Whereas Scott had an unwavering self-belief that he was right.

Recently, she'd sometimes wondered if Scott might have mild OCPD. She didn't know a whole lot about it, apart from a few things David had told them years ago. Scott had that perfectionist streak, the determination to follow a process to the letter. Especially if it was a process that he had designed and deemed the best course of action.

At first, that had been attractive. After the split from Callum, Lily had needed dependable and solid. She'd had enough drama and depression and self-destruction.

And the word "doctor" in Scott's Tinder bio had helped. Their first date was three weeks after the break-up, and her workmates at the school were surprised at how quickly she moved on. But it had felt right, at the time.

Her phone timer went off and made her jump. Scott had her on a regimen of supplements, anti-nausea meds and ibuprofen.

He looked at her from over his book. 'Time for more medicine?'

She nodded, queasy.

He got up from the sofa, leaning over to put a palm on her head. 'Still no fever. Great.' He withdrew his hand and let out a big breath. 'I – think you'll be feeling much better by tomorrow morning.'

# Chapter 59

## Friday | Evening

## Callum

While Maxwell went to make himself a coffee, Callum looked around his office. In a weird way it reminded him of his dining room at home. Everything was worn out, a bit grubby. The shelves were dusty, Maxwell's desk was covered in piles of crap and the bin was full of crisp packets.

There was a clock on the wall and even though looking at it was painful, Callum hadn't asked Maxwell to take it down. After the last few days, it didn't seem as terrifying as it would have before.

Talking to someone new was a bit of a revelation.

David knew it all, everything since Callum was fifteen. Maxwell was a stranger, but after his support today, and the way he stood up to Field, Callum felt safe speaking to him. Plus, the poor bloke was still here, despite starting at God knows what time this morning.

So far, his questions were straightforward and cut to the heart of the matter:

*If you had to pick one, which is scarier: the number itself or the perceived consequence?*

*You said in the past you did a lot of research to prove that these existential coincidences don't exist. Have you ever considered that the researching itself could be a compulsive behaviour?*

*You believe you could never move out of your nan's house? Why not? And why do you still call it her house?*

After a while Callum got so engrossed in Maxwell's questions, he forgot to count them.

Maxwell came back from the ten-minute break looking knackered. He settled himself into his desk chair with a cup of coffee and took a sip. 'Are you sure you don't want anything?'

Callum shook his head.

'Where were we?' Maxwell picked up his pen and surveyed his notes. 'Oh yes. I was about to ask you about the book. *Darlings, Obsessed.* You can count me a fan. I really enjoyed it.'

Callum tensed. 'Thank you. You read that quickly.'

The doctor looked puzzled for a moment, then laughed. 'Oh, I didn't read it especially. I read it ages ago. A patient recommended it.'

He leaned back in his chair, mirroring Callum's hands-on-knees posture.

Cal crossed his arms.

'How did you find the writing process? Partly it was written while you were in hospital, yes?'

'Yeah. I wrote the first half when I was sixteen. Paige and I—' He faltered, but Maxwell waited patiently. 'We wrote a lot. She wanted to be an actor, but it was a waste, if you ask me. She could have been the next—'

220

He stopped, embarrassed that he couldn't think of a playwright. Brain fog, just one side effect he hadn't missed.

Callum swallowed. 'But yeah. I wrote the second half after I got home, from my second stay in hospital. Then I redrafted the kid stuff and found my agent.'

'And did you always want to be a writer?'

'Ever since I was little. And I guess the only not-shit bit of having OCD was that by the time I was fifteen and in David's little support group, I actually had something worth writing about.

'Plus, you know, it was a good publicity angle,' Callum said, with a wry smile. 'The whole sectioned teenager thing. Very romantic.'

His agent, Dominic, had taken a punt on him. Spun Callum as the working-class and mental Sally Rooney. After strong hardback sales and a good publicity campaign, Dominic sold the film rights to *Darlings, Obsessed* to an American outfit for so much money, Callum wouldn't have to write another novel for six years yet.

Unless Lily moved out. Then it would be three.

'It's a remarkable work. I've got a copy here somewhere.' Maxwell got up from his chair and rooted around the bookshelves, moving stacks out of the way and scanning the spines. Callum pulled at the sleeve of his T-shirt six times.

Finally, Maxwell found it. The familiar purple cover was dog-eared, and the spine had been cracked. Cal liked books to look well-thumbed.

Maxwell flicked through the pages. 'Do you mind if I read my favourite passage out loud?'

'Go for it.'

Callum leaned back in his chair and closed his eyes. He was knackered.

Dr Maxwell read aloud in a low, soothing voice.

'Daniel packed his few possessions into his rucksack. Battered tobacco tin. A handful of birthday cards. When the bag was full, he drew the strings tight and hoisted it onto his shoulder.'

Callum kept his eyes closed, enjoying the shifting levels of darkness behind his eyelids.

In his mind he could still see his skinny sixteen-year-old self, packing to leave his little room – except when he left it hadn't been a tranquil solo experience. Paige had been discharged the month before but was back for a visit, sitting on the bed learning the "*the play's the thing*" soliloquy from Hamlet. Lily was picking out which of his posters she wanted to keep.

'And then he stood, alone at the threshold of the room. Doorways had always been hard things,' Maxwell read on. 'Counting how many times he'd walked through them. How often others had. But—'

'For this room at least,' Callum took over, from memory, 'his count was done. He wouldn't see the four magnolia walls again, and the only thing he'd leave behind were the Blu-Tack stains.'

Maxwell stayed silent.

Callum opened his eyes. 'I'm not an egomaniac who memorised their own book, by the way. It took fucking ages to get right.'

Maxwell was still looking down at the page. 'It's lovely. A beautiful end to the first act.'

'For most people, it was the high point.' Callum held out a hand for the paperback and Maxwell passed it to him. He flicked the pages, enjoying the sound. 'Most people prefer the half where the main character is completely off his nut. It's more romantic.'

He froze, book in hand. He'd taken it without thinking,

stared at the words as he flicked the pages – not the numbers in the corners.

They sat in silence for a moment. Callum was too hot – the book heavy in his hands. He passed it back to Maxwell, who hadn't noticed him spinning out, like David would've.

As soon as the book was on the other side of the desk Callum felt better.

He was about to ask if they could call it a night, when Maxwell leaned forward.

'How did *you* feel about David Moore's paper? At the time, in 2010.'

Callum stretched his arms above his head, then stood up and moved to the window. He knew that, on the fourth floor of this particular ward, it wouldn't open. The sky outside was a brilliant indigo, and he could feel the last of the day's heat radiating from the glass.

'Well, obviously, I told him he could write about me. And he did offer me the chance to read it before he published it, but said I didn't want to. Pretended I didn't care.'

He turned back to the room.

'I thought it would just be the details of how many doctors cocked up giving us an OCD diagnosis, but . . . it was personal. Really fucking personal. And it was my own fault for not reading it first, but that made me angry.'

Maxwell's eyes strayed back to *Darlings, Obsessed* and Callum laughed.

'I know, I'm a hypocrite, right? I gave my anonymity up anyway, didn't I? I published that—' He pointed.

'It's not the same—' Maxwell started, but Cal spoke over him.

'But now, I'm glad he did it. And if you read that paper, underneath all the bland academic speak, David was so *angry*. And in hindsight, I'm fucking fuming too: at all the doctors who fucked us over; at the families who dropped us because they thought we were making it up; at the therapists who didn't know shit about OCD.'

He swayed slightly on his feet, feeling like he could drop on the spot, fall to the carpet.

Maxwell sat still in his chair, his attention unwavering.

'Paige summed it up to me once. After the paper was published, she said: "David is worried that if the paper doesn't go down well, we'll all think we don't matter." But it did go down well. It made a difference, because we *did* matter.'

His eyes were unfocused, staring at a point over Maxwell's head. 'Paige, she was the youngest, but she was the cleverest.'

Usually, he couldn't talk about Paige without crying, or nearly crying. And David – David was dead now too.

'She was a fucking good liar – did I tell you that already?' He looked at Maxwell, who shook his head. 'Well, she was. She would have been a famous actor by now.'

The medication was turning him zombie, and his voice sounded flat and tired.

'And I'm remembering *why* I wrote the book. Why I worked so hard to get it published. Because I wanted to *help* someone, Dr Maxwell. That's what David did, and that's what Paige would have done, if she'd lived past fucking nineteen. I thought that if one person could read it and find it useful or see some part of their own experience in it, then—' He threw his arms up and let out one bark of laughter. 'Well then maybe it wouldn't all have been for nothing.'

Maxwell gestured to Callum to sit back down, and he did.

'That's very noble, Callum.'

'No, it's not. Or maybe it is, I don't know. I go back and forth.' His eyes were closing again, heavier this time. He could feel himself slipping back into sleep. 'But that's what we were all doing, Dr Maxwell. All along.'

'What who was doing, Callum?'

'David,' he murmured, feeling sleep overtake him. 'And us. *The five anonymous patients*. We were trying to help.'

# Chapter 60

## Saturday | Early hours

## Field

She desperately needed sleep, but Field couldn't bring herself to actually close her eyes.

With every minute that crept by, she felt more tightly wound, convinced the phone would ring at any second – there would be a third attack, all because she hadn't figured this out fast enough.

Her bedroom was cool, a fan whirring on the bedside table.

The minute hand on the clock ticked over.

One a.m.

David Moore had been dead twenty-four hours. Sam for forty-eight.

'Fuck's sake,' she muttered, sitting up and flicking the lamp on. Her handbag was packed next to the bed, and she dragged it over. It was almost as bad as Young's, and she pulled things out, hunting for the slim purple paperback.

If she wasn't going to sleep, she might as do something

useful. For all she knew, Mulligan's novel might contain something relevant to the case.

It wasn't in there. She flopped back onto the pillows, suddenly treated to a vision of it, smack bang in the middle of her desk.

Field pushed herself to sitting, swung her legs over the edge of the bed and got to her feet. Toby's room was the other side of the thin corridor. A few years ago, she'd painted it a motherly shade of beige and bought neutral bedding, in case she ever had guests.

The door creaked as it opened, and she groped for the light switch.

Tobes was a big reader – always had a book stuffed into a pocket or under his arm. He still had a Billy bookcase full of paperbacks in one corner of the room. Michael Morpurgo and *The Worst Witch* were crammed in next to the YA zombie series he got into in his early teens.

She was about to give up, when the purple spine winked at her from the bottom shelf.

The book had Post-it notes sticking out of the top, and when she opened it to a random page, she found annotations in Toby's cramped writing, and whole passages underlined, with exclamation marks in the margins.

It would be better, she thought, to wait for tomorrow. Read the clean copy.

She turned her head to read one note, repeated twice.

*It's not just me*

*It's not just me*

A lump rose to her throat.

She didn't bother going back to her room, or turning off the big light to put the lamp on instead.

Field lay down on the spare bed, bent the cover back on Toby's copy of *Darlings, Obsessed* and started to read.

# Chapter 61

**D:** How are you feeling now?
**P:** How do you think?

*Pause*

**D:** Sorry.

*Pause*

**D:** I am. Sorry.

*Pause*

**P:** So not a one-off, then?
**D:** No. No, I guess not.

*Pause*

**D:** But you know we can't do that again, don't you?

*Pause*

**P:** Yes.

*A breath exhaled.*

**D:** Okay. It never happened.

**P:** It never happened. Twice.

*Pause*

**P:** I should get dressed. Pass me that – under the desk.

*Pause*

**P:** Thank you.

*Pause*

**D:** And you know you can't tell the others, don't you?
**P:** I'm not an idiot, D—.
**D:** I know. I know you're not an idiot.
**P:** I can't find my other sock.
**D:** Because they wouldn't understand. You know that don't you? That they wouldn't understand?

*Pause*

**D:** And they wouldn't believe you. No one – they just wouldn't.

# Chapter 62

## Saturday | Early hours

### Lily

She woke up drenched in sweat.

'Scott,' she said, weakly. He didn't wake.

Lily tried to reach for him, but her arms felt weak. The nausea was back, her stomach rolling and pitching.

The sickness was made worse by imagining Callum alone on the ward, and David's wife dealing with her grief, and the thought of Sam in the morgue.

'Scott,' she said again, and this time he woke with a start, sitting bolt upright. He turned the lamp on, and she winced away from the light, head pounding.

'Shit,' he breathed. 'Let's get you sitting up for a second. Let me look at you.'

He stood up from the bed and came round to her side. Smoothly, he slid one arm under her shoulders, the other under her knees, and gently turned her, until her legs were off the bed.

'Ready?' he asked.

'Yeah.'

As he sat her up, her vision blurred.

'Fuck—' Scott said, catching her under the armpits as she pitched forward. 'Babe?'

'Sorry,' she mumbled. 'I sat up too fast. Feel faint.'

'Put your head between your knees.' Scott put a large palm on her back, his voice business-like suddenly.

But as soon as she was in position, she experienced another wave of nausea. She couldn't sit up, because Scott was rubbing slow, forceful circles on her back.

'Scott—' she said, needing him to stop, because he was making it worse.

But before she could say anything else, she was throwing up, all over the white rug.

He hadn't dodged out of the way in time, and she was apologising and trying to stand all at once. She was burning up, and her throat was raw from the vomit. Her balance went. She dropped like a stone, hitting her head on one of her knees, and wailed.

'Okay, okay—' Scott lifted her head with one hand. 'Here's what we're going to do.'

He lifted her, gently. Like a baby.

Carried her sideways through the bedroom door into the dark hallway, then laid her on the cold tiles in the bathroom. They felt good against her skin and the nausea subsided a little.

There were turning taps and then the sound of the bath filling.

'You need to soak the rug,' she said, weakly. 'Or it'll stain.'

He let out a low chuckle. 'I always hated that rug. White is impractical.'

He kneeled in front of her, tipping his head sideways. From this angle she could see his vomit-spattered T-shirt.

'Oh no,' she whispered, putting out a hand to his chest. 'Sorry.'

'Stop apologising,' he said, with a smile. 'I'm a doctor, getting thrown up on is kind of my day job.'

Scott pressed a cold flannel to her head. He kept talking to her, the whole time, in a low soothing voice. Wiped her face and then sat her up. Gently lifted her shirt over her head. Eased her PJ shorts off. Even picked her up again to put her in the bath.

She felt better in the warm, scented water.

'It might be shock,' Scott said, stripping off himself and putting toothpaste on her toothbrush, so she could clean her teeth in the bath. 'From what's happened.'

Lily shook her head. 'It's not just today though, is it? I've been throwing up for a week. It must be a bug.'

'The fainting worries me.' He frowned. 'Maybe we should get you a CT scan.'

'*Almost* fainting.' Lily smiled at him, accepting her toothbrush. She held it in her hand, too weak to lift it.

The sickness had left her feeling exhausted, and she could feel a headache coming on, a dull pain at the base of her skull.

She let her head lean against the edge of the bath, and Scott sat cross-legged on the bathroom floor, at her eye level, examining her face with a worried expression.

It was his eyes. The guilt on his face.

And then she knew.

# Chapter 63

## Saturday | Morning

### Lily

She'd insisted on sleeping on the sofa last night. Scott wanted to stay with her, but she sent him away, scuttling back to his bed.

It had been tempting to confront him, there and then – but she was too weak. She needed to rest first.

So far, he had denied it all.

'What have you been giving me?' she asked him again, fighting to keep her voice level.

Scott ran a hand through his hair. His jaw was tense, and he looked cornered, pacing the living room like a caged animal.

'Just tell me, Scott.' Lily gripped the back of a dining chair, supporting her weight but refusing to sit down. 'What have you done?'

Weeks of feeling not quite right, like she had a cold or a bug coming on. Then the first pangs of nausea, the cramps. The late period that had made her panic, take multiple tests.

Lily's hold on the chair was so tight she thought it might splinter in her hands. She had goose pimples on her arms from adrenaline.

Scott let out a nervous shriek, half-laugh, half-cry, and threw his arms up. 'Just say it. What are you accusing me of?'

'*This*. You did this to me.' She looked down at herself, her blotchy legs, thin and spammy below the hem of his black T-shirt. 'I'm not ill, am I? I've been on meds before. These are side effects.'

He turned, and she saw he had tears in his eyes.

'Don't lie to me, Scott. Please don't lie to me.'

Scott took three strides across the room and put one hand around her waist, the other in her hair. He looked down at her through his wet eyelashes.

Lily wanted to push him away, but she needed to hear him admit it, so she didn't.

'I love you, so much.' Scott squeezed his eyes closed and a tear rolled down his cheek. 'I love you, so much, and I wanted to keep you safe.'

He let go of her and sank into a dining chair, his head in his hands. Lily was still faint and unsteady but her anger – no, her *rage* – kept her upright.

'I was going to tell you. I swear I was going to tell you,' he said into his palms.

'I can't believe—' Lily said, swaying slightly on her feet. 'What right did you have to make that decision for me?'

Scott exhaled sharply and pulled another chair out. 'Sit down, Lil. Please. You look like you're about to collapse.'

Lily didn't move.

'I'm sorry.' There was a wobble in Scott's voice. 'I didn't realise you would—'

'Scott.' Lily shook her head. 'What were you giving me?'

'Beta blockers,' he said, in monotone.

The heat of the morning hung between them, charging his confession.

'Is that all?' she asked. 'Nothing else.'

'Diazepam, just the last few days. First two milligrams, then five.'

Her stomach swooped again. He turned his face away from her, his palms on his knees, staring blankly at the remote on the coffee table.

'It's my job, isn't it?' he said, his voice cracking. 'Making people better.'

A beat.

She had to get away from him.

Lily walked to the bedroom, on legs that were steadier. She pulled on a pair of jeans. Scott followed her, babbling an explanation she wasn't listening to. She spotted her rings on the bedside table and slipped them onto her fingers, then looked around for her bag.

'Please don't go.' Scott dived in front of her, arms wide, blocking her from leaving the bedroom. 'Let me explain.'

'What is there to explain, Scott?' Lily's voice was calm, the same deadly tone her mother had used when she was a child. 'You *drugged* me. You gave me drugs without telling me.'

He shook his head, his face screwed up in pain but no tears falling.

'Scott, let me get past.' She wasn't asking – would never ask him for anything again.

'You don't understand.' Scott took a step towards her, and Lily backed away.

He looked at her in sheer disbelief, backing away, before collapsing to the floor of the bedroom and clutching the back of his head. 'You don't get it.'

Lily stayed still. Now she knew what the nausea and weakness were caused by, it was easier to stand up, easier to make herself move. She looked down at Scott, curled up and crying, and felt nothing but cold fury.

'I was trying to help,' he said, still turned away from her. 'That's all – I thought it would help you.'

'Four *fucking* years – that's how long I was on and off meds. Do you know what it's like to be out of control of your own body? Have you ever had a doctor make your decisions for you?'

She looked around the room. The vomit-stained white rug, the bare walls. The hardback non-fiction books he claimed to have read, with brand-new-looking dust jackets. And Scott crouching in the middle of it – snivelling.

He looked up at her from the floor. 'You can't see how ill he's making you. How much you need help. But I saw it, and I knew you'd never leave that house unless you could *think*.'

Of course it was about Callum.

'He manipulates you, Lily. You've been in it so long you don't realise, but he does. He says things to make you feel shit about yourself. You're just as trapped in that house as he is.'

'You *drugged me* because you were trying to get me away from Callum?' Lily threw her arms wide. 'You wanted to be in control.'

'Control?' Scott's voice was a shriek. 'When I have been in control of anything? When we first started dating, I had *no idea* – no idea how fucked up the two of you are. How far back this co-dependent bullshit really goes.'

She took a step away from him. 'I only told you about my OCD two days ago . . .' Lily paused for a beat as her thoughts caught up. 'But you've been giving me that shit for weeks.'

Scott ran a hand through his hair.

'You accessed my medical records, didn't you?' Her stomach sank. 'When?'

'Last month,' he said, voice hollow.

She had felt so *guilty* for not having told him yet. She'd felt bad, when all along he'd read her notes. The write-ups from her teenage GP visits, the list of symptoms her despairing mother had reeled off while begging for them to hospitalise her, so Lily would be out of the house.

It was too much.

Scott was right. Callum did manipulate her. Over the years they had both said awful, hurtful things to each other. He could be jealous, petty, mean. Cal always knew how to most upset her, what he could say to get the maximum reaction and cause the most hurt.

And Lily had learned a lot from him.

She bent down, kneeled in front of Scott, and took his face in her hands. He gazed soulfully back at her, his cheeks still dry.

'You're right,' she said softly, and Scott's bottom lip trembled. 'Callum is bad for me.'

Scott nodded, opened his mouth to speak—

'No, let me finish.' She stroked his cheek with her thumb and maintained eye contact. 'Callum is bad for me. But I still love him.'

The knife found its mark. Scott's shoulders stiffened, and she leaned in closer. 'No one will ever love you, Scott, not like I love him. Not me – not anyone.'

Scott forgot to look hurt or pained. He just looked shocked.

Lily stood, tried to leave the room again, but Scott grabbed at her leg, catching the hem of her jeans.

'Don't tell anyone,' he said. 'I'll lose my job – my medical licence. Please – please don't tell anyone.'

Lily eyed him coldly. 'I'm going to tell anyone who will listen. Your boss, the medical board.' She pulled her leg free from his grip. 'How dare you think I wouldn't.'

# Chapter 64

## Saturday | Morning

## Field

Field got to the station at quarter past seven. She'd showered, straightened her hair – even put on make-up. Everyone else looked rested, but after finishing Callum's book at gone four, she'd had a few hours' fitful doze before her alarm went off.

Day four – and another night with no reported incidents. They had two days before the super reassigned the investigation, and still had no name for Patient C.

Field needed to concentrate on the case, but she kept thinking about Toby.

She wanted to tell him that she'd read Callum's book. All these years, she'd never been able to fathom what might have been going on in Toby's head, when he was a teenager. All she knew was the terror and the confusion of being trapped on the outside.

But then she read *Darlings, Obsessed*.

Riley and Wilson were in before eight, both looking for

fresh links between David and Sam, convinced that if they were the only intended victims, there had to be something going on between them. Their chatter and speculation finally snapped Field out of it.

She was waiting for the results of the DNA comparison between the semen sample found on Sam and David's DNA, but then Riley dropped a print-out on Field's desk. It was Sam's phone download, back late last night from Digital Forensics.

Field skimmed a string of messages between Sam and a man saved in her phone as "James Hinge". They'd been messaging for over a fortnight, and met for a first date on Tuesday. There were messages from Wednesday morning, thanking Sam for breakfast, suggesting he'd been with her overnight, when David was attacked. A DC was already on the way to follow it up.

The team had completely taken over the whiteboards in the conference room. Furthest left were David and Sam's photographs, surrounded by their known movements and personal information.

In the centre of the board was their list:

PATIENT A: LILY STEWART
PATIENT B: SAMANTHA HUGHES
PATIENT C: ?
PATIENT D: CALLUM MULLIGAN
PATIENT E: PAIGE JACOBS

They had pictures of Lily and Callum – a smiling Lily at a wedding, in a formal dress, next to Callum's book headshot, moody in black and white.

On the same board, Wilson had started a neat list of periphery players, with accompanying photographs printed much smaller: Penny Moore; Sam's family members; David's receptionist; an ex-boyfriend of Sam's that Riley uncovered from Instagram; Lily Stewart's boyfriend, Scott, a junior doctor. James from Hinge was another recent addition.

Field frowned and made a mental note to ask Young and Prof if they'd ever heard of Lily's boyfriend, since they all worked at the same hospital. It was unlikely that Scott, in Cardiology, had crossed paths with David Moore, but it was yet another coincidence.

Overall, it was a relatively small pool of suspects and players, which made Field more uneasy. She was missing something, some vital piece of information.

Riley knocked on her door, stuck his head round it. 'Boss?'

She nodded at the chair opposite her desk, and he took a seat, laptop on his knees. His lip looked better today.

'I've just sent you an email,' he said. 'I've found Paige Jacobs. Well, her family.'

He carried on talking as she navigated to her inbox. Riley was struggling to look at her with the sun in his eyes, from the window behind her.

'There was no address on the RTC report, but I cross-referenced the time and date with local news stories and got in touch with a few of the people who left comments on the *News Shopper*'s Facebook post. Two of them got back to me this morning.'

'Good,' Field said, scanning the clippings he'd sent over.

'Mr and Mrs Jacobs, her parents, are selling up. They've already moved to Hastings, into a little bungalow. It's just Paige's sister in the house now. I spoke to her, too. She's in all day today, and she's happy to speak to you.'

Field scanned the email again. 'Ruby Jacobs?'

'Twenty-nine-year-old pharmacy technician. Still lives at home, no priors or anything.'

He broke off as Field got out of her chair to wrestle with the blinds. His pained squinting was getting on her nerves.

'What did you make of the report?' The cord finally gave way and the blind shot down. 'Anything they might have missed?'

He looked down at his laptop and shrugged. 'I can't see anything obvious. She went off the road in Thamesmead – you know the dual carriageway? There are some big dips in the road near the industrial estate that flood all the time.'

'Oh, that's where it happened?' Field was surprised it was so close to home. For some reason, she'd imagined Paige far away somewhere unfamiliar, on a winding country road.

She glanced at the Jacobs' address again. At a guess, Paige was maybe ten minutes from home.

'The car aquaplaned. The RTC report mentioned a mechanical fault, which Wilson and I couldn't make head nor tail of. I spoke to a mechanic on the phone last night.' Riley sucked in a breath. 'It was a faulty drive shaft. That was all. No suggestion the brakes had been meddled with or there was any foul play. Apparently, she must have been going too fast, skidded on the water – then the fault meant she couldn't regain control in time.'

'Cause of death?' Field asked.

'Cranio-cerebral injury,' he replied, automatically. 'Died six hours after she was admitted.'

Her poor parents.

Field sat up in her chair. 'How old was she? Nineteen?'

Riley nodded.

'Did she have drugs or alcohol in her system?' Field asked.

'Nope.'

'And no one else was in the car with her, right?'

Riley closed his laptop. 'No. She wasn't found for over an hour. It was dark and the car had flipped over, down a verge.'

He hesitated. 'There was a suggestion that it could have been suicide, because of her past mental health issues. But the parents were adamant that was all behind her.'

Field swallowed. 'Right. I need to get ready for the case call. I'm just going to make a quick coffee.'

'Do you want me on that call, boss?' His voice was slightly higher than usual.

'Yeah.' She nodded. 'Fine.'

Field escaped to the solitude of the kitchenette, mercifully empty this early on a Saturday. The limescale-ridden kettle rattled as it boiled, but Field didn't hear it. This case was like two fistfuls of sand, and Field was desperately trying not to let it slip through her fingers.

# Chapter 65

## Saturday | Morning

## Field

'Thank you for joining the Zoom, especially on a Saturday,' Field said, exhaling. 'I have DS Riley and DS Wilson in the room with me here.'

Her internet connection wasn't great, and some of the faces were frozen. Riley and Wilson were next to her, hands clasped around steaming mugs.

Bellamy was using his phone, walking through Callum's house with headphones in.

Zara was in Penny's garden. Professor Robinson – Prof – had a backdrop of books, on ancient-looking oak shelves.

Young was in her modern, Scandi living room, sipping from a Le Creuset espresso cup Field had got her as a set last Christmas.

Last to join the call was Dr Maxwell, frowning down the camera from his cupboard-sized office.

Field addressed Maxwell first, keen to get his take and then invite him to leave the call, so they could speak openly about Mulligan.

'Dr Maxwell, can I ask – is it still your intention to discharge Callum tomorrow?'

'Yes,' he said, curtly. 'I spoke to him at length last night. My assessment is that on his normal medication Callum is perfectly lucid, and doesn't pose a threat to himself or others. He's recovered from the stress he was subjected to at the scene. The social worker will be here tomorrow to sign him out.'

Wilson made a note, as Riley sat up straighter.

'When will he be able to go back to his house?' Maxwell asked.

Bellamy, who had turned his camera off, suddenly reappeared. 'I'd expect us to be out of here by tomorrow morning. Obviously, if we find anything it could be longer.'

'That's good,' Maxwell said. 'Staying in a hotel wouldn't have been an option for Callum.'

'In your opinion, has he been affected by the attack on Sam, beyond witnessing it?' Field asked.

'Well, yes.' Maxwell shifted in his seat. 'She was a friend, in the past. They hadn't been in touch for some time, but he was still upset.' He sighed. 'I can't really say any more than that, without breaching my patient's confidentiality.'

Field added a line on her "patient confidentiality" tally.

'If we want to speak to him again today—' Field said, letting her question hang in the air.

Maxwell looked reluctant. 'Yes, it would be admissible.'

'Right, okay,' Field said, with a smile. She did a quick mental calculation of exactly how many people she needed to speak to, and how many different places she had to be in. 'In that case, we will see you tomorrow morning. Before the social worker. Thank you, again, Dr Maxwell.'

'No worries.' He added a curt goodbye and signed off.

'Nice chap,' Prof said, cheerfully.

'Right, so we believe we've traced Paige Jacobs' family address,' Field said. 'We're going to head there next. Riley has spoken to—'

'The sister,' he said, keenly. 'Ruby Jacobs.'

Field nodded. 'She'll be expecting us, Wilson. The RTC report suggests the accident was caused by a combination of deep water on the road, a mechanical fault with the car and possibly excessive speed. It was a long time ago, so nothing to suggest it's related to this case.'

'I'm happy to take a look at the pathology report,' Prof chimed in. 'If that would be useful.'

'Great, thanks. Riley – get that sent over please.' Field took a sip from her mug. 'So, we still haven't found any recent messages between David and Sam. Sam had been on a date with a man from Hinge, and she seems to be his alibi for the night of David's murder. I've got a couple of DCs heading to speak to him.'

'Anything I've missed?' she asked Riley and Wilson, who shook their heads. 'Great, so I think that's my update. Bellamy, can you give us a summary of what you've found at Callum Mulligan's house, and on the street?'

'Morning, boss,' the voice down the line said, sounding chipper, despite the all-nighter. 'We've not turned anything up inside the address. All the kitchen knives appear present and correct, and they're all blunt. I've bagged all the dark clothing, as requested. Shoes too, although UV checks aren't showing blood on any of the soles, and they don't look like they've been worn out of the house recently.'

Bellamy was speaking delicately, because he knew about Callum's "housebound" alibi.

'But we did find something outside.'

245

Field sat up in her chair, as Bellamy fiddled with his phone and swapped to the back camera, so they could see the evidence bag in his hand.

'Look familiar?' he asked. 'It's page 2.'

Through the clear window of the paper bag, they could see a typed sheet of A4.

'So that looks like a match for the sheet found at the David Moore scene. Where was it, Bellamy?'

'Under a neighbour's hedge. Found it during the final fingertip search. There's blood on it, which we can safely assume belongs to your victim.'

'Let's get it to fingerprints today,' Field breathed. 'Riley, phone ahead and get it flagged as urgent. Excellent work, Bellamy.'

'No worries. Final crime scene log and all the paperwork will be with you tomorrow morning. There is one other thing,' Bellamy said. 'I'll have to board the back door up. Bloody thing keeps blowing open, and he'll get robbed otherwise.'

'Fine,' Field said. 'Penny Moore – have you had anything back from Digital Forensics? Has there been *any* contact between David and Penny, since he moved out?'

'They've checked again – nothing that we can see. Also, I know you were concerned that she had her phone off, so we couldn't use cell site to put her at home on Thursday night.'

'Oh yeah?' Field said.

Bellamy shrugged. 'Well, I've downloaded the data from her Ring doorbell – and the one over the road too. Both ran all night, and there was no movement. She doesn't leave the house, car doesn't move. Lights are off.'

'So, I think we're pretty close to ruling her out as a person of interest,' Field said. 'Thank you, Bellamy. Appreciate the attention to detail, as always.'

He nodded. 'No worries – cheers all.' Bellamy signed off the call.

Field looked to Young's rectangle on the screen. 'Anything back from the lab tests at the post-mortems?'

Young shook her head. 'You're looking at mid-week, earliest, for the fingernail scrapings. Preliminary reports from the clothing by Tuesday, at a push.'

'Ever the optimist, Young,' Prof boomed, leaning forward. 'I'm sure you're not surprised, DCI Field, but not much has changed our side since yesterday. I have taken a second round of swabs today, of Samantha Hughes.'

Unbidden, the image of her lying on the mortuary table sprang to Field's mind.

'I'm still hopeful we may have contact DNA from the slip in the blood,' Young said.

'Thank you, both. Sorry to drag you onto the call,' Field said.

'Not at all.' Prof waved a hand. 'It's useful, keeps us up to date. I'll have David Moore's prelim PM report for you by end of the day today. Samantha's tomorrow.'

Young nodded, and Field's eyes swivelled to Zara Ayres. 'How does Penny Moore seem?'

'I got here about an hour ago. She's sleeping.' Zara was speaking in hushed tones, and Field upped the laptop's volume. 'Dr Simon Dawes is planning to stay on for a few more days, says he'll keep an eye on her.'

There was a brief pause.

'Right,' Field said. 'Today is going to be busy. We need to speak to Paige Jacobs' sister, Lily Stewart – and ideally Penny Moore, too.'

She thought for a moment. 'Let us speak to Ruby Jacobs first, then we'll head to the Moore house. Wilson, you're with me again today. Riley, I want you to update the decision log and collate any additional victimology we've turned up in the last twenty-four hours.'

Everyone on the call knew it was a snub, the ongoing repercussions of his fuck-up with Callum.

She thanked them all, the civvy support worker promised to get the notes over in the next hour or so, and Field closed the laptop.

# Chapter 66

## Saturday | Morning

### Field

The Jacobs' home was in Erith, a large detached red-brick house.

Wilson pulled onto the drive, parking next to a smart little Corsa.

There were no curtains in the downstairs windows, and as they approached the front door, Field could see straight into the bare living room. The driveway was neat and well maintained, no weeds sprouting through the cracks in the paving – a war Field had long given up on in her courtyard at home.

Ruby opened the door within a few seconds, and Field wondered whether she'd been waiting in the hall for them.

'Hi, Ruby, I'm DCI Field, and this is DS Wilson.'

They held out their warrant cards, but the girl didn't look at them.

Ruby was a tiny wisp of a girl with big dark eyes and

dyed-purple hair. She was wearing a long-sleeved black dress and, despite the weather, black tights.

'You spoke to my colleague, I believe?' Field asked, gently. 'You were expecting us?'

'Yes, God. Sorry. I don't know what's wrong with me. I think it's the heat.'

She led them through the hallway, which was stacked high with moving boxes. There were marks on the walls, where pictures once hung, and a large mirror was on its side, leaning against the bottom banisters.

'You'll have to mind the mess,' Ruby said, her voice a squeak. 'Mum and Dad are getting the new place sorted. They complain about all the DIY, but—' she kicked a black bag out of the way '—I think I drew the short straw, packing this place up.'

'Moving house is the worst,' Wilson said with feeling, as they made it to the kitchen. 'My housemates and I are looking for somewhere at the moment. Total nightmare.'

Ruby seemed to relax a little. Gold star, Wilson.

The kitchen was empty too – nothing on the sides, apart from a kettle and a tea cannister. A temporary-looking dining table was set up against the far wall, consisting of a cheap white desk and a few garden chairs. Ruby didn't offer them a drink.

'Hopefully we won't take up too much of your time, Ruby,' Field said, as she sat down.

Wilson pulled her daybook from her bag, and produced a pen from her breast pocket.

Ruby nodded, went to speak, hesitated. 'You already know about my sister, don't you?'

She looked crestfallen. Field kept her voice gentle. 'Yes, Ruby. I think DS Riley explained on the phone, that in the course of our investigation, we've been looking into Dr David Moore's past patients.'

'And the trial?' Ruby pressed.

'Yes,' Field answered. 'And the trial.'

The girl's hands were on the table. They looked dry and painful, like she'd scrubbed at the skin. The fingernails were bitten down to painful-looking stubs, the skin around the nail beds picked at and raw.

Ruby flopped back into her seat. 'I thought so. I was shocked when I saw the news about David, but then Sam too—'

Sam's name hadn't hit the press yet.

Ruby must have caught Field's expression, because her eyes went wide, and her mouth opened a little. 'I saw it on Facebook. I'm friends with Sam on there.'

They were going to need to tread carefully. Ruby could clearly give them valuable information, but if Field wasn't careful she'd clam up like Lily.

'I wanted to ask you about Paige's time at the Maudsley, Ruby. Did you visit Paige in the hospital?'

'Every week,' she said, looking away from them, towards the door. 'Wednesday evenings and Saturday mornings.'

'That must have been hard,' Wilson said.

Ruby wiped a tear from the corner of her eye, but didn't say anything. It had to take a toll, being the child your parents weren't terrified for.

'Look, Ruby. I'll be perfectly honest with you. We know the attacks were linked. That means we're looking for a double murderer.'

Ruby's head cocked in her direction.

'There's good reason to believe it's linked to the trial. We've traced some of the patients, but—'

'Oh no.' Ruby shook her head firmly. 'Paige wouldn't want me to betray her – her friends.'

Field's silence was Wilson's signal to pick up from her. Ruby had already shared a moment with her; they were closer in age.

'It's not betraying them, Ruby,' Wilson said earnestly. 'You could be keeping them safe. We can't protect them, not when we don't know who they are.'

Her voice was a whine, more tears falling. 'I don't know if I should tell you.'

Wilson passed the notebook and pen to Field, and leaned forward to hold one of Ruby's battered hands. 'We've spoken to Callum Mulligan—' a sharp intake of breath from Ruby '—and Lily Stewart.'

Ruby nodded miserably, wiped her face with her free hand. Field had the pen poised.

'That last person, whoever they might be, that could be the key to us finding out what happened to Sam.'

Ruby tipped her head back, and Wilson let her hand go. 'Okay.'

Field's jaw was clenched. This was it – the last of the five.

'His name is Andy.' Her voice was steadier. 'Andrew Levey. He lives in Blackheath. Works in IT or software, or something.'

*Patient C.*

Field tempered her relief and exhilaration.

He was in Blackheath. That meant they'd all stayed local to South East London. Unusual, maybe, these days. Most young people wanted to live in Clapham or Dalston, somewhere things were happening.

Field wrote it down as Wilson spoke.

'Andy was at the hospital with your sister? And he was part of the trial?'

'Yes.' Ruby tugged the hem of her short dress closer to her knees. 'He was my favourite, if I'm honest. Quiet, a bit shy. Like me.'

'Have you had any contact with him recently? Or anyone else from the trial – Callum, Lily, Sam?'

'No.'

Field gave her a warm smile. 'I know this is hard for you Ruby—'

'Yeah it is. I don't know – I wasn't expecting—' Ruby's voice rose, hands clenched on the table. 'I just thought you'd want to know about Paige.'

'This situation, it must be incredibly difficult for you, and your family—' Wilson started, but Ruby cut her off.

'I dug some photos of her out of the boxes, because I thought you'd want to see. I even—' Her breath hitched. 'I thought you might be looking into what happened to her.'

Surprise was written all over Wilson's face.

Ruby chewed the inside of her cheek, then her anger seemed to pass. 'She had her whole life ahead of her.'

'I've seen a photo of her,' Field lied. 'She was beautiful.'

Ruby nodded, miserably.

'It was actually Lily, who told us about Paige,' Field said, watching closely for a reaction. 'Lily spoke very highly of her. It sounds like she was a force to be reckoned with.'

'She was,' Ruby squeaked. 'She was amazing.'

'And she was in the Maudsley for just under two years?'

'Yes.' The girl exhaled. 'She went in a kid, and then it was like she came out a grown-up. It changed her, being in there. I missed having her at home, even if life was easier—'

She broke off, looked stricken.

'I understand. It can be hard, watching a loved one go through something like that.' Field's voice cracked, and she reddened, clearing her throat like she had a frog in it. 'Did you see David Moore there, when you visited?'

'Yes, of course.' Ruby picked at her nail varnish. 'And Paige never stopped talking about him, even after she came home.'

Field wasn't really sure where to take their conversation next. The big win had been Andrew Levey's name.

'It must have been very hard for your parents, Ruby. Losing Paige, after she'd worked so hard to get better.'

Ruby waved a hand around the kitchen. 'Well, look how long it took them to move out of our house.' Ruby sniffed. 'Her room was the same as it was. Totally untouched for years, until a couple of months ago. They couldn't face it, so—'

'You had to pack her things away?' Field asked.

'Yeah.'

Field couldn't blame them for staying on in the house for so long. Losing a child, especially in an accident—

It seemed like Ruby wasn't happy about the move. Field wondered what she saw when she looked at the empty rooms, whether she visualised them full of their old belongings.

'Are you going with them, Ruby? To the coast?'

'Yes, I am. Someone has to look after them. I work in a pharmacy, so I should be okay.'

With her gothic look and dark eye make-up, Field couldn't imagine Ruby offering out cheerful greetings alongside prescriptions.

Field needed to wrap up the interview. She needed to call Bellamy, get him onto tracing Andrew.

But it was clear Ruby was wrestling with something.

Ruby chewed the inside of her cheek, then let the words out in a torrent. 'It's hard to explain, but the five of them were so close. Like they knew each other inside out – and I find it weird. They all went their separate ways after the trial, like it was just all done, you know?

'Paige didn't really speak to them anymore, and I wonder if she was struggling. The car accident – it was raining and she'd seemed tired that week, like she was getting ill.'

Field didn't need to ask what kind of ill Ruby meant.

Ruby reached across the table, gripping Field's hand, with

surprising force. 'You have to understand, I'm all she's got. My parents have this golden view of her, off to RADA, cured – but I think there was more to it all.'

Ruby's intensity was unsettling.

'More to it all?' Field echoed.

Ruby puffed out her cheeks; her grip went limp. 'I sound crazy. I don't know.'

Field waited.

'I just think, if there was something to know – they'd have all known it.'

# Chapter 67

**P:** My sister gets up every morning. Gets dressed, goes to school. She just had her first kiss, got her first boyfriend. She's getting good grades.
**D:** We've talked about this, about comparing yourself to others.
**P:** I'm not comparing myself to just anyone though, am I? Because we're both a product of the same environment.
**D:** P—
**P:** I was always the dramatic one. The one who had meltdowns in the aisles of the supermarket. The one who needed all the attention.

*Pause*

**P:** That's why no one believed I was ill.

*Pause*

**P:** That's why even if I did tell, no one would believe me.

# Chapter 68

## Saturday | Morning

## Callum

Maxwell put a coffee down in front of Callum, then took a large gulp of his own, and sat down heavily.

'How did you sleep?'

'I should probably say I slept really well,' Callum said, trying to suppress a yawn. 'In case you don't let me out. But to be honest, I had a shit night. I kept seeing – you know. What happened.'

'That's a totally normal trauma response,' Maxwell said. 'And the fact you're able to talk to me about it – that's good. That's really good, Callum.'

He wanted to shrug off Maxwell's praise, like it didn't mean anything to him – but it did.

Callum looked past Maxwell, out the window. The tree outside had yellow leaves, scorched by the sun over the last few weeks.

'I want us to come up with a plan, before you leave

tomorrow,' the doctor went on. 'Steps we can take to process what you saw happen to Sam, and what happened to David. Early warning signs that you're not coping, strategies that might help when the anxiety builds.'

'Can you speak to Lily? About when I get out?' Callum picked at the skin around his index finger.

'Of course.' Maxwell leaned back in his chair. 'I have a question, actually. Relating to Lily.'

The flap of skin gave way and a bloom of crimson slid down his nail bed. Callum sucked the blood from his finger and nodded at Maxwell to continue.

'You said yesterday that you ended it, with Lily. I'm interested to know why.'

Callum went back to examining the leaves, adding up how many were visible in the top-left pane of glass and focusing on the iron taste in his mouth.

'I hadn't been well for ages, and then about two years ago, I just stopped going out. I don't even know why, or where it came from. I just knew I couldn't do it anymore. At first, I thought it would be a few weeks, or a few months, but after a year—' He had to stop for a second, catch his breath. 'It was draining her. Working all day, looking after the kids in her class and then coming home to me—'

Every evening the door would slam, and she'd call out to him. Every day she'd try and mask the fear in her voice, the terror that she might find him crying or covered in blood, or in the middle of a full-blown psychotic break.

And some days he didn't call back. Stayed silent, in his room, letting her panic for those few extra seconds, to remind her that he needed her.

'It wasn't fair.'

Maxwell laid his pen down. Waited for more.

Callum sighed. 'Have you ever read any Edward Thomas?'

258

'No,' Maxwell said. 'But he features quite heavily in *Darlings, Obsessed*, doesn't he?'

Callum nodded. 'There's one story, about this guy who is going to kill himself. He says something horrible to his kid, and he feels so guilty that he takes his gun into the woods to, you know—'

'Seems like an overreaction,' Maxwell said, and Callum studied his face. It wasn't said judgementally, or critically. If anything, Maxwell sounded intrigued.

'There's a line in the story, where the guy says that he "could not believe they would ever be more unhappy than they often were now."'

Callum let the quote hang in the air, and he felt the same tug, same pressure on his chest, as he had the first time he'd read it.

'Because of his depression, he'd made his family so unhappy. And he couldn't imagine, couldn't fathom what else it would take to make them *more* unhappy. Isn't that the saddest fucking thing you ever heard?'

'It's—' Maxwell trailed off. 'Is that why you broke up with Lily? Because you felt like the man in the story?'

Callum downed the coffee. 'I need a shower and a shave. What time is Lily getting here? Do I have time?'

Maxwell looked at his watch, a silver face on a battered leather strap. 'If you're quick.'

Callum eased himself up out of the chair and walked the four paces to the door. He turned back to Maxwell, who was already typing away on his laptop.

'It's called "The Attempt", by the way.'

'What?' Maxwell said, looking up. 'What is?'

'The short story,' Callum said. 'It's called "The Attempt", and the guy doesn't shoot himself, in the end. He survives.'

259

# Chapter 69

## Lily

Lily thanked the driver as she got off the bus, outside the Maudsley.

The crowd of people who'd got off behind her streamed towards the park. It was another cloudless afternoon, sun beating down. The perfect Saturday.

She didn't have sun cream at Scott's, and her shoulders would burn if she didn't get inside soon.

Her legs felt heavy and unsteady, but now she knew what had caused her symptoms, they were easier to ignore. She wasn't sick, and she'd start to feel better as soon as all the shit was out of her system.

She was buzzed into the building, and gave her name at reception.

Lily couldn't connect the Maudsley now to the hospital she'd been in as a teenager. Partly, it was because all her memories of that time had an otherworldly quality. Not a whole picture, more like snapshots and fragments. Vignettes.

It could also be down to the extensive refurb and paint job.

It was Erin, the nurse from the other day, who let Lily onto the ward. She kept up a stream of chatter as she guided Lily down the corridor, to the dining room.

Callum was sat at a table reading a book.

Lily stopped in the doorway, and as if sensing her presence, he looked up and smiled.

He was holding the book at the corners, thumbs over the page numbers, like he used to. But reading was reading.

'Hey,' she said, slowly. 'You okay?'

'I'm out-of-my-head anxious,' he said, with a laugh. He dropped the book onto the table and pushed it as far away as he could reach. 'How're you?'

'You seem better.'

Cal's smile slipped. 'Lil?'

She was tearing up. It was stupid, and selfish – but the sight of him reading a book was going to make her cry. She did a big sniff, pressing the heel of her hand to her nose. 'Hay fever.'

'O-kay.' Callum folded his arms.

She'd made it awkward.

'What book is it?'

'It's a Vonnegut. Maxwell is a fan too. I don't think I've taken a word of it in. Just stared at the same sentence over and over.' His tone was conciliatory.

Maybe it was the side effects, or the lack of sleep. Or maybe she was just a bitch.

Because she wasn't happy to see him reading. She felt jealous.

How many years had she spent trying to help him? Christ – how many years had David tried? Ten minutes on this ward, with this new doctor, and he was tackling one of his biggest compulsions.

He didn't need her. Maybe he never had.

# Chapter 70

## Saturday | Afternoon

### Field

'Zara? Can you hear me?'

Field waited, then heard a sliding door open.

'Can you hear me now?' Zara asked.

'Yeah, that's better.' Field accepted her coffee from the barista, and moved away from the noisy coffee machine. 'How's Penny doing?'

'She's okay,' Zara said. 'She's actually been talking today. What time will you be here?'

Field grimaced.

Wilson took her cup from the server with a smile, and came over to stand next to Field, avoiding the many prams and toddlers in her path.

Riley had promised that he'd have an address for Andrew Levey inside the hour, so they'd stopped at a little caff in Erith, just for a breather. Wilson had tapped away, typing up the notes from her daybook, while Field composed a detailed update for the super. It shouldn't have taken her as long as it had, but it took a lot of edits to tone down her obvious dislike.

'I don't think we're going to make it there today.' Field walked outside and scanned the tables on the pavement for a spare seat. 'Depends on how it goes with Andrew Levey, when we find him.'

The only free table was covered in dirty plates and mugs, but it'd have to do.

'I can let her know,' Zara said.

Field appreciated that there was no sulk in her tone. 'What have you been chatting about? Anything useful?'

Wilson was stacking the plates and tidying the table, to make it easier for the servers. Thoughtful, but annoying.

'Well.' Zara lowered her voice. 'She admitted to me this morning that she knew Callum had been at the trial. Partly because David was still treating him, but also because of the book.'

It made sense.

'I think she's worried we're going to charge her with obstruction, for not mentioning it on the first day. And she's convinced herself that if she had told you, Sam wouldn't be dead.'

'Jesus,' Field said.

She suddenly felt like a piece of shit for not trying to cram a visit to Penny in, between visiting Ruby and knocking for Andy.

'That's not all. She also knew about Paige.'

Field sat up in her chair. 'How?'

'Well, she was married to David by then, when Paige died. Apparently he was devastated. She never saw him that upset, before or since.'

Field frowned. That made it two names that Penny had held back.

'She's adamant that that's it. David used to talk about them as a group, sometimes, but he always called them "the kids". Simon Dawes is back today, and he's confirmed that.'

'Okay,' Field said. 'Well, it is what it is. Try and reassure her.'

'Will do, ma'am. I'm going to stay here for another hour, and then drive over to Rickmansworth. Check in on Mr and Mrs Hughes. They've asked to see Sam, so I'll try and get that arranged for tomorrow.'

'Ask Professor Robinson to have a word, if you're struggling to get through to anyone on a Saturday. Oh, and Zara?'

'Yes, ma'am?'

'Make sure Penny knows that we're doing everything we can. Tell her I'll be by in the next few days, and to try not to worry, okay?'

They said a hasty goodbye.

Field had kept an open mind when it came to Penny, suspecting she knew more than she'd let on, but never sure how much.

She was left-handed, and she'd had odd reactions to the news of her husband's attack – but Field didn't believe she was a suspect.

The super was still keen for them to have a prime suspect, something he could sell on to his superiors, but Field wasn't going to pester a grieving widow, just because they had nothing more solid to go on.

Her phone buzzed in her hand, and Wilson's screen lit up.

Wilson snatched it up, then gave Field the nod. Andy's address.

Andrew Levey's door was answered almost immediately by a twenty-something blonde girl, in tiny pyjamas. She was dabbing at her chest with a bag of frozen peas. 'Yeah?'

Field was surprised. She seemed an unlikely housemate. 'I'm DCI Field, and this is DS Wilson. Is Andrew Levey home please?'

'Andy?' The girl's eyes widened, and she crossed her arms over her chest. 'He's not here. Why?'

'Could we come in?' Wilson hesitated. 'Sorry, I didn't catch your name.'

She turned to her, answered frostily. 'It's Lisa.'

If Riley was here, he'd have charmed his way in by now. Field took the lead. 'Are you Andrew's girlfriend, Lisa?'

She let out a bark of laughter. 'Andy? God no.'

Field smiled. 'So, who is Andy to you? A housemate?'

'He's a friend,' Lisa said slowly. She leaned against the banisters. 'We're five of us here – we went to uni together. He's got the top room.' Lisa's eyes widened. 'Shit. Has something happened to him?'

'Let's do this inside the house, shall we?'

Lisa took them inside, to a messy living room, and Wilson told her about the two attacks, keeping the link to Andy vague.

'An OCD doctor? Andy has OCD,' Lisa said, frowning. 'I mean – he's fine. We're all used to it. It's not like it stops him working, or anything.'

Field was surprised at the frankness. Clearly Andy hadn't hidden his illness from his uni friends, now housemates.

'What does he work as?' Field asked.

'He's a software engineer.' Lisa pointed to the pile of laptops on the dining table. She was rambling, nervous. 'We all did computer science at UCL. I'm a UX designer at a start-up. Andy works for Microsoft. He's the front-end lead on a major software upgrade to SharePoint. He earns silly money.'

Wilson's pen hovered above her notebook. 'And Andy's OCD, it doesn't affect his work?'

'No,' Lisa said firmly. 'He finds it hard when we're noisy, sometimes – and there's still the odd thing we do around the house to make life a bit easier for him, but most of the time you'd never guess, not nowadays. I'm not sure his work even knows.'

'And when you said he's not here—'

'He's gone to stay at his mum's place for a few days. She passed away, a few months ago. He's doing it up, to sell.'

'And when did you last see him, Lisa?' Field asked, already getting her phone out to send an urgent email.

'Thursday morning, when he left for work. He was in bed by the time I got back on Thursday night, and I think he left for his mum's early on Friday. What is this about?'

'You've been really helpful,' Wilson soothed. 'We just want to make sure Andy's safe.'

Lisa let them go up into his room. They were pushing it, without a search warrant, but Field wanted answers, and they'd wasted enough time.

The room would be easy to search, when they did get a warrant. It was almost completely bare. There were shelves holding a few books and some well-cared-for houseplants. He had an open wardrobe rail, a small chest of drawers and a desk.

The bed had been stripped, the bare duvet folded on top of the mattress.

Wilson snapped on a pair of gloves and opened the desk drawer. Field leaned over to look inside.

Neatly laid out were his phone, his laptop, his bank cards.

'Anything that could be used to trace him,' Wilson said grimly, sliding the drawer shut without touching anything.

Field rubbed her temple. 'So, he was last seen early on Thursday morning – the morning after Sam's attack. He was one of David's patients, but as far as we know, he's not been in treatment for OCD since.' Field hesitated, tapping her phone against her hand. 'And at some point between Thursday morning and today he's disappeared without his phone, bank cards – anything.'

Wilson still had gloves on, moving aside the trailing houseplants to peer at the books.

Field caught sight of the laundry basket, at the end of the bed. She used her pen to lift the lid. 'Wilson—'

Field looked down at the white T-shirt, crusted with blood. The bedsheets beneath it were filthy – the light blue pinstripes stained black.


'The Territorial Support Group are being briefed as we speak.' The super sounded energised, full of praise for their initiative in tracing Andrew Levey through his work.

'Thank you, sir,' Field said down the phone, throwing a thumbs-up at Wilson. 'That's great.'

He'd handled the warrant for Andrew Levey's house personally, and he'd called DCs from MIT5 and MIT2 into work, for extra support.

'Make sure you nail the bastard, Field,' he said, happily. 'Wrap this up nice and quick and, well—'

It might bring the Met some positive press for once, and earn him major brownie points with the commissioner.

For once, Field didn't care what his motivations were. They were making progress, and all she wanted was to bring Andy into custody – safely.

# Chapter 71

## Saturday | Afternoon

### Andy

He jumped at the knock on the door.

The journey over to it cost him a great effort. Dragging each foot, hearing the scrape of his socks against the threadbare carpet. It made his heart pound, the friction of it making the roof of his mouth itch. He could feel the noise in the soles of his feet.

The scrape of the metal key in the lock was a momentary relief from the memory of the carpet sound.

He pulled the door back. Wood noises he liked.

He shouldn't be paying this much attention. Hadn't, for a long time. It was the solitude. The quiet of the room. It was toying with him.

Andy watched the woman's mouth move but couldn't make out what she was saying.

This was bad. He could hear the floor, so why couldn't he hear words?

'Sorry,' he croaked. 'Could you say that again? Please?'

This time he caught something about towels, and he could almost hear the muscles in her forehead contracting, bringing the soft skin of her face into deep, concerned wrinkles.

'I'm okay,' he said. He tried to smile but it felt strange, and he was worried he was doing a horrible leer. 'Thank you.'

Her eyes shot to his bandaged arm.

*Fuck*. He hadn't put a jumper on. Beetroot stains were spreading along the neat white package.

The veins in his arm throbbed extra hard, like they were calling out to the woman, shouting *look, look, look at what happened*.

Andy took a step back, his foot rasping against the floor again. He needed to shut the door.

Her mouth was moving, the deep lines in her head moving with her eyebrows, up with wide eyes and then crashing back down. He shook his head again. It was hard to breathe. Air was coming in with no oxygen in it, nothing reaching his brain, anyway. His lungs were burning.

'Thank you,' he said again, but he couldn't hear it. Maybe he'd said something else; his ears weren't working. He might have said something obscene, and how would he know?

The door shut with a resounding echo that shook the walls of the room. They fluttered like sheets on a washing line, and then settled back down with the silence.

Andy slid down the door, an avalanche down a mountain that came to rest on the scratchy, Velcro-sounding carpet, and stayed there.

# Chapter 72

## Saturday | Evening

### Lily

Visiting hours ended at four, but Lily wasn't ready to go home. Not to Scott's.

She'd walked through the park for a while, her thoughts swimming. When she felt too tired to keep going, she sat down on a bench.

Lily hadn't told Cal what Scott had done.

In her imagination, Callum would have demanded to be discharged early, and stormed from the hospital without even bothering to change clothes. She'd be following him, pleading with him – but he'd ignore her. Then a fist, slamming into Scott's door, and Callum would have him up against a wall.

Instead, they made small talk, and told stories about Sam.

On the ward, Sam was always the mischievous one. It was like she couldn't help it; she just itched to do the one thing that wasn't allowed.

She had a game in group therapy, where she would earnestly

deliver lines from the previous night's rerun of *The Simpsons* as though they were deeply profound. Per Sam's own rules, she got double points for Homer, triple for Mr Burns. After a week, David was so confused, he was proposing a review of her medication.

Sam doodled on her slip-on shoes. Dyed her hair fun colours. Bribed the nurses to bring in contraband Red Bull.

There was no doubt that Andy was the smartest when it came to maths and science, but Sam ran rings round them at other subjects. Her recall for dates and historical events was insane.

They did a lot of weird shit to pass the time.

Paige used to love testing Sam on the dates of the Shakespeare plays, which she learned one weekend when she was bored. To help Paige prepare for her future career-defining turn as Ophelia, Sam learned all of Hamlet's lines.

By the time they were discharged, Callum was cast as Claudius and Lily was Gertrude. Sam also memorised Laertes and the Ghost. On a good day, David could even be persuaded to read Polonius.

The sun had finally set, and for the first time in weeks, there was a slight breeze.

Lily had goose bumps on her arms. The park had emptied out quickly once the sun went down. In her hurry, Lily came out of the wrong entrance – God knows how far from the bus stop that would take her back to Scott's.

Her phone was dead. She had no Google Maps, no Uber.

Footsteps came up behind her. Lily glanced round, but there was no one there.

*You're being paranoid.*

She looked back over her shoulder. Maybe she should cut through the park – she'd be back at the bus stop in ten minutes, rather than thirty.

Apart from a few biscuits with a cup of tea, it had been a full twenty-four hours since she'd eaten, and that had all been thrown up in the night. She was exhausted and emotionally wrung out, and even if it meant getting back to Scott's and having to face him faster – at least she could rest.

She heard the sound again, and felt a little prickle of fear at the back of her neck.

A few seconds later, a whistling man appeared from behind her with an excitable beagle on a lead. He smiled and nodded, and was off down the road.

She *was* being paranoid.

Lily mentally shook herself, and set off on the long way round, down the lit street.

# Chapter 73

## Saturday | Evening

## Field

Andy's mother's house was a tired two-up two-down in Thamesmead. The grass in the front garden was dead and brown, and tall weeds below the front window provided the only greenery.

They were parked two hundred metres up the road. Field was in the Territorial Support Group vehicle, air-con blasting. They'd been watching the house for an hour, and a plainclothes TSG officer had already done a reccy. So far there were no signs of life. She had Wilson on one side, the TSG inspector on the other.

Bellamy, and every DC the super could call in, were waiting in buses further up the road.

Field's phone vibrated, and she snatched it from the dashboard. It was hot from the glare of the late-afternoon sun, and the email loaded slowly.

'Is that the green light?' Wilson asked, hand on the door.

'No,' Field said. 'Riley's forwarded the statement from Paige's parents.'

Phrases from the email jumped out at her, and Field's head swam.

*David Moore gave us our daughter back*

*The helplessness of watching your child suffer with mental illness*

*The work he did with those kids was transformational*

Beside her, Wilson huffed. 'Obviously he didn't bother CCing me in.'

Then both of their phones buzzed, and it *was* the go-ahead.

'Let's go,' Field said, opening the car door and stepping out.

In under a minute, the small house was surrounded.

Field and Wilson hung back, thumbs looped into their vests, as the inspector gave the signal, and the door was smashed in on the first try with an enforcer.

Shouts of *"Police"* ripped through the night.

Faces appeared at windows up and down the street. A few doors opened.

Field tapped her foot, waiting for the inspector to reappear – either dragging Andrew Levey along in cuffs, or totally deflated.

The radio crackled constantly.

*Living room clear.*

*Kitchen clear.*

*Bedroom clear.*


The front door was still hanging on by one hinge when Field entered the small house. It sagged into the hallway at a drunken angle.

Field was surprised by the décor. She'd been expecting to step back in time, into an old person's house with flocked

275

wallpaper and a musty body-odour smell. But the hall was painted white, with thick cream carpet.

A white sideboard, probably from IKEA, was the only piece of furniture downstairs. There was nothing on the top. Field opened the first drawer. Inside were a few framed photos and a trinket dish, which presumably had stood on top of the sideboard at some point.

Field picked up one of the photographs. It was of Andrew in his mid-twenties. He obviously didn't like having his photo taken. His shoulders were high about his ears, and the shadow of the camera had fallen across one half of his face. His closed-mouth smile looked like a grimace.

He probably wasn't a bad-looking lad, in person. Mothers did tend to love terrible photos of their children. But, if they did need to circulate a photo of him to the press, Field knew it would get picked up. In the case of two brutal stabbings, Andrew's face just fit.

The first room they checked was the kitchen, but there were no kitchen knives. In fact, there was no anything. The cupboards were empty – her second empty house of the day.

The living room was bare, with a TV-sized patch of brighter wallpaper on the chimney breast.

The PolSA team were on the way, but Field couldn't wait for them to get here.

Field, Wilson and Bellamy went room to room. Upstairs was tidy, sparsely furnished, and free of clutter. The master bedroom was empty, and had been stripped of wallpaper, scarred walls waiting to be finished.

Bellamy called to them from the second bedroom. It was blue and had a single bed rather than a double – probably Andrew's childhood bedroom.

Bellamy pointed to two cardboard boxes stacked on the bed. 'Stuff he was planning to save, maybe?'

Field pushed her sleeves up. 'Let's take a box each.'

'What're we looking for?' Wilson asked, heaving the first one down, and lifting the lid. It was stacked with books.

'Anything that might give us a location,' Field said. 'Or an idea of where he might go.'

Bellamy carefully removed bubble-wrapped figurines from his box.

Wilson rummaged through the books. 'He doesn't have any other family, does he?'

'Not that we know of.' Field pulled a red photo album from her box and started to flick through it. 'It must've been hard for him. Losing her.'

Lily didn't speak to her family. Field wasn't sure where Callum's parents were, and he'd lost his nan a decade ago. Andy was alone now, too. But Sam and Paige had both been part of loving families, so there was no pattern there.

'Grief makes people do all sorts,' Wilson said.

Field considered this for a moment, and again her thoughts went to Toby. How would he cope, if something happened to her?

In her box, Field found family photo albums and Andrew's degree certificate. First-class honours from UCL.

Wilson was scanning a bundle of letters. 'I've got postcards from Brighton here.'

'Any Brighton photos in there?' Bellamy nodded to the photo album.

'He needs somewhere he can go to ground,' Field thought aloud, as she checked. 'And Brighton makes sense. It's close enough that he could get there quickly, but it's out of London.'

A series of family photos caught her eye. A tiny boy, Andrew presumably, standing between his mother and father on the steps of a B&B or a hotel. She'd found a similar picture in the drawer downstairs. The boy Andrew looked serious and worried, squinting up at them. The same photo was recreated over the years, the boy getting taller and a little broader in each one, until he was about twelve.

Field extracted a few of the clearest ones from the sleeves. 'Call Riley. Send these over to him, and see if we can enlarge it. Tell him to get the name of whatever hotel that is.'

Wilson took a picture of the photograph with her phone, then bagged it.

'If the hotel is still there, get Riley to phone and ask if they've had anyone matching Andy's description check in.'

# Chapter 74

## Saturday | Evening

### Field

Young was sitting in Field's usual booth at the back of the Volly, a bottle of wine in an ice bucket in front of her. She'd already filled her own glass, and a second stood ready and waiting.

The balmy weather and lack of football meant most of the patrons were in the beer garden. Apart from Field and Young, the only people inside were the staff and a few old blokes on bar stools.

'Heya,' Young said, breezily. 'I got Pinot – hope that's okay.'

Young didn't meet Field's eye as she sat down. She busied herself pouring the wine, and mopping up the drips from the ice bucket with a tissue from her cavernous handbag.

'I thought this was going to be about the case,' Field said. 'I didn't realise we were on the lash.'

Young shrugged. 'Well, you haven't had a break since Tuesday. I thought you might need a breather.'

'Right.'

They sat in an awkward silence, sipping from their glasses. Field had a headache starting, behind her eyes.

'So, the raid on Levey's house was a washout then?' Young asked.

'Yep. He's disappeared without a trace. I've got Riley on a few wild goose chases, but I'm not hopeful.'

'You never know.' Young stared down at the table.

As they lapsed into silence again, a bloke at the bar opened a bag of crisps. The sound of him eating set Field's teeth on edge.

She had a creeping suspicion that something was going on. Young was acting like a parent about to break bad news to a five-year-old. Field took Toby for a spontaneous trip to McDonald's before she told him Jimmy the hamster had died.

Field didn't really want to be sitting in the Volly drinking Pinot.

Wilson was ordering the tests on the bloodied clothing found at Andy's house, filling out the forms that Field would need to authorise when she got home. She should have just ignored Young's text, pretended she hadn't seen it.

And now she was here, her friend was distracted. Field could sense that there was something she wanted to talk about, that she was working her way up to.

'Found anyone interesting on the apps lately?' Field asked.

Young shrugged. 'If they've still got their hair and their own teeth, they're looking for someone twenty years younger. My last date cried about his divorce over pudding.'

Field grinned. 'I told you not to go for the fresh divorcees.'

Young's face stayed deadpan. 'They'd split five years ago.'

Field snorted. 'Well, you do know how to pick them.'

Young's voice dropped to a whisper. 'I can't move for, like, twenty-eight-year-olds.'

'What?' Field's mouth fell open. 'You can't date someone younger than your son. Your mother-in-law could be, well. Our age.'

'I know, I know.' Young put a hand on her chest. 'I don't talk to them. It's just – you know. A nice ego boost.'

Field snorted again.

'So—' Young took a deep breath. 'Toby called me.'

For one bizarre moment, Field thought it was an extension of their previous conversation. That her son was betraying his boyfriend of five years, to flirt with a woman who had been like a second mother.

'Toby called you?' she repeated, blinking.

Young threw her hands up. 'Don't be mad at him. Please don't fly off the handle—'

'Fly off the handle? When have I ever *flown off the handle*?' Field's voice was rising.

'He's just worried—'

Field spoke over her. 'When? When did he call you?'

'This morning.' Young spoke quickly. 'He's just worried about you. It's not like we discussed you at length or anything. He just wanted—'

'Worried about me?' Field screwed her face up in exaggerated confusion. 'I haven't seen him since Wednesday night.'

'I know—'

'Why didn't he say anything when I called him on Friday?' Field shot back. 'Why didn't *he* ask me for a drink tonight?'

She felt drunk with anger, like she'd downed the whole bottle, not a few sips. Her pulse was thundering in her ears, the ache behind her eyes getting worse – and only pissing her off more.

Young was going red, and the old blokes at the bar were staring now. One had a crisp frozen halfway to his face.

'I just think—'

Field cut her off again. 'He's so worried about me, he decided to skip speaking to me altogether, and go straight to one of my work colleagues, did he?'

At this Young scoffed, and rolled her eyes. 'Oh, come on, Liz. I'm hardly a *colleague* am I? We've known each other twenty years.'

'And we're working a fucking murder investigation together, Debbie.' Field was shouting now.

*I need to leave.*

If she didn't get out soon, she was going to say something she regretted. She grabbed her phone and swung her bag up onto her shoulder.

Young had flopped back into the booth seat, clutching her wine to her chest, eyes closed.

The defeat on her face took some of the heat out of Field's anger. But not enough to stop her turning on her heel and marching out of the pub.

# Chapter 75

## Sunday | Midnight

## Lily

It was gone midnight, and Scott still wasn't back at the flat. She'd left her phone off, so if he'd messaged her she hadn't seen it.

She had nowhere else to go. DS Wilson had called to say she should stay safe indoors tonight and keep the doors locked.

Lily didn't feel safe in this flat, not anymore.

If he was still out this late, on his night off, then Scott would be getting shit-faced. Usually he was pious, sipping one low-calorie bottled beer for an hour and then moving on to slimline tonic. But there had been a handful of nights out with his old med school mates. Scott swore he was just hungover, but Lily recognised the signs of a comedown.

A few months ago, he'd had a difficult shift at the hospital. A patient put in a complaint about something – Lily never got the full story. He'd gone out on his own and she hadn't heard from him for two days.

On the bus home tonight, she'd thought of a thousand scathing things to say to him when she got in, and then he was just gone. It was unnerving, being on her own in his flat, waiting for him to get back.

She'd looked everywhere for the pills he must have been giving her. Taken the flat apart as thoroughly as DCI Field's team would have. He must have got rid of them today, or kept them in his car, because she didn't find anything.

She did find a bag of coke, right at the back of his bedside drawer. He always said anyone who did drugs was pathetic.

She flushed it down the toilet. Fucking hypocrite.

Lily didn't need the pills themselves. There'd be her medical records, and his prescriptions. She would tell them how violating it was, finding out that someone had been trying to regulate your moods for you. Putting powdered tablets in her tea, or her food.

Her tote bags were packed, at the end of the bed.

She couldn't wait up much longer, but she didn't want him to come back in when she was sleeping.

Eventually, when her eyes kept closing on the sofa, she dragged one of the dining chairs into his bedroom, and wedged it under the handle. Lily hadn't really expected it to work, but it did.

She left the lights on, just in case. Crawled into his bed for the final time, and fell asleep.

# Chapter 76

**D:** You know you're not ready to form romantic attachments. You're not in a place to have healthy romantic relationships.

*Pause*

**P:** I think you're wrong.

*Pause*

**P:** I'm ready. I am – I am ready.

*Pause*

**D:** Who is the doctor?

*Pause*

**P:** You.
**D:** And who is the patient?

*Pause*

**P:** Me.
**D:** So, are you ready for a romantic relationship?

*Pause*

**P:** (*Quietly*) No.

# Chapter 77

Sunday | Early hours

## Field

Field paced up and down her small concrete patio, ears straining for the sound of Toby's key in the lock. She desperately wanted a cigarette, but she hadn't passed anyone to bum one off on the way home, and she refused to buy a packet.

She wasn't just angry. She was hurt.

Four days into a double murder investigation, and Toby had decided she was cracking up. Toby *knew* Young was working the case and he went to her.

Young was probably her closest friend, but that had never impacted their working relationship. Field didn't bring her private life to work. Even if it was fucking with her head, all the stories about those teenagers, the case hadn't suffered. No one on her team could tell.

But Toby had gone behind her back. After everything they'd been through, everything she'd done for him – they were supposed to be close. He could have come to her first.

A small voice in her head, one she was ashamed of, couldn't let go of the fact that it was Toby's fault. If he hadn't got ill when he was fifteen, she wouldn't be finding it all so fucking much.

Field let out a long breath. She needed to calm down before he got here.

She went back into the kitchen, locking the back door behind her. Poured herself a glass of tap water in the half-darkness and drank it over the sink, hoping it would soothe her headache.

'Mum?' Toby called – and it made her jump. She dropped the glass, and it bounced off the edge of the counter, smashing on the floor.

*For fuck's sake.*

'Don't come in here without shoes,' she called, bending down to pick up fragments of glass.

Apart from a few shards, it had broken cleanly in two.

'Mum?' he said again, putting his head round the corner.

It was hard to see the glass in the dim light, but she thought she'd got it all. As she stood up, she put her free hand on the counter to steady herself – and felt a stray chip bed itself deep into her palm.

'Shit—'

'For God's sake, Mum,' Toby muttered, flicking the light on.

They stared at each other for a second, Field with one hand full of glass, the other bleeding. Toby was still in his uniform, hair rumpled, dark circles under his eyes.

'It's fine.' Field moved to the bin and dropped the glass into it, hiding how red her cheeks had gone.

Toby sighed and retreated to the living room.

She ran her palm under the tap, picking the shard out with her nail. The running water swept it down the plughole, and she ripped off a sheet of kitchen roll, clenching it in her fist to stem the bleeding.

When she went into the living room, Toby had put the big light on. He was sitting at the dining table, chin in his palm, eyes down. Like he was resigned to his fate.

'You know, I don't have time for this,' she said, voice icy. 'I'm investigating a double murder. I don't have time for your – theatrics.'

His eyes flicked to her. 'Theatrics?'

'All this—' She waved a hand. 'Letting yourself in to my house and leaving plates of food out, like I can't feed myself. Calling Young to tell her I'm off my head – what was that all about?'

'That's not what happened.' Toby's voice was monotone. His face had lost all its softness. 'I'm allowed to worry about you.'

Field scoffed.

He rubbed his temples, one of her mannerisms. 'I'm not a fucking kid anymore, Mum. I can see when you're struggling.'

'I'm not struggling,' she snapped.

'You are.'

Her cut hand was stinging. 'You can't walk into my house and tell me how I'm feeling. It's a double murder; it's going to be stressful—'

'You're allowed to be stressed.' His voice was thin and high. 'Be stressed, but let me help. I can cook dinner or just, fucking, *be* here.'

'Why are you acting like the injured party?' she demanded. 'You're the one contacting my colleagues and asking them to what? Check up on me? Do you know how fucking embarrassing that is?

'I have to look Young in the eye next week. What if it had got back to the super, eh? "DCI Field's *son* is getting in touch with people working on an active investigation because he's concerned for her welfare." I am already on the receiving end of so much *shit* from him—'

She paused for breath, unsure who she was even angry with.

'Whatever,' Toby said. 'I can't talk to you when you're like this.'

Toby had always sulked. As a toddler, chubby arms crossed, facing the wall. When he got his first boyfriend and they had their first fight, Toby sulked for a week, mooning about the house, pointedly refusing his calls.

It infuriated her. He could never just *have* the argument. Sort his shit out. He had to brood on it, let it stew and poison everything.

Toby picked up his phone, and turned in a half-circle looking for his keys. 'I'm going home. Get some sleep, okay?'

That was it. He was dismissing her. The fist not clutching the kitchen roll clenched too.

Field waited until he was unlocking the front door, before she spoke.

'I'm not like *you*, you know? I'm not fragile.'

The words hung in the air.

Her voice had sounded normal. Unbothered, like they were having a typical conversation.

Somehow that made it worse.

A trickle of shame extinguished her anger. She wanted Toby to turn round and hurl abuse at her. She wanted to have the fight she knew she deserved.

Toby didn't say anything else before he left, but he slammed the front door so hard his school photos rattled on the wall.

# Chapter 78

## Sunday | Morning

### Field

Field felt sick, when she woke up.

It was like a bad hangover. Her stomach was churning, her skin was hot to the touch and her head was pounding. Last night's dreams were replays of the conversation with Toby. Twisted versions, where she was more hurtful, took it even further.

Field sat up in bed, punching her pillow into a more comfortable shape.

Yesterday they'd had their biggest breakthrough yet, with Andy's bloody clothes and the raid on his mum's house. Even if they hadn't found him yet, they were closing in.

There was no reason for her to go off at Toby like that.

She leaned over to the side table and put Radio 4 on, to alleviate the silence. Her back was stiff, but before she could luxuriate under the waterfall shower for fifteen minutes, she needed coffee.

Field opened the back door to let some air into the kitchen. The August heatwave still hadn't broken, although the radio presenters kept saying they were due a storm.

A fat ginger tabby with no discernible owners sauntered into the kitchen, winding its way around her legs. He looked pleadingly up at her as she sipped her coffee, as though it was something he was certain he'd enjoy, if only she'd make him one.

Field kneeled down to stroke the cat, and noticed several large chunks of glass that she must have missed the night before.

'I need to apologise, don't I, tabby?' she said, scratching behind the cat's ears.

Sensing there was no food on the horizon, the cat left again with a flick of its tail.

She busied herself showering and getting dressed, then gave the kitchen a proper sweep and hoover.

Before she knew it, it was already quarter to eight, and she was jumping into the car. She had to be at the Maudsley by nine, latest, to interview Callum.

She would text Toby. She knew she needed to say sorry – but later. First, she needed to find and speak to Andrew Levey, the last patient on their list.

# Chapter 79

## Sunday | Morning

### Callum

DCI Field was back, on her own this time. Maxwell stayed as his appropriate adult. He had the same lawyer as the other day, in the same cheap suit.

They were in the dining room, sitting in the same places. It was like a grim parody of last time, except he didn't feel out-of-his-brain anxious. Just his usual anxious.

'How are you, Callum?' Field asked.

'Been better,' Callum said, glancing at Maxwell. 'But I'm okay, today. Thanks.'

'Callum, I want to go into a bit more detail on a few things,' Field began. 'You understand that anything you say today is admissible in evidence?'

Callum nodded.

'Good.' DCI Field looked less tired than yesterday, and her hair was pulled back in a neat ponytail. 'When did you last speak to Andrew Levey?'

He'd been expecting her to go through his alibi for each night, or ask why Sam might have been outside his house.

Clearly not giving them Andy's name hadn't stopped the police finding his details.

Field was clicking and unclicking her pen. He closed his eyes, screwed them up. Tried not to count.

*Click.*

He realised he hadn't actually answered her yet.

'Andy?' Callum rubbed a hand over his scalp. He coughed, buying thinking time. 'I don't know. Maybe five years ago? A new year's text or something.'

*Click.*

'Why didn't you stay in touch?' Field asked.

The small room was heating up.

'I don't know—'

*Click.*

'—I think Andy wanted to distance himself from the study, and from his illness.'

Callum could feel sweat gathering in his armpits.

*Click.*

'By the time we left he was much better, and he wanted to get on with his life.' He shifted in his seat, unable to get comfortable.

*Click click.*

Was that one or two?

He forced himself to concentrate. 'Andy was always the quiet one. He got a lot out of being around us four, but I think in the end, he wanted a fresh start. We all did.'

Field put the pen down and relief flooded through him – chest lighter, hands unclenching.

Field pulled a book from her bag and put it on the table. A well-read copy of *Darlings, Obsessed*.

'Andy isn't a character in the book, is he?'

Callum gripped the edge of the table. 'I didn't base the characters on those guys.'

'Oh, I don't know,' Field said, picking it up.

Dr Maxwell was making eyes at the solicitor, but Callum shook his head, to indicate he could go on.

'There's a character with an eating disorder.' Field looked up to gauge his reaction. 'Like Lily Stewart. Counting and magical thinking, like you – that's the term, isn't it? And skin picking, like Sam. The youngest character has contamination OCD, like—'

'Okay,' Callum interrupted. 'I didn't use misophonia.'

'Remind me, what is misophonia?'

He'd lost count of her questions – did they start from "How are you?" or when the recording started? Were they at nine yet? Maybe she was counting to see if he would react to question nine – trying to test him.

Before Callum could answer, Maxwell interrupted.

'Fear of sound, or an extreme anxious reaction to certain sounds.' Maxwell crossed his arms. 'But Callum wasn't the psychologist treating this patient, so I don't think it's pertinent to question him on medical terms.'

The latest anxiety spike flattened. Maxwell answering for him was like a stay of execution.

Field gave Maxwell a frosty look. 'Big picture, Callum. Do you think Andy is capable of these attacks?'

'No.' He didn't want to look at her. He stared at a spot on the wall behind her left ear. 'Not the Andy I used to know. But it's been a long time.'

Field looked down at her notes. 'What about Lily? Could she be capable?'

'Lil? No. No way.' He suppressed an eyeroll. The police must be desperate, Callum thought, if they were looking at Lily.

'What makes you say that?'

He went through a rolodex of examples in his mind. The fact she never let him kill spiders, even though she was terrified of them. Her fear of blood. The pervading *goodness* of her, that he relied on as much as it infuriated him. Took advantage of.

'She just wouldn't,' he said, finally. 'Why would she? What possible reason?'

He took a sip of water, the tremor in his hand making it hard not to spill any. They must be past nine questions now.

It was fine.

It was all going to be fine.

He sensed Field's next question before she asked it.

'If you don't mind, Callum,' Field said. 'I'd like to know more about Paige. It must have been difficult for you, when she passed away. Could you tell me about her?'

*Tell me about Paige.*

A simple request. One of the easiest things she'd asked so far.

He closed his eyes.

'Paige was the youngest – two years younger than me, with a proper baby face. We all saw her as a little sister.'

Strange lights danced against his eyelids. He couldn't picture Paige's face anymore. He could summon the essence of her, how she threw her head back and laughed, the cadence of her voice, but her face was a blank, apart from the big, dark eyes and elfin Irish features. He'd never had a very visual memory – and he didn't have a photograph of her.

He opened his eyes. Field was looking at him dispassionately. Not brimming with empathy, but not shooting daggers either.

'What was her OCD like, Callum?'

'Contamination,' he said, mechanically. This was more solid ground. 'Not so much bins and germs, although there was that. Specifically, she thought people she didn't know very well were contaminated. So, we were safe, she could touch us – just. But the cleaners, new nurses, other visitors. Anything they touched, she couldn't.'

'That sounds hard.'

The blandness of the statement pissed him off. 'It was. If her mum popped to the shops for a pint of milk, it'd take Paige two hours to "decontaminate" her, because she'd come into contact with things strangers had touched.' His voice stuck in his throat. 'There was one day, not long before Paige was discharged, when her mum and sister came to visit. When they got there, before they'd even used the hand sanitiser, Paige walked over and hugged them. Her mum was so happy, she couldn't stop crying.'

Callum had envied Paige in that moment. Her enduring, enabling mother who only wanted the best for her. Her supportive little sister.

'Paige was a better writer than me,' he said, for something to distract himself. 'I can tell you that for free.'

'Did she write during the trial?'

'Yeah. We were quite competitive.' He laid his hands on the greasy table.

'What did you both write about?' Field asked. She seemed in no hurry to move the interview on.

He exhaled, staring at his hands. They felt useless, disconnected from him. 'We wrote about our experience of OCD, illness, hospital.' He looked up. 'Have you read my book?'

'Yes,' Field said, without hesitation. She cleared her throat.

He nodded. 'Then you'll know. It's *tiny*. It's a very small book, about small, sad people. It's *minuscule*. I write horrible narcissistic characters who are different slices of me. I give them my flaws and I crank up the pressure and I try to make them crack.'

Field was frowning at him. If she was following his thread, it was only just.

He sighed. 'Paige didn't write like that. She was younger and less cynical and cleverer. She wrote in this big broad way. She wasn't afraid to go deep, you know? She made you think about big themes, big issues.'

There was a gentle hum from behind the shutters. The staff would be prepping lunch, warming up the big oven for the trays of soft food.

'People who claim they are "so OCD" have no idea what OCD is actually like.' Callum sighed. 'But Paige's writing, she helped people to get it – to put into context what the worst possible experiences felt like.'

When Callum looked up, Field looked pale. He frowned. 'Are you okay?'

Field gave him a bland smile. 'Yes. Fine – you were saying? Did Paige want to be a writer?'

'God no, she wanted to be an *actress*.' He let out a hollow laugh. 'For her RADA audition, they let her perform an extract of her own play. That's unusual. It normally has to be something pre-approved, I think. When they offered her a place, she was the only person who was actually surprised. She texted me – sent me "RADA" and then about a thousand crying emojis.'

He'd got her text on the train and jumped out of his seat. There'd been no one, before or since, whom he'd loved like Paige. Like a sister, fiercely protective but also scared for her. He wanted to push her to achieve big things but also keep her wrapped up in cotton wool.

'Did you go to her funeral, Callum?' Field asked, quietly.

He shook his head and wiped his hands on his jeans.

'Why not?' She prompted. 'Couldn't face it?'

'I got as far as the grounds of the crematorium.' He sighed.

298

'But I'd spent a year and a half with Paige, and the others, just us.'

Callum struggled for the words to explain, looking up at the stained ceiling. 'I couldn't be there, with her family. I didn't want to see her mum and sister again.

'My parents blamed me, for getting ill. I moved in with my nan, and apart from a card at Christmas we don't speak. Lily hasn't spoken to her mum or her sisters since she was sixteen.'

No one spoke. He was aware of Maxwell next to him, aware that this would be fodder for future therapy sessions.

'Paige was so loved. I didn't want to meet her school friends, and her cousins and all the other people in her life – all the people who never abandoned her. I didn't want to compare my grief to theirs.'

He took a big breath of air, and met Field's eye. 'I told you. I'm selfish.'


'Here's your medication,' Maxwell said, handing over a bulging paper bag. 'They've given you enough for two weeks. There are beta blockers in there, in case you need them, but try and only take them in emergencies.'

'Sleeping pills?' Callum asked, peering into it.

Maxwell folded his arms. 'They've actually given you a high dose of amitriptyline. It should make you tired but won't be as addictive as a sleeping tablet, short-term.'

Callum nodded, and pushed the pills into his rucksack. As long as he could close his eyes without the image of Sam bleeding to death in the street, he didn't care what the pills were.

They left Maxwell's cramped office and walked towards the ward's entrance, Callum carrying his rucksack and his red parka in his arms, a protective bundle between him and everything else.

'The police have been in touch. You can go home. Everything should be cleaned up, so – so you should be all right. You know they've offered to put an officer outside your house tonight? Just in case—'

'No,' Callum snapped. He couldn't face seeing the bloke from that night. 'No police.'

'Okay.' Maxwell raised his hands. 'But keep your phone turned on, in case they need to get hold of you. Plus, you've got my number. If you need anything over the next few days, you call me, okay? Or get Lily to ring.'

Callum nodded. 'Have you spoken to her? Lily?'

The urge to count as they walked was overwhelming. His footsteps, the floor tiles, the squeak of Maxwell's right shoe.

'I haven't heard from her.' Maxwell shot him a worried glance.

He'd have liked to have her here, for this bit, but Callum shrugged. 'It's okay. She'll be at home, I guess.'

They stopped by the doors to the ward, and a few of the other patients eyed him with interest.

'Thanks, Doc,' he said quietly. 'I didn't think I'd—'

Guilt rose in him. How many hours had he spent with David, over the years? How long had they spent together, working through Callum's many regressions?

'I didn't think there would be another doctor who would get this stuff,' he said, weakly.

Maxwell shrugged. 'I'm sure there's a lot I don't know yet. Ultimately, you're the expert on what's going on and how you feel, Callum. But I'm here, and I'm on your side, okay?'

Callum shrugged his rucksack over one shoulder. It was only light – some clothes the police had brought him from home yesterday, some leaflets from Maxwell, and the meds.

Maxwell sensed that he didn't want to prolong the goodbye and held the door open for him.

Callum walked through it.

The hospital was quiet. There were a few people Callum assumed were relatives or visitors, clutching flowers or bags of food. Some looked harassed or stressed but most seemed upbeat.

He followed the signs for the exits without thinking about it, keeping his mind deliberately empty.

A woman in shorts glanced at the winter parka he was holding with a mildly amused expression. He wanted to tell her to fuck off.

But he didn't. The cool air-conditioned corridors finally gave way to baking afternoon heat, as he took a deep breath and walked through the Maudsley's front doors.

*Three.*

The number popped into his mind automatically.

The third time he'd been discharged from this hospital.

# Chapter 80

## Sunday | Morning

### Lily

After barely sleeping all night, she slept through her alarm.

Lily had missed Callum's discharge from the Maudsley. He was going to think she'd rather be here, with Scott. The rush of guilt was quickly overtaken by rage, when she stood up too quickly and felt the familiar sicky sensation in her stomach.

She'd slept fully clothed, shoes still on. All she had to do was put her rings on, and give her hair a quick brush.

The chair was still wedged under the door. Lily had a vision of Scott standing on the other side, waiting silently for her to emerge. She put a hand over her pounding heart, taking a few deep breaths.

She dislodged the chair and opened the door in one swift move.

Lily dragged the chair back into the living room and found Scott passed out on the sofa, an arm thrown over his face.

There was a bottle of Jack Daniel's on the coffee table, only a third of it gone.

Lightweight.

Lily checked the travel app on her phone. She would never make it to Denmark Hill in time. It would be quicker to travel back to theirs, and hope Cal would be there.

Scott's phone was on the side in the kitchen, the battery dead. Lily looked down at it, weighing up her options. She desperately wanted to get out of the flat, escape the white walls, white furniture and the overpowering scent from the nine reed diffusers in five rooms. But she could stand ten more minutes.

*Fuck it.*

Lily carried his phone to the bedroom, and plugged it in.

While she waited for it to charge, she decided to strip the bedsheets. She took them back to the kitchen, stuffed them in the washing machine and set it off on the first setting she landed on. Lily didn't want Scott to smell her on his sheets when he eventually went to bed.

By the time the washing was rolling round on its cycle, his phone had turned itself on.

In a few taps she'd entered his passcode and opened his emails. Lily flicked through his sent items, taking quick photos on her phone of the email addresses he'd been in touch with, including that of his boss, and someone important-sounding who'd sent a hospital-wide memo on patient confidentiality.

Scott's phone was on four per cent battery, so she unplugged it again.

He was still asleep when Lily left.

No fanfare, no final row – but she had several emails she needed to send on her bus ride.

# Chapter 81

**P:** Do you wish we could take it back?
**D:** Look, P—
**P:** Because I don't, okay? I don't regret it.

*Pause*

**D:** It was wrong. It was my fault.

*Pause*

**D:** I don't know. I don't know how it happened.

*Pause*

**D:** I'm a monster.
**P:** You're not. It was me—
**D:** You're underage, P—. And you're my patient.

*Pause*

**P:** I wanted it.
   Transference. It's called transference – I looked it up. When you develop feelings for your therapist. Or your lawyer, or doctor, or teacher whoever.

So, I'm not special. There's a name for it. Add it to the long list of my diagnoses.

*Pause*

**P:** I'm the one who's wrong, D—. There's something wrong with me, not you. Okay?

*Pause*

**D:** Okay.

*Pause*

**P:** I'd die, you know. I'd die before I let anything bad happen to you.

# Chapter 82

## Sunday | Morning

## Field

Tomorrow, that was their deadline. Monday morning, and without Andrew Levey in custody or a decent new lead, the super would reassign the case.

Field had barely got back and sat down at her desk, before Riley sprinted into her office.

'Boss, I think we've got him.'

She stopped short. 'Already? What, in Brighton?'

Riley exhaled. 'Yeah, in bloody Brighton. In the exact B&B you thought he'd be in.'

She was stunned. It was never that easy, never this straightforward to apprehend a suspect. Even the stupid ones were harder to catch, and Levey was a well-paid software engineer.

Riley looked a little crestfallen that his news hadn't been met with a bigger reaction.

'We've told the owner of the B&B not to go near him for

now,' Riley said. 'Apparently he's totally out of it – might have taken something. Are you going to blue-light it down there?'

Field shook her head. 'If we get caught in traffic and he gets away, we're fucked. Let a Brighton car bring him in.' She stood up, sweeping her notebook back into her handbag. 'Let's grab Wilson and start planning the interview.'

When she looked up, Riley was smirking. 'What?'

'Aren't you forgetting something?' he asked her, and she could have slapped the smug smile off his face, until the penny dropped.

'When did he check in?' she asked, but she knew the answer from Riley's expression.

'Friday afternoon,' he said, with a flourish. 'And his housemates hadn't seen him, had they? So, he's got no alibi for either attack.'

*It's never this easy*, Field thought again.

# Chapter 83

## Sunday | Afternoon

### Andy

It didn't come as a surprise.

Andy was always listening, and no amount of therapy or CBT could stop him. And as quiet as they thought they had been, they weren't quiet enough. The soft tread of boots on the stairs, the squeak of the banister taking someone's weight.

It was a relief.

His whole arm was on fire, radiating out from the wound on his forearm, up to his shoulder blades. The paracetamol and antiseptic weren't cutting it.

Andy slipped his noise-cancelling headphones on and lowered himself to the ground. The pain of putting his injured arm above his head made him feel sick, but it was the only way he could think to protect himself.

Even with the headphones on, the sound still reached him. The door smashing in and the shouting, all faint and muffled and far away, until someone ripped the headphones off, and he could hear the roar of it all.

Metal bit into his wrist and Andy was dragged upwards. He couldn't see who was behind him and the pressure of the noise in the room – shouting stamping doors banging – meant he probably couldn't have processed it anyway.

He twisted, trying to ask someone to pick up his neatly packed rucksack, but he was shoved forward again, and this time there was a hand on his bad arm. Andy screamed in pain, and it was a strange noise, one he'd never made before.

The yelling intensified, and whether Andy planned to resist arrest or not, within seconds he was being slammed into the wall next to the door, his face pressed hard into the embossed, flowery wallpaper.

Andy didn't know how many hands were on him. His shoulders, his head – pushed into the wall with a force he thought he probably deserved, although he couldn't say why. He couldn't understand the words, the sounds the voices were making – but their tone was angry and urgent, buzzing in his ears after they'd finished speaking.

Hot tears stung his eyes, and he closed them.

And it was David's voice he heard, in his head, telling him not to panic.

# Chapter 84

## Sunday | Afternoon

### Lily

Part of her hoped that Cal would be there, and part of her didn't.

The police had left a voicemail to say they were done, and Lily could go back home. She didn't want to go inside yet, but she wanted to see it – the house.

Their street was quiet. Windows were open in every home, curtains hanging limply in the still air. There was nothing to indicate the horrors of a few days ago.

The house looked the same as it always had. Middle of a terrace of identical little houses. Scruffy front garden, with a pop of colour from the pot of geraniums she planted for Paige, every spring.

But behind the house, over the roof, the sky was shot through with orange. A warning colour, caused by dust from the Sahara, according to the News app.

Lily's stomach rolled and pitched, and she stopped walking

for a moment, sitting down heavily on a crumbling brick wall opposite, a few houses down. She wasn't going to be sick – she was almost sure the actual vomiting was over. She just had to breathe through it.

The feeling was so familiar, now she knew what it was. When she was younger, beta blockers had made her feel ropey, but it was diazepam that had really fucked with her.

Three separate doctors had tried her on diazepam, prescribing more pills for the side effects. No one listened when she asked, begged, not to go back on it. Patronising smiles promised that if she could power through for a few short weeks, her body would adjust, and she'd start to "really feel the benefit".

The worst had been the second time, just after her thirteenth birthday. She was painfully thin already, and the pills set off a chain reaction of sickness, fever and migraines that blurred her vision for days.

*Another deep breath in.*

It wasn't the same. Scott couldn't have been giving her the pills more than once a day, and she was fitter, healthier and stronger than her thirteen-year-old self.

'Lil?'

Her eyes opened, and she had to blink Callum into focus. He frowned down at her. 'You okay?'

She gulped down the question and tried to form an answer. Angry. She should still be angry. Scott had *pitied* her – that was the worst thing. Diagnosed her and then, like the doctors before David, made decisions for her.

'What's happened?' Cal demanded.

And although Lily had been so sure that Callum would fly off the handle, potentially even assault Scott, there was a worse option. Worse – she might catch a glimpse of I-told-you-so in his expression, and have to watch Cal judge her for making such a shit choice.

She couldn't answer. She shook her head, and looked up at Cal.

He was wearing one of his own T-shirts, a white Cure band tee with a faded logo, too big on his shoulders and across his chest. There was a patch of sweat below the collar.

She'd expected him to look thinner and distraught, but he seemed solid. His shadow was blocking the sun. He was trailing the red parka behind him like a comfort blanket.

Then it dawned on her.

He was outside. Callum was out of the house.

The thought hadn't really occurred to Lily, when she visited him on the ward, but seeing him in the street, in natural light, it felt huge.

'David and Sam—' Her voice came out as a croak. 'I can't believe they're dead.'

'I know.'

'Sam was one of us,' Lily said, limply. It was a nothing comment. It didn't convey the depth of everything she felt, but she couldn't think of another way to say it.

Cal spread out the parka like a picnic blanket. As he sat down, the sunlight hit her face again. He was cross-legged on the dusty pavement, his elbows on his knees, chin in his cupped hands.

Lily was glad she didn't have to stand up yet. She glanced at the house again. There was a stray tendril of crime scene tape caught on their hedge.

'Do you remember,' Cal said abruptly. 'The session where David got us all to write those letters?'

Lily remembered.

David picked up on their fears about leaving the ward, their fear of getting ill again when they weren't wrapped up in the safety of the group.

It was a trauma, what they'd been through. David's answer

to trauma was to confront it. Put pen to paper and write to the people who let everything go so wrong in the first place.

'Paige let me read hers,' he said. 'It was to her sister – because she was so *angry* that she got to be the normal one. We set fire to it with my Zippo, behind the bins.'

'I never knew that,' Lily said, quietly.

'Who did you write to?' Cal asked.

'My parents, obviously.' Lily sniffed. The conversation was distracting her from the lump sitting low in her oesophagus. 'Some of the doctors I had. I never posted mine, either. Did you?'

'I only wrote one letter,' Callum said. His eyes were shining. 'I tried to write so many of the ones David wanted, to the people I was angry with. But I couldn't.' He laughed – a bitter, twisted sound. 'I think I'd already put all of that into the book.'

Lily eased herself off the wall, joining him on the ground. She picked up one of his hands and turned it over, resting her palm on his. Not holding hands, just palm to palm. Something they hadn't done for a long time.

'I wrote to the house,' he said.

She looked at it over his shoulder. 'You were angry with the house?'

'No.' He brushed a tear away with his other hand, then covered his eyes with it. 'I wrote to the house and asked it to keep me safe.'

He stayed hidden behind his hand, and Lily noticed that he was gripping the side of his face so tightly that the skin beneath his fingertips was bright white. The sinking in Lily's chest had nothing to do with the diazepam. She wanted to wrap her arms around Callum, stop him talking, take his pain away.

'I'm outside. I'm outside again, Lil, and I just want to call David to tell him.'

Lily clenched her jaw, every muscle in her face, trying to repress her own tears. She leaned backwards so the wall was digging into her back, above her shoulder blades.

'But I can't tell him, now. I can't call him, and I can't thank him.' Cal let his hand fall from his face, his usually dishwater-coloured eyes bright green. Another gargled laugh. 'I felt like I was cheating on him, with that new doctor.'

Lily wiped tears from both their faces. 'You can't think like that, Cal.'

He nodded, then lay backwards on the pavement, arms splayed, head on the thick ridge of the kerb.

She had a moment of hesitation, thinking of neighbours and passers-by, then lay down next to him, and looked up at the bloodshot sky.

Callum left his parka on the low wall of their house, like leaving flowers at the side of the road after a car accident.

They walked up and down residential streets. They had easily been walking for over an hour, in no particular direction.

Cal read the door numbers and gave her hand a squeeze whenever they passed a "9". He was crying, silently, the tears falling down his cheeks and onto the chest of his T-shirt, where they dried quickly.

She didn't remember choosing to hold his hand, or him taking hers. His palm was dry, despite the heat of the afternoon. He only let go to roll cigarettes.

It'd felt like this before, between them. A long time ago, when they were both ill. They were only able to speak about the hardest things, only able to deal in truths. Every conversation tore something from them or opened an old wound.

So – they didn't speak. They spent whole days, before, in total silence. It wasn't allowed, but most nights Lily would go into Callum's room and sleep in his bed. Both fully clothed – nothing ever happened. They just needed to be near each other.

Finally, as Lily's feet were starting to ache and the sun was dipping behind pink cotton-candy clouds, they were back on their road.

'Lil—'

Cal stopped walking and she turned to him, her anxiety sparking at the thought of having to go back into the house, to sit down and talk about what had happened with Scott. Try and figure out what would happen next, or pick through their memories of Sam and David.

'Lil—' he said again, and his voice broke.

She lifted her free hand to wipe away a tear and Callum trapped her palm against his cheek.

Lily looked up at him. Nodded. 'Okay.'

Then he kissed her.

# Chapter 85

## Sunday | Afternoon

## Callum

They staggered into an alleyway between two houses. Lily was against the wall, and despite the urgency between them, he was careful not to let her head hit the bricks.

It wasn't lust; it was something else.

Something more desperate and more needy. She needed him and he needed her, and as his hand formed a fist in the hair at the back of her neck Lily pressed closer. It was like they could undo the last few days – kiss away the last year of being apart.

Lily's knee pushed between his legs.

He knew she was going to bite his lip a second before she did it, and as the pain registered, as she drew blood, he pulled away, his breath ragged.

She was pale, her eyes glassy.

He let go of her hair. 'You don't look great, Lil. Are you sure we should be—'

She cut him off with another kiss. She was pressing against him again and the sticky heat of the afternoon welled in his chest, and he was somewhere else.

A bead of sweat slipped down his back, and it made him shiver.

Lily pulled away this time and Callum took a step back, slightly dazed. He looked up and down the alleyway. On either side were the graffiti-covered back fences of semi-detached houses.

Callum clenched his jaw and focused on the pain in his bottom lip. 'Let's go home.'

Lily took his hand, and they stumbled up the street. As soon as they were out of the alley Callum saw his red parka, still on the wall.

He fumbled with the lock, struggling to get the key in the door, Lily's hands were under his T-shirt, her nails raking his chest. She was kissing his neck, down his spine.

'Stop.' He laughed, and Lily took a step back, his skin tingling where her hands had been.

The key found its home and he turned it. He fell forward as the door opened.

It smelled of her.

The spell broke. The hallway smelled like Lily, like soap and lavender. Callum had never noticed it, because he lived in it. But it was like walking into her room at the Maudsley. Just like he was fifteen again, knocking for her on their way to dinner. Popping in to borrow a book or a biro or to bitch about the nurses.

It felt wrong. He took a step backwards.

If he went back in, would he ever come back out?

'Callum?' Lily asked, uncertain.

He was frozen on the doorstep.

*What were they doing?*

Sam was dead. David was dead.

Lily put a hand between his shoulder blades. 'Cal?'

Doorways. Always a point of OCD, always something to count.

*How many times had he been through this door?*

*Which doors were safe, and which needed to be counted?*

*Would something awful happen if he went through the same door nine times in one day?*

*Nine times in one month?*

*Did you count going in and out as one time or two times?*

*Why were some doors fine and others significant?*

*Why was it sometimes okay to lose count and sometimes not?*

His ears were buzzing, and his hands were numb.

He turned and looked at Lily. At her heart-shaped face, flushed from the walk.

Callum took a step backwards, through the doorway and into the house. He pulled Lily in after him.

# Chapter 86

## Sunday | Afternoon

### Andy

It was a relief when the handcuffs were taken off.

He was in a small square room, with a high bed and a first-aid station. Detective Field was by the door, arms crossed, next to a uniformed officer.

The doctor turned his arm gently as she unwound the last of the bandage.

'Now, you don't need to tell me specifics, Andy,' Dr Young said, softly, with a glance at Detective Field in the corner. 'And I've got a nurse on standby to re-dress your arm properly in a minute—'

'So, you're not a doctor?' he said, without thinking.

Andy was embarrassed by his rudeness, but she didn't seem to mind.

'Well, yes, I am. But these days I work as a forensic medical examiner. My job is to examine victims and perpetrators of crimes – I look at their injuries and advise the police, and sometimes the pathologists, involved in a case.'

Andy looked down at her dainty hands and wondered how many dead bodies she'd touched. He'd never had contamination OCD, but he wouldn't want to hold Young's hand in a hurry. These thoughts, paired with the pain as the bandages came away, made him feel sick.

The last stretch of the bandage was stuck to the hot skin and pus underneath it, and he let out a sharp hiss as she pulled it.

'So, as I was saying,' she went on, kindly, 'you don't have to go into specifics with me, because Detective Field will question you shortly.'

Young picked up a large camera.

She took a few pictures, twisting the lens to zoom in and out. He liked the sound of camera shutters. The scratching of her pen as she made notes on her clipboard wasn't pleasant, but it was bearable.

'Are you left- or right-handed, Andy?'

'Right,' he answered.

The doctor's eyes flicked to the detective in the corner.

Then she mimed drawing a line down her own arm, then made another note, which he couldn't read upside down.

She took photos of the back of his arm, then got very close to the edges of the wound. Pressed the skin of his arm with a gloved finger, so that the cut widened, for a second.

Andy heard the air above the hot red skin sizzle.

# Chapter 87

## Sunday | Afternoon

## Field

Andy was pulling his T-shirt back on, after Young had examined his torso and back for any other injuries.

From the meek character his housemates described, Field had expected Andrew Levey to be short and slight-framed. But he had to be at least six foot three, and he dwarfed the custody sergeant. He was broad-shouldered, and he wasn't just naturally big, Field was sure he must go to the gym daily.

Earlier Riley had called him a "fucking unit". He was cheerful – glad that on a day of desk duty, the case had found its way to the station.

Field was standing in the corner of the sterile medical examination room, as Young packed away her equipment and samples.

If the cut to Andy's arm was the self-inflicted injury from the night of Sam's attack, Young's testimony would be crucial evidence.

Andrew ducked his head and looked down at his shoes as he was cuffed again, thanking Young as he was led out of the room.

'Okay,' Young said, stiffly. 'Shall we go over my thoughts in your office?'

They walked through the station in awkward silence, a few of the team raising a hand to wave at Young as they passed. Field had a knot of dread in her stomach. It reminded her of walking to the headmaster's office, knowing you were in for a bollocking.

Once the door was shut, Field turned round to face her, and saw Young had her arms crossed, a pissed-off expression on her face.

'What the fuck is wrong with you?' she hissed.

Field appreciated that she wasn't yelling.

'Honestly? I don't know.' She made sure to look Young in the eyes. 'But I'm sorry. For how I spoke to you at the Volly – I really am.'

'You know it's not me you should be apologising to.' Young's shoulders dropped and she sighed, flopping into the chair opposite Field's desk. 'I spoke to Toby – and before you fly off the handle, *I* called him. He told me about last night.'

Field's face was hot. She'd delivered terrible news to hundreds, maybe thousands, of people, but the thought of facing her son was making her squirm.

'He's okay, you know,' Young said.

'That's good. I'll apologise to him tonight. We haven't had an argument since he was—'

Young shook her head. 'I don't mean about the row.'

Field took a beat.

'I mean he's *okay*, Liz. You don't need to torture yourself worrying about him, not anymore.'

Hearing it out loud – it was such an instant, visceral relief. To Field's horror, she felt tears spring into her eyes.

'I fucking hate it when you call me Liz,' she said, pressing her index fingers into her tear ducts.

'Would you prefer *Elizabeth*?' Young asked, grinning.

Field snorted.

They were going to be okay. Young didn't hold a grudge. She said life was too short, after spending hers dealing with dead and dying people.

Young rolled her eyes, and held up her notebook. 'Right, can we get on with this, please?'

'Oh shit, your date with the hot plasterer,' Field said, still sniffing. 'Weren't you going to the cinema?'

'Sunday roast.' Young laughed. 'And I can still make it, if we get a move on.'

She pulled up a photo of Andy's wound on the camera, and zoomed in. 'It's not a defensive injury, in my opinion. It's too deep, for starters. But also, with a defensive injury, he would be moving his arm, so it'd be more erratic. This is a clean line.'

'So could it be self-inflicted?' Field asked, leaning in to look at the small screen.

Young shook her head. 'Typically, a self-inflicted wound starts near the wrist, and then the knife moves towards the body.' She mimed her closed fist moving from her wrist towards her elbow.

Field's eyebrows raised. 'Typically?'

'Well, in the cases where a self-inflicted wound goes towards the wrist, they don't tend to be this deep. And you'd see hesitation marks here—' She pointed to the crease of the elbow. 'Also, if they start deep, they get shallower near the wrist.' Young mimed again. Elbow to wrist, flicking up towards the end. 'People doing this action tend to want to avoid the vein – consciously or sub-consciously.'

'And you're saying Andrew Levey's wound was—'

'Inflicted from elbow towards the wrist and got *deeper*.'

Field rubbed her forehead, which was sticky with sweat. 'You think Andy was stabbed?'

'It veered to the right at the end, so I'd say if it was someone else, they were standing opposite him and they were left-handed. I'd say it was a downward, sweeping motion, which is very different to the stab to the abdomen, which was the first injury to Sam and David.

'But could Andy have done that to himself, as a sort of alibi?' Field asked.

'Sure.' Young shrugged. 'Without the knife, it's hard to say. Have you found one?'

It was yet another thing that was making Field feel uneasy. 'No. Not among his possessions in Brighton, anyway.'

'Well, there's not much else I can give you from a single knife wound that's partially healed,' Young said, with a hopeful shrug.

'Go on,' Field said. 'Get out of here. Knock him dead.'

They both cringed at her choice of words.

Young gathered up her things. 'Well you know, I could be wrong. There are always exceptions; can't take anything for gospel, yada yada. I'll send you my report first thing tomorrow.'

'Thanks. I appreciate it.'

'Any time,' Young said.

Before Young could open the door, Field caught her in a quick firm hug.

'It'll all be fine,' Young said under her breath, before Field let her go.


Field hesitated before dialling, reluctant to ask the petulant doctor for help. However, part of being a good DCI was knowing when you were in over your head.

His mobile only rang twice before Maxwell answered. 'What?'

'Hi – Dr Maxwell, it's DCI Field—'

'Is this about Callum?' Maxwell snapped. 'I'm telling you, it's time to leave the guy alone.'

'It's not Callum,' Field said quickly. 'I need your advice. As in, your medical opinion.'

There was a pause on the other end of the line. Field spun in her desk chair and looked out of the window. The sky was stained orange, pink clouds hanging in the air, no breeze to move them.

'I've got a suspect in custody,' she went on. 'He fled London, he has links to the victims, and we found blood in his house.'

She could hear Maxwell's breathing, but he didn't speak. He was waiting for her to get to her point. The doctor was probably used to people getting things wrong. Walking onto his ward, making assumptions. It was exactly what she was trying *not* to do.

'The suspect has—' she double-checked her notes '—harm OCD. I'll be honest, I have no idea what that is. He's distressed, and I don't want to make him more anxious, but this is critical—'

She heard a familiar grinding squeak from a desk chair on the other end of the line.

'Harm OCD stems from a person's fear that they will do something awful. For example, a new mother is on a train platform and, for a split second, she imagines pushing the pram off the edge, in front of the train.'

Field blinked. When Toby was born, she sometimes imagined stepping onto a bus, leaving the pram behind at the bus stop. She'd always known she'd never do it.

'People with this form of OCD aren't able to dismiss these intrusions as we might,' Maxwell went on. 'So, the new mother starts to avoid train stations. Soon she's avoiding roads, and bridges. The more she worries about the intrusive thoughts, the more frequent and disturbing they become.'

'Okay,' Field said, slowly. 'I'm following.'

'Harm OCD stems from people's desire *not* to cause injury.' Maxwell's tone was firm, like he was talking to an idiot. Field used that voice on new recruits.

'So, harm OCD doesn't lead people to actually hurt anyone?' she proffered.

'No,' Maxwell said quietly. 'If they hurt anyone, it's usually themselves.'

# Chapter 88

## Sunday | Evening

### Field

The interview room didn't have air-con, and it felt like Field was sealing them all in as she shut the door.

Andrew had refused a solicitor. Field had agreed that Riley could sit in on the interview, partly because Wilson was knackered and needed to get her head down for an hour. But Riley had also been working his arse off to make up for his fuck-up with Callum Mulligan. He'd lost some of his swagger in the last few days, and she could tell he was grateful to be there.

'Hi, Andrew. I'm DCI Field, and this is DS Riley. Are you ready to answer some questions? How's the arm feeling?'

'It's better.' He looked down at his neatly parcelled forearm. 'I feel okay. I want to help. And you can call me Andy – if you like.'

Riley introduced the recording and asked a few opening questions.

Andy liked his job, said he had a team to manage but for the most part he was lost in code all day. He was close to his housemates, although they went out a lot and he preferred being at home. Andy had loved his mother, and they'd always had a good relationship. Her death wasn't wholly unexpected, but yes, it hit him hard.

When Riley got to the end of his easy openers, Field leaned forward.

'I want to start with how you got that injury, Andrew.'

Riley gripped his pen tighter, poised to take notes.

Andy took a breath. 'I was walking home, across Blackheath common. It was late but not totally dark yet, and there were a few drinkers about—'

'Which day was this, Andrew? What time?'

'Sorry—' he stammered. 'Thursday night. I was walking home. It was just before midnight.'

Field glanced down at the timeline in her notebook.

*Wednesday 00:20 – David attacked*

*Thursday 01:00 – Sam attacked*

'And where had you been, that evening?'

'I went to see a play, at the Old Vic,' Andrew said, looking down at his lap. 'Then I had a few drinks in a pub in Bermondsey and came home.'

'On your own?' Field prompted.

Andrew nodded.

There would be plenty of CCTV at the theatre. It was an easy alibi to check.

'Okay, thank you,' Field said. 'Carry on – you were walking across Blackheath common?'

Andy paused. 'So, there's a place off the common, a little nook. Surprisingly few people know about it. It's called Point Hill. When the pubs and stuff are busy and there's loads of people around, I go there. To think and enjoy the quiet.

'I struggle with noise. Even now – after the therapy and stuff.' He twisted his hands in his lap. 'I don't let sound rule my life anymore but it's still nice, having quieter places to go.' His breathing hitched and he closed his eyes, his broad frame folding in on itself. 'Places that feel safe.'

Next to her, Field could sense Riley was humming with excitement, impatient to get to the root of Andrew's story.

Nonchalant, she turned the pen in front of her ninety degrees, so it was facing Riley. He saw the action and registered her warning not to interrupt.

Andy carried on. 'From Point Hill you can see all across the city. Sit on a bench and watch the world go by, and even if you can hear the noise from the common, it's all muffled.'

His speech was speeding up, the sentences running into each other. Field trusted Riley not to interrupt. They needed Andy to tell this in his own words, however rushed and garbled. His eyes were still screwed shut.

'But I can't switch it off, even there. David—'

'It's okay. Take your time,' Riley said, after the pause dragged on.

Andy took a deep breath. 'David said that was okay. People with hay fever are sensitive to dust and pollen, and I might always have a sensitivity to noise. It makes my chest go tight and my heart races, my palms sweat – I might not be able to control that *physical* response. All I can control is how I react to it.

'Do you know I used to pray that one day I'd go deaf?' Andy's eyes flew open, wet with tears. 'How fucked up is that? How selfish?'

It chimed with something Callum had said. He'd called himself selfish, too.

'What happened on the hill, Andrew?' Field asked, gently.

'Even all these years later . . .' his voice was barely a whisper

'. . . I still do what David taught me. I was anxious that night – I can't even remember why now – and I wanted to put my headphones on. Cancel the noise out. But I didn't let myself. I sat with the anxiety. Let myself feel it.'

They were inching closer, Field felt. Riley was rapt.

She added a line to the timeline: *Friday 00.00 a.m.*

'Sometimes you have to let yourself get anxious,' he said. His shoulders were so hunched, so clenched, that he must be in physical pain. 'You've got to prove to yourself that you can *listen* to the noise and not block it out, and even though you'll be anxious, you'll be okay.

'So that's what I was doing. And that's why I heard them coming.' A sob escaped him. 'David saved my life. Again.'

Field gave him a second to wipe his eyes.

'I need us to go through that again, Andy. Step by step, if you can.'

# Chapter 89

## Sunday | Evening

## Andy

Andy tried to describe it to the detectives – that moment on the hill, before it all happened.

He'd almost convinced himself that he was imagining the footsteps, that it was anxiety playing tricks on him, that he was hearing his own heartbeat pounding in his ears.

But he'd got up off the bench and spun round and seen the slight figure, hood up, knife in hand.

'I asked what they wanted,' he said, looking up at Field. 'I assumed they were going to mug me. Wanted my phone or something.'

He focused on Field's stern face. The flecks of grey at her temples, the studious expression. If he listened, and he always listened, he could hear the rustle of her starched white shirt.

'It was like something out of a film. She circled the bench, and I was edging away—'

'She?'

He hesitated. 'I think it was a girl. I mean, it could have been a small guy, but they moved like a woman.'

Field nodded for him to continue.

'I kept my eyes on the knife and kept asking: "What do you want? What do you want?", but she didn't say anything, and then she . . . ran at me.'

It had happened quickly, and he was embarrassed. Someone his size shouldn't be scared of someone so small. If he'd had his wits about him, if he hadn't been so bloody anxious when it happened—

'She lunged at me with the knife, and she must have cut my arm.' He held it up, then felt stupid. 'To be honest, I didn't even feel it, I just kept stepping backwards and then I tripped and fell and—'

The male detective was taking notes without looking down at the paper.

He needed them to believe him. The story had seemed too strange to report to police, had happened too quickly, and now speaking it out loud it sounded ridiculous, made up.

'Someone came round the corner, and she ran for it, sprinted past them. I got up and walked away and it was only when I got home that I realised I'd been—'

*Stabbed*. He couldn't say the word – it sounded too melodramatic.

'That I was bleeding.'

The scratching on the paper was distracting him. He rested his head on one hand, to muffle the sound, an old trick. An old coping mechanism that only half worked because he could still hear the pen. He'd done something to try and block the noise out, and because he'd given in to this small action, his anxiety was already tugging at him, trying to get him to do another.

'The attacker, were they left- or right-handed, Andy?' she asked.

He tried to picture it. Put himself back in the moment. 'Left.'

'Good, well done,' Field said. 'So, you got home, and then what happened?'

He could hardly hear the question over the sound of the pen, but then the writing stopped. Andy breathed again.

'I don't know what time it was exactly. I tried to sleep, but the bleeding wasn't stopping. I was awake most of the night, until I decided to just leave.'

When he got home, his main concern was the blood. Not dripping blood on the carpets or leaving smears on the walls. He was confused and upset, and it felt important, so important, not to leave blood anywhere.

'And why did you decide to go to Brighton?' the man asked, and Andy sensed his pen hovering above the pad.

He clenched his fists and focused on the question.

'I don't know,' he said, with a sigh. 'I knew David had been attacked. I saw it in the news. I didn't know about Sam, not until earlier when they arrested me.'

*Sam.*

Sometimes, on the ward, it had felt like Lily and Callum and Paige were all so similar, and so *exuberant*, that he was the outsider. He didn't mind – it wasn't their fault. They never left him out on purpose.

But Sam always made sure he was included.

'But it was like I could feel that someone was coming for us. I was in my room, and I kept hearing footsteps, imagining they were creeping up on me all over again. It felt important to get somewhere they couldn't find me,' he said, looking up at them both.

Field had a closed expression on her face, all buttoned-up. He had no idea whether she believed him.

# Chapter 90

## Sunday | Evening

### Field

'Fuck.' Field slammed the door to her office, and it rattled the hinges.

'It wasn't him,' Riley said, again. 'It wasn't Levey.'

Field tried to marshal her thoughts.

They'd wasted a full day tracking him down, pouring all their efforts into finding him. It'd felt too easy to track him down because it *was*. He wasn't hiding from the police; he was hiding from his attacker.

'Unless he's lying,' Riley said, and she opened her eyes. He was pacing in front of their main board, one hand over his eyes. 'Could he be lying?'

The door opened and Wilson stepped in, breathless. She'd been watching the interview over the CCTV. 'Boss, you'll want to see this.'

She held up an image on her phone. 'The Brighton team just found it in his room, shoved behind the bed.'

It was another page of the *Disordered Diagnosis* paper. Page three, for the third attack in three days.

'I think he's telling the truth.' Field stared at the newly printed photograph of Andrew, underneath the heading "PATIENT C".

She picked up the whiteboard eraser and wiped away the word "Suspect" below his photo.

'Riley, get hold of the Old Vic. See if they had a ticket booking for Thursday night under his name, and then I want someone in Waterloo, looking at the CCTV from that night. Wilson, put out a call for witnesses on Blackheath for between 10 p.m. and 1 a.m. And get onto the CCTV from that area. There's got to be decent coverage – it's high footfall.'

Andrew Levey wasn't their perpetrator. He was the third victim.

# Chapter 91

**P:** I'm so tired.

*Pause*

**P:** I want a break, just one day where I don't have it. This *disorder*.

*Pause*

**P:** I want to wake up normal. I want to worry about whether my hair looks nice, not whether touching my hair will make my hands greasy because it's been two weeks since I last had the energy to wash my fucking hair.
I'm so tired.
I can't do it anymore.
I can't get up tomorrow morning unless you take this away. Give it to someone else.

*Pause*

**P:** Give it to anyone. I don't deserve it. I haven't done anything wrong.
**D:** No. You haven't done anything wrong.

# Chapter 92

## Sunday | Evening

### Callum

A shiver ran down his spine, as the sweat on Lily's skin cooled against his.

The cracked leather sofa was clammy and uncomfortable, and the scratchy blanket they'd thrown down tickled his thighs, but Lil hadn't been in his bedroom since the break-up, and Scott's stuff was still scattered around Lily's.

Callum drew soft circles on her shoulder blade.

She was breathing normally, but he could feel her heart was still thumping.

'Are you okay, Lil?'

She turned her head so she could see him. 'I don't know.'

He shifted, and they spent a few awkward moments trying to get comfortable, the sofa not wide enough for them both to move easily. Callum settled back down with his hands behind his head, and Lily lay on his chest, her hand over his heart. He noticed how thin her wrists were.

Lily closed her eyes. 'I think, maybe, when I thought I was better, maybe I wasn't.'

Callum made a noise in his throat.

'Like, maybe all this time, when I thought I was keeping my head healthy, I was kidding myself.'

He twisted a lock of her hair around one finger, going cross-eyed as he considered it. 'Or are you overthinking it now? Are you trying to find evidence that you haven't been okay all this time, when you have?'

'I mean, that does sound like me, sure,' Lily said, with a smile. Her smile – the one that could cut to the core of him. 'But I don't know. I've been thinking about it for a while.'

The sun passed behind a cloud, and the room was suddenly greyscale.

She sighed. 'I'm just tired.'

'Don't do that,' Cal said, sharply. 'Don't dismiss it.'

The new edge in his voice, that he hadn't meant to use, felt like coming back to reality. Lily sat up, put one arm across her chest, and groped on the floor for her T-shirt.

'I shouldn't be putting my shit onto you. Not when you're struggling.'

Cal laughed and didn't move to cover himself. 'When am I not struggling?'

Her T-shirt had rolled itself into a tube, and she wrestled with it, her back to him. Once it was on, she pulled on her pants and sat on the edge of the sofa, facing the bookshelves, her face in profile.

Her features were so familiar to him. The slight frown lines between her eyebrows. The vulnerability of the white skin of her neck below her hairline, when she had her hair up.

There was a brief flash of longing. Not for them now, not for the Lily in front of him. He wanted to be seventeen again, the punk version of himself, watching Lily set fire to her old food diary and give it a Viking burial down the Thames.

'How's your head, Lil?' he asked. 'Explain it to me.'

She stayed silent.

'Please,' he said.

'I just feel like I'm on the defence. Always.' She laughed, but it had no humour in it. 'I'm constantly on my guard. For the next behaviour, the next intrusive thought. Whatever it is that would send me on a spiral.' She blew air up onto her face and put a hand on her stomach. 'And being on my guard worked, didn't it? Because I haven't spiralled. I've been okay, I've looked after both of us—' She hesitated and looked down at him.

He nodded his assent. He wouldn't make her feel guilty for saying what she had to say.

'I've gone to work and got out of bed and got my nails done and read the Booker prize winners.'

'You got promoted to head of Key Stage 1,' Callum added. 'You survived being dumped by me. You cleaned the oven last year.'

'I got a tattoo I don't regret. I do meal prep, and I sort your benefits. I phone my grandparents once a week. I stopped buying scratch cards.' She paused. 'And I haven't blacked out or skipped meals or made an embarrassment of myself. So – I thought, yeah. Success.'

There were tears in her eyes. Cal didn't say anything.

They just sat, and then the sun came back out, picking out the bright accents among the spines of the bookshelves.

'I'd beaten it. I *was* beating it. I'd won.' She sank her toes into their fluffy green rug. 'But that wasn't "better", was it?'

Cal shook his head. 'It's not cancer, Lil. You don't get an "all clear". But look at where we were, and look at how far you've—'

'I know.' Lil rubbed her eyes with her fists. 'I've come so far. I'm a mental medical fucking miracle.'

He didn't know how to help her. Had never gotten well enough to struggle with the grey area of being "fine".

He put his boxers and his T-shirt back on in silence, then sat up next to her.

The closeness – the madness that had overcome them, was gone.

She sighed. 'Normal people aren't on the defensive every day, are they?'

Lily jumped at the same time Callum did – and turned towards the noise from the back of the house. The back door had blown open and smashed into the kitchen wall.

'To be fair,' Cal said, standing up to go and close it. 'What the fuck would we know about normal people?'


The back door slammed again.

He navigated the hallway in the dark, feeling for evidence that the search people hadn't put things back properly, but not finding any. He'd replace the light bulb tomorrow.

The back door continued to smack into the wall, and he gritted his teeth, stepping into the dining room.

It was tidier than they'd left it. The chairs were tucked under the dining table, and the empty cans and bottles had been removed.

Callum wanted to rush, run into the kitchen before the ninth time the door hit the wall. But that was irrational, because he would get there before the ninth time anyway, and it didn't *matter* if there was a ninth time.

The evening sun was streaming into the narrow kitchen. The grass needed sorting. Callum hadn't been out into their little garden for over a year.

He'd go out there tomorrow and cut the grass. He loved

the smell, and he wasn't going to waste the ability to get out, now he had it.

As he closed the door and slid the top bolt across, a shadow fell across his arms.

He turned, expecting to see Lily, but all he saw was the knife.

# Chapter 93

## Sunday | Evening

## Callum

He put both hands up. She must have been standing behind the door.

The girl was about a foot shorter than him, vivid dyed-purple hair. Thick make-up circled her dark eyes, and her skin was pale, like she hadn't seen the sun for a long time. She was standing in the kitchen doorframe, blocking off his access to the rest of the house.

'What do you want?' he asked, quietly.

He didn't want Lily to hear, to come in and startle the girl. Callum took half a step back, so he was leaning against the back door.

Their kitchen was a narrow galley layout, with a row of ancient cabinets on each side. The knife block wasn't in its usual spot by the sink.

To Callum's left was the tiny bathroom, always freezing cold in winter. To his right was his nan's big ancient fridge.

The girl was standing by the oven, at the far end nearest the door to the dining room. They were at a stand-off, at either end.

Even if Callum rushed forward and tried to get the knife, she'd have the advantage. There was no room to get round her or perform some elaborate tackle – the kind he'd seen on telly but never even attempted in a playfight.

He was weirdly calm. A life spent killing yourself with stress over the completely illogical must mean you've run out of adrenaline by the time something truly fucked happens.

She tossed her hair over one shoulder, speaking in a half-whisper. 'What's wrong, Callum? You don't recognise me?'

Callum frowned. He didn't know her – where would he know her from? He hadn't left the house or used the internet for two years.

His phone was in his jeans, on the living room floor. Callum pulled the edge of his T-shirt down. The girl registered the action and smirked.

Someone was pointing a knife at him, and he was in a T-shirt and his fucking boxers.

He didn't have many options. He'd just bolted the door to the garden. The lock was stiff, and he'd never undo it fast enough. The chipboard door to the loo wouldn't keep her out, and while he was cowering behind it, what would she do to Lily?

All his instincts, his gut – everything was screaming the same thing:

*Protect Lily.*

When *Darlings, Obsessed* was first published, he got intense fan mail and messages on social media, girls sending photos of themselves. Was it better to lie? Pretend he knew who she was?

'Let's call your girlfriend in, shall we?' the girl hissed. 'Let's see if Lily knows who I am.'

The calm feeling, the illusion – fell away at once.

'Shout for her,' the girl said, holding the knife higher. The sun caught the tip of it and it glinted gold for a second. A cinematic detail that only added to the unreality of the situation.

'You can do what you want to me,' he said, voice urgent. 'But don't touch Lily. She's done nothing wrong.'

The smirk disappeared, and the girl's expression hardened. She took two steps towards him in the small space.

He could make a grab for the knife, from this close. Even if she ended up fucking stabbing him, he could shout at Lily to get out, to get away.

Before he could stop it, his brain filled with an image of Sam – bleeding to death, choking, begging him with her eyes to save her, to not let her die. The feel of her blood slipping over his fingers, the smell of it—

'Call her,' the girl hissed again.

Callum didn't want to die like that.

'Lil?' he shouted, and his voice was strangled, caught in his throat. 'Lil – come here.'

Lily shouted back, but he couldn't make out the words.

He was a coward.

But there were two of them – and only one of this crazy bitch. Maybe together they would be able to overpower her.

His last, desperate thought was to grab the toaster as a shield, but even that was too far to reach.

Lily was talking as she came to find him. The girl pointed with the knife, and Callum backed away, hands up again. She stood behind the door, so Lily would walk past her and into the room.

Then Lil was there, in front of him, frowning.

'Well?' Lily said, hands on her hips. 'What?'

Callum reached forward and grabbed her by the forearm,

yanking her towards him, away from the blade. Lily's protest died in her throat as she saw the girl.

Callum's grip on Lily's arm tightened, hard enough now to leave bruises, but if he let go of her, if their skin broke contact, then something might happen, and he'd be responsible.

He pushed Lily behind him, putting his body between her and the knife.

'How fucking sweet,' she said, her voice a drawl. 'So protective.'

'What is your fucking problem?' Callum snapped.

'You,' she said evenly. 'Both of you. *You* are my problem.'

Callum didn't speak. He could feel Lily trembling.

*It's okay*, he tried to say to Lil, with his mind. *I won't let anything happen to you.*

He would keep her talking, keep the situation calm. The neighbours would hear, or he'd be able to hold her off long enough for Lily to escape.

'You're both hypocrites,' the girl spat, and the knife sliced through the air as she spoke. 'Hypocrites and liars.'

He could see the pain on her face, and the fear – and it was then that he recognised her. So different to the Paige he'd known, the child in the unit, the girl with the wicked laugh. But at the same time, they were so similar, Callum didn't know how he hadn't seen it straight away.

'I recognise you,' he said, in a low voice. Lily took his hand. 'I know who you are.'

# Chapter 94

## Sunday | Evening

## Field

Wilson hung up. 'Lily Stewart's boyfriend said she left his flat this afternoon, and he hasn't seen her since.'

They didn't have a suspect in custody, they had another victim. Their perpetrator hadn't broken from the schedule for the first three nights – one a night – even if they had botched it with Andrew Levey.

That meant someone else on their list was in danger.

*Callum Mulligan. Lily Stewart. Penny Moore.*

'Callum was in hospital on Thursday night,' Riley said, a defeated note in his voice. 'He can't have been wielding a knife on Blackheath common, and he doesn't fit the description.'

This was a make-or-break moment. Field could either give in to the pressure and crack up, or she could go back to basics.

Motive.

'*Why?*' she asked, her voice steady. 'Why, all these years later, is someone picking them off?'

Her eyes darted from Riley to Wilson.

'*Why?*' Field asked again.

They stared back at her, eyes blank.

'The paper,' Wilson said, finally. 'It's got to go back to David Moore's paper, his write-up of the trial.'

The paper that told semi-famous writer Callum Mulligan's teenage story and earned Dr Moore his career. The paper left at all three of the stabbings.

Unless it wasn't about the paper itself. Unless – it was about something that happened at the Maudsley.

What had Penny said?

*He had closer relationships with some of his patients than with me.*

*He loved being their doctor more than he loved being married.*

'They're panicking,' Wilson said, quietly. 'They fell and got injured when they attacked Sam, then they botched it with Andrew.'

'But there was no break for three nights.' Riley was staring at the floor. 'It's like they didn't want to keep going, but—'

'But maybe they had to,' Wilson finished. 'Like it's a compulsion.'

Three stabbings in three days. Then nothing in the early hours of Saturday or Sunday.

Lily safely locked away at her boyfriend's house. Callum in hospital.

The adrenaline was leaving her, now. The analytical part of Field's brain was taking over, method and logic. Field had grown up on Sherlock Holmes and Poirot, knew that the only way through the confusion was cold reason.

She held up a hand. 'Andy was sure it was a girl who attacked him.'

The room was stifling, the boards of half-baked information mocking her from the walls.

She should never have let Maxwell release Callum.

'Let's go with his theory, and say our perpetrator is a woman. She must have been involved in the trial, or linked to it in some way.'

Riley and Wilson shot a glance at each other, knowing Field was building up to her big rhetorical question.

'Who would be most likely to put off attacking Callum Mulligan? Who would leave him until last?'

'Lily Stewart,' they answered, in unison.

Field swore and raked her hands through her hair.

Was that right? Was it Lily?

She'd sat in on Callum's interview. Lily had no alibi for Sam, and Callum was an unreliable alibi for David.

But it didn't *feel* right. Something was still nagging at her.

Wilson and Riley were speaking in low, urgent voices. Field tuned out their conversation and stared at the board, eyes moving from photograph to photograph.

Her gaze lingered on a name, towards the bottom of the board—

Something slotted into place.

'Boss?' Riley prompted.

'She knew where Andrew lived.' Field breathed. 'How did we miss that? She said it – Blackheath. No social media profiles and it took us a day to trace him, so how would she know?'

They stared back at her.

'She knew them, when they were teenagers. She visited the hospital. Ruby – the sister. She knew them all.'

348

# Chapter 95

## Sunday | Evening

### Andy

He'd been sat in the room for so long, he was pretty sure they'd forgotten about him. They'd paused the interview and left him with a bored uniformed officer. Andy sat still and tried not to listen to his heavy breathing.

Eventually, Detective Field came back in, with DS Riley and a female officer he hadn't seen before. Field looked harried, and Riley was clutching armfuls of folders.

'Interview resumed at—' Field glanced at the clock '—6.58 p.m. We'll put you somewhere more comfortable and process your release tonight, Andy. But first—' Field took a seat, but on the very edge of the chair – like she'd be up again at any moment. 'When did you last see Ruby Jacobs?'

'Ruby?' Andy frowned. 'It would have been Paige's funeral, I guess.'

Paige's funeral had been one of the worst days of his life.

All the rows of people, and the sounds of sniffling, orders

of service being fanned in front of damp eyes. The long groan of the church doors in the wind, the rustle of black clothes.

He didn't hear any of it. None of it mattered.

He remembered sitting in the back row, holding Sam's hand and watching Paige's family walking through the church, to their pew at the front.

There was no way that many people would turn up for his funeral. The priest spoke about rebirth and Paige's sister got up and read the eulogy. Neither of her parents could face it. They stayed sitting, clutching each other.

Paige was a talented actress. She was a writer. She was an *OCD survivor*.

Was he an OCD survivor? He supposed so.

'Andrew?' Field said, snapping him out of his thoughts. He was back in the room, back at the table, in the station, being interviewed. 'Are you in contact with her?'

'No.'

'Does she know where you live? Has she been to your house?'

He looked between the detectives. 'No?'

She turned and Riley handed her a file. The female detective shifted from foot to foot. Field spread the file open, and a familiar face looked up at him.

Older than last time they'd been in the same room. At the church.

Andy's vision blurred, and then he blinked the big dark eyes back into focus. Took in the uneasy, familiar smile of the girl in the photograph.

'You haven't seen her?' Field pressed. 'Not even walking past her in the street.'

'What is this?' Andy shook his head, eyes going back to the photo of Ruby. 'No—'

It was surreal, how similar they looked. Sam said so too,

after the funeral. There was only ten months between them. Basically twins, Paige said in a group session once.

Riley had a hand on the door, poised to dash out.

Andy put his hand out for the photo and stared down into the face.

'Is that who you think did this?' he asked. 'Paige's sister?'

# Chapter 96

## Sunday | Evening

## Field

Wilson was on the phone to Control. Riley was calling Callum, putting the phone down when it went to voicemail and hitting redial.

'TSG and Firearms are at least forty minutes away,' Wilson said, slamming the phone down. 'Major incident ongoing in Orpington.'

Wilson and Riley stood next to each other, waiting to be told what to do.

'I need one of you to stay here, co-ordinate the support,' Field said. 'I'm going to Callum Mulligan's – in case they're there.'

Riley and Wilson exchanged glances.

'Take Riley,' Wilson said. 'He's stronger than me – and he's a better driver than either of us.'

'Are you sure?' Riley asked. 'I don't mind—'

Teamwork – better late than never. But Wilson was right, Riley drove faster than either of them.

'Okay, fine. Riley – we'll blue-light it to Plumstead,' Field snapped.

He reached for his suit jacket, on the back of his desk chair.

'Leave that,' Field said. Riley froze, one arm in the jacket. 'You'll need a stab vest.'

# Chapter 97

## Sunday | Evening

## Callum

'Tell me why you're doing this.'

The girl ignored him, pacing back and forwards in front of the door to the dining room. She held the knife in her left hand, but he noticed she winced whenever she lifted her arm above elbow height.

He couldn't remember her name. It was there, on the tip of his tongue, but he couldn't remember it. Paige had spoken about her sister a lot. "Basically twins" – ten months apart. Callum couldn't believe he hadn't spotted it from the start.

Her eyes – she had the same big dark eyes as Paige.

Lily whispered something behind him, but he missed it. He turned his head slightly towards her, indicating he needed her to say it again.

'Ruby,' she hissed, and the girl turned around.

'Remembered my fucking name then?'

*Ruby.*

Callum took a breath. 'Look, Ruby. I don't know what you think we've done or why you're here, but we can work this out.'

'Yeah,' she said, with a laugh. 'Yeah, we can.'

Ruby stopped pacing.

'Can I say something?' Lily said, softly, trying to push past Callum, and stand in front of him. He put an arm out to stop her.

'No. Actually you can't.' Ruby pointed. 'Move the fridge.'

'What?' Callum frowned. 'The fridge?'

'Don't you know what a fucking fridge is?' Ruby's voice rose to a shout, and she pointed at their old, heavy fridge with the knife. 'Push it in front of the back door. *Now.*'

Callum looked at Lily. She was shaking with fear, and it hardened his resolve. He wouldn't get anxious. He wouldn't fuck this up. All he had to do was keep Ruby calm, find out what she wanted, and protect Lily. At any cost.

The fridge hadn't been unplugged since his nan installed it in the early Nineties, and he strained to pull the plug from its socket. It gave way suddenly, and he stumbled backwards.

Ruby flinched, raising the knife instinctively, but Callum caught himself, hands up again.

Lily had to press herself against the cabinets, so Callum had room to push the fridge in front of the back door. He could hear jars sliding around on the shelves, clinking into each other. The muscles in his arms strained with the effort.

One of the fridge's feet caught on the lino, tearing a chunk out of it and sending the whole thing teetering, almost straight through the kitchen window.

Lily put her hands up to help steady it, and finally Callum got it into position, in front of the broken back door.

'Good,' Ruby said.

He hadn't noticed the bag at Ruby's feet, until she leaned

355

down and dug around in it. She pulled out a handful of cable ties and threw them onto the kitchen floor, where they scattered around his feet.

'Tie your girlfriend's hands together.'

'Ruby. Let Lily go – we can sort this out between us. I just want to talk to you.'

Ruby put the index finger of her left hand onto the tip of the knife, and Callum watched as a bead of blood formed.

She was fucking cracked in the head.

'It's okay,' Lily whispered, holding her hands out to him, her wrists touching each other. 'Do what she says.'

Callum blocked Ruby's view as he did the cable tie up, trying to communicate through his eyes that Lily should hold her wrists apart, so she could slip her hands out.

Lily looked up at him, and despite her fear, there was a glint in her eye. It was a look she'd given him many, many times before.

*Be careful, Callum.*

'Hurry up,' Ruby snapped.

He pulled the tie tight, but not too tight. Before he moved out of the way, Lily gave an experimental movement of her wrists, and gave him a tiny nod.

'Good,' Ruby said. She beckoned Lily towards her. 'Time to split you two up, I reckon.'

Lily shot Callum a look.

Ruby laughed. 'Not like that – you can be star-crossed lovers if you like. I don't give a fuck.'

Callum's whole body was vibrating. He didn't understand what was going on, or what he was supposed to do next. His feet were cold, and he looked down at them, amazed he had even noticed.

Next from the bag was a dark purple silk scarf. Ruby threw it on the floor at Callum's feet. 'Gag her.'

Callum picked it up and stared at it. It was Paige's, he was sure of it. Sometimes she would scratch at her throat when she was having a panic attack, and she'd wear the purple scarf to cover up the marks.

*Why is she doing this, P?*

Callum held an end in each hand and passed the scarf over Lily's head.

Lily squeezed her eyes closed as he tied the gag at the back of her head. When she opened her eyes again, her lashes were wet with tears.

Ruby gestured. 'Come here.'

'Wait, leave Lil here, and we can—'

Ruby took two steps towards Lily and seized the end of the cable tie, pulling it as tight as it would go. Lily let out a yelp, as the plastic cut deep into the skin of her wrists.

'Don't move,' Ruby snapped at him, pressing the knife against Lily's neck. 'And don't fucking speak, either of you.'

Ruby led Lily into the dining room by her hands, pushed her towards the stairs. From the doorway of the kitchen Callum saw Lily fall forward, unable to catch herself with her tied hands. She hit the stairs with a sickening thud, her arms twisted at awkward angles.

'Oops,' Ruby said, with a laugh, pulling Lily backwards by the hair so she could right herself. 'Now get upstairs.'

Lily was whimpering in pain.

'Don't follow us,' Ruby called over her shoulder. 'And don't move, or I'll slit her throat.'

He listened for the steps on the stairs and dashed into the dining room.

Callum didn't dare run to the living room for his jeans. He wrenched open the door of the tumble dryer, and pulled out a pair of jogging bottoms. When they were on, he felt instantly better, less vulnerable.

He should make a dash for his phone, call the police. He should run out of the front door, screaming for help.

*Should*

*Should*

*Should*

He couldn't focus long enough on one train of thought to weigh up a rational decision.

And then Ruby was back.

She blew air upwards, but her hair was stuck to her forehead with sweat, and didn't move.

He hated her, Callum realised. He hated her, and if he got the chance, he'd kill her.

'Front door,' she said, simply.

Callum didn't move.

'Move that big cabinet in front of the front door,' she said. 'Now.'

She made sure she stayed a few metres away from him, knife raised.

As he walked through the dining room, Callum looked up at the ceiling. Imagined Lily lying on her bed upstairs, straining to listen to what was happening.

He didn't bother taking the crap off the sideboard, letting things fall from it as it moved. It wasn't as heavy as the fridge, but it was another narrow space to navigate.

Ruby swiped at her fringe with the back of the hand that was holding the knife, and inspected his work.

The cabinet was slightly wider than the hallway, so it wasn't flush against the door, but it was wedged against each wall. The door wouldn't open more than an inch from outside.

Two years. He'd finally escaped the house after two years.

And now he was trapped inside it again.

# Chapter 98

## Sunday | Evening

## Callum

For the first time, Ruby looked unsure.

They were sat at opposite ends of the dining table, Callum at the far end, away from the doors and the stairs up to Lily. She hadn't cable-tied his hands. He just had to keep her calm, and make her think he wasn't a threat.

Ruby's grip on the knife was so hard, her knuckles were turning white.

It'd probably only been ten minutes, since he found Ruby in the kitchen. He couldn't check, because his pathological fucking fear of clocks meant there were none in the house. But moving the fridge, Lily being led upstairs, the front door – it felt like time had slowed down for all of it.

'I watched you, you know. At the hospital, when I came to visit Paige with mum. I'd see you all. You never gave me a second glance.'

Callum felt drained, and he didn't speak, didn't want to make it worse.

'Paige talked about you, Callum.' Ruby's voice had dropped an octave, and she didn't look up at Callum as she spoke.

'She did?'

Ruby nodded. Wiped a tear from her eye, smearing eyeliner across one cheek. 'She was in awe of you.'

His heart swelled a little, and he closed his eyes. 'She was the strongest of all of us. By the time we got to that ward, we were all broken. Completely shattered. And it didn't matter, what she was going through, how much she was hurting – she was always there. Always.'

Ruby sniffed. 'It was scary. Watching her get sicker and sicker. When I was ten, she used to wake me up in the night and make me get up and – and she'd make me shower. Downstairs, so Mum and Dad wouldn't hear.'

'She told us about that,' Callum said, quietly. 'She always regretted the impact it had on you, her OCD.'

'She did?' Ruby turned to him, her eyes wide.

'She talked about you a lot.' He kept his voice light, but he didn't want to hear about Paige's OCD from Ruby's point of view.

Callum couldn't sit opposite the girl who had killed David and Sam, and feel sorry for her. Poor Ruby, how hard for *her*.

'I can't imagine how you felt when she died,' he offered. 'But you should know, she was like a sister to me.'

Callum jumped – Ruby had leapt to her feet and knocked her chair over.

'She wasn't a sister to you, or you'd – you would have *stopped it*—' She took a shuddering breath. 'She was *my* sister. I would have protected her.'

He leaned backwards in his chair, trying to put a few centimetres of extra space between them. 'Protected her? From what?'

# Chapter 99

**P:** You should have stopped me.
**D:** I know.

*Pause*

**P:** But you didn't, and I didn't want you to.

*Pause*

**P:** It's all right, D—. It is.
**D:** It's not all right. How is it all right?
**P:** It's not that big a deal. It doesn't have to a be a big deal, okay?

*Pause*

**P:** I promise I won't tell anyone.

# Chapter 100

## Sunday | Evening

### Lily

Lily stared up at the ceiling.

She'd looked up at it so often. Knew where all the cracks were, where they intersected. Her own set of constellations.

There was no noise from downstairs, and she closed her eyes – as though it would make her hear better.

Every slight movement made her feel sick, made her wince in pain.

She was so tired.

*Callum.*

She shouldn't have closed her eyes, because despite everything, the panic and her fear for Callum, she was sinking into the mattress and falling asleep.

# Chapter 101

## Sunday | Evening

## Field

Sunday night and the roads were clear.

Riley flew through Greenwich and blue-lit it down the straight road through Charlton, Woolwich, Plumstead.

She had failed to look into the sad, helpful sister. Failed to properly investigate the family of the dead girl.

En route Field made call after call. Lily's number, then Callum's. Control had promised to divert a support vehicle when one became free, but with nothing concrete, they'd be lucky to get more than that.

As they reached the end of Conway Road, Riley turned the lights off and slowed to a crawl, looking for a parking space that wouldn't be visible from Callum's house.

Riley switched the car off and looked across at her. He was pale, but his jaw was set as he looped his thumbs into the thick vest over his shirt.

Only a few days ago, the street was bloodstained and swarming with forensics.

But now the house looked empty, the lights off. The small front garden was still overgrown, the paint peeling off the front door. Perfectly ordinary.

# Chapter 102

## Sunday | Evening

## Callum

'She was only *thirteen*. It was abuse.'

He was bewildered. He'd seen people manic, people in full-blown psychosis, and this wasn't it. Ruby was still on her feet, chest heaving now, tears rolling down her face.

At least Lily was safe, out of sight upstairs.

'Do you think I wanted this?' She spread her arms, knife pointed at the ceiling. 'I never knew, I never fucking knew, because she didn't tell me. But *you* were in the hospital with her. You were there with her and *him* and you should have known—'

'Ruby,' Callum said. He lifted his hands up in front of his chest. 'You're not making sense—'

Ruby's tears were carving inky black trails down her face, and she wiped her cheeks with her sleeve, smearing most of the eyeliner away.

Callum tried again. 'Is this about the accident? About what happened to Paige?'

'Don't say her fucking name,' Ruby screamed.

The neighbours had to be hearing this. They knew what had happened on Thursday, so surely someone would phone the police? He needed DCI Field to smash through the front door and—

'I always thought it was an accident,' she said, her voice a whisper. 'So fucking cruel, after everything she went through, to die just as she was better. But do you know what I think killed her?'

'The car. It was raining, she skidded—' he stammered.

'It was him,' Ruby cried. 'What he did to her. She must have wanted to make the pain stop—'

Callum wanted to screw his eyes closed but he didn't. Ruby was pointing at him with the knife.

'She was all on her own. Maybe she didn't want to die, maybe the crash was supposed to be a cry for help.'

He was lost again.

'I think you knew, all of you.' Ruby was staring at a point past his head. 'But even if you didn't, it's not fair, is it? That you all got to go on living your lives, being happy. An author. A teacher. Sam studying a PhD. Andy and his well-paid job.'

He stayed still. Perfectly still – like playing dead with a bear, in case his breathing, or flinching or anything set her off again.

'But, yeah. I think she did it on purpose. After the trauma, she wanted to die—' Ruby wiped more tears away, shrugged at Callum, helplessly. 'I don't know. I don't know any more.'

'What trauma, Ruby? I don't know what you're talking about—'

She snorted, then turned and walked to the kitchen, bending down for the bag, and in the few seconds she wasn't looking at him, Callum threw desperate looks around the room. No phone, nothing he could use as a weapon. If he screamed or cried out, she'd probably go for him.

Ruby came back, holding a plastic wallet stuffed with paper, starting to split down the edges from being overfilled.

'What is that, Ruby?' he asked, hoping he could keep her talking.

Ruby threw the folder over to him, and it landed between them, on the table.

'Pick it up,' she barked.

'No,' he said, flatly.

Ruby's eyebrows disappeared into her fringe. 'Excuse me?'

'I said no,' he said, more loudly. 'Tell me what it is.'

He met Ruby's eyes, and she didn't blink.

If she was going to stab him, she'd have burst in and done it. She was toying with him, but Lily was okay. If Ruby was focused on him, maybe he'd buy enough time to figure out how to get them out of this.

'What is it?' he said, pointing at the folder. 'Tell me.'

'That file is the reason David Moore is in the fucking morgue,' Ruby said quietly. 'Where he belongs.'

'So – this *is* about David?' Callum said, trying to keep his voice level and failing.

'It's her record, of what happened,' Ruby said. 'I found it a few months ago, when Mum and Dad had decided to move. They asked me to pack up Paige's room.'

He looked at the papers, but the side facing upwards was blank.

'And this was in there, the whole time. I found it at the bottom of the bag she was planning to take to RADA, because she couldn't leave it behind, could she? She couldn't let go.'

He kept his eyes on the knife as he stretched forward. He dragged the document towards him and flipped it over.

'She kept a record, of their conversations.' Ruby exhaled.

He didn't recognise it at first. Was used to seeing flowing handwriting instead of neatly typeset words.

His eyes scanned the front page, then flicked back up to Ruby.

It was like all the adrenaline was slowly leaving his body, replaced with ice-cold water. Starting in his chest, spreading through his veins.

It was starting to make a sick sort of sense. Ruby's fury, the tears – the violence.

He'd had the answer the whole time, he just didn't know it. Detective Field had even asked him.

*What did you write about?*

And he'd told her.

*Paige was a better writer than me.*

*She wrote in this big broad way.*

*She made you think about big themes, big issues.*

Callum cleared his throat, and read out loud. 'I suppose this is my record.'

He was numb with shock. Paige used to read it to him. The bits she wasn't happy with, usually. They worked on them together.

Callum chose a different line. 'The rules don't work. There aren't enough rules. There are too many rules to cope with.'

He felt sick.

'It's all there,' Ruby choked out. 'Everything he – he did to her. He was supposed to make her better—'

'He did,' Callum whispered. 'We all got better.'

'She was *thirteen*,' Ruby screamed, kicking her fallen chair. 'And he abused her.'

Callum flinched at the noise and closed his eyes. 'Ruby. Tell me this isn't why you killed David—'

'She was thirteen when she arrived on that ward and that animal, that pig – he was supposed to be looking after her.' Ruby let out a sob. 'I read those papers, over and over, and I realised – that *animal* picked her. If he'd chosen one of you, maybe she would still be alive—'

'Ruby—'

'No – I am *talking*,' she cried. 'My sister is dead—'

'It's a play,' Callum said, loudly enough to interrupt her.

He turned the pages, recognising a phrase here, the opening of a scene – even after all these years.

His ears were ringing. Ruby took two steps towards him, now within arm's reach, the knife at her side. Her pupils were pinpricks.

'You killed David, killed Sam, because of this?' he asked quietly, fighting to keep his voice level.

'Yes.' There was snot running down Ruby's face, but she didn't wipe it away. The other hand joined the first on the handle of the knife. 'She was my sister.'

Callum counted to six in his head.

'It's not real, Ruby.' He held the papers in front of his torso, like a shield. 'It's not real.'

'You're lying.' She'd stopped crying. Seemed frozen to the spot. 'You're always lying.'

His rage, always just below the surface, overwhelmed him.

He threw the papers across the table and stood up, took a step towards her.

'I'm lying?' He laughed, the cruel laugh he had when he was drunk. He felt drunk. He felt high, completely fucked – because this couldn't be real. 'I'm fucking lying?'

He took another step towards her, and Ruby backed off.

'Your sister was an artist,' he said, in a low voice. 'She was an actress, yeah? In the end, Paige decided that she wanted to act, go to RADA, but when she was with us?

'She wrote.' He laughed again, throwing his hands up and making Ruby flinch. 'To make herself feel better, she wrote about an even shittier situation than the one she was in. It was a *fucking* play.'

Ruby shook her head and the last of his control snapped.

He didn't care what she did – she could stab him too for all he fucking cared.

'It's not real,' Callum said. He punctuated each of his words with a step forward, pushing Ruby back towards the kitchen door. 'It's fiction. "D" stands for doctor, and "P" stands for patient.'

'A play?' Ruby looked shell-shocked, her eyes darting to the folder on the table.

'It was part of her RADA audition. *Disorder*, a play by Paige Jacobs. How did you not know that? Did you not fucking care?'

'I—'

'A good man is dead because you didn't know your sister,' Callum yelled. He was in Ruby's face, the knife forgotten.

Everything happened at once. The hammering on the front door, the shout of "*Police*" from outside and the pressure, below his ribs.

Callum looked down. It was like she had barely touched him, maybe a firm push backwards, but the knife was buried in his stomach, up to the handle.

# Chapter 103

## Sunday | Evening

## Field

'Callum,' she called through the door. 'Callum, are you there? We need to speak to you. We need to know you're safe.'

She stepped back and waited, listening hard. Riley was holding an enforcer, ready to break the door down. The other cars were still five minutes away at least.

'What do you want to do, boss?' Riley asked.

Field rubbed her forehead with the heel of her hand.

It could be an empty house. She could smash the door down and find that Callum and Lily weren't home, that she was in the wrong place entirely.

But if they were home, if Ruby had found them—

'Do it.'

The door, the flimsy front door that probably hadn't been changed for forty years, splintered on the first impact.

Raised voices from inside the house told her they had made the right call, and Riley hit it again.

But the door that should have swung open straight away didn't yield. It was open, just a crack—

'There's something behind it,' Riley said, dropping the enforcer into the weeds, and throwing his shoulder against it.

They pushed, together, but whatever was behind it was the width of the hallway and wouldn't budge.

Riley turned to her again, desperate, waiting for her to make a decision.

'Break a window.'

# Chapter 104

## Sunday | Evening

## Callum

He backed away from Ruby, the knife still in his stomach. She was distracted, trembling and facing the hallway, clutching her shoulder.

'She called them,' Ruby spat, looking at the ceiling. 'That fucking bitch must have called them.'

Callum looked down. It didn't hurt. He couldn't feel it, beyond a sharp scratch and a stinging sensation, and he was still on his feet.

*Keep the knife in* his instincts were screaming.

'It's over, Ruby,' he said, trying to stay calm. 'It's over – it's okay.'

'Okay?' she turned to him, eyes wild, make-up still smeared across her pale skin.

'I'll tell them, I'll explain. It was a play – you thought it was real.'

'It is real,' she screamed. 'She wrote down everything the bastard said.'

The police were pushing at the door now, and he could hear Field calling out, but couldn't make out the words.

'I – I stabbed Moore, because—' She was frantic, her hands in her hair and her eyes on the knife in his stomach. 'And Sam knew – she must have done. She was in the room next to Paige's. She must have seen something, or heard something.'

'Ruby—'

But she had turned, and she was running for the stairs, to Lily—

Callum made a grab for her, and the sudden movement made the blade twist in his abdomen. A swell of a pain and his vision went black, but he kept stumbling forward, reaching for Ruby with his other hand.

'Not Lily,' he cried. 'It's over, Ruby – it's over.'

Glass smashed somewhere, but the noises were confused – he was disorientated.

He caught hold of Ruby on the stairs, got a fistful of her clothing and dragged her backwards. She lost her balance and fell onto him. They hit the wall and Callum let out a scream of pain as Ruby's weight drove the knife further in.

She was scrabbling, trying to get away, and he clung to her jumper, but she was twisting, trying to get out of it.

Callum turned his head and could see Field, trying to push through the gap in the door. She was shouting into a radio, still trying to get in but the cabinet was wedged at an angle, and they couldn't move it, there was no way Field would get through.

It was so loud, and he couldn't tell where the sounds were coming from, but he couldn't let Ruby get upstairs, couldn't let her reach Lily.

Callum breathed deeply and took hold of the handle with

his right hand, pulled the knife out, and lunged at Ruby's back.

He couldn't tell if he'd made contact, because everything went black.

# Chapter 105

## Sunday | Evening

## Field

Riley was through the living room window, and she watched through the crack in the door as he tackled Ruby, pinning her arms and snapping the handcuffs on.

Field followed him, cutting her shin on the shards of glass still in the window frame.

It was mayhem. There was no light in the hallway, but light from the dining room illuminated the two figures.

Riley had subdued Ruby, who looked unhurt, lying face down on the hallway floor, hands underneath her, sobbing into the carpet. Field kicked the knife away, and it went skittering into the dining room.

Riley was shouting into Callum's face, pressing down on his stomach.

Field shouted into her radio. 'Control, Hotel Charlie Six-Four. Request LAS and emergency backup to 56 Conway

Road. IC1 male with stab wound to the abdomen. Suspect apprehended.'

A crackling voice said the paramedics were two minutes away as Field pushed into the dining room. She pulled a towel from the drying rack and threw it to Riley, to press onto Callum's wound.

'Lily?' Field called.

She'd heard Callum shouting Lily's name – she must be in the house.

The narrow galley kitchen was clear, the fridge pushed against the back door. Field checked the downstairs toilet and found nothing.

'He's not responsive,' Riley said, desperately, as she got back to the hallway.

Field sank to her knees and pressed her fingers to Callum's neck. A weak pulse fluttered.

'He's got a pulse, Riley. Stay calm, keep talking to him—'

She was cut off by Ruby, who had pushed herself to her knees and had thrown her body into Riley, knocking him off balance.

Riley righted himself, scrabbling to apply pressure to the wound again. Callum groaned and coughed, and Field stepped over them, hauling Ruby up by the handcuffs.

Ruby was screaming, thrashing as Field pulled her backwards into the living room. By wrenching the girl's arms, Field managed to use a second set of cuffs to connect the first pair to a radiator. As she clicked them into place Ruby threw her head back and caught Field in the face.

'Fuck—' She felt her nose break.

She pulled her shirt up to stem the blood, as blue lights filled the room from outside.

Field backed away. Ruby's baggy T-shirt had slipped down

over her left shoulder, and Field could see the edge of a large plaster.

'Ambulance is here,' she shouted to Riley, her words muffled through the broken nose and her shirt, pressed into her face. He was still dealing with Callum's wound. She edged past them, up the stairs.

'Lily?' Field called. 'Lily?'

Field could remember the layout of the house and she tried Lily's room first, throwing the door open. The curtains weren't drawn, so flashing blue lights bounced off the wall, like crude nightclub lighting.

There was a slim figure on the bed, face up, hands bound. Her skin was grey.

Lily Stewart was lying in a red-black pool of blood. Field crossed to a window and threw it open. Paramedics were spilling out of two ambulances, and she called down to them.

'Second victim, upstairs. I need help – *now*.' In two steps she was back by the bed. 'Lily? Lily – can you hear me?'

Lily's clothes were so blood-soaked Field had to tear Lily's shirt away to find the wound. A single deep gash to her abdomen.

With one hand, Field pushed a pillow down onto the wound. She felt for a pulse with the other hand. It was barely there.

Field gently slapped Lily's cheek, and the girl shrank away from her hand, but didn't regain consciousness.

Field could hear heavy boots on the stairs.

'Help is coming, Lily, okay? Hold on for me, darling.'

Field waited for the paramedic to take over, and then backed away.

Another medic pushed the bedding out of the way, and as it fell to the floor, Field noticed the swipes of blood on the duvet, where Ruby must have cleaned the knife.

# Chapter 106

**P:** I'm tired.

*Pause*

**D:** Yes.

*Pause*

**P:** It's not my fault.
**D:** No. None of this is your fault.


*Blackout*

# Chapter 107

## Monday | Early hours

### Field

When Field got home, she was ready to sleep for a hundred years.

Toby was in his usual spot on the sofa, reading a book with two fans trained on him. He looked up and smiled. 'I thought I'd give it a reread.'

The purple cover of *Darlings, Obsessed* caught the fading light. Field dropped into an armchair and closed her eyes. If she never saw the book again it would be too soon.

Her head was pounding, and she couldn't breathe through her nose. The epicentre of her headache was behind her left eye, which was already a glorious purple.

Field sat down. 'I'm sorry, Tobes.'

'It's okay,' he said.

'No.' She squeezed her eyes shut tighter, trying not to let the tears fall – but making her eye hurt even more. 'I handled it badly then, when you were ill, and I'm doing the same again now, aren't I?'

He didn't say anything.

She opened her eyes. Drank him in. He covered her hand with his.

Field took a breath. 'Ever since you got better, I've just been terrified you'll get ill again. And I know it's stupid – believe me, I know. You're a grown man, you have a gorgeous partner, you're training for a job you're bloody good at.' She brushed her tears away with her index finger. 'You're doing better than I ever could have hoped.'

A tear curved across Toby's cheek.

'You're not fragile,' she said, emphatically. 'You're one of the strongest people I know.'

'I take after you,' he said, with a smile.

She laughed, and it turned into a sob.

'But you've got to talk to me, Mum,' Toby said, his voice firmer.

She nodded.

'You want to know if I'm going to get ill again?' He put his head on one side.

*No. Yes. Maybe.*

'Because I might.' His tone was matter-of-fact. 'I don't think it's likely to happen any time soon. I've got a great support network, and I know a hell of a lot more about depression and anxiety than I did then—'

She forced herself not to wince at the word. *Depression.*

He got up and sat on the arm of her chair, wrapped her in a hug. She breathed in the scent of him. 'But, Mum, if we can't talk about this stuff when I'm fine, how are you going to help me if I do get ill?'

She closed her eyes. 'I'll try. I know I need to try.'

Toby pushed her away from him, holding her at arm's length. 'Are you going to be okay?'

She nodded. 'I'm sorry,' she said again. 'For everything.'

'You have nothing to apologise for, Mum.' He leaned over and kissed her hair, then stood up, suddenly business-like. 'Now, you'll be very pleased to know that dealing with people who've been decked in the face is literally, like, day one of paramedic school.'

Field touched the bridge of her nose and winced.

Toby's eyes narrowed. 'Put your feet up. I'm going to find you some peas.'

# Chapter 108

## Monday | Morning

## Field

Field met Maxwell in the station's reception. They stood awkwardly for a second, before she buzzed him through, and they made their way towards the cells.

'That looks nasty.' He nodded to her black eye, inexpertly covered up with Young's concealer.

'I've had worse.' Field shrugged.

Field was replaying the bollocking she'd given Riley. The warnings she'd dished out to everyone about being small-minded – before she took an immediate dislike to the therapist.

She stopped in a quiet stretch of corridor. 'Look, Maxwell – I know we didn't get off to a great start—'

He snorted.

'—but I really appreciate you coming in for this,' she finished.

He shrugged. 'Apology accepted.'

Field narrowed her eyes. She hadn't apologised as such – but then she caught the smile at the corner of his mouth.

'It's a good job I need you this morning,' she grumbled, half laughing.

The team were in two minds about whether Ruby Jacobs warranted a 132 – whether they should section her. Field had wanted to bring Maxwell in as the doctor for the assessment. The approved medical practitioner had already arrived.

'Wilson gave you the context, right?' she asked, as they descended the stairs to the basement.

'I've had the exec summary, yeah,' Maxwell said. 'And I've got a rough idea of the questions you want me to put to her.'

'She's not even "no comment" when we speak to her.' Field pressed her ID to the scanner at the bottom and held the door open for Maxwell. 'She just screams.'

They went through three more doors, and then they were at the cells. At the furthest end there was an open door, with a PC stationed outside looking in – a twenty-four-hour constant watch.

'You can get a break now, ta,' Field said to her, as they approached.

She jumped up gratefully, stretching out her legs. 'Thanks, ma'am.'

The AMP shook Maxwell's hand, notebook and pen at the ready.

'I'll wait out here, okay?' Field said. 'Any sign of trouble, don't engage with the suspect, just get yourselves out of the way.'

Maxwell nodded, straightened his collar.

Ruby was sitting in the middle of her bunk, hands gripping legs. From Field's vantage point outside the door, she could only see the back of Maxwell's head, but she could hear perfectly.

'Hi, Ruby, I'm Dr Maxwell. This is Celia Garfield, she's a community mental health nurse.'

Ruby didn't lift her head, but Field watched her fingertips start to scratch at her legs.

'Can you tell me where you are, Ruby?' Maxwell asked.

A long pause, then: 'Police station.'

'Good,' Maxwell said. 'And do you understand why you've been arrested?'

She nodded. 'David Moore. Samantha Hughes.'

'And can you tell me, Ruby, why you attacked Callum Mulligan and Lily Stewart in their home this evening?'

Now Ruby did lift her head. Her body seemed to rise with it, like she was about to get up onto her tiptoes. Field braced herself, ready to launch herself into the cell – but Ruby stayed sitting.

'Would you sleep with a patient, Dr Maxwell?' Ruby's voice was a rasp.

'No, I wouldn't,' he said, evenly.

'Would you sleep with someone underage?'

'No, Ruby. I wouldn't.'

Ruby gave an exaggerated shrug. 'Well then.'

Maxwell considered her for a moment. 'Can you tell me, Ruby, did anyone tell you to attack those people?'

'I'm not mad,' she spat.

'Okay.' Maxwell held up a hand.

'If I was mad, I couldn't have planned it all, could I?' Ruby threw her hands into the air. 'I followed them. I made notes.'

Field sighed. None of what she said could be admitted as evidence, or even recorded – not if it was part of a 132. But Christ – it was quite something to hear Ruby say it.

'And why did you plan it?' Maxwell kept his voice low.

'Because I know the crash was deliberate.' Ruby matched his volume, leaning towards him.

Field got up from the chair, standing in the door of the cell. From this angle, she could see Maxwell's face in profile.

'Back then, I knew Paige had crashed the car deliberately, but no one believed me, because there was no note,' Ruby said. 'But she didn't need to leave a note, did she? Not when we had that – that whole record of their conversations.'

'You believe your sister's death was suicide?' Maxwell asked.

A firm nod.

'And you blame David Moore?'

'Him, and the brats that covered it up for him.'

It angered Field, that Sam's killer could sit there and call her a *brat*. Lily was clinging to life in a hospital bed.

Callum had managed to tell Field about the play, from his hospital bed in A&E, before he went in for surgery. They'd recovered it at the scene – the second time in a week his house was swarming with forensics.

'If they'd spoken out, she might have got help,' Ruby said.

Ruby might be deluded about her sister's play, but she wasn't mad. She was calculating, and her crimes were premeditated. There was nothing preventing them from taking her to court and seeing her remanded in Belmarsh.

Maxwell kept his voice calm. 'Why did you leave those pages at the scene, Ruby? From the paper about the trial?'

The last question on Field's wish list.

'I wanted the others to work it out,' Ruby whispered. 'They knew what they did. I wanted them to know I was coming for them.'

# Chapter 109

## Monday | Morning

### Field

Field squeezed the car into a space on the busy street and turned the engine off. She felt the lack of air-con immediately.

Riley and Wilson unclicked their seatbelts, but neither of them moved.

Field flipped the mirror down. She'd sweated off another layer of cover-up and the bruises around her eye were, if possible, darker than they had been earlier.

Zara opened the front door, and they followed her into the dining room. It was full of light, bouncing off the whitewashed walls and tiled floor.

Simon and Penny were sat at the one end of the kitchen table, a pot of tea waiting under a cosy. The large windows were open, floral scents wafting in from the garden.

Field, Riley and Wilson took their seats.

Penny cleared her throat. 'You've made an arrest?'

No one touched the teapot.

Field nodded. 'Yes, we've got the perpetrator in custody.'

It was important to take these conversations slowly.

'You've got him,' Simon said, almost to himself.

Penny nodded several times, then her face crumpled, and she addressed her next question to the ceiling. 'Who was it?'

It was hard to know where to start.

'It was a relative of one of the trial participants. The girl who died in a car accident, Paige Jacobs – it was her sister.'

Penny pulled at the collar of her blouse. 'Paige's sister? But—' Her voice was thick with emotion.

'Ruby Jacobs has confessed to David's murder,' Field said. 'And the murder of Samantha Hughes.'

'We appreciate how difficult this is,' Wilson added. 'Take a minute, if you need it.'

'Yeah, actually, I will—' Penny hesitated. 'Help yourselves to tea, I'm just going to—'

The chair scraped against the tiles and she left the room. Simon followed her into the hallway and closed the kitchen door.

Field sagged against the dining chair and suppressed a yawn.

'Are you going to tell her?' Wilson asked quietly. 'What Ruby thought David had done?'

Zara poured the tea, passing them each a cup.

Field sighed. Penny would have to know, eventually. There would be a trial, and from the brief conversation Maxwell had managed to have with her this morning, Ruby was still convinced that the whole thing was a true account.

'I'd tell her,' Zara Ayres said in a low voice. 'She wants to understand, and she's going to be frustrated if she thinks you're holding something back.'

'Okay,' Field said.

It was ten minutes before Penny and Simon re-entered. Her eyes were red, but she looked composed.

'Shall we sit in the garden?' she asked, hovering by the door. 'David's wildflowers have bloomed. He'd want us to enjoy them.'

They took their tea to the walled garden, and Field explained how Ruby found the playscript among Sam's things, when she was packing up the house. How she believed David had abused her sister, when she was admitted onto his ward. Taking the play as truth, Ruby assumed the other four knew about the abuse, or at least suspected it.

A faint breeze ruffled the vines climbing the brick walls.

'I've read it, by the way. It was called *Disorder*,' Simon said, quietly. 'David used extracts from the play as a teaching aid, for a time,' Simon said, clearing his throat. 'Along with an early draft of *Darlings, Obsessed*. Paige and Callum gave him permission. He'd get students studying CBT to read it. To give them a real-life insight into the complexities of OCD.'

Riley topped up Penny's glass of water from the jug on the iron table and Penny nodded her thanks.

Silence settled on the garden.

'Before we could make the arrest,' Field said, carefully. 'Ruby also attacked two other patients from the study. Callum Mulligan and Lily Stewart.'

Penny sat up. 'Are they okay?'

'Callum is doing well. He's stable. Lily is still in critical condition, and she'll be undergoing a major operation this afternoon. The blood loss was severe and—'

Field felt Wilson's and Riley's eyes on her, and knew she had to tell the truth. No sugar-coating; that's what she always told people. 'It's a very risky procedure. The doctors say she might not make it.'

The four officers waited in silence while Penny sat, eyes closed, hands in her lap. Finally, Penny stood up from the table.

'Why?' she demanded. 'If Ruby thought – she thought David could do *that* to a patient, I understand attacking him. But why the others?'

Field hadn't fully wrapped her head around that herself yet. She let Riley answer.

'She thought they must have all known, and helped cover it up to protect David,' Riley said. 'As you know, Paige Jacobs died in a traffic accident. It seems Ruby always suspected it was deliberate – a suicide. After she found the playscript, she took it to be, well, evidence.'

No one spoke.

The tiny courtyard garden could have been suspended in time.

Finally, Penny spoke. 'David loved those kids, you know? Even though he worked with hundreds of children later, they were always special to him.

'I know David and I weren't – we weren't together when he died. But I loved him. He was a good person, to his core, and he'd be—' her voice caught '—be devastated by all this.'

'We're so sorry, Penny,' Zara said, taking Penny's hand across the table. 'So sorry for your loss.'

Penny squeezed it.

'I don't know if I told you this,' Field said quietly. 'But as well as wearing his wedding ring, David was carrying a photo of you in his wallet.'

Penny tipped her head back, looking up at the sky and pressing the heels of her hands into her cheeks to stem the tears.

Field realised it was the first time she'd seen Penny cry.

'At least it wasn't one of those kids,' Penny said at last. 'It's not much, but it's something. He wasn't killed by one of his kids.'

# Chapter 110

## Two weeks later

## Callum

He stabbed the button for the lift with his thumb and looked up and down the corridor. Tried not to look at the sign for the ninth floor, which was giving him heart palpitations.

Sunday should have been a busy day for visitors, but after it had been cloudy all week, the sun had finally broken through the clouds, and Callum supposed sick family members were coming second to barbecues and sunbathing.

The lift rattled, pinged and then the doors slid open.

A doctor shot a bemused look at the red parka in Callum's arms. He had the same thick dark hair and posho in-bred features as Scott, and Callum hated him instantly.

Hospitals smelled like shit, and too many tones of *beep* followed him along the corridor to Lily's room. He was walking quickly, and the pain in his stomach throbbed like a second pulse.

He knocked. Through the window he saw her flinch away from the sound, raising her arms above her chest.

'Fuck,' Lily groaned. 'You scared the shit out of me.'

He threw his parka onto the end of the bed and took the wing-back plastic armchair, easing himself into it with a hand on the spot where his dressings were.

Lily eased herself back onto the pillows and raised an eyebrow. 'Milking that little scratch, a bit, aren't we?'

He stuck his middle finger up.

They fell into silence, and Callum examined her face. 'You look like shit.'

'Charming.' Lil had dark circles under her eyes, and her skin had a slightly yellow, sun-deprived tone. She looked small in the big bed.

Her hands were trembling where they lay on the blanket. He'd bought her favourite hand cream from the Boots downstairs, but it was unopened on the bedside cabinet.

He picked up one of her hands. 'I'm worried about you.'

She didn't answer.

*Trauma*, Maxwell kept saying. *You don't go through a trauma like this and bounce back in a few weeks.*

Callum ran his free hand over his hair, finally growing back post-buzz cut. 'Have they given you any meds for the panic attacks, Lil?'

He couldn't see her expression. Her profile was a silhouette against the sun.

'It's not a step backwards, you know, if you do go back onto meds. While you process all this shit – while *we* process this shit. They might really help—'

'It's not that,' she said, leaning back.

Suddenly she wasn't blocking the light, and his vision was spotted with bright daubs of orange, rippling into blues and purples.

'Cal – I've been thinking. I've not been able to do anything but think, in this shithole.' She rubbed the dark bruise-coloured skin under her eyes. 'And – I don't really know how to say this—'

The brave face he was putting on, the steely optimism he'd summoned that morning in front of the mirror – both deserted him – replaced with a pressure on his chest, a crushing sensation. He gripped her hand tighter.

Tears were running down her cheeks, her nose. They both cried easily, now.

'Lil—'

'No, I have to – let me speak, Cal, please.'

The smile she gave him broke his heart. Pitying, both for him and for herself. She squeezed his hand back, and he was starting to lose the feeling in his fingers. He forced himself to stay silent.

'We can't do this, anymore,' she whispered. 'It's not fair to either of us. When they discharge me, I'm going to go home. My parents have been in to see me, and they want me to move back to theirs. I'll see my sisters again.'

His throat was thick, seized up with emotion, and the weight on his chest was making it hard to think clearly.

'I love you. I'll always love you, Callum, but – all of this?' She lifted her arms, and his hand was suddenly empty. 'Neither of us are going to be okay, for a long time. We need help, and I love you – I do love you, but—'

She was blurred, now – he was looking at her through tears.

'I love you too.' It was like someone else's voice. He was in his body, trapped inside it, but also watching from afar.

Lily let out a grunt of pain as she twisted in the bed, reaching for him. She put her hands on his face and Callum closed his eyes. His cheeks were hot, and his tears ran over her fingers.

'Cal, look at me,' she whispered.

He couldn't look at her, didn't want to open his eyes, but he was in pain – and she was the person he wanted when he was in pain.

Lily's face was close to his, and now she wasn't against the hospital pillows and in the bright glare of the sun, she looked more like herself.

He shut his eyes again and counted the seconds of silence. Made himself get to nine.

'I don't know how to be okay without you,' he said, finally.

She took her hands away, wiped his cheeks first, and then hers. Let out a little bubble of laughter. 'Oh, and I do?'

Lily was having hourly panic attacks, wouldn't be able to walk for weeks. After the years she'd spent looking after him – Callum wanted to be able to step up and hold them both together.

But he couldn't look after himself yet.

They both knew this conversation was coming. But he was a coward, as usual, and had waited for her to pull the trigger.

He pressed his knuckles into closed eyes and growled.

'What?' Lily huffed, a hint of the old tease back in her voice.

'I can't believe—' Callum said, with a sigh. 'I can't believe you're breaking up with me, right after I've been stabbed.'

She let out a bark of laughter, the first properly joyful sound he'd heard for weeks, and then they were both laughing, crying – clutching the stitched seams of their healing wounds.

# Chapter 111

## December | Four months later

### Lily

They had originally tried to think of somewhere meaningful to meet, somewhere that had a connection to David, but eventually Cal took over and told her to meet him in a pub in Greenwich.

They'd invited Andy, but to their great surprise, he was travelling. Seeing in Christmas and the New Year in Silicon Valley. Not everyone's dream destination, but he was happy.

The pub was deliciously warm, especially after the bitter December weather outside. Fairy lights glittered from the ceiling and the large tree in the corner. She'd already bought herself a red wine, and a pint of Diet Coke for Cal.

'Fancy seeing you here.'

She turned, and saw Cal behind her.

He looked so different she couldn't speak for a moment. Lily had only seen him a few times in September, as she slowly moved her stuff out. She had deliberately not let herself look at his newly set up Instagram.

He'd put on weight, and his shoulders were broader. He was wearing a light checked shirt over a white T-shirt, and he even had a little bit of a belly under the layers.

'You look – you look good,' she said, finally.

'Don't sound so surprised,' Cal said, laughing and taking his seat.

Lily frowned down at her jeans and battered pink Docs with the over-long green laces, wishing she'd made a bit more of an effort.

'So,' he said. 'How are you?'

'You know—' She shrugged.

He raised an eyebrow. It was such a typical Callum mannerism, but at the same time, his whole manner, the way he carried himself – it was different. Lighter.

'How are you?' she asked, clearing her throat.

'Oh, well, you know.' He let out a comically long sigh. 'OCD-wise I'm like, stirring my tea six times and irrationally terrified of it being September again for a whole month, but I go out every day. I've got a dog to walk, now.'

He said this with an extra-smug note, and Lily grinned. She'd always vetoed the idea of getting a dog. 'Pretty good, then?'

'Yeah,' he said. 'Although, for the first time in my life, I've developed fucking chronic insomnia.'

A harassed-looking barmaid leaned over them to grab the empties that had been on the table when Lily sat down.

'Insomnia?' she said, when she'd gone back to the bar. 'But you've always gone out like a light.'

'Being up all night is productive for writing, but yeah – it's shit.' He shrugged, a shadow passing over his face. 'I get nightmares.'

Lily's own night terrors were getting better, but she still found herself asleep-awake, pinned to the bed, staring at the ceiling, imagining her blood pooling out of her. Unable to move, or cry out – slowly sinking into darkness.

'How's the house?' she asked, forcing some brightness into her voice.

'It's lush.' He leaned back in his chair. 'New kitchen is being fitted next year. You'd fucking love it. I'm knocking through to the dining room and everything. No more rusty cupboard doors.'

'I never minded the creaking cupboards,' she said with a smile.

'Really?' He blew out a breath. 'Well, you learn something new every day. How are things with your parents?'

'We're getting there,' Lily said. 'They still find it hard to talk about everything that happened, but we're in family therapy now.'

'Seriously?' Cal's mouth fell open.

'Yeah,' she laughed. 'It's been a bit of a revelation.'

They both looked around the pub, watching people coming and going, laughing over their drinks and steaming plates of fish and chips.

'Lil – I just wanted to say—' Cal broke off.

She nodded for him to continue.

'I'm glad we took the time, and it's so fucking good to see you, and you look really well, and—' he sucked in a breath '—I hope it's okay for me to say this, but I really missed you, you know?'

Colour rushed to her cheeks, and she smiled. 'It's okay – I missed you too.'

'This is weird, isn't it?' Cal said, finally.

The noise and bustle of the pub carried on around them, but seemed muted.

Ruby's trial was due to start in March. Zara had prepared Lily and her family for the renewed press interest.

The NHS were planning to name a new CAMHS unit after David, somewhere in Central London. Penny was setting up a foundation in his name, sponsoring students from less privileged backgrounds who wanted to become CBT practitioners.

Hundreds of former patients, and parents of former patients, had shared their thanks to David Moore on the page that was raising money for the OCD Action charity, in his memory.

There had been a lot less focus on Sam in the press, but Zara said her parents had requested that. Sam was going to be awarded her PhD next summer, as part of the graduation ceremony, and Lily had agreed to go – as had DCI Field.

'Paige always said once she got out, she'd look after Ruby,' Callum added, quietly. 'It was one of the things she was looking forward to doing, when she was better, remember? Being a big sister again.'

Lily knew she should feel pity for Ruby – but her eyes went to Callum's waist, where his scar would be under his T-shirt, the mirror of hers, and she couldn't summon any.

'Maybe if I'd made more of an effort with Ruby. If I'd stayed in touch with her—'

'What was that line?' Lily said, and Cal blinked. 'What was Paige's favourite line from *Hamlet*?'

'*There is nothing either good or bad but thinking makes it so*,' Callum said, without hesitating.

'Exactly,' Lily said, forcefully, leaning across the table. 'It wasn't your fault – you can't let yourself think like that. If Paige was here, that's what she'd be saying.'

They took a fortifying glug of their drinks.

'Paige will be up there,' Lily said, smiling. 'Bending David's ear.'

'The poor man will be lucky to get a moment's peace,' Cal muttered.

Lily had already sunk half her wine.

'Fuck,' Cal said. 'Can we get this over with? David never liked it when we dragged out the tough bit.' He raised his glass.

And despite the fact they were both older, with new scars and new fears – despite the fact Callum was out of the house, and he seemed properly better – as Lily raised her glass, she could also see the scrawny sixteen-year-old punk, scribbling his novel in an exercise book and smoking roll-ups behind the hospital bins.

'To David—' Callum said.

'And to Sam—' Lily added.

'—and to Paige.'

# Author's Note

*Breakdown.*
*The rules don't work. There aren't enough rules.*
*There are too many rules to cope with.*

Like Paige and Callum, when I was a teenager suffering from OCD, I turned to writing.

I wrote a two-hander play called *Soap and Water*, which was performed at the Assembly Rooms Theatre in Durham, during my second year of university. It was a play about my OCD, but it was also very much a play about being misunderstood, misdiagnosed and on the receiving end of constant, very diminishing stereotypes.

This novel came more than ten years later, but lots of my original play – including the lines above – found its way into the book.

I have met a lot of incredible people with all kinds of OCD over the years. My characters' OCD experiences are only a few examples of how OCD can present itself, but I hope they begin to illustrate what a hugely varied illness it is.

# Acknowledgements

I have to begin by thanking my agent, Donald Winchester. He is unflappable and endlessly patient, and this book wouldn't exist without him. The whole Watson, Little team have made this process a joy!

I'm lucky to have found the most wonderful editor in Emma Grundy Haigh. Emma – thank you for making the book infinitely better, and for championing Field since day one. Working with you is a dream.

It takes a lot of people to bring a book to life! Thank you to Sean Garrehy for designing the incredible cover, Molly Lo Re, for bringing Field to audio – and Jess Zahra, Helena Newton and Tania Charles for their fantastic editing. Then the powerhouse of sales, marketing, rights and more – Hannah Lismore, Angela Thomson, Emily Gerbner, Jean-Marie Kelly, Sophia Wilhelm, Emily Hall, Jessie Whitehead, Francesca Tuzzeo, Melissa Okusanya, Hannah Stamp, Katie Buckley, Emily Scorer, Becky Hunter, Zoe Shine, Aisling Smyth, Anda Podaru and Ashton Mucha. Thank you all – it's my incredible privilege to be an Avon author!

Enormous appreciation to all my fellow Greenwich Writers,

especially George, for captaining our ship, and Andrew, Kingsley, Nat, Liv and Nick. A special thank you to Katie, for everything.

The Harry Writers! You are all a constant source of advice and inspiration. Special thanks to Tania Tay, C.L. Miller, Kate Wells, Jessica Bull, Jennie Godfrey, Fiona McPhillips, Teri Terry, Kristen Perrin and Annette Caseley.

I'm so grateful to the authors who have given the book lovely quotes, and everyone who has supported it online and left reviews. Thanks also to you, the reader! I hope you enjoyed it.

My incredible friends! Charlotte and Rosanna, for the calendar moments. Aisling – thank you always, for your help with the *Soap and Water* script. Paul Webb – it'll be you soon! Tashko, for aesthetic book nights, and Kirstie – who'd have a cob on without a special mention. Thanks to Leanne, for the paramedic's view of a stabbing, and Saša, who was expecting a quiet drink. Josie, Dan and Thomas – my best friends for over half my life. I don't know what I'd do without you.

To the Durham lot – Flo, Ed, Alex, Kirsty, Becka, Lily and Rory – your support then and your support now means the world. Lily and Rory acted in a production of *Soap and Water*, as did Anna and Will. And thanks to Hild Bede Theatre, for letting me direct lots of dark, twisted plays!

Clare, who generously read the novel and gave a therapist's viewpoint. The next decade looks very different, because of you.

About a year and a half ago, a police officer and an aspiring crime writer met for a drink in a Wetherspoons. Writing police procedurals is much easier when there's a copper next to you on the sofa. Thank you for everything, Max.

Love and thanks to my whole family, especially everyone

who read early drafts – Jason, Debbie, Pat, Maggie and Dave. Riley – who finally has a character named after him. Edie – for my treasured writing desk. Nisey – for filling my childhood with creativity. Nan and Grandad – the most loving grandparents I could ask for.

And then my mum, who I owe the biggest thanks of all. Thank you for teaching me never to give up. *Of course* the book that got me published would have a main character inspired by you. I love you.

# Read on for an exclusive extract from Hannah Brennan's next novel, *Nothing Left Behind . . .*

# Chapter 1

## Wednesday | Midnight

PC Hunt rapped on the glass. 'All right, sir, could you wind down the window for me?'

He tried not to look bored as the Vauxhall Corsa's window receded into the door. The sheepish boy at the wheel looked too small for the car, like he'd been caught trying on his dad's overcoat.

'Do you know how fast you were going, there?' He injected a little more menace into his voice. Couldn't hurt to put the shits up the boy.

'Um, thirty?' the kid said hopefully.

Hunt knew he must not roll his eyes, but Jesus.

'You were doing forty-five down a residential street.' It was always tempting to stick a "mate" on the end of those sentences, but Hunt tried not to. Once you got to a certain age you could start saying "son".

'Oh.' The boy looked forlornly at the dashboard, like it had deceived him.

'Have you been drinking today?'

The boy shook his head with a wide-eyed panic that looked

genuine. 'What? No. I just borrowed the car off my mum to go to Bluewater for the midnight release of this game—' He lifted a plastic bag off the passenger seat as Hunt's radio crackled into life.

'Control to all units. Report of a house fire at 35 Dahlia Road. Is anyone available to respond?'

The boy's eyes went to the radio and Hunt put a hand to it, giving it a second in case someone else answered.

'Control, this is Delta November Nine-Two. It'll be a false alarm. Known hoax caller.' Hunt turned back to the kid in the car. 'Right, step out of the vehicle for me, please. We're going to do a quick breath test—'

Another interruption. 'We're aware of that, Nine-Two, but it's an I-grade. Are you available to respond?'

Hunt blew a breath through his nostrils. The boy had picked up on his indecision and was hovering halfway out the car.

'I said get out,' he snapped and the boy scrambled onto the street, dropping the keys in the road.

The last thing he needed was one of Anne's calls, tonight of all nights.

'Control,' he said, through gritted teeth. 'I'm telling you, it will be a false alarm. Put it on the jobs list. I'll get to it later.'

They'd been promised cover from community support, which never turned up. Even the skipper was out from behind his desk, in a long custody queue with a drink drive. They had one car on the border of Lewisham supporting with an ABH and at least two officers were stuck at Queen Elizabeth, waiting in A&E with suspect for an injury he had caused to himself, pissed, on a railway line.

'Control to Nine-Two – can I show you en route?' The controller was speaking slowly, condescending.

'Wait there,' Hunt snapped at the kid. He strode a few

paces back towards his own vehicle and changed the radio's channel. 'This is Delta November Nine-Two to Borough CCTV Command.'

A different frequency squeal before a gruff response. 'Unit calling CCTV, go ahead.'

'I need you to get visuals of the houses on Dahlia Road. I want to confirm no sight of house fire, or suspicious activity.'

There was a long pause, while the imbeciles at Borough CCTV worked out what way up their keyboard went. Finally: 'Dahlia Road coverage is down, Nine-Two. None of our cameras are online. Over.'

The first flicker of unease. 'Go a road along, Command. It should be visible from Fuchsia Street. You—' He pointed at the boy. 'Stop driving like a prick. I'll send your parents a ticket.'

The kid didn't move.

This time Hunt did roll his eyes. 'Go on – go home.'

The boy leapt into action, scooping his car keys up and slamming the door shut, before pulling away at five miles an hour and crawling down the road.

Hunt got into his own car and stuffed the key into the ignition.

It choked a couple of times, as he impatiently turned it over. He counted to five, tried again, and it finally started.

A different voice spoke on the radio, a woman this time, slightly breathless: 'I've got a view from Openshaw Road. Looks like there's a column of smoke rising above the street—'

Hunt's siren drowned out her next sentence.

# Chapter 2

## Wednesday | Early hours

By the time DCI Field arrived at half four, the fire was out.

Three homes had been gutted by the blaze. The glass in the windows had shattered. The frames were black, and so were the rooms beyond them.

The hoses were being retracted. Water still seeped out from under the front doors of the houses that weren't caught in the fire. Those would be ruined too.

It was hard to make out precise details. The power had been cut for the whole road, so there were no streetlights. Clouds were blocking the moon, and threatening rain.

Field ducked under the cordon, ignoring the twinge in her back.

The air was acrid, and she had to remember to breathe through her mouth. She hadn't been anywhere near the building yet, but her paper suit was already covered in soot.

Standing around the scene were whole crowds of firefighters – she still had to remind herself not to say fire*men*. Field weaved through them, trying to get to the front. Usually, the atmosphere among fire crews was jovial, jostling. Field had met plenty who would peacock for onlookers, basking in the adulation the public reserved just for them.

But not tonight. Not when there'd been a death.

The crew from Eltham, who had been the first on scene, were soot-stained and wearier than their colleagues.

It was an unusually cold night, and while the fire crews were solemn, they were also all holding cups of coffee and packets of biscuits. It didn't look like the neighbours had offered the police officers at the scene anything. The standard treatment of the Met versus the heroic LFB.

Then she caught sight of the house's blackened bricks, and her irritation ebbed away.

Field hated working fires. In her first few months on response, almost thirty years ago, she'd followed her training officer into a burning flat. The mother and son got out okay, but they lost everything they had over a lit cigarette butt in an overturned ashtray.

'Ma'am?'

Field turned and saw a CID detective she recognised from a past case. 'Morning, DS Birch.'

'You can call me Sarah, ma'am.'

Field forced a smile. She'd probably never refer to Birch as "Sarah".

It was incredibly old-fashioned that Field called everyone by their surname, but it was a habit she'd had for thirty years. Most people assumed that it was because her father was in the military – but actually she just hated her first name, and the overfamiliar way her superiors used to call her "Liz".

'Have you been filled in, ma'am?' Birch hesitated. 'We don't have much detail on the cause of the fire yet, I'm afraid.'

The fire should be a CID case, and they both knew it. How

they got it escalated to MIT without definitive proof there had been a murder, Field didn't know.

But she was here now, and if it did turn out to be an accident, all Field had lost was a night's sleep. If it wasn't . . .

She realised Birch was waiting for her to answer. 'I think I'm up to speed. Did you ever meet her? The victim.'

Birch nodded. 'Yep. I was here a lot, when I was on response.'

'What was she like?'

'Anne? She was nice, most of the time. Made me a cup of tea, once.' Birch stared at her hands.

The fire crew hadn't been able to get a visual ID on the body, but everyone guessed it was Anne. She lived alone, with no known next-of-kin – and she had a reputation for nuisance calls to 999 going back years.

The response team had been called to the property too many times to count. Some of the fire crew too. They all knew Anne Evans by name, knew her address when it came over the radio.

Part of the fabric of the response team's day-to-day. A job to be ticked off the daily roster.

When she did call in, Anne's pleas were always the same.

*Please come quick. He's trying to burn my house down. He's going to kill me.*